Jeebee tensed as he climbed. True, Wolf had not so far tried to take from him anything that he was actually holding, even the bits of porcupine meat that were merely close to him. But that was no guarantee. Moreover, Wolf was really an awesomely dangerous animal, with those teeth and the speed and power Jeebee had seen him show over the past few weeks. If it came to a real contest between them ... Jeebee had come to love Wolf, but now, somehow, everything had changed.... Deep in him a primitive decision was stirring. He had food now, and no one, not even Wolf, was going to take any of it from him.

He went on up the ladder.

As his head rose above the earth, and his eyes met Wolf's, only a half a dozen feet away, something seemed to touch him at the base of the back of his skull. A chill flooded out as if it was some powerful dye; spreading forward to the back of his ears, down his neck and into the muscles of his back and down his spine. As he continued to come up the ladder and step out at last on level ground, his vision focused more and more tightly until he saw nothing but Wolf directly ahead of him—and all this time his eyes had never left Wolf's....

"Dickson's skill at storytelling combines painstaking research with a craftsperson's love for his work in this novel of faith in humanity's ability to learn from the wild."

— Library Journal

GORDON R. DICKSON

WOLF AND IRON

A TOM DOHERTY ASSOCIATES BOOK
NEW YORK

WOLF AND IRON

Copyright © 1990 by Gordon R. Dickson

A Tor Book
Published by Tom Doherty Associates, Inc.
49 West 24th Street
New York, N.Y. 10010

ISBN: 0-812-50946-3

Library of Congress Catalog Card Number: 90-2953

First edition: May 1990
First mass market printing: April 1991

Printed in the United States of America

0 9 8 7 6 5 4 3 2 1

This book is dedicated to Harry Frank and Martha Frank, without whom I could never have hoped it to be what it is.

ACKNOWLEDGMENTS

Chris Clayton
Juanita Coulson
John Fentriss—Dalhousie University, Halifax, Nova Scotia
Harry Frank—University of Michigan–Flint
Michael Longcor
Peter McLeod—University of British Columbia, Vancouver,
    Canada
John Miesel
Sandra Miesel
Kenneth S. Norris—University of California–Santa Cruz
Anne Passovoy—Chicago, Illinois
Robert D. Passovoy—Chicago, Illinois
Irene Pepperberg—Northwestern University, Evanston, Illinois,
    Department of Anthropology
Edward O. Price—University of California–Davis

FOREWORD

I can't remember when I first read something by Gordon Dickson. Every now and then (usually when the basement floods and I have to move my paperbacks to high ground) I thumb through an old issue of *Galaxy* or *Astounding* and run across a story that I remember clearly and with fondness and "discover" that Gordon Dickson wrote it. I guess you go from reading a particular author to being a reader of that author when you begin to look for his books and stories. That happened over twenty-five years ago.

But if I can't say when I began reading Dickson's work, I certainly know why I have continued to do so. First, he's a dandy storyteller. Even in the mid-1960's, the Dark Ages when a lot of first-rate science-fiction writers produced a lot of second-rate imitations of avant-garde "mainstream" literature, you could count on Dickson for good, basic storytelling. Stuff with a beginning, a middle, and an end in plausible settings with characters you'd like to meet.

Secondly, the science in Dickson's work is often behavioral science rather than physical science. This is not to say that his futuristic novels lack the usual trappings of hyperspace travel, disintegration beams, and the like, but these are mere technological furnishings. He never bothers the reader with tiresome lectures about how they actually work, and I can't remember a single plot that depended on curious properties of neutron stars or the paradoxes of faster-than-light travel. It's not that I don't enjoy these plots. Asimov and Niven do it splendidly, and I enjoy it very much—but I don't know enough about physical science to appreciate it.

Also, I freely admit to a behavioral scientist's bias in such matters: I spend less time wondering about how we're going to get to the stars than I spend wondering about what we'll do when we get there.

I not only find it congenial that Dickson looks to behavioral science for the "hook" in many of his plots, but also that he does so with scrupulous integrity. He doesn't take liberties with the meaning of a scientific concept just to exploit its current popular appeal. *None but Man,* for example, is less a science-fiction novel than it is a parable about the clash of cultures. It illustrates far better than many cultural-anthropology texts the role that culture plays in equipping us with glasses through which we interpret reality, and how difficult it is to realize that others with other values, or glasses, can view the world differently but with perfect validity.

Similarly, the solution to the problem confronting the central character in *The Alien Way* was ultimately resolved by recognizing that different evolutionary pathways—even if they lead to similar end products—can leave very different instinctual residues. Indeed, Dickson hung the plot on the character's recollection of work reported by Peter Krott in *Natural History* magazine on foraging patterns in bears. The research was reported faithfully, the pivotal connection with the plot was plausible, and even the citation was accurate.

Consequently it was with more than my usual sense of anticipation that I settled back to read the title story in the Dickson anthology *In Iron Years.* The cover illustration showed a man carrying something vaguely similar to the Finnish version of the AK-47 assault rifle and accompanied by a rather medieval, but recognizable representation of a wolf. I had worked with wolves and compared wolf and dog social behavior for several years and looked forward to seeing how Dickson would weave into his plot the complex subtleties I'd found to be so elusive and fascinating. When I finished the story, I was not merely disappointed—I was downright angry. Dickson had given his reader nothing but an overgrown dog wrapped in wolf's clothing!

Exit the reader; enter the pedagogue. The setting in one of Dickson's novels had described enough of the local landscape and downtown area for me to surmise that the locale was his own hometown. With nothing more to go on, I called information and, to my surprise, was given a listed telephone number for one Gordon R. Dickson. I called, spoke to one of his assistants, left my name—complete with academic affiliation, which I thought might pique his interest—and to my surprise got a return call in less than an hour.

Exit the pedagogue; enter the reader. I don't recall much of our conversation. I only remember how congenial and self-effacing and gracious was the person on the other end of the line. I sent him a few reprints of some of my early wolf-research papers, casually dropped his name for a few days with students and colleagues I knew were science-fiction readers, and promptly filed the conversation away under "interesting people I've met."

A few years later I received another telephone call. Gordon told me that he was expanding *In Iron Years* into a novel and wondered if I would be willing to read the passages describing wolf behavior and check them over for authenticity. I promptly agreed, and so began my role as Gordon Dickson's wolf consultant.

I was flattered, and I looked forward to the satisfaction of contributing even in a minor way to a work by a favorite author. Gordon doesn't know it, but most of my colleagues I told about the project were very dubious. I won't catalog the list of pitfalls they envisioned for me. I don't really remember them—I only recall that they were pretty gloomy. But I thought it would be great fun. They were wrong. I was right.

In retrospect, I can see all sorts of problems that might have cropped up and made the project a painful chore. That it turned out to be—as I had blithely expected—great fun was because Gordon is the person he is. I don't mean this to sound condescending—but he is the sort of student every teacher hopes for. He is interested in everything, immerses himself in technical and theoretical details, asks questions that I have to think about for several days, and comes out of the whole thing with a sure and confident grip on essentials. It is fortunate for his fans that he made fiction his life's work. But if he had not done so, I feel certain that he would have had an equally illustrious career in any of the sciences.

John Le Carré said that authenticity is less important than plausibility. For Gordon, authenticity is the way to achieve plausibility, and it's not just a means to an end. It's a passion. It was not sufficient that he understand enough about certain aspects of wolf behavior to ensure that these were presented faithfully. He had to know everything about wolf behavior. He not only read books and papers I recommended, but questioned me about them to be certain he had understood them properly. And he went way beyond the books I recommended. He went way beyond what I could tell him with any firsthand confidence and sent me scurrying to the telephone to call friends and colleagues who had more experience with wolf behavior in the wild, who knew someone who knew someone who had once reported on wolves interacting with horses, with bears . . .

On other questions, I sent him to the telephone armed only with the name of someone I knew slightly (or not at all, save by reputation) who could tell him everything he might ever want to know about, say, the dietary habits of grizzly bears in Montana.

And it didn't stop with reading and with questions. I suggested with some hesitation that Gordon join the Animal Behavior Society and attend the annual meeting, which in 1988 was held at the University of Montana in Missoula. Many of the researchers whose work and thinking I was reporting to him secondhand would be there, and he could talk to them personally. Since he wanted to scout the territory where most of the action in the story would occur, he did.

Nor did it stop with wolves. Gordon takes an intense and detailed interest in everything he writes about. A call from Gordon could lead me into a description of the organizational structure of a university or an overview of current theory in behavioral ecology—or send me scurrying to the pages of *The Shooter's Bible* to compare the ballistics of a .308 Winchester with a .30/06 or *Blade* magazine for a definitive, scholarly article on Bowie knives.

Certainly, what appears in the book represents only the tiniest fraction of what Gordon read, what went into our conversations, exchanges of letters, and—eventually—our appropriately science-fictionesque transmissions from computer to computer. I recall once reviewing several hundred pages of material on one minor issue in a scientific paper I was writing. These hours of work were ultimately represented by only a single sentence in the paper. This is typical in the world of scholarship, but I would imagine it is rare in the world of fiction. Scholars must be productive, but their livelihood is only indirectly tied to the absolute volume they produce, and the positions they advance must be supported by a broad understanding of previous work. This is the nature of the peer-review system. Professional, working writers have neither the mandate nor the luxury of exhaustive research and judicious, deliberative selectivity.

Nevertheless, the passages involving wolf behavior in *Wolf and Iron* represent the same sort of distillation. The upshot is that Gordon has produced not only a typically fast-paced and interestingly peopled Gordon Dickson futuristic adventure novel, but also a credible and, in my best judgment, wholly scientifically supportable portrait of wolf behavior and wolf–human interactions.

Virtually every one of the scenes in which Wolf is an actor has its precedent in either published research or in unpublished reports by scientific observers.

The explanations presented for Wolf's behavior are a different matter. Explanations are essentially theoretical in nature, and theories do not exist in the real world. They exist only in the mind of the scientist. Consequently, the actions that Wolf (or any wolf) performs can often be explained in many ways, and the explanations can be quite different from one another. Sometimes this is because the question why can mean different things. In other cases, different explanations are based on different sets of assumptions and are just plain contradictory.

When Gordon asked me to sketch an explanation for one or another of Wolf's actions, I was guided by two things: First, I generally tried to go with an explanation based on theory that has fairly widespread currency in the scientific community. If this left me choices, I tried to offer the explanation that was most consistent with plot development. To do otherwise would be to have the wolf wagging the tale.

Harry Frank, Ph.D.
Professor and Chair
Department of Psychology
The University of Michigan—Flint

CHAPTER 1

A man, failed and unfit, moved west and north. Jeebee had made it safely this far on the electric bike—a variation on the mountain bicycle with an electrically driven motor—moving at night through northern Indiana, Illinois, Iowa, and Minnesota. Partway across South Dakota, however, the heavy skies that had been with him since yesterday moved lower; and a late April rain began to come down, cold and bitter on the north wind.

His outer clothing, of a breathable, but waterproof fabric, kept the wet from reaching most of him. But even with the long brim of his baseball cap and riding gloves, the rain laid an icy mask on his face and icy chains around his exposed wrists.

He stopped at the first abandoned building he could find—a recently burned and partly fallen-in farmhouse. There was a way among the charred and fallen timbers, however, into a part of it where he could shelter from the rain.

He moved in, accordingly, after covering the motored mountain bike with a plastic tarpaulin from his backpack. He ate some of the cold canned stew he had found in another ruined habitation only a day or so earlier; then lay for hours, waiting for the rain to end.

Eventually, he slumbered. But his dreams were bad, about the running and hiding in a world bankrupt and collapsed. He woke groggily and shifted; and sleep came again, at once. This time he dreamed the old nightmare that he had carried with him out of Michigan and westward. He dreamed that he was back working in the study group; and that the computer screen in front of him was full of the symbols of his equations.

Suddenly a darkness, just a pinpoint at first, appeared near the middle of the screen to obliterate some of the symbols. The blackness grew, spreading and wiping out all his work. It was, he had long since realized, his awareness of the inevitability of the coming Collapse, even though he juggled symbols to prove that it need not come. Now, the inevitability of it invaded his dreams, in retrospect coming to interrupt and destroy all that he had tried to do—he and the others in the study group at Stoketon, Michigan.

His dream shifted. The darkness came out from his screen and became a black shape that pursued him. He found himself in one situation after another, backed into a corner, with no place to go and the darkness approaching; growing enormously to blot out everything as it came closer and closer, to blot him out also.

He woke, sweating. In the lightlessness of his sleeping place, he felt like a naked animal; like a shelled creature stripped of all its normal protection. After a long time, he fell asleep again. This time he slept steadily, the sleep of exhaustion. He did not wake until early afternoon of the next day.

Outside, he found the day scene hardly brighter than the night had been. The thick cloud cover had broken finally, here and there, to let down occasional beams of sunlight. He was so unreasonably cheered by seeing the sun that, since the surrounding territory seemed to be as clear of people as he had found it to be the last week, he took a chance and moved on for a change in daylight.

Slightly after midafternoon, however, the clouds closed down once more; and the rain began again.

Jeebee pulled the visor of his cap down against the falling moisture. Although this plains country, with its sparse patches of timber and only an occasional devastated farmstead, seemed deserted enough, nothing could be certain. His outer clothing, made for camping, continued to keep him dry underneath. Also, today's rain was not as cold on his face and hands, so he was not uncomfortable.

But as the afternoon wore on, the darkness of the clouds increased, the temperature dropped and the rain turned to sleet. It whipped against the naked skin of his face as the wind strengthened from the north.

Like an animal, he thought again of shelter and began to cast around for it. So that, when a little later he came to another pile of lumber that had once been a ranch house, before being dynamited or bulldozed into a scrap heap, he gave up travel for the day and began searching for a gap in the rubble.

He found one at last, a hole that seemed to lead far enough in under the loose material to indicate a fairly waterproof area inside. Laying the bike on its side under an overhang of shattered timbers that would shield it from the rain, he crawled in. He pushed his backpack before him as he went, bracing himself for the possibility of having stumbled on the den of some wild dog— or worse.

But no human or beast appeared to dispute his entrance; and the opening went back farther than he had guessed. He was pleased to hear the patter of the rain only distantly through what was above him, while feeling everything completely dry and dusty around him. He kept on crawling, as far in as he could; until suddenly his right hand, reaching out before him, slid over an edge into emptiness.

He stopped to check, found some space above his head, and risked lighting a stub of candle from the bike pack. Its light shone ahead of him, down into an almost untouched basement garage; with no car in it but walls of cinder blocks and a solid roof of collapsed house overhead.

He memorized this scene below as best he could and put the candle out to save as much of it as possible. He let himself down into the thick, dust-smelling darkness until he felt level floor under his boot soles. Once down, he relit the candle for a moment, and looked around.

The place was a treasure trove. Plainly no one had set foot here since the moment in which the house had been destroyed, and nothing had been looted from this part of the building's original contents.

That night he slept warm and dry with even the luxury of a half-filled kerosene lantern he found there, to light him for a while. The next day he enlarged the entrance, and pulled the bike in out of sight. When he left the place, once more in daylight, two days later, through a separate, carefully tunneled hole much larger than the one by which he had entered, he was rich.

He left still more riches behind him. There was more than he and the bike could carry; but it was not just a lack of charity to his fellow human beings that made him carefully cover and disguise both openings to the place he had found. It was the hard-learned lesson to cover his trail so that no one would suspect someone else had been here and try to track him for what he carried. Otherwise, he would not have cared about the goods he left behind. For his path led still westward to Montana, to his brother Martin's Twin Peaks Ranch—still eight hundred miles distant.

His riches, however, could not help going to his head a little. For one thing, he was taking a calculated risk, riding off in daylight, once more, on the bike. It was true that its motor was almost soundless. But it was an experimental, state-of-the-art device from the days when only those who knew him well had called him Jeebee.

To all others in those days—incredibly, only months before—he had been Jeeris Belamy Walthar. Even then the bike had been an experimental prototype of a vehicle under research, its battery rechargeable daily by sunlight falling on a blanket of miniature solar cells. A blanket which could be unfolded to create thirty-six square feet of energy-gathering surface, exposed to sunlight. Together, blanket and bike were priceless nowadays. It was also true that on it, in open country like this, he could probably outrun anyone else, including riders on horseback. But it was also an open invitation to attack and robbery in these catastrophic days; as a fat wallet had once been, flourished in a den of thieves.

Besides the bike, however, Jeebee had selected well. The

compass that hung from a cord around his neck was sturdy and versatile; and his backpack contained, in addition to the precious solar-cell blanket, a Swiss army knife, some rope, twelve square feet of heat-reflecting plastic tarp, a medical kit, shaving kit, and a little food. Also a pair of binoculars—opera glasses—plus a thick, pencillike device containing a ceramic filter able to take out most bacteria down to two microns, some candles, a waterproof container of matches, an extra sweater, and extra underwear.

Now, as well, from the garage he had just left, he was wearing some other man's old but still solidly seamed leather jacket. His belt was tight with screwdrivers, pruning knives, and other simple hand tools.

Canned food from looted houses and small game had fed Jeebee on his trip so far. But he had been running short of bullets—never having been much of a shot. Now, a small supply of additional ammunition for the take-apart .22 rifle he had been carrying was in the other pack on the bike's rear-fender carrier. As well, in the cellar garage he had picked up a few canned goods, some of which might still be edible.

You could never tell until you opened a can and smelled its contents.

A final find, wrapped now around his waist above his belt, was a good twenty feet of heavy, solid-linked metal chain, taken from the cellar garage.

He had learned enough by this time not to follow any roads that might lead him to inhabited houses, or even small towns. So he cut off between the hills, on the same compass course westward that he had been holding to for the past two weeks, ever since he had run for his life to get away from Stoketon.

Even to think of Stoketon now set a cold sickness crawling about in the pit of his stomach. It had taken a miracle to save him. His buck fever had held true; and, at the last, when Buel Mannerly had risen up out of the weeds with the shotgun pointed at his head, he had been unable to shoot, though Buel was only seconds away from shooting him. Only the dumb luck of someone else from the village firing at Jeebee just then and scaring

Buel into diving to the ground had cleared his way to tree cover and escape.

It was not only lack of guts on his part that had kept him from firing, Jeebee reminded himself now, strongly, steering the bike along a hillside in the sunlight and the light breeze. He, more than anyone else, should be able to remember that like everyone else, he was the product of his own part of the quantitative sociodynamics pattern; and it was that, more than anything else, which had stopped him from shooting Buel.

Once, in a civilized and technology-rich world, reactions like his had signaled a survival type. Now, they indicated the opposite. He glanced at his reflection in the rearview mirror, on the rod projecting from the left handlebar of the bike. The image of his lower face looked back at him, brutal with untrimmed beard and crafty with wrinkles dried into skin tanned by the sun and wind. But above these signs, as he tilted his head to look, the visor of his cap had shaded the skin and his forehead was still pale, the eyes still blue and innocent. The upper half of his features gave him away. He had no instinctive courage, only what was left of a sense of duty, a duty to a fledgling science, which had barely managed to be born before the world had fallen apart.

And a desperate, instinctive need to survive.

It had been fury over that failed duty that pushed him originally in the first few days of his escape from Stoketon. Without that, his spirit would have failed at the thought of the hundreds of unprotected miles between him and the safety of the Twin Peaks Ranch; where he could shelter behind a brother more adapted to these times. But what he had learned and worked at had driven him—the importance of a knowledge that must be saved for the future.

All around the world now there would be forty, perhaps as many as sixty, men and women—applied mathematicians and behavioral scientists like himself—sufficiently expert in the complexities of quantitative sociodynamics to have come independently to the same conclusion as he had. For a second the elegant mathematical notations danced before his mind's eye, spelling out the unarguable truth about the human race in this spring of dissolution and disaster.

Like him, the others would have come to the conclusion that the knowledge of QSD must be protected, taken someplace safe, and hidden against the time—fifty or a thousand years from now—when the majority of the race would begin to change back again toward civilized patterns. Only if all those understanding the mathematics of QSD tried their best would there be even a chance of one of them succeeding in saving this great new tool for the next upswing of mankind.

It was a knowledge that could read both the present and the future. Because of it, they who had worked with it knew how vital it was. It must not be lost. Otherwise future generations could suffer another cycle like this one, of disintegration and chaos.

It was a bitter thing that the others, like himself, were non-survivors under these conditions. The very civilized intellectual nature of their own individual patterns unfitted them for the primitive, violent world that had now recreated itself around them. It was a cruel irony that they were the weakest, not the strongest, vessels to preserve what they alone knew needed to be preserved.

But they could try. He could try. Perhaps he could come to some terms with this time of savagery. It was ironic, also, after all the fears of worldwide nuclear destruction, the "greenhouse effect" and the like, that the world had actually died with a whimper, after all.

The world's currencies had been interlocked, interdependent. This much had been widely understood by those in money markets since the nineteen-fifties. Also, therefore were the economies of the world's nations.

It required only one domino to fall under the right conditions, to set a whole ranked row behind it tumbling. It fell with the collapse of a single obscure bank. The run on this by mobs of people for money it did not have, drew in its creditors. Other banks began to tumble. The panic spread and governments intervened with funds to shore them up—only to find even their funds inadequate for this, as defaults became universal. The world economic web drew the collapse from nation to nation. Central governments fell: and the process of the world splitting into small and smaller self-sufficient pieces began.

Phone systems were the first to die. Then electric services. Then transportation, with furnaces grown cold and refrigerators, like air conditioners, stilled for lack of fuel. Food ceased to reach the cities from outside. Supplies from anywhere else had become nonexistent; and people had begun to fight for what the stores still held; or to take what they had not and needed. It was the nineteenth century again.

The whimper became a snarl.

All this had been predicted in Jeebee's QSD computer screen. Like everyone, he had not believed it could come so quickly.

It was something now for bitter inner laughter in Jeebee. Sociodynamics was new, but it had its roots in the pitifully simple, and artificially static, optimality models, by which behavioral ecologists of an earlier time had predicted the foraging behavior of animals.

But when it had been applied to human society and the problems of modeling dynamic processes, the conclusions were as inevitable as they were terrifying. Independently, but almost simultaneously, the predictions had appeared in the literature from around the world—from people like Piotr Arazavin, Noshiobi Hideki . . . and Jeeris Belamy Walthar, yours truly. . . .

They had disagreed only on the degree of social entropy—chaos—required to trigger the leap to this new, savage expression of social organization. It was no one's fault that the threshold turned out to be lower than any of them had suspected.

So cities became battlefields and stood now as silent, ravaged testaments to the dead left by riot and revolution. Isolated communities developed into small, primitive self-fortified territories. And the Four Horsemen of the Apocalypse were abroad once more—heraldic symbols of the new order.

So it had become a time of bloodletting, of a paring down and reshaping of the population—the pattern that QSD predicted would optimize the restoration of social order in those with the QSD patterns for survival under fang-and-claw conditions. A new medievalism was upon the globe. The iron years had come again; and those who were best fitted to the immediate task of survival were those to whom ethics, conscience, and anything else beyond the pure pragmatism of physical power, were excess baggage.

And so it would continue, the QSD models predicted, until a new, young order could emerge once more, binding the little village fortresses into alliances, the alliances into kingdoms, and the kingdoms into sovereign nations that could begin once more to treat with one another in systems. Fifty years, five hundred years, a thousand years—however long it would take.

And meanwhile, a small anachronism of the time now dead, a weak individual of the soft centuries struggled to cross the newly lawless country, carrying a precious child of the mind to where it might sleep in safety for as many centuries as necessary until reason and civilization should be born again—

Jeebee caught himself up at the brink of a bath in self-pity. Not that he was particularly ashamed of self-pity. Or, at least, he did not think he was particularly ashamed of it. But emotional navel-contemplating of any kind took his attention off his surroundings; and that could be dangerous. In fact, no sooner had he jerked himself out of his mood than his nostrils caught a faint but oily scent on the breeze.

In a moment he had killed the motor of the bike, was off it, and had dragged it with him into the cover of some nearby willow saplings. He lay there, silent and rigid, trying to identify what he had smelled.

The fact that he could not, did not make it any less alarming. Any unusual phenomena—noise, odor, or other—were potential warnings of the presence of other humans. And if there were other humans around, Jeebee wanted to look them over from a distance before he gave them a chance to see him.

In this case the scent was unknown, but, he could swear, not totally unfamiliar. Somewhere he had encountered it before. After lying some minutes hidden in the willows with ears and eyes straining for additional information, Jeebee cautiously got to his feet and, pushing the bike without starting the motor, began to try to track down the wind-borne odor to its source.

It was some little distance over two rises of land before the smell got noticeably stronger. But the moment came when, lying on his stomach with the bike ten feet back, he looked down a long slope at a milling mass of gray and black bodies. It was a large flock of Targhee sheep—the elusive memory of the smell of a sheep barn at a state fair twelve years before snapped back into his mind. With the flock below were three boys, riding bareback on small shaggy ponies. No dogs were in view.

The thought of dogs sent a twinge of alarm along his nerves. He was about to crawl back to his bike and start moving away when a ram burst suddenly from the flock with a sheep dog close behind it, a small brown-and-white collie breed that had been hidden by the milling dark backs and white faces about it. The sheep was headed directly up the slope where Jeebee lay hidden.

He lay holding his breath until the dog, nipping at the heels of the ram, turned it back into the mass of the flock. He breathed out in relief; but at that moment the dog, having seen the ram safely back among the other sheep, spun about and faced up in Jeebee's direction, nose testing the wind.

The wind was from dog to Jeebee. There was no way the animal could smell him, he told himself; and yet the canine nose continued to test the air. After a second the dog began to bark, looking straight in the direction of where Jeebee lay hidden.

"What is it, Snappy?" cried one of the boys on horseback. He wheeled his mount around and cantered toward the dog, up the pitch of the slope.

Jeebee panicked. On hands and knees he scrambled backward, hearing a sudden high-pitched whoop from below as he became visible on the skyline, followed by the abrupt pounding of horses' hooves in a gallop.

"Get him—*get'm!*" sang a voice. A rifle cracked.

Knowing he was now fully in view, Jeebee leaped frantically on the electric bike and kicked on the motor. Mercifully, it started immediately, and he shot off without looking backward, paying no attention to the direction of his going except that it was away from those behind him and along a route as free of bumps and obstacles as he could find.

The rifle cracked again. He heard several voices now, yelping with excitement and the pleasure of the chase. There was a whistling near his head as a bullet passed close. The electric bike was slow to build up speed; and its softly whining motor did not cover the sound of the yells behind him. But he was headed downslope and slowly the bounding, oscillating needle of the speedometer was picking up space above the zero-miles-per-hour pin.

The rifle sounded again, somewhat farther behind him; and this time he heard no whistle of a passing slug. The shots had been infrequent enough to indicate that only one of the boys was armed; and the rifle used was probably an old single-shot, needing to be reloaded after firing—not an easy thing to do on the back of a galloping horse with no saddle leather or stirrups to cling to. He risked a glance over his shoulder.

The three had already given up the chase. He saw them on the crest of a rise behind him, sitting their horses, watching. They had given up almost too easily, he thought—and then he remembered the sheep. They would not want to go too far from the flock for which they were responsible.

He continued on, throttling back only a little on his speed. Now that they had seen him, he was anxious to get as far out of their area as possible, before they should pass the word to more adult riders on better horses and armed with better weapons. But he did begin, instinctively, to pay a little more attention to the dangers of rocks and holes in his way.

There was a new, gnawing uneasiness inside him. Dogs meant trouble for him, as one had just demonstrated. Other humans he could watch for and slip by unseen, but dogs had noses and ears to sense him in darkness or behind cover; and sheepherders meant dogs—lots of them. He had expected cattle, but not sheep, out here. According to the road maps that were all he had to direct him, he should be no further west than a third of the way into South Dakota, by now.

A feeling of utter loneliness flooded through him. He was an outcast; and there was no one and no hope of anyone to stand by him. If he had even one companion to make this long hazardous journey with him, there might be a real chance of his reaching his brother's place. As it was, what he feared most deeply was that in one of these moments of despair he would simply give up, would stop and turn, or wait to be shot down by armed riders like the ones just now following him. Or he would walk nakedly into some camp or town to be killed and robbed; just to get it all over with.

Now he fought the feeling of loneliness, the despair, forcing himself to think without emotion. What was the best thing for him to do under the circumstances? He would be safer apart from the electric bike; but without it he could not cover ground anywhere near so swiftly.

With luck, using the bike, he could be out of this sheep area in a day or so. With the solar blanket to charge its battery, he could cover ground at the low speed of eight miles an hour for some ten hours, before needing to recharge. Four hundred miles—it was like thinking of some incredible distance; but it was actually only fifty hours of such travel away. The bike would get him there, if he just trusted it. It was a case of simply pushing on through; and simply hoping to outrun trouble, as he just had, when he ran into more of it.

But he must go back to hiding out somewhere during the days and traveling nights only. This daytime travel was too dangerous. Starting right now—but even with a good moon he would have trouble spotting all the rocks and potholes in the path of the bike, off-road like this. And road travel increased his chances of being seen. But the yearning for even a rainy daytime like this one was too strong. No, he would make as much time as he could while the day lasted. When night came, he would decide then whether to ride on. . . .

Thinking this, he topped the small rise he had been climbing and looked down at a river, a good two hundred yards across, flowing swiftly from north to south across his direct path west.

Jeebee stared at the river in dismay. Then, carefully, he rode down the slope before him until he halted the bike at the very edge of the swiftly flowing water.

It was a stream clearly swollen by the spring runoff. It was dangerously full of floating debris and swift of current. He got off the bike and squatted to dip a hand in its waters. They numbed his fingers with a temperature like that of freshly melted snow. He got to his feet and remounted the bike, shaking his head. Calm water, warm water, he could have risked swimming, pushing the bike and his other possessions ahead of him on a makeshift raft. But not a river like this.

He would have to go up- or down-stream until he could find some bridge on which to cross it. Which way? He looked downstream. In the past, it had always led to civilization—which in this case meant habitation and possible enemies. He turned the bike upstream and rode off.

Luckily, the land just beside the river here was still-uncovered floodplain, flat and open. He made good time, cutting across sections where the river looped back on itself and saving as much time as possible. Without warning he came around a bend and saw ahead the end of a bridge; straight and high above the gray, swift waters.

It was a railroad bridge.

His first reaction was pure reflex, out of a civilized time when it was dangerous to try to cross a railway bridge for fear of being caught halfway over by traffic on the rails. Then common sense took over, and his heart and hopes leaped up together. For his purpose a railway bridge and the way along further rails, beyond the bridge, was the best thing he could have encountered.

There would be no traffic on these rails nowadays. And for something like the bike, the right-of-way beside the track should be almost as good as a superhighway. He rode up the sloping bank of the river to the railway grading, stopped to lift the bike onto the ties between the rails just for the bridge crossing alone, and remounted. A brief bumpy ride took him safely across what, moments before, had been an uncrossable barrier.

On the far side of the river, as he had expected, there was plenty of room on the grade top beyond the ends of the ties, on either side, for him to ride the bike. He lifted the machine off the ties to the gravel and took up his journey along the track. He was among cottonwoods now, which blocked his view of the surrounding countryside. The embankment top was pitted at intervals where rain had washed some of the top surfacing down the slope and away, but for the most part it was like traveling a well-kept dirt road, and he made steady time with the throttle at a good ten to fifteen miles per hour.

He was now back into the open landscape he had been passing through earlier, although then the land had nourished few stands of trees. Now, on either side of the track, the land was obscured to the near horizon; until, in the far distance ahead, it curved out of sight entirely among some low hills. And nowhere in view were there any sheep, or in fact any sign of man or beast.

For a rare moment he relaxed and let himself hope. Anywhere west of the Mississippi, across the prairie country, a railroad line could run for long distances between towns. With luck, he could be out of this sheep country already. Further west, Martin had written two years before, in the last of the rare letters Jeebee had gotten from his brother while there had still been mail service, the isolated ranchers of the cattle country had been less affected than most by the breakdown of the machinery of civilization. Law and order, after a fashion at least, was still in existence. But in order to reach there, Jeebee needed to trade off the loot he had picked up from the cellar for things he needed.

First would be a more effective rifle than the .22. The .22 was a good little gun, but it lacked punch. Its slug was too light to have the sort of impact that would stop a charging man or large beast. Wolf, bear, and even an occasional mountain lion, still existed in the Montana area toward which he was headed. To say nothing of wild range cattle, which could be dangerous enough.

Moreover, with a heavier gun he could bring down cattle—or even deer or mountain sheep, if he was lucky enough to stumble across them—to supplement whatever other food supplies he was carrying. Which brought him to his second greatest need, the proper type of food supplies. Canned goods were convenient, but heavy; and impractical to carry by backpack. What he really needed was some irradiated meat. Or, failing that, some powdered soups, plain flour, dried beans or such, and possibly bacon.

He had started with some supplies of that sort in his back-pack, when he had finally made his escape alive from Stoketon. In fact, when he had packed to go, it had never actually occurred to him that the locals would not just let him leave, that they might really intend to kill him. In spite of his previous three months of near isolation in the community, he had still felt that after five years of living there, he was one of them.

But of course, he had never been one of them. What had led him to think he knew them was their casual politeness in the supermarket or the post office, plus the real friendship he had had with his housekeeper, Ardyce Prine. Mrs. Prine had lived there all her life, and, in her sixties, was in a position of belonging to the local authoritative generation.

But when the riots became too dangerous for him to risk traveling into Stoketon itself, to the building housing his study group—think tank, his Stoketon neighbors had called it—the local folks had begun to consider him an outsider they were better off without. There was, in fact, no real place for him in their lives. Particularly, as those lives began to shift toward an inward-looking economy, with local produce and meat being traded for locally made shoes and clothing. Jeebee produced nothing they needed.

While Ardyce had still been his housekeeper, they had tolerated him; but the day came when she did not appear; only a short stiff note, delivered by her grandson, saying that she could no longer work for him.

After that, he had felt the invisible enmity of his neighbors beginning to close about him. When he did try to leave and head west to Twin Peaks, he found them lying in wait for him with guns. At the time, he had not been able to understand why. But he understood now. If he had tried to leave naked, they might have let him go. But even the clothes he wore they now regarded as Stoketon property. Buel Mannerly, the druggist, had risen like a demon out of the darkness of the hillside, shotgun in hand, ready to bar his going; and only that lucky misshot from somewhere in the surrounding darkness had let Jeebee get away.

But then, once away, he had foolishly gone through his supplies like a spendthrift, not understanding then how hard it would be to replace them with anything edible at all, let alone more of their special and expensive kind.

He had learned differently the hard way, living off vegetables in abandoned gardens and what he could find in the ruins of isolated and looted houses. There was never much to be found in either kind of place. Now, three weeks later, at least part of him had become bearded, wise, and wary—ears listening, eyes moving, all the time; and a nose sensitive to any scent that might signal danger. . . .

He fell to dreaming of the things he would want to trade for as soon as he found someplace where it was safe to do so.

In addition to a heavier rifle, he badly needed a spare pair of boots. The ones he wore would not last him all the way to Montana, if the bike broke down or he had to abandon or trade it off for any reason. Also—a revolver and ammunition for it would be invaluable. But of course to dream of a handgun like that was like dreaming of a slice of heaven. Weapons were the last thing anyone was likely to trade, these days.

He became so involved in his own thoughts that he found himself entering a curve between two low hills almost unexpectedly. The railroad track curved out of sight ahead between two heavy, grassy shoulders of open land and disappeared in the shadow of a clump of cottonwood trees that lay at the far end of the curve. The rain had stopped sometime before. He followed the tracks around, chugged into the shadow of the cottonwoods and out the other side—to find himself in a small valley, looking down at a railroad station, some sheep-loading pens, and a cluster of buildings, all less than half a mile away.

CHAPTER 2

As it had when he had smelled the sheep, reflex led him to kill the motor of the bike and get both it and himself down on the ground beside the track. He lay where he was on the rough stones of the track ballast, staring through a screen of tall, dry grass at the buildings ahead and a little below him.

Even as he lay there, he knew his hitting the ground like this had almost certainly been a futile effort. If there was anyone in the little community ahead, they could have heard the whine of his electric motor even before it came into view from under the trees. He continued to lie there; but there was no sign of movement in or around the small community he had before him. Nor any sound, although the tin chimneys on several of the buildings were sending up thin streamers of gray smoke against the blue of a now mostly clear, late-afternoon sky.

Overall, what he was looking at seemed like some sort of sheep-loading station that had grown into a semivillage. There were two buildings down there that might be stores; but the majority of the structures he saw—frame buildings sided with gray unpainted boards—could be anything from homes to warehouses.

He rolled half on his side and twisted his body about to get at his backpack and take out the pair of binoculars. They were

17

only four-power, actually a pair he had bought the previous Christmas to give to a friend in the study group; only to find that the friend, with his wife and son, were gone, hastily and in the night, before that holiday.

They were all he had been able to get his hands on before his own departure had been hurried by the antagonism of his neighbors; and they were something that in ordinary times he would not have bothered to put in his pack. But they did magnify, although the material of their lenses seemed hardly better than window glass.

He put them to his eyes now and squinted at the buildings. This time, with their help, after a long survey, he did discover one dog, apparently asleep beside three wooden steps leading up to a long, windowed building he had guessed might be a store. He stared at the dog for a long time, but it did not move.

Jeebee held the glasses to his eyes until they began to water. Then he lowered them and took his weight off his elbows, which had been badly punished, even through the leather jacket, by the gravel and stones beneath him. He tried to estimate what sort of place and people he might have stumbled upon.

If it had not been for the ascending smoke, the wild wishful thought came sliding into his head, he could almost believe he had stumbled across some community where disease or other cause had killed off the population—including the dogs. In which case, all he would have had to do was step down there and help himself to whatever property might be lying around.

The ridiculousness of such good fortune coming his way helped him push the fanciful notion aside. But certainly, the buildings seemed almost too quiet to be true. Of course, it was late in the afternoon now, and most of the people here could be peacefully indifferent to the arrival of some stranger.

But that, too, was a farfetched notion. No one in these days would be unconcerned about strange visitors. No, there were people below, just like those in Stoketon now and everywhere else. The only question was how they would react once they knew he was here. On that, he needed more evidence.

He lay and waited. In about twenty minutes the door of a

storelike building—not the one where the dog lay—opened, and
people began to come out. With their appearance, the dog was
on his feet, in what, as far as Jeebee could tell from this distance,
was a friendly greeting. The dog trotted toward them. They continued emerging until half a dozen men were out, to scatter toward and into other buildings. What they might all have been
doing inside the one structure was a question impossible to answer. But it indicated an importance to the building.

Jeebee lay, watching. Shortly after the last one had disappeared, the door opened again and a final figure in skirts
emerged, threw something to the dog, and went back inside. The
dog ran over and lay down to chew on whatever it was.

Jeebee stayed where he was, thinking. He could hold his
position until night and then push the bike around the station
and continue on down the track beyond at some safe distance.
While he was still thinking this, the rattle of iron wheels on rails
broke open the silence below him, and a moment later a hand-
propelled railcar, with two men pumping opposite ends of the
seesawlike propelling lever, rolled into sight, moving away from
him on the track beyond the buildings. It continued up the track,
away from him and the station until it was lost to sound and
sight.

Jeebee chilled, looking after it. A car like that, pumped by
two men, could get its speed up to twenty or more miles an hour
along good railway track. It could run down his motorcycle if his
battery was as low as it must be by now.

He had been fortunate that it had not come out earlier and
been headed toward him, instead of in the other direction. Of
course, he could probably have gotten off the embankment and
into the cottonwoods before he could have been spotted. But all
the same . . .

Suddenly he had made up his mind. It was a decision out of
a sort of emotional exhaustion. He had to stop guessing, sometime. Somewhere, he would have to take a chance on trying to
trade and this place looked as good as any. He found he no
longer cared what the results of his meeting these people might
be.

He lifted the bike and got on it. Taking the .22 out of the bike pack, he fitted it together and loaded it.

Openly, with the rifle in one hand, he rode down the track and off, in among the buildings.

A clamor of barking broke out as he entered. A near-dozen dogs of various breeds, but all of sheepherding type, gathered around him as he rode the bike directly to the steps of the building from which all the people had emerged earlier. The original dog was one of those now following him clamorously. Like the others, it seemed content to voice alarm and challenge, but showed no inclination to bite, which was—he thought—a good sign as far as the attitudes toward strangers of those owning the dogs were concerned.

He stopped the bike, got off, leaned it against the side of the steps where the dog had lain, and climbed the steps, shrugging his backpack higher on his shoulders. He knocked. There was no answer.

After a moment, he knocked again. When there was still no answer, he put his hand on the knob. It turned easily and the door opened. He went in, leaving the yelping of the dog pack behind him. Their noise did not stop once he had disappeared from their view, but went on, only muted by the walls and windows of the building.

Jeebee looked around himself at the room into which he had stepped. The place was barely warmer than outdoors, probably unheated. This particular room, at least, was fair-sized. It held six round tables with four chairs to each. Along one wall was a short, high bar, with nothing but some glasses upside down on the shelves behind it. Beyond the bar was a further door, closed, which Jeebee assumed to lead deeper into the building. Stacked on one end of the bar were some dishes, cups, and silverware, looking as if they had just been left behind by diners.

The barking of the dogs outside had taken on an eager, high-pitched quality interspersed with excited yips, then unaccountably faded to silence, with a few isolated whines. Jeebee moved swiftly to the nearest window and looked through it.

Coming toward the steps of the entrance was a strange

female figure. A woman who must have been as tall as, and heavier than, Jeebee himself, unless most of her bulk was extra clothing underneath that dress. She was dressed in a muffling, nineteenth-century-style dress, of rusty black cloth that fell to the tops of her heavy boots below and ended in an actual poke bonnet at the top. Broad-shouldered, bent-shouldered in the black dress, she walked with long and heavy strides, leaning back against the strain in the taut chain leash one end of which was looped around a dog's neck and secured by a snap lock that just showed above the thick ruff of hair and the nape of that neck.

It was the dog itself that had aroused the rest of the pack. It was an unlikely sheepherding dog, resembling a German shepherd more than any other breed. Also, there was some kind of difference Jeebee could not pin down, in its appearance and the way it walked. It was long-legged and had a loose-gaited, almost shambling way of moving. Its massive body was half again larger than most of the other canines around it, its coat rough with the thick hair of a dog that had spent most of its winter out in the weather.

It paid no attention to the other dogs at all. It ignored them as if they did not exist, walking ahead of the big woman, its head low and thrust forward as if on some purposeful errand. Most of the other dogs had pressed forward at its approach but now drew back and sat or lay down and were watching the newcomer with intense interest. But there were four larger dogs who stood, still on all four legs, out of the path to the steps, but just barely. Foremost of these was the largest, a dog collielike in its markings, but short-haired and heavily boned with a broad skull that reminded Jeebee of the European sheep-guarding dogs he'd seen pictures of in *National Geographic*.

It did not withdraw as the leashed animal, pulling forward on the chain in advance of the woman, passed it. As the leashed animal went by Jeebee saw it raise its head and look left for a moment to meet the eyes of the collie. Then the leashed dog turned away again, without other movement or expression, and, still pulling on the leash, led the woman ahead and up the steps to the door.

Jeebee saw the door handle turn. The door opened and the two of them stepped into the room where Jeebee waited. The woman closed the door with a deliberate movement, behind her. The dog on the leash turned immediately to her, and she, feeling into some sort of deep pocket in her voluminous dress, pulled out something that seemed to be a tidbit of some kind, which she palmed into the dog's open and waiting mouth.

The dog swallowed it at a gulp and turned toward Jeebee. He tilted his long nose up and tested the air with several deep sniffs.

"Guard!" the woman ordered to the dog, then looked toward Jeebee herself. She spoke again in a hoarse, deep voice like the voice of a very old person: "I saw you on your way in. I just stepped out to get my watchdog, here."

Jeebee felt the metal of the trigger guard of the .22 slippery in his right hand. The woman, he saw now that she was close, was wearing a black leather belt tight around her waist, with a small holster and the butt of what looked like a short-barreled revolver sticking out of the holster. She smelled, a dirty-clothes sort of smell. He did not doubt that she could and would use the handgun, if she thought it advantageous to do so. And, flooding all through him, was the old doubt that he could lift the .22 and fire back, even to defend his own life.

The German shepherd–like dog lay down, hind legs tucked under his body, his head erect and his weight resting lightly on his elbows and forelegs. His gaze remained on Jeebee, but that was all. The woman lifted her head, looking directly at Jeebee. Her face was tanned, masculine looking, with heavy bones and thin lips. Deep parentheses of lines cut their curves from nose to chin on each side of her mouth. She must be, Jeebee thought, at least fifty.

"All right," said the woman. "What brings you to town?"

"I came in to trade some things," said Jeebee.

His own voice sounded strange in his ears, like the creaky tones of an old-fashioned phonograph record where most of the low range had been lost in recording.

"What you got?"

"Different things," said Jeebee. "How about you? Have you or somebody else here got shoes, food, and maybe some other things you can trade me?"

His voice was sounding more normal now. He had pulled his cap low over his eyes before he had come into town; and hopefully, in this interior dimness, lit only by the windows to his right, she could not see the pale innocence of his eyes and forehead.

"I can trade you what you want—prob'ly," the woman said. "Come on. You too."

The last words were addressed to the dog and reinforced by a tug on the leash. The dog rose silently to four feet again, and once more took the lead as she led Jeebee to the further door. They went through it into another room that looked as if it might once have been a poor excuse for a hotel lobby. A dingy brown corridor led off from a far wall, and doors could be glimpsed, spaced along either side.

The lobby-room was equipped with what had probably been a clerk's counter. This, plus half a dozen more of the round tables, and a few plain wooden chairs, were piled with what at first glimpse appeared to be every kind of junk imaginable, from old tire casings to metal coffeepots that showed the dents and marks of long use. A closer look showed Jeebee a rough order to things in the room. Clothing filled two of the tables, and all of the cooking utensils were heaped with the coffeepots on another.

The woman led the dog to the end of the counter. There were two different lengths of chain, a long and a very short one there, with one end of each bolted to the thick wood of the countertop.

She started to snap the end of the lead chain to the shorter of the bolted-down ones, then apparently changed her mind. She connected it instead to the long chain, which Jeebee noticed would let the dog range anywhere in the room.

"Guard," the woman said to the dog again. The dog, this time, remained standing almost as if it had not heard her. Its gaze stayed on Jeebee.

She, also, was looking at Jeebee. When he looked back at

her, she nodded at the dog. "Pure wolf, he is, so don't try taking anything."

"Let's see what you've got." Jeebee kept his voice emotionless.

She motioned to an end of the clerk's counter that was clear. Jeebee unbuckled his recently acquired leather jacket—the dog's nose tested the air again—and began unloading his belt of the screwdrivers, chisels, files, and other small hand tools he had brought. When he was done, he unwrapped the metal chain from his waist and laid it on the wooden surface of the counter, where it chinked heavily.

"Maybe, you can use this, then," said Jeebee, nodding at the dog as casually as possible.

"Maybe," said the woman, with a perfect flatness of voice. "But he don't need much holding. He does what I tell him."

"You said he was a wolf?" Jeebee asked skeptically as she began to examine the tools.

She looked up squarely into his face.

"That's right," she said. "He's no herder. He's a killer." She stared at him for a second. "What are you—cattleman?"

"Not me," said Jeebee. "My brother is. I'm on my way to his place, now."

"Where?" she asked bluntly.

"West," he said. "You probably wouldn't know him." He met her eyes. It was a time to claim as much as he could. "But he's got a good-sized ranch, he's out there—and he's waiting for me to show up."

The last, lying part came out with what Jeebee felt sounded like conviction. Perhaps a little of the truth preceding it had carried over. The woman, however, looked at him without any change of expression whatsoever, then bent to her examination of the hand tools again.

"What made you think I was a cattleman?" Jeebee asked. Her silence was unnerving. Something in him wanted to keep her talking, as if, so long as she continued to speak, nothing much could go wrong.

"Cattleman's jacket," she said, not looking up.

"Ja—" He stopped himself. Of course, she was talking about the leather jacket he was wearing. He had not realized that there would be any perceptible difference in clothing between sheep- and cattle-men. Didn't sheepmen wear leather jackets, too? Evidently not. Or at least, not in this locality.

"This is sheep country," the woman said, still not looking up. Jeebee felt the statement like a gun hanging in the air, aimed at him and ready to go off at any minute.

"That so?" he said.

"Yes, that's so," she answered. "No cattlemen left here, now. *That* belonged to a cattleman." She jerked her thumb at the animal, swept the tools and the chain together into a pile before her as if she already owned them. "All right, what you want?"

"A pair of good boots," he said. "Some bacon, beans, or flour. A handgun—a revolver."

She looked up at him on the last words.

"Revolver," she said with contempt. She shoved the pile of tools and chain toward him. "You better move on."

"All right," he said. "Didn't hurt to ask, did it?"

"Revolver!" she said again, deep in her throat, as if she was getting ready to spit. "I'll give you ten pounds of corn and five pounds of mutton fat for it all. And you can look for a pair of boots on the table over there. That's it."

"Now, wait . . ." he said. The miles he had come since Stoketon had not left him completely uneducated to the times he now lived in. "Don't talk like that. You know—I know—these things here are worth a lot more than that. You can't get metal stuff like that anymore. You want to cheat me some, that's all right. But let's talk a little more sense."

"No talk," she said. She came around the counter and faced him. Jeebee could feel her gaze searching in under the shadow of his cap's visor to see his weakness and his vulnerability. "Who else you going to trade with?"

She stared at him. Suddenly the great wave of loneliness, of weariness, washed through Jeebee again. The thinking front of his mind recognized that her words were only the first step in a bargaining. Now it was time for him to counter-offer, to sneer at what she had, to rave and protest. But he could not. Emotionally he was too isolated, too empty inside. Silently he began to sweep the chain and the hand tools into a pile and return them to his belt.

"What you doing?" yelled the woman, suddenly.

He stopped and looked at her.

"It's all right," he said. "I'll take them someplace else."

Even as he said the words, he wondered if she would call on the wolf-dog to attack him; and whether he would, indeed, make it out of this station alive.

"Someplace else?" she snarled. "Didn't I just say there isn't anyplace else anywhere near? What's wrong with you? You never traded before?"

He stopped putting the tools back in his belt and looked at her.

"Look!" she said, reaching under the counter. "You wanted to trade for a revolver. Look at it!"

He reached out and picked up the nickel-plated short-barreled weapon she had dumped before him. It was speckled with rust. When he pulled the hammer back, there was a thick accumulation of dirt to be seen on its lower part. Even at its best, it had been somebody's cheap Saturday-night special, worth fifteen or twenty dollars. Jeebee did not really know guns, but the value of what he was being offered was plain.

His head cleared, suddenly. If she really wanted to trade, there was hope after all.

"No," he said, shoving the cheap and dirty revolver back at her. "Let's skip the nonsense. I'll give you all of this for a rifle. A deer rifle, a .30/06 and ammunition for it. Skip the food, the boots, and the rest."

"Throw in that motorcycle," she said.

He laughed. And he was as shocked to hear himself as if he had heard a corpse laugh.

"You know better than that." He waved his hand at the pile on the counter. "All right, you can make new hand tools out of a leaf from old auto springs—if you want to sweat like hell. But there's one thing you can't make, and that's chain like that. That chain's worth a lot. Particularly to somebody like you with stuff to protect. And if this is sheep country, you're not short of guns. Show me a .30/06 and half a dozen boxes of shells for it."

"Two boxes!" she spat.

"Two boxes and five sticks of dynamite." Jeebee's head was whirling with the success of his bargaining.

"I got no dynamite. Only damn fools keep that stuff around."

"Six boxes, then."

"Three."

"Five," he said.

"Three." She straightened up behind the counter. "That's it. Shall I get the rifle?"

"Get it," he said.

She turned and went down the corridor to the second door on the left. There was the grating sound of a key in a lock, and she went through the door. A moment later she reemerged, relocked the door, and brought him a rifle with two boxes of shells, all of which she laid on the counter.

Jeebee picked up the gun eagerly and went through the motions of examining it. The truth of the matter was that he was not even sure if what he was holding was a .30/06. But he had lived with the .22 long enough to know where to look for signs of wear and dirt in a rifle. What he held seemed clean, recently oiled, and in good shape.

"You look that over, mister," said the woman. "I got another one you might like better, but it's not here. I'll go get it."

"Guard!" she said to the wolf, or whatever it was. It was a male, he saw. It did not move, and its gaze remained fixed on Jeebee. She passed through the door, closing it behind her.

Jeebee stood motionless, listening until he heard the distant slamming of the outside door reecho through the building. Then, moving slowly so as not to trigger off any reflex in the dog, he slid his hand to one of the boxes of cartridges the woman had brought, opened it with the fingers of one hand, and extracted two of the shells. He laid one on the counter and slowly fed the other into the clip slot of the rifle. He hesitated, but the dog had not moved. With one swift move, he jacked the round into firing position. . . .

He could hear it click loosely inside the gun as he lifted it.

Slowly, he took the shell out again and laid the gun thoughtfully down on the counter. The proper-size ammunition, probably, would be in that room down the corridor, but his chances of getting there . . .

On the other hand, he might as well try. He took a step away from the counter toward the corridor. The wolf-dog did not move.

It stood like a statue, its tail motionless, no sound or sign of threat showing in it, but neither any sign of a relaxation in its watchfulness. It was the picture of a professional on duty. Of course, he thought, of course it would never let him reach the door of the room with the guns, let alone smash the door lock and break in. He stared at the animal. It must weigh close to a hundred and twenty pounds, and it was a flesh-and-blood engine of destruction. Some years back he had seen video film of attack dogs being trained.

The distant sound of voices, barely above the range of audibility, attracted his attention. They were coming from outside the building.

He laid down the .30/06 and took a step toward the door to the outer room. This moved him also toward the wolf-dog, and at this first step the animal did not move. But when he stepped again, it moved toward him. It did not growl or threaten, but in its furry skull its eyes shone like bits of golden china; opaque, he thought, and without feeling.

But his movement had brought him far enough out in the room so that he could squat and see at an angle through the windows and glimpse the area in front of the building where the three steps stood to the entrance door. The woman stood there, now surrounded by five men, all with rifles or shotguns. As he stood, straining his ears in the hot, silent room, the sense of their words came faintly to him through the intervening glass and distance.

"Where y'been?" the woman was raging. "He was ready to walk out on me. I want two of you to go around back—"

"Now, you wait," one of the men interrupted her. "He's got that little rifle. No one's getting no .22 through him just because you want his bike."

"Did I say I wanted it for myself?" the woman demanded. "The whole station can use it. Isn't it worth that?"

"Not getting shot for, it ain't," said the man who had spoken. "Sic your wolf on him."

"And get it shot!" the woman shouted hoarsely, deeply.

"Why not?" said one of the other men. His beard hung down to his belt. It was as black as Jeebee's, but there was a thickness of body to him and wrinkles around his eyes that suggested he was as much as twenty years older than Jeebee.

"You're soft on that wolf," he went on, "always have been, ever since you bought it as a pup from that trapper and raised it for the first few days before Callahan bought it off you—"

"That's enough!" said the woman.

"No, I mean it," the man went on. "If you weren't soft on it, why'd you stop us killing it when we trashed Callahan's place? It's no damn good, that wolf. Killed my Corduroy, and he was next to being the top dog here—"

"I said, that's enough!" The woman seemed to grow until she towered over all the men, and her voice chilled even Jeebee, through the glass. "I'm soft on nobody, Jim Carlsen! Remember that! At Callahan's none of you had the guts to kill his wife and baby? No, but you'd shoot his wolf! You want to find out for yourself how soft I am?"

There was a moment of absolute stillness and silence outside the building, that stretched out. Then the black-bearded man looked away from her, cleared his throat, and spat on the ground to his side.

"Hell! Have it your own way," Jeebee barely heard him say. The man kept looking away from the woman.

"All right!" she said. "I don't want to hear anything more about killing it. That's a valuable animal! Like this's a valuable machine!"

The woman waved at the motorcycle. "You got to take some risks to make a profit."

"All the same, you go in and send that bastard out here!"

one man said stubbornly. "You send him out not suspecting, and give us a chance to shoot him, safe."

"If he comes out," said the woman, "he's going to want to come out traded, with a loaded .30/06 instead of just that .22. You want that to face after I let him go? I did my share, facing him. Now it's up to all you—"

The argument went on. The loneliness and emptiness mounted inside Jeebee. He closed his eyes, wanting everything in the present crazy world just to go away. . . .

And opened them again on a feeling of instinctive urgency, to find the muzzle of the dog almost touching him and the golden eyes fixed on his own—not sixteen inches between their faces.

For a moment the animal stood there. Then it extended its neck and sniffed at him once more. Its black nose began to move over his body above the waist, sniff by sniff exploring the leather jacket. Casually, he closed both hands on the .22 still in his lap, and with his left one tilted the rifle's muzzle toward the head of the wolf-dog above it as his right hand felt for the trigger. At this close range, even a small slug like this ought to go right through the brain of the animal. . . .

His finger found the trigger and trembled there. The wolf-dog paid no attention. His nose was pushed into the unbuttoned opening at the top of the jacket, sniffing. Abruptly he withdrew his head and looked squarely into Jeebee's eyes.

In that moment Jeebee knew that he could not do it. Not like this. He could not even kill this creature to save himself. It had done him no harm. It was now even acting almost friendly. His buck fever was back on him . . . and what did it matter? Even if he killed it, the men outside would kill him, eventually. What kind of an idiot guard animal was it, that would let him put a gun directly to its head and pull the trigger?

The questing nose had now changed its attention and was working down his right sleeve. It reached the end of the sleeve, the long jaws gaped, revealing teeth twice the size of those Jeebee had seen on any dog, and these teeth closed gently on the cuff of the jacket and tugged. It shifted the grip of its jaws on the cuff to further back in its mouth, so that the wide carnasials now closed on the leather. It chewed for a moment; then let go and tilted its head back, looking up at Jeebee with golden eyes.

Jeebee's mind suddenly made sense of the situation. It was the jacket, of course, his mind told him. The jacket, and the dog alike, must have come from the ruined house where he had found the chain and taken shelter that night. The jacket must still smell of the cattleman the woman had mentioned, who had no doubt been killed by the woman and her friends. A man who had owned this wolf-dog originally. Now, several days of wearing the leather garment had mingled its original owner's scent with Jeebee's; until they were one scent only. Also, above all, the jacket and Jeebee both would not smell of sheep and sheep handling, of which all this station, its people and buildings, must reek to the creature's sensitive nose.

However else the wolf-dog might react to him, it seemed—tentatively, at least—ready to accept him, and should not attack mindlessly. For the first time he remembered what he had noticed but paid no attention to in this room. Around the end of the counter where the two chains were stapled, around the space of the short line, particularly, everything within reach of the chain had been chewed or torn by canine teeth. The heavy wood of the counter had been pitted, a brace to one of the legs of a nearby chair had been gnawed almost in half. For the first time it occurred to Jeebee that this animal might be as alone and friendless as Jeebee himself.

On a sudden impulse he reached down and unsnapped the closure that fastened the chain around the other's neck.

The wolf-dog shook himself, like one of his kind coming out of water, but briefly, and looked again curiously up at Jeebee.

Now, however, Jeebee felt time pressing on him. He was reminded of the danger close by, in which he still stood. Still holding the .22 in one hand, he snatched up the .30/06 from the counter in the other and ran with both rifles to the door of the room the woman had entered. The wolf-dog went with him.

The door resisted opening when he reached it. But a blow of the butt of his .22 was all that was needed to break the cheap lock of the door handle; and the door itself swung open to show him a rack of rifles and shotguns. He found boxes of ammunition for the .22 and changed the .30/06 rifle the woman had given him for one that also accepted the same ammunition but had been customized to have a square magazine about the size of a box of kitchen matches under it, that would hold sixteen shells instead of the ordinary clip.

He stuffed his pockets full with ammunition for both the .22 and the .30/06.

He would have to give up the bike and the carrier pack that was on it, with all its contents; but perhaps he could still get out of this with his life. Hastily, he loaded the rifle's box magazine. He went to the single window in the room and found, as he had hoped, that it looked out on the back of the building. Through its dirty pane he saw a slight, grassy slope upward to trees that crowned a low hill, trees that were the beginning of a wood that stretched northward. They were part of the same woods the railroad tracks had curved through before emerging here.

Taking a rifle in each hand, he used their butts to smash out the window glass, then clean as many as possible of the glass shards from the bottom and sides of the window frame. He threw the rifles out, and taking a grip on the inner edge of the window sill, he made a twisting jump out and down onto the grass about four feet below.

He snatched up the rifles and began to run for the trees. The wolf-dog appeared beside him, having clearly followed him out. Although Jeebee was running at top speed, the other was barely loping along with him, and still looked more interested than concerned. *Run, you idiot!* thought Jeebee, but did not have the breath to say it.

He heard a shout behind him, and glancing briefly back over his shoulder, saw the man with the belt-length black beard had come out around the corner of the house behind him, carrying a rifle. The shout was unintelligible. Jeebee ignored it, continuing to run as fast as he could.

The outer line of trees loomed close before him, perhaps only a dozen more strides away, but now there was also the clamor of barking dogs behind him, and Jeebee knew that dogs could run him down easily. A sudden panicky fear made him skid to a stop and swing around. At least he would go down looking as if he was willing to fight.

The man he had seen a moment before had been joined by another, this one holding a pistol in one hand hanging down at his side. But between those two and Jeebee was a good-size pack of the local dogs he had seen earlier.

They swarmed up the slope after him, the large, short-haired collielike dog in the lead. The two men were merely standing with their firearms, apparently content to let the dogs catch Jeebee and pull him down. It was plain that it was more agreeable to them to have him as a captive, to explain the workings of the electric bike, than it would have been to bring him back as a nontalking corpse.

Now, he thought, was the time when he should shoot. When the two before him were not ready. But he could not do it. He could, however, fire on the dogs.

But, now that he had halted, he saw the collielike dog well in advance of the rest of the pack. The wolf-dog, stopped beside him, had also turned back. Suddenly it moved. It became a blur of gray rushing toward the oncoming dogs. The awkward-looking, shambling gait he had noticed through the window was gone. The wolf-dog, its head and ears erect, was closing the distance in great fluid bounds that reminded Jeebee of dolphins he had once seen, breasting the bow waves of a cruise ship—"lads, before the wind," Herman Melville had called them in *Moby Dick*, and those words, strangely right in this moment, came unexpectedly back into Jeebee's mind.

The dogs right behind the collie spun and bolted, tails between their legs. The collie, however, which Jeebee recognized as the one who had stood forth against Wolf's entry to the store, checked, lowered its body into a half crouch, and sprang for the wolf-dog's throat.

The wolf-dog made no effort to evade the attack. He simply closed his jaws around the back of his attacker's neck. There was no sound, but the collie's legs suddenly went stiff and its body jerked once as the canine teeth pierced the spinal cord.

It fell.

The wolf-dog stood over it for a moment. The man with the rifle had lifted his weapon to aim at Jeebee after all. Now his aim swung instead to point at Jeebee's companion, who was now turning from his dead opponent.

Jeebee dropped the .22 and jerked the .30/06 to his shoulder. The imaginary line across the horns of the rear sight and the tip of the front blade bisected the beard above the man's chest. This time Jeebee fired without hesitation.

Then he snatched up the .22 and turned away himself, hearing the pistol bark behind him, and made it into the shadowed protection of the woods. The wolf-dog had run at the sound of Jeebee's rifle. Now he was far ahead of him into the trees and out of sight.

CHAPTER 3

Jeebee plodded on through the woods. He had put a good two hours of walking behind him, since he escaped from the station. But now the westering sun was just above the horizon, and he was looking for a place to camp for the night.

He had heard two more shots from the revolver after he was among the trees and out of sight, but none of the bullets evidently came anywhere near him. Nobody, it seemed, had made any effort to follow him. Nor was there any great reason to, he had thought to himself. They had his bike; and going into the woods after him would be to risk the almost certain chance that he could kill or badly wound more than one of them before they killed or captured him.

Nor had he seen any further sign of—abruptly he found he could not think of the creature he had freed as a wolf-dog any longer. No dog had ever covered ground the way he had seen his companion do so in turning back to his attack on the collie. Dogs did not bound like deer. He, whoever he was, could only be an actual wolf, and nothing else.

Jeebee came upon a little opening in the trees, a sort of pocket-sized glade. Beyond it, the trees thinned out and he could see into more open country beyond. There was little point in trying to go further today, in any case. He congratulated himself on still having an emergency flask of water in his backpack.

He found a pair of trees on the edge of the clearing close enough together so that he could fasten his heat-reflecting plastic tarp between them. Some six feet out from the tarp, he put together the materials of a fire and lighted it. Gradually, as the small twigs with which he had started it picked up flame, he added larger and larger dead branches that he had gathered from the woods around him. At last he had a small, but warm, fire going; as well as a pile of more wood handy to see him through the night.

His first buoyancy of spirit, which had come from escaping from the people in the station, reinforced by the fact that he now had a heavier rifle and more ammunition, began slowly to leak out of him.

He took off his backpack and settled down to make an inventory of what he now owned in the world.

Beyond what was in the pack, his pockets held only the boxes of ammunition for the .22 and the .30/06 and a few packages of irradiated foods, and some underwear and socks. The great value lay in the ammunition he had picked up, and the .30/06.

Even so, he reminded himself, the store of ammunition was not inexhaustible. The farther west he got, the more difficult it would be to find any ammunition at all.

He ate a little of his irradiated emergency food, washing it down with water from the plastic flask. When he was done, the flask was only a little more than half-full; which meant that his first search tomorrow must be for a source of drinkable water. Also, he must check the next ruined buildings he came across for blankets to replace the ones that had been carried on the bike and now were gone for good. For tonight he would roll himself in the solar-cell blanket. It did not have the qualities of the heat-reflecting tarp, but it would at least help to conserve his own body heat.

Meanwhile, he found himself sitting, staring into the fire, not ready to sleep yet, but with his spirits as deeply fallen as it seemed possible for them to fall, and an exhaustion of the mind that mirrored the exhaustion of his body.

It was completely dark now. The light from the flames of the fire leaping before him made a wall of darkness around him, so that he caught mere glimpses of the trees surrounding the little clearing. He forgot about his surroundings and sat gazing only into the flames dancing above the burning branches and before the backdrop of utter blackness that was the night.

The snap of burning firewood snatched him from the uneasy doze into which he had slipped, and through the red, upleaping flames of the fire he became aware that Wolf had appeared, having approached him noiselessly, curiously, until he was almost upon Jeebee. His ears were folded back, and he stretched his long neck cautiously toward Jeebee's boots.

Wolf— Jeebee said internally, speaking the name he had given the other in his mind, but not daring to break the spell of the moment by speaking the name out loud and possibly scaring him away.

Jeebee did not move; and Wolf's exploratory sniffs finally gave way to an almost explosive exhalation that tickled the hairs on Jeebee's shin. Jeebee had to fight down the impulse to pull back his leg. *So!* the crazy thought came to him. *Wolves do huff and puff!*

Little by little, Wolf's investigation proceeded up Jeebee's body until their noses were only inches apart. The eyes that looked like golden china from a distance, up close were kaleidoscope mosaics of brown and yellow and green. Jeebee found it difficult to breathe. The coarse fur of Wolf's chest brushed the back of his hand, and unconsciously he began to scratch the thick ruff.

A small part of his mind noted with some surprise that the collie's teeth seemed to have left neither scratch nor puncture. Hesitantly, almost shyly, Wolf's tongue flicked the end of Jeebee's nose. In that instant of contact, the exquisite tension that had held Jeebee, burst.

Impulsively, overwhelmingly, grateful for this tiny hint of trust, he threw his arms out to hug Wolf's neck.

Wolf jerked away with a growl of startlement and a clack of jaws that closed on empty air. He hesitated for just an instant with one foreleg raised. An uncertain, quizzical expression was written momentarily on his face and form. Then, suddenly, he was gone, vanished from the small circle of firelight.

For a moment Jeebee could not believe he had lost Wolf again. Slowly, the reality of the other's going dawned on him as he sat waiting, listening, hoping in spite of himself that Wolf would return. But he did not. After a little while, Jeebee rolled himself in the solar-cell blanket and slept.

When he woke, stiff and chilled beside the dead fire in the early morning, Wolf was there, lying on the other side of the clutter of burnt wood and ashes. When Jeebee sat up, however, Wolf was instantly on his feet and lost into the brush and trees surrounding the campsite.

Nonetheless, Jeebee felt a great upbounding of happiness inside him. The other had come back. He had not been driven away for good by Jeebee's attempt to hold him.

I don't blame him, Jeebee thought as he got to his feet and began to urinate on the gray, dead ash of last night's fire. If someone he hardly knew tried to grab him, he, also, would have avoided the attempt. He wondered if there was any chance of Wolf staying with him. He must remember to let Wolf make the advances, in his own time. If he was not scared off, the other just might share Jeebee's travels—for a way, at least. Jeebee had not realized until now how hungry he had grown for any kind of company at all.

The sun was barely up. Jeebee drank as little as possible from his water flask, took a strip of irradiated beef from his pack to chew on, and began to move. Awake and revivified, his mind was at work again. He had perhaps half a pound more of the beef in his pockets. Enough for two light meals for him—probably a gulp and a half to Wolf. They would both need food; but if Wolf was going to share his journey for any distance at all, he surely could be trusted to find his own food.

Jeebee could concentrate on his own needs. Water was the most urgent of these. But while looking for water, he could also watch for signs of game. Anything—squirrel, porcupine, groundhog—along their way. It was too much to hope for signs of deer, or any prey at all large. But if it appeared, he now had the .30/06.

Even if he found, and could shoot, something as large as a deer, it would only be a temporary solution. So far, he had been lucky in finding food as he went in looted houses and their storage places. But that was a luck that probably would not last in this less populated country.

He dreamed of Wolf choosing to stay in touch with him. If Wolf did, Jeebee wondered, would there be any way, assuming they could become a team, that Wolf could help him find game? He now remembered reading that a pair of lions would work together in their hunting, one driving game toward where another was lying in wait. Did wolves work together that way? Or, if not, was there still some way Wolf could be brought to drive meat animals into his gun sights?

He sighed. The whole idea was nothing more than wishful thinking. Wolf was clearly no dog to be either controlled or trained. In any case, until Wolf would trust him more, it was all supposition. But the working engine of his mind stored the possibility for future reference, in the days that followed, as Jeebee moved on westward and Wolf continued to touch base with him, most twilights and dawns.

There was only one realistic answer for him now, Jeebee realized. He had been avoiding the more traveled east-west routes for fear of being ambushed. Such routes sometimes used—but more often paralleled—one of the old highways. Most road surfaces were still good, but beginning to be overgrown with vegetation from lack of use. Still, they usually indicated the best route across the countryside. Unfortunately, such routes were usually the most direct way to the next town or city.

He could not risk entering any inhabited or formerly inhabited place, again. His last experience was a gentle example of what might be encountered. But along any road, with the weapons he now had, he could possibly find other travelers from whom it would be safer to trade—or buy.

Or rob. He put that thought from him. He had not yet become that desperate. Not yet, at least.

Luckily he had not dared show it to the woman back where he had gotten the gun, but in a money belt around his waist under his shirt were twenty-three gold coins he had bought long ago, as a result of casually answering a coin-of-the-month plan in a magazine advertisement. He had paid for the coins regularly until, one day, he had realized he really had no great interest in belonging to such a plan and had dropped out.

But now, they were there, under his shirt. If he could find someone safe to buy from, he would rather do that than rob—and perhaps have to kill.

But he told himself now that if necessary, he would do even those things to stay alive and get safely to the ranch.

His knowledge of QSD must live, therefore he must. Life had no meaning for him otherwise, now.

He began to scheme as he walked, a rifle in each hand. He badly missed his maps, most of which had been with the motorbike. But memory said the nearest large east-west highway had been south of where he was now.

It was strange how the study group at Stoketon had already become almost dreamlike in his mind—like a childhood memory of a home lived in once, but for a short time and long ago. Jer Shandeau, Peter Wilbiggin, Kim Allen—these and all the others he had worked with there—had acquired the sort of sunset aura that had always seemed to surround people in fables and fairy tales. It was hard now to believe that they, and the life he had shared with them, had been real at all.

He caught his thoughts sharply up from their wandering. A necessary change of route was what he had been thinking of. This day would be warmer than the one before. The gentler weather of spring was moving inevitably northward. So far, today was a day of sunshine and an occasional cloud, and the warmth caused his spirits instinctively to rise.

He had become used to using the sun as a timepiece. Though he still wore his watch with an experimental hundred-year battery, he had gotten out of the habit of glancing at it. The sun told him that the morning was perhaps one quarter of its way toward noon. South would be less than a half turn to his left.

To check that fact, he lifted the cord holding his compass around his neck and took the compass itself on the palm of his hand. It agreed with what he had read from the sun's position, but was a little more precise in what could be read from its poised needle.

He had instinctively been moving within the woods since they had left their camping spot of last night. The turn south would take them out into the open grassland.

He regretted more than ever the loss of his South Dakota map.

What would be the type of east-west road he would encounter first, going south? He wanted a former freeway, or some kind of road that ran far to the west, not just something that had been a two-lane strip of asphalt joining two small towns together.

The routes of the former interstates would attract more travelers and give him a greater choice. He was, he thought, somewhere below what had once been the city of Pierre, South Dakota.

Pierre was too large a place to approach safely, these days. If anything was left of it at all, those leavings would be divided into territories by well-armed and watchful gangs at feud with each other, and all on the lookout for any easy prey such as he, alone, would be.

The change in direction unfortunately took him out of the occasional cover of trees in which he preferred to travel, when these were available. Wolf seemed to do so, too. One thing was certain; he could come and go like a shadow.

But he was clearly following a roughly parallel course to Jeebee's; and sometimes, now that nearly two weeks had passed since they met, he stayed the night.

Jeebee was now traversing land that had once been largely farm- or pasture-land. Occasionally he crossed country roads, and every so often he sighted farm buildings in the distance.

It made for swifter, if more open, going.

But as if to compensate for this, the rainy weather that had given frequent showers, let up, and he went through a succession of days that were both warm and sunny. The dead grass in the untilled fields was drying out and a few blades of new green were among it.

These fields he circled, staying under cover or below the horizon as much as he could. It was in the process of going around one such that Jeebee learned his first lesson from Wolf. It was mid-to-late afternoon and for once Wolf had joined him early. They had come to a narrow band of brush and trees stretching off to his right, and without thinking, Jeebee had turned into it with the intention of bypassing the farmhouse he could see ahead, behind the leafy cover.

Wolf had hesitated. After a few steps Jeebee had realized the other was not with him and looked back to see Wolf standing and looking after him. Jeebee stood still; and after a moment of uncertainty Wolf trotted forward to join him.

But Jeebee was beginning to be able to read Wolf's body signals. Right now, they were broadcasting definite wariness about going this way.

Jeebee himself had stopped. Now he studied the four-legged form beside him to figure out exactly what was giving him that impression of wariness. He recognized after a moment that Wolf was standing very tall, craning his neck, ears pricked forward to hear and see and smell anything that might signal danger, but his hind quarters were just a little crouched and his tail was down, indicating what Jeebee had learned to recognize as uncertainty. Overall, his body was tense, and Jeebee thought that he read in Wolf's expressive face—and Wolf's face as well as his body was very expressive now that Jeebee had come to know the other better—an expression that Jeebee read as reluctance or hesitation.

Jeebee frowned, looking ahead through the impenetrable screen of trees. At that moment there suddenly began the barking of a dog distantly ahead but off to the right someplace.

Jeebee looked back for Wolf, but Wolf was gone. Jeebee had developed his own wariness over the months since he had left Stoketon. The wind was roughly from the direction of the barking to him; nonetheless, Wolf had seen fit to steer clear of it, and it would do no harm for Jeebee to do likewise. He turned and went off in the direction Wolf had taken. If nothing else, the barking of the dog ahead had signaled the possible presence of living human beings. And any humans at all were likely to treat him as those back at the station where he had lost the electric bike—and there was no telling how they might react to Wolf.

Wolf did not appear again until Jeebee had camped for the night and was putting a last log on the evening fire he had built within a protecting patch of trees. Over the days they had been together, Wolf's evening and morning greetings had progressed from the cautious sniffing that had marked his behavior both in the store and at the campfire of the first night after their escape from the station. Now Wolf appeared as silently and as suddenly as he always did. He walked slowly up to where Jeebee was sitting, sniffed at him, examined him for a moment, and then advanced a little further—enough so that he was within reach of Jeebee's hand.

Jeebee slowly put out that hand and scratched in the ruff under Wolf's neck—that ruff seemed to fairly call out to be scratched. From the neck, as Jeebee had gradually ventured to do over the days, he moved down Wolf's chest and rib cage—cautious about handling this volunteer partner of his more freely than that. As his fingers moved, he scratched and plucked out the tufts of loose fur that were signs that Wolf now was beginning to shed his winter undercoat.

Wolf moved closer, to let himself be touched. His air was one of relaxed anticipation. His tail wagged briefly, just a little from side to side—but it was a wag. Jeebee continued now to scratch and groom him on both sides, but when he plucked a few tempting tufts from his lower ribs, Wolf swiveled his head toward the intrusive hand, drew back, stared at it for a long moment, then moved away and lay down beside where Jeebee was sitting.

The move was a clear statement that Wolf had had enough of being touched. Respecting it, Jeebee merely sat where he was, occasionally poking the fire and thinking his own thoughts while feeling a pleasure from the simple fact that Wolf was with him. It occurred to him now, sitting here before the fire with Wolf beside him, how much he was changed from the man he had been when he had fled from Stoketon.

When Jeebee had left that town with Buel Mannerly's pellets whistling over him to speed him on his way, he had thought of himself as leaving with only a handful of the tools he needed to survive in this newer, crueler world. Now he found himself surviving with even much less.

Of course, it had never occurred to him that he would have to protect even this little he now had from his best and only friend, as he had come to think of Wolf. By now Jeebee had discovered that his tarp, and everything else he carried, ran the risk of being shredded by a curious Wolf, if he left them available to the other. He had learned from experience that the gnaw and chew marks he had seen in the woman's store were not entirely, if at all, signs of Wolf attempting to escape, but simply an expression of his kind's instinctively perverse, destructive nature.

He had believed then—and, in fact, he still thought so in retrospect—that he had less than was necessary of the muscle, the skills, and necessary combative instinct to survive in the new world that had come. But it was undeniable that he was toughening up and learning. It was curious that in some ways, survival in this harsher world required more sensitivity, rather than less.

Life had not trained him to fight his fellowman for survival. But it had trained him to be a superb and close observer, to note everything that was to be seen and put the observations together to produce conclusions that were based on the best understanding he was able to achieve; and this was a possibly critically useful ability.

Now, Wolf *was* equipped to be a survivor. From the first night when the attention of Jeebee's mental engine had engaged itself with the question of whether Wolf was a dog or not, Jeebee had automatically noted, and tried to make sense of, everything he had seen the other do. Following that moment of escape from the station, and Wolf's killing of the collie, he could not do otherwise than accept the fact that Wolf was, indeed, a wolf. On the testimony of the words Jeebee had overheard through the window from the black-bearded man, he had been caught by a trapper, then hand-raised from a pup by the same man who had owned the leather jacket Jeebee now wore. That same leather jacket that had caused Wolf to take to him in the first place. But if he had come to learn more about Wolf, what he had learned had merely opened the door on even greater puzzles. There must be a specific reason for Wolf's continual leaving—as there must be a reason for his coming back. Just as there would be a reason for the meeting and touching ritual he expected to go through with Jeebee every time he showed up.

There was, Jeebee's mind told him, a great deal more in meaning to Wolf's facial and body expressions than he had ever expected in any animal. Dogs might or might not learn to read human facial expressions. Certainly they learned to read human tones of voice. But Wolf was an observer to a degree Jeebee had never seen in a dog.

It would be up to Jeebee to learn to act like a wolf, to think like a wolf—in the end, to "talk" as wolves talk, if he wanted to really communicate with Wolf. He could make a start by beginning to try to see things the way a wolf would see them.

Putting two and two together now, it struck him that Wolf had to be hunting on these absences of his. But the hunting must not take him too far from Jeebee's line of travel, or else it would be more work than it would be worth to come back and find him—particularly if the reward was no more than Jeebee's companionship. In short, he must gain something from being with Jeebee, since he was so superbly fitted to survive on his own. But what?

His thoughts were interrupted by Wolf just then getting to his feet. His head lifted, testing whatever odors the breeze brought him for a moment. He lowered his head but stayed standing.

Twilight was giving way to the darkness of night beyond the illumination of the fire. Suddenly, from far off, a banshee cry rose on the still air, quavered, and dropped, ending in a series of yips. For once, Jeebee recognized something heard or seen. It was the howl of a coyote. Radio and television shows had made it familiar.

Wolf got to his feet, lifted his own muzzle into the air, and opened his jaws. A howl, less full-bodied than Jeebee had expected, came from the furry throat. It was, in fact, a high, trilling, almost soprano howl. There were no yips at the end of Wolf's howl; and, hearing it, something bone-deep stirred in Jeebee. He found himself tilting back his own head, cupping his palms on either side of his mouth, and howling back, himself, at the distant coyote—a long, drawn-out howl.

Wolf immediately howled again, with Jeebee—his voice harmonizing, working in and around Jeebee's.

Silence flooded in. Jeebee looked over across the fire to see that Wolf had lain down again on his side, his eyes looking once more at Jeebee.

"You know what I hate—" Jeebee began softly and lovingly, then corrected himself, "what I hate and envy about you, you bastard? It's your damn matter-of-factness about everything!"

For a long moment more the golden eyes continued to watch him while the silence about them filled with the little sounds of the night wood. Then the lupine eyelids drooped sleepily and the eyes closed. Jeebee settled down himself with his pack as a pillow—both for that purpose and to protect it from Wolf's teeth.

When he woke, somewhat after sunup the next morning, Wolf was gone again. The fire was out and the ashes cold. He felt both cold and grumpy himself, and the thought came that somewhere, right now, Wolf might be finding food, while he had nothing. It put him in an ill humor.

He folded his solar blanket, which he had wrapped around him for sleep, and stowed it in his pack, put the pack on his back, then slung the heavier of the two rifles also over his back with a length of cord hacked from the coil he had carried to make a tent out of the reflecting tarp.

But the .22 was always in one hand or the other, ready for small game or any other use. He carried it loosely, by its middle, in his right hand at his side. More and more, he carried it this way, as he became more and more expert at reading the ground over which he passed, for signs of animal passage over it. So far he had gotten nothing but a couple of ground squirrels or gophers—he was not able to tell one from the other; and these he had eaten hastily, raw, before Wolf might happen to return and he would feel obligated to share his kill with the other.

As he took up his travels again, however, the walking began to warm him and some of the ill humor left. His mind began to work to some purpose.

Somehow, he must come to grips with the food problem. He chewed on dried grasses as he went along, having read somewhere that this would help. But it did not seem to. There was an answer to his need to fuel his body, if only he could think it through.

As usual, however, his mental engine, faced with one problem, immediately went off on another. As it frequently did, it had to do with Wolf. How far afield did the other go when he was gone like this? On impulse, Jeebee stopped, lifted his head, and cupped his hands around his mouth.

As he had done the evening before, he howled.

The sound lifted, hung, and died on the soft morning air. It was another bright day with only flecks of clouds to be seen; and howling seemed ridiculous. The long moments went by, and Jeebee was about to stop listening and go on. Then, from some distance, but so obviously an answer that Jeebee's hair stood up on the nape of his neck as he heard it, a howl came back in answer. But it was not the high-pitched trilling response Wolf had made to the coyote, the night before. This, while lower in pitch than last night's, had more in common with the mournful plaint of a train whistle.

Was it Wolf—his Wolf who had answered? It could be another wild one of the same breed. Jeebee lifted his hands to his mouth to howl again, but something very like an instinct seemed to caution him against pushing his luck.

Not now. Later, sometime, he could try again, and if he again got an answer, he would be ready to see if he could be sure it sounded like the answer he had just gotten. It would be unlikely that there would be a strange wolf answering close to him and Wolf far off—and if Wolf was likewise close, why had he not likewise answered?

The question was suddenly wiped from his mind by the glimpse of a small form scurrying out of his sight into the tall grass ahead and to the right of him.

The .22 he had carried in his right hand so long leaped to his shoulder and fired almost before he had registered the movement. Jacking another shell into the chamber, he went forward as cautiously as if he was stalking a wounded bear and came upon a porcupine with its head almost torn off by the .22 slug.

Carefully, he flipped the carcass on its back with the muzzle of the gun. He had read about porcupines. In some states they had been protected as "survival food," since they were slow enough for a human to run down and kill with a club or heavy stone.

Now, remembering what he had read, he slit the carcass down its belly, hooked a finger in the slit and dragged it back to an open space where he could build a fire. He was overjoyed by the dead weight of it pulling against his finger.

He built a small, hot fire with his tinder sticks and some dead branches from a nearby bush. Then he began, unskillfully but more or less successfully, to get the meat of the animal out of its quill-protected body. He had nearly managed to complete this job when Wolf appeared.

Jeebee stiffened in reaction, knife in hand. He had literally forgotten the other's existence in the glory of suddenly having a possible full meal in hand. Whether Wolf had returned as a result of the exchanged howls, or simply chanced to come back, this was one time Jeebee intended to fill his own belly first, before anyone else. Wolf approached, but came to a stop less than two feet from him. He whined.

Jeebee tensed, expecting Wolf to make a try for the porcupine meat. Ready for anything, but determined to hold on to his food, Jeebee finished loosening most of the chunk meat from the bones and cut off as much as he thought he could eat at one sitting. He dropped the rest back in with the carcass and pushed it with his rifle barrel toward Wolf.

Wolf buried his nose in the carcass. Jeebee set about trying to cook the chunks of raw meat he had, by impaling them on sticks that he held out over the fire.

Wolf went through the eatable parts of the porcupine that had been given him in what seemed to be no more than a couple of seconds. Finished, he moved close to the opposite side of the fire; and Jeebee warily withdrew the sticks he held, holding them as close to himself as possible while still keeping them in the heat of the flames. A sort of madness of hunger was on him and he found he regretted having only the knife in his hand that did not hold a food-laden stick. In that moment he was quite ready to kill Wolf if the other tried to take the food from him.

Wolf did not try, however. Instead he stretched out his muzzle with laid-back ears and made a series of small whines, almost puppyish whines.

Jeebee did not trust him. He took one stick from the fire and gulped down the half-burned, half-raw meat that was on it, then devoured the other one. Wolf continued his appeals until all the food was gone; but once it had disappeared, he stopped, stared companionably at Jeebee for a moment, then turned and disappeared off into the brush again.

Jeebee sat back, conscious now of singed fingers and a burned tongue, but with an incredible sense of satisfaction in him. He had never before known such a feeling. To have his belly filled, as it was now, was like being lord of all the world.

CHAPTER 4

They had reached the interstate highway Jeebee had set as a goal for himself, nearly five days before. But now that they were there, he was taking time to explore up and down a twenty-mile length of that double ribbon of concrete before settling on a position of observation, to make sure of both his knowledge of the area and a food supply.

The food-supply question had reached the critical stage. Wolf, gone most of the time, had not shown any signs of suffering from a lack of it. It was impossible for Jeebee to tell how well fed he was simply by looking at him. Underneath his almost ragged-looking summer coat of fur, dark on back and sides but lightening almost to white on the belly, he had appeared lean, almost skinny, since he had shed his winter coat. But without any real proof of the belief, Jeebee felt fairly sure that Wolf, unlike him, had been able to find and hunt down some kind of prey, even if it had been no more than hare or ground squirrels.

In Jeebee's case, however, the small supply of emergency irradiated food was long since eaten. He had found little to put in his stomach since the porcupine, except for a few mushrooms he had been able to identify safely as morels—one of the three species he could recognize from possibly deadly kinds—that he found growing on the decaying roots of a tree in a wood clump. But these were quickly eaten and not very satisfying to his clamorous belly. He was conscious of a sort of continuous hollow feeling. It could be ignored, if necessary, but in fact it was always with him these last few days. More troubling was a general weakness of body. He tired more quickly than he liked, after even a few hours of walking.

Now, however, on his fourth day of exploration he had come across a farmhouse, abandoned and half broken down, that had at first looked promising. If he could find even some sprouted grain that had been originally stored for feed animals, he could cook and eat that. . . .

But after a thorough search of the barn and what was left of the house, he had found nothing. He was about to leave when he suddenly caught sight of Wolf, who had not been with him since the dawn, also nosing around the place. He paid no attention to Jeebee, but seemed intent on his own investigations.

Jeebee suddenly felt something like resentment. He had been about to give up this place as having nothing worth taking. But now that Wolf was investigating it, he was suddenly reminded of the fact that his comrade's keen nose and intense curiosity might be able to find things he had missed.

Accordingly, Jeebee went back to searching, himself. He had pretty well examined the house and felt sure he had not over-looked anything at all that he could eat, but now he would look again. He began to search the immediate perimeter of the former dwelling.

His searching took him on a spiral outward from the foundations of the building until it brought him to a fairly large patch of foot-high, year-old dead grass.

It had seemed to be nothing more than that; but as soon as he began searching through it, to his annoyance Wolf came also to nose about in it a few yards from him. Abruptly Wolf appeared to have found something. His tail and ears went up and his muzzle dipped out of sight below the tops of the grass stems. He seemed to be engaged with something.

Jeebee went hastily to join him. After a couple of strides, he saw that Wolf was standing in an open patch in the grass, worrying with his teeth at some kind of bolt that had to be first turned up, then slipped back from a hasp to free up a metal cover that lay level with the ground around it, its gray surface splotched with rust, but having the appearance of a fairly thick piece of sheet iron.

Jeebee knew better by now than to try to push Wolf away and simply take over the hasp himself. Wolf was extraordinarily protective of anything that he had near his mouth. On the other hand, there was that curiosity of his. . . .

Jeebee backed off a little way out of the patch of grass and quietly picked up a couple of plum-sized rocks. Wolf's head was down, still worrying with the hasp. Jeebee chucked one rock into the grass about fifteen feet beyond Wolf and another one as much again further on a second later. Wolf's head came up, his ears pricked, and he bounded forward, searching into the grass about where the first rock had fallen, and then continued on, searching further out. In four quick strides, Jeebee reached the metal plate lying in the ground. He reached down and took hold of the hasp, just as Wolf's muzzle poked back into his circle of vision.

But Jeebee was holding the hasp now, and if Wolf was protective about things right under his nose, he had so far likewise seemed to respect Jeebee's ownership of anything he held. Of course, this respect had not been tested with anything that Jeebee suspected Wolf really wanted.

Now that the bolt was back, it was obvious to Jeebee that the metal plate had been a trapdoor over something. He looked for what must be there and now saw the two hinges, overgrown with grass in the edge opposite the one in which the bolt had been set. He took hold of the bolt and lifted. The cover was heavy, but it came up without too much trouble, though with some squealing that signaled long unuse.

Wolf backed away. Ahead of them and beneath Jeebee was a black hole of unknown depth in the ground. The top of a ladder led down into it.

Jeebee looked over at Wolf. He was five or six steps back. His posture was a picture of conflict between timidity and curiosity; and his raised and furrowed eyebrows gave a humanlike impression of concern as he craned his neck toward the darkness below.

It occurred to Jeebee he would be wise to get down the ladder as soon as possible, before Wolf overcame his original reaction at finding what was underneath the metal.

He turned, cradling the .22 in the crook of his arms, and began cautiously to back down the ladder. The .30/06 was in its sling on his back and pressed against him in unusual fashion as he descended. He went down into the darkness.

A moment later the toe of his left boot, searching downward, encountered something solid, and he stepped down on to what had enough give to feel like a dirt floor. He searched around with the toe of the boot to make sure there was adequate standing room at the foot of the ladder, then came all the way down with both feet.

For several long moments he could see nothing. He heard an almost querulous whimpering above him and looked up at a suddenly blinding patch of blue sky framed by the opening, and just a slice of Wolf's muzzle, still some few feet back from one edge of the opening, looking down after him. A gray-furred paw reached tentatively down to the ladder's topmost rung, and was swiftly withdrawn.

Jeebee made a mental note that Wolf was either not happy about entering unknown dark places belowground, or did not like descending ladders.

Whether the other could even see him or not down here, Jeebee did not know. And it did not matter.

Gradually his eyes, adjusting to the gloom, revealed to him, like a picture developing in a darkroom in its first tray of fluid, a cavelike area lined on all sides with shelves loaded with cans, some boxes, and even a few sealer jars.

Jeebee's mouth suddenly watered. This was something that used to be common at every farm before rural electricity had come in, bringing with it refrigerators and freezers—a root cellar. Back in that time, these shelves would have been filled with glass sealers like the few he saw. Now, just before or at the time the house was deserted and damaged for whatever reason, its owners must have gone, leaving it still filled with the many things they had not taken with them. What was down here was food. And the canned stuff, at least, might still be edible.

Ignoring the little sounds from time to time of Wolf above him, Jeebee reached over his shoulder to fish in his pack and come up with a candle stub like the one he had used in the cellar where he had found the leather jacket.

Briefly he lit the two-and-a-half-inch piece of candle and began examining the cans closely. With the heat from the candle flame almost searing his eyes and the can at the end of his nose, he was at last able to find that most of them had been dated on the metallic circle of the bottom of each one. To his joy, the date stamped on there was no more than nine months earlier, and in only a couple of cases a year or more beyond what his multimode watch told him was the present date.

Hastily, he stuffed as many of the safely dated cans as he could into his backpack, filled his pockets, was about to pile more in his arms when a thought made him pause.

Wolf's jaws, from what Jeebee had seen him do with them, would have no problem at all puncturing and tearing open one of these cans.

Slowly, he put back the few extra cans he had just picked up, reached back to take the .30/06 from the sling and replaced it with the .22. He gathered cans again into the crook of his left arm and looked once more about the root cellar before blowing out the candle. It had a wooden roof, braced by two-by-fours, about five feet above the floor, and with stoutly built shelves all around the sides. He would be back.

He blew the candle out, replaced it in the backpack, and took the .30/06 in his right hand, butt foremost, holding it balanced by the middle with the first three fingers while he used the last two to cling to the ladder rungs as he went up them. He mounted slowly and awkwardly. It was not unlikely, he thought, that Wolf had smelled the food that was in the glass sealers, if not that which was in the cans. The food in at least some of the glass sealers had probably gone rotten and the odor of them— detectable to Wolf's sensitive nose, if not Jeebee's own—had seeped out. If so, Wolf could not help but know that what he was now carrying up was at least potential food.

Jeebee tensed as he climbed. True, Wolf had not so far tried to take from him anything that he was actually holding, even the bits of porcupine meat that were merely close to him. But that was no guarantee Wolf would not try to appropriate the cans he was now carrying, or contrive to make him drop them.

Moreover, Wolf was really an awesomely dangerous animal with those teeth and the speed and power Jeebee had seen him show over the past few weeks. If it came to a real contest between them . . .

Nonetheless, as he approached the top of the ladder, he became aware of the strange change inside of him. For days now he had been deeply and sincerely grateful to Wolf for staying with him. Even with the other's undoglike strangeness and what might fairly be called selfishness, it was hardly an exaggeration to say that Jeebee had come to love him.

Until this moment. Now, somehow, with the prospect of food for his starving body in his pockets, backpack, and arm, everything had suddenly changed. First and foremost, he had become aware of the huge force of the hunger in him. From the equivalent of a sharp pain, the hunger had become more like a deep but steady ache, always with him, but so familiar that it would almost have felt strange to be without it. It was like a vicious animal that had been asleep in his belly but was now awakened. Deep in him a primitive decision was stirring. He had food in his possession now, and no one, not even Wolf, was going to take any of it from him.

He went on up the ladder.

As his head rose above the earth level, and his eyes met Wolf's, only half a dozen feet away, something seemed to touch him at the base of the back of his skull. A chill flooded out from that part of him as if it was some powerful dye; spreading forward to the back of his ears, down his neck and into the muscles of his back and down his spine. As he continued to come up and step out at last on level ground, his vision focused more and more tightly until he saw nothing but Wolf directly ahead of him—and all this time his eyes had never left Wolf's.

Wolf's tongue licked his lips uncertainly and he backed up five or six steps, still watching Jeebee. Jeebee waited but he made no other move. Jeebee stood, prepared to club Wolf with the stock of the rifle if the other made a try for the cans he held.

After a moment of waiting, Jeebee turned, keeping his eyes on Wolf while he put down the cans, pulled the lid up on its hinges, and closed it again over the root cellar, shooting the bolt home. He gathered in the cans once more, the rifle in his hand still pointing in Wolf's direction, and turned away. Slowly he started off in the direction of his camp, tense and ready for Wolf either to approach him suddenly with that fantastic bounding speed, or move behind him to get at the root-cellar door again.

But Wolf did neither. As Jeebee continued to move away, Wolf turned out in a circle around him to come back in fifteen to twenty feet ahead of him. He continued at a slow trot, looking back over his shoulder at Jeebee every so often; and in this way they both returned to the campsite.

Jeebee had set it up in a patch of woods, not directly overlooking the superhighway, but a good five hundred yards behind the clump on the hill that did; that clump from which he could observe traffic on the highway while lying with the opera glasses, out of sight, himself. When the two of them reached the camp, now, Wolf circled the dead ashes of the previous night's fire. He stood on the other side of them, watching, as Jeebee went to a cottonwood tree not ten feet from the ashes and lifted, one by one, the cans he had been carrying as high as he could reach, to perch them along several thick limbs coming out from the cottonwood.

He had leaned the .30/06 reluctantly against the tree so that he could put up the cans. But Wolf merely stood watching, making no move to approach. It was as if he had lost interest in the cans as food and was merely being his old, usual, curious self with his constant observation of everything that happened around him.

With all the cans safe, Jeebee laid the rifle down and pulled himself up onto the lower limbs of the cottonwood until he could get a leg over one of them and hang there. Then he transferred the cans from their present limbs to higher branches—ones to which Wolf could not possibly jump or climb. This done, he let himself back down onto the ground. While he had been in the tree, Wolf had flopped down on one hip, with his muzzle resting across his forelegs and his deceptively sleepy eyes following Jeebee's every movement. Cautiously, Jeebee produced one of the cans from his pocket—it was a can of stew. His mouth watered and his hands trembled as he held it.

Reaching down for his large hunting knife, he untied the thong that held it firmly in its sheath, pulled it out, and with the heavy blade punched through the lid. He sawed raggedly around the rim of the can until he had it off. All this time, he was watching Wolf, but Wolf seemed to have lost interest. He yawned once or twice, then got to his feet and, angling off to one side of Jeebee, at the edge of the clearing, began to sniff and after a while to dig busily at the foot of a tree.

Jeebee resheathed the knife, placed the open can of stew up in one of the recently vacated lower crotches of the tree limb, and followed it with the .30/06, which he laid across two limbs. Then, careful not to disturb either can or gun, he climbed back up into the tree. Once he was seated on one of the branches, he retrieved the rifle in his left hand, put the open can between his knees, and began gingerly to reach between the ragged edges of the can to get at the stew inside with two fingers.

He began to scoop up fingers loaded with the stew and push them into his mouth. The porcupine meat, as delicious as it was, was a pale memory compared to the reality of what he held in his hand. The fat he licked from his fingers drove him almost wild with hunger even as a nausea began to rise from his shrunken stomach.

He fought to keep the nausea down, but vomited in spite of himself onto the ground beneath. Like a flash Wolf was underneath the tree at what had come up.

Jeebee sat miserably above the other. His body cried out for more food, but his stomach still roiled with upset at the thought of receiving it. But after a while it calmed, and he ventured to feed himself some more, taking small amounts at intervals and working them thoroughly in his mouth before he risked swallowing them.

Eventually, he managed to keep some down. It was not surprising, he told himself, that his stomach, so long empty, should be unable to handle a sudden onslaught of fat and meat.

Regretfully, he threw the empty can down to the ground. It made barely one bounce before Wolf was on it. Jeebee left the rest of the cans still in the tree, took the .30/06, and climbed down. By the time he reached the ground Wolf was lying down with the can held between the toes of his two front paws with a suppleness that was almost that of human fingers, his long tongue having polished the interior until it looked like it had been just washed.

Jeebee felt a momentary pang of conscience.

"Maybe later on—" he began, taking a step toward Wolf. But at Jeebee's first movement toward him, Wolf growled protectively, leaped to his feet, holding the completely empty can in his jaws, and ran off among the trees. Jeebee sighed and sat down. He took the small whetstone from its leather holster on his belt and began to sharpen the mistreated edge of the knife.

He sat so, sharpening the knife, for about fifteen minutes, then waited another fifteen. But Wolf did not return. He had probably, thought Jeebee, taken the can and hidden it somewhere, then gone off on one of his own hunting expeditions. Though what there should be about the can once Wolf had licked out what little Jeebee had left, stuck to its inner sides, Jeebee had no idea. There could hardly be even a smell remaining of the food that had originally been in it.

He sighed. There was very much more he had to understand about Wolf.

There was also no point in continuing to sit here himself. Jeebee took his two rifles and slung the .30/06 on his back once more. Carrying the .22 in his right hand, he left for the place he had picked out as an observation post, from which he could keep a watch for the sort of traveler along the highway whom he had decided he needed.

CHAPTER 5

Jeebee lay between two hackberry trees in a little woods just at the crest of a rise of ground about a hundred and fifty feet to the north of the interstate highway. He was using his cheap and inadequate binoculars to scan the twin roadways below him, east and west, as far as they could help him to see.

For a moment the thought of Wolf intruded. Jeebee had meant what he had felt in their moment of confrontation, earlier in the day. He would do exactly the same if he faced the situation again. But maybe he had pushed Wolf permanently away from him? He put the matter out of his mind. At least the good weather was holding.

The afternoon looked to be clear and bright at least until sunset. There was little breeze and almost no clouds at all—none on the horizon. The day before it had rained; but except for that, they had had nearly a full week of dry weather now, and spring was rushing the growth of new vegetation. Already, the fresh young grass was a good six inches high among the dead brown stalks left over from the year before.

So far, since his arrival half an hour before, there had been no sign of traffic on the interstate. It stretched, a gray double-ruler line before him, from right horizon to left horizon. Nothing moving was to be seen in either direction at the moment. This small hill with its clump of trees was only one of many such for some miles; but it was the one closest to the road, so that other clumps of vegetation did not cut off his further view of the concrete strips in both directions.

Former interstates like this were not ordinarily traveled even at night, let alone in daytime as it was now. Anyone so doing could be seen coming clearly from some distance. Any such travelers would appear while still far enough off for Jeebee to make up his mind about them.

If the individual or group traveling looked dangerous, he could lie quiet until they had passed. Or, if they sent someone to scout the woods before they passed, he should be able to see the scout coming in time to fade back off the crest and put a safe distance between himself and them.

Most of those who came by in daytime were much more likely to be in groups, to risk such visibility. Only a complete fool would travel alone under such conditions and risk attracting the attention of any looters or marauders in the vicinity. His plan was to give his afternoons to watch for traffic. Mornings, as he had today, Jeebee could give to the other necessary duties of finding food and staying alive.

But today the first requirement had been pretty well taken care of by his very lucky find of that root cellar. He had looked for that sort of underground storage at every clump of abandoned farm buildings he had investigated ever since he had left Michigan. Undoubtedly, it was now clear, he had passed some by without knowing they were there. If it had not been for Wolf's curiosity, he would have missed this one.

Of course, there still remained the problem of finding some kind of bag or container he could put up in the tree and fill with as many of the cans as possible. Wolf, he had found, was wary of anything unknown. The trick would be to keep it unknown. So Jeebee's trips to the root cellar for loads of cans had better be at times when Wolf had gone off on his own business—hunting or otherwise—as he had just a while ago.

Of course, there was no certainty Wolf might not show up unexpectedly at any time. His most routine appearances were at dawn and twilight. But he had also shown up without warning at all other hours. Jeebee would just have to take his chances of getting to the root cellar and back without encountering him.

Meanwhile, Jeebee's belly was full now, and there was the highway to watch.

The most dangerous possibility in the way of daytime travelers would be a gang all armed and mounted. A raiding group. These were literally latter-day horse nomads, who lived continually on the move and sometimes numbered enough to threaten even small settlements.

That sort of gang would also be the most likely to send scouts ahead to explore the only cover in sight—in this case, his woods. Moreover, on horseback, they could easily run him down if they caught sight of him. They would be interested not only in everything he had, but in everything he could tell them about things they might want. That meant that as a matter of course, they would torture him to get whatever answers he might be able to give them; after which they would kill him.

In such a situation he could look for no help from Wolf. Not only would his companion be timid of any strangers—strange how an animal so potentially lethal and so armed by nature could also be so cautious and ready to run under unfamiliar situations—but, even if he did, a single bullet would take care of him, probably a shot on first sight by anyone taking Jeebee prisoner.

So Jeebee would be wisest to start leaving the minute he identified any such group moving down the highway. Even a couple of rifle-armed men on horseback were potentially dangerous . . . unless they were careless, drunk, or drugged enough to ride by these trees without thinking of the danger of being shot from ambush. Jeebee wondered, if it came to that, whether he actually could bring himself to shoot down two such men, merely for what they possessed.

He had shot before at an armed man aiming his rifle at Wolf. But if his shot had killed the man, it had been done in hot blood. Could he do the same in cold?

He thought again about the depth of his hunger and his sudden complete readiness to turn on Wolf, himself, back at the root cellar. The sudden, deep, instinctive emotion of that moment touched him again in raw memory. Yes, if a parallel need occurred with humans in front of him, he could kill his own kind, too, if that was the only way to survive.

But deeply he still hoped and believed what he wanted could be got without killing. It must be a matter of just picking the right traveler, or travelers.

Ideal would be a family with women and children and only one person armed. Probably too ideal. A group like that would have sense enough to travel at night, and as much out of sight as possible.

Whoever it ended up being, he must pick a group with which there was some reason to believe he could risk showing himself and trying to parley. Also a group that had what he needed to trade for or buy.

His mind drifted as he lay in the warmth of the sun. It had now sent fingers of light among the trees to uncover him from shadow. It was hard, even now, for him to realize how much he had changed since he had fled from Stoketon—

The even current of his thoughts, almost drowsy in the warming noontime, was broken abruptly as he caught sight of movement at the far end of the nearest strip of highway to his left. It was not possible yet to tell who or what was causing it. But it was undoubtedly movement, and it was toward him.

He waited, watching patiently, as it got closer, and the movement resolved itself into a gaggle of adults on foot, moving forward more as a loose mob than anything else.

As they came closer Jeebee studied them carefully. They were not a prepossessing bunch. Some of them had rifles, some showed no weapons at all, and in between there was everything from kitchen knives stuck through belts to axes in hands. They were rather a tatterdemalion bunch. One large man, surprisingly clean shaven in a time when most men had simply let their beards grow, marched at the front and seemed to be as much in charge of the others as anybody else was. He was flanked by two slightly smaller, bearded individuals, who could be subleaders of some sort.

Jeebee thought he had not a great deal to fear from them. They clearly were not sending out scouts to protect their flanks, apparently depending simply on their numbers for protection. There must have been between forty and fifty of them, equally divided between men and women. The latter were hardly distinguishable from the men, wearing roughly the same assortments of clothing—pants, shirts, jackets, and hats—and in most cases had their hair cut short. In addition, the layers of clothes nearly everybody wore nowadays, including Jeebee himself, disguised bodily differences.

There was something famished looking about the whole group. Jeebee felt a touch of coldness at the thought of being discovered and captured by them; but if in any strange case they did pay attention to his hillside, he could simply head back off the crest and into the folds of the land. He was pretty sure that he could outrun them. At least he could keep away from them for long enough so that it would not be worth their while to keep chasing him. Otherwise, if he could string them out in chase until there were only two or three of them dangerously near, then firing from the ground with a steady rest for the rifle, the .30/06, he should be able to take care of them.

Accordingly, he watched them pass with some tenseness, but no extreme alarm. They moved on westward, to his right, until they began to dwindle in the distance, and he slipped back into his thoughts.

Now that they had gone by he was pleased that he had been as little frightened by them as he had. He had indeed changed.

It was hard to say how much, but it was not a small change. He was as ready to bolt now as he had been on leaving Stoketon, but there was the difference that now there might be situations in which instead of running, he might turn and become an aggressor. Hard to believe. At odds with everything his whole life had taught him up to the moment when he had first begun this run for safety to Martin's ranch.

That had been the Jeebee that was. But now—he took a hand momentarily from the binoculars to touch the thick curly black beard on his chin. Perhaps growing the beard had something to do with it? No. He took his hand away. That was ridiculous.

What was actually making him different was the mere fact that he had survived this long. The process of continuing to live had taught him daily lessons that made his chances of living better. The old Jeebee, running from Stoketon, packing much more in survival gear than he owned in the world now, had given himself almost no chance at all to last in this new world. Now he was beginning not only to think he might make it safely to Martin's ranch, but to take it for granted he would, and concern himself only with the problems along the way.

Greatest of these had been his sudden discovery of the necessary savagery in himself under the patina of twenty-five years of civilization—

Hold it. Some movement in the eyepieces of his lenses had brought him abruptly back to the present.

He squinted hard to make out what it was. Something else was coming into view at the eastern end of his view of the highway. Damn these little opera glasses! All he could make out was movement; and since it had not been visible a moment before, he assumed it was movement toward him. He would have to wait for it to reveal itself in finer detail.

Slowly, while he watched with a tension that in the end had his eyes beginning to blur with protective tears, it resolved itself into not one, but a group of figures on horseback. They were still too far away to count, but it seemed as if there must be four of them at least, if not more.

There were more. Slowly, it became clear in his binoculars that there were six of them, all but one of them men and all of them riding at a trot with the unconscious ease of people long used to horseback. Behind them trailed a number of packhorses, each with its load. More important, from his point of view, as they came more clearly into focus, he could see that each rider had a rifle scabbard fixed to his saddle, and the butt of a weapon protruded from each one.

These were exactly the sort of travelers he had been fearing, though in a smaller group.

There was a chance, of course, that they were a perfectly harmless group simply traveling the old right-of-way because its shoulders and median made for more open, smoother going than an off-road route.

But anybody who would bet on that would be willing to believe that a grizzly would enjoy having his ears pulled.

Jeebee was up, squatting on his toes, ready swiftly to rise and retreat. But he found curiosity holding him in his place. The group was still a distance from him.

He decided to stay where he was for the moment.

The riders came on. As they got closer to the woods, one of them suddenly separated from the others to ride off to Jeebee's left, to investigate something. The rider disappeared in some trees farther down the road which hid the area back from the highway.

Jeebee began to become uneasy. He was aware that the rider could be circling to investigate his patch of woods from behind. If so, he had perhaps made a mistake in letting himself get too interested in these riders. He might no longer have time to escape back across the open patch between these woods and those where he had camped.

He got to his feet quickly and went deeper into the clump he was in, looking for an appropriate tree to climb. It had to be one with limbs low enough for him to get started up on, and yet big enough so that he could get high enough that the leafy branches below would hide him from anyone passing beneath.

After a few minutes he found one, a cottonwood. The lower limbs were ideal in that they were within reach of him if he jumped up and caught hold of one, but not so close to the ground that they would suggest the tree was easily climbable. He pulled himself up—suddenly grateful for the extra arm muscle that the past few months had built into him.

He commenced his climb. Cottonwoods were usually easy to climb and this was no exception. He made it high into the tree, into the crotch of a limb where it joined the trunk. He was a good twenty-five to thirty feet off the ground, and while he could look down through the leaves and see the immediate ground area, he doubted that anyone looking up would easily make out the shape of his body through the intervening greenery.

He sat, and time went by slowly. But the past three months had conditioned him to patience. He had carried the .22, moving it ahead of him to keep laying it between the next two limbs above him as he climbed. Now, seated near the tree top and hidden, he traded it for the .30/06 slung on his back, put the .22 in the sling, and held the .30/06 loaded, across his knees.

If the single rider did have suspicions about the tree, he wanted to be able to take whoever it was out with a single shot. He was still far from being as good with a rifle as he would have liked, with shells as hard to come by as they were. But he was fairly confident of his ability to fire a killing shot from this short a distance, at a slowly moving target.

When the rider finally came, he heard hoofbeats in the distance, from deeper in the woods behind him. For a moment he thought horse and stranger would pass beyond the area of ground he could see through the leaves below him. But in the end they both came almost directly below him. The rider was a woman.

Though he would not have been sure of this if she had not glanced up—at the sky, as it happened, rather than into the tops of the trees around her. She was lean as a man, and dressed pretty much as a man from the jeans and heavy checkered shirt and the wide-brimmed hat, which may have had long hair tucked up under it, or may have had hair cut short. A very serviceable rifle rode in the saddle holster by her right knee.

Jeebee had her in the sights of his rifle almost from the first moment he saw her, and tracked her until she passed out of sight farther on. She was not riding as if she really expected to discover anything, but rather as if this was half a duty to be done, and half a pleasure to ride alone by herself for a change.

It was not until long after her hoofbeats had faded from his hearing that he ventured to begin the climb down.

He kept the .30/06 free, and ready to use, however, until he was safely on the ground, and even then changed his mind about putting it back into the rope of the sling on his back and instead carried it as he went cautiously toward the front of the woods and looked up and down the road with the opera glasses to see if the group of riders was still in view.

They were, at the very limits of identification by the cheap binoculars he was using.

Slowly he put the opera glasses away. It was time to be heading back to camp soon, anyway. He might as well go now. As he turned about and struck back through the woods, he wondered if she had been the only woman in the group, one of several—or whether, perhaps, the group might consist all of women, which was also a possibility.

He concluded there was no way of telling. If she was the only woman, the reason the rest had probably chosen her to search was probably because either she was the most likely to find any watcher in the woods, or possibly she was the one who could most easily be spared, in case there was an ambush waiting.

He would never know, just as he would never know the composition of their group. The next few following days had little to offer. One was completely void of travelers. On another the only passersby were a family with a father and mother and three children about half-grown, two girls and one boy. Jeebee considered approaching them, for they were leading packhorses that seemed to have a fair amount of possessions upon them and therefore might be willing to enter into some kind of a trade.

But there was a wild gaunt look about them and an impoverished air to both them and the horses. They were not exactly what he was looking for, and now he had food from the root cellar to supply him. He could wait.

The next day it rained and there was no movement until late afternoon, when the rain let up and then an old man went by on a bicycle, alone and wearing short pants, dressed rather like a Boy Scout, but with untidy gray hair flowing halfway down his back. His hair mixed with the gray beard that fell almost as far down his chest in front. He seemed to have no other possessions except what might be in his pockets, or concealed about the red-and-black lumberjack shirt, tan shorts, and tennis shoes he wore.

Even though he had nothing worth taking, except the bicycle, anyone wanting to along the road could have killed or taken him prisoner simply for the sport of it.

Just before Jeebee was about to stop and the sun was on the horizon, a line of five well-made, heavily laden, horse-drawn wagons went by, each with its own driver and accompanied by somewhere between fifteen and twenty armed riders, male and female, as well as a number of fit-looking horses for remounts and wagon pullers, herded along behind by some of the riders.

For a moment Jeebee was tempted. They did not quite have the appearance of a raiding group, though their weapons and discipline made them look formidable enough. Rather, they seemed more like a group of people who had decided to travel in convoy, like the wagon trains of the nineteenth century during the settlement of the west. Such a group should be the least likely to be spooked by a single man coming toward them making peaceful intentions clear with his hands holding his rifle over his head.

Then as they got close, his binoculars picked up something very interesting. The man driving the front wagon had a chain attached to his ankle and to the footboard of the wagon seat. Jeebee checked as he got a better look at the rest of the wagons and saw that all the drivers were chained.

Instantly his understanding of the whole picture changed. Plainly, the drivers were people who had been enslaved, leaving the others, who must be a sort of modern version of the Comancheros of north Texas in the mid–nineteenth century, all free to use their guns or pursue anything interesting, if necessary. After they were gone, he got up, somewhat stiffly after his long hours in a prone position. There was a chill in him from what he had just seen. He had come close to driving one of those wagons with a chain around his ankle—or worse.

Soberly, he returned to his camp and busied himself starting a fire. Later in the evening he piled several larger logs on the fire, slung the .30/06 across his back, and moved off, away from the flames. He counted off fifty paces, then, relying on the luminous dial of his compass, made a full circuit about his campsite. If slavers were in the neighborhood he wanted to be trebly certain that the light of his fire could not be seen.

He had just returned to the campsite and settled down in front of the fire—now a small, comfortable blaze—when Wolf returned. Jeebee barely nodded his acknowledgment of the other's arrival. The rush of pleasure he ordinarily felt when his companion appeared was blunted by the haunting memory of the slaver procession. He stared unblinkingly through the wisps of smoke, through Wolf and the trees beyond, unable to shake the vision of chains.

The sound of deep, throaty vocalizations mixed with whimpers brought him sharply back to the present.

Wolf was approaching him in a strange, half-sitting crouch with his back hunched and tail tucked between his legs. His head was low and the corners of his mouth were drawn back in the mockery of a smile that exposed the ivory expanse of his back teeth. Jeebee's first thought was that he'd been injured, perhaps shot by one of the armed travelers he'd seen today. He reached out an exploratory hand, and the moment he did, Wolf folded onto his side and rolled over on his back, whimpering abjectly. Jeebee ran his fingers through the coarse hair of Wolf's exposed chest and belly looking for wounds and his heart sank as his hand encountered warm, sticky wetness he first thought to be blood.

Wolf was urinating copiously, his half-closed eyes and fixed grin signaling an absolute relaxation and utter contentment.

CHAPTER 6

During the next week a number of travelers passed Jeebee's lookout point. But they all fell into one of two categories. Those who were too dangerous to approach because they were possible aggressors, and those whom it was not safe to approach because they might be too fearful.

However, he had food from the root cellar; and in another old abandoned farm he had found a length of canvas that he made into a rough bag and hung up in the tree, so that now he could have quite a store of food by him without making too many trips to its source. Wolf made no attempt to attack the root cellar on his own. Clearly there were no scratch or dig marks around it other than there had been at the first moment of Jeebee's discovery, and Wolf had not followed him to the root cellar on any of his trips to it, or surprised him when he was there.

Also, Jeebee was aware of a subtle change in Wolf's behavior toward him. Some sort of watershed had been passed with the moment of Wolf's peculiar and abjectly solicitous behavior that night—the urgent, but hesitant approach, for the first time rolling over on his back and exposing his belly to be scratched.

Jeebee had pondered this without being able to define the full significance of it. He could only feel that their relationship had changed. They were now closer and their respective positions were more sharply defined.

They had become partners in a more important sense, rather than just traveling companions, and Wolf had apparently accepted a junior role in that partnership. He still went about his own business during the day. But he had not, since that night, left before Jeebee awoke, and not until Jeebee had shown an agreement with his leaving—almost a "permission" to leave, with at least a few reassuring words and a perfunctory scratch behind Wolf's muttonchops.

In spite of recognizing this change, Jeebee put aside any temptation to take for granted whatever new authority the other might have acknowledged in him.

He was no more ready than before to try to take food away from Wolf or to impose his will upon him in other ways. Indeed, he felt instinctively that this might now be even riskier than before, when Wolf's most likely response was, simply, to leave.

At a deeper level, he felt that any such behavior on his part would be a betrayal of trust. But his life since Stoketon had taught him much about the economics of trust. Whatever the nature of Wolf's allegiance to him, anything that could be eaten, pilfered, broken, or ripped would be something Jeebee would keep, as before, securely stowed out of the other's reach. For the moment, Jeebee's "trust" extended only so far as the luxury of no longer worrying that Wolf might leave one morning for no apparent reason, and never return. But the fact that he was able to have even that much faith, he realized, in itself was a major milestone.

In other areas, however, he began to be concerned, particularly as he went into the second week at his observation point. He still had an ample food supply. But the traffic on the road had varied widely in character, day after day, and as yet he had seen no one he trusted to approach.

He still held to his original belief that someone approachable would eventually turn up. But increasingly he felt time's clock ticking away the minutes and days while he waited. Time was on its march. His brother's ranch in Montana was in higher country and would be under snow as early as October. He had only the summer and early fall in which to travel, and a good ways to go yet.

Then one day as he was lying, watching the road just before noon, he got a glimpse of movement out of the corner of his eye. It was not on the road but in the patch of woods around him, to his left and about twenty yards off among the trees.

He looked, and saw Wolf. His partner seemed to be dodging about in play behavior with some four-legged companion, but Jeebee could not make out at first who or what the companion was.

But as the romping brought the two of them closer to him, he saw that the other animal was not a wolf. It was a short-haired, yellow dog, as large and almost as lean as Wolf.

Jeebee sat up to watch. The two came quite close, and eventually Wolf, in his bouncing around, ended up facing Jeebee. Apparently reminded by this of his new obligation to his senior partner, he stopped playing to trot over and greet Jeebee.

The dog followed after a moment, slowly and warily. Coming to about a dozen feet from him, it stopped, and stood, now clearly visible.

Jeebee concentrated on scratching Wolf's neck. The dog hesitated a moment more where it stood; then slowly it moved forward again to come level with Wolf's hindquarters. Here it hesitated once more, looking at Jeebee. Jeebee was careful not to look directly back at it. He saw, however, that it was a female. After another moment, she apparently made up her mind to trust him. Decisively, she pushed forward and nosed Jeebee's arm.

"Well, hello there," said Jeebee, looking at her now.

She wagged her tail and pushed herself past Wolf to sniff at Jeebee's jacket. He ventured to stop scratching Wolf and turned to stroke her head. She pulled back out of reach for a second, then pushed forward again and wagged her tail again, more confidently.

Jeebee spoke to her soothingly again and reached out a hand to stroke the top of her head. Wolf crowded his body between them and wedged his head under Jeebee's hand. Jeebee found himself beset by an unaccountably frantic bout of face licking, but there was an odd undercurrent of tension in Wolf's behavior. His tail wagged uncertainly, and his eyes flickered back and forth between Jeebee and the yellow dog. Despite the clearly audible whimpers, Jeebee could feel Wolf's rib cage vibrating with suppressed growls. He couldn't tell if they were intended for himself or for Wolf's new friend.

Jealousy, thought Jeebee? He chided himself for the suggestion—arrant anthropomorphism. But, he thought then, it was as convenient a tag label as any. *Something* about the situation was disturbing Wolf. Still, jealousy did not fit his character as Jeebee had seen it displayed up until now. On the other hand, his relationship with Wolf *had* changed, in ways he did not fully understand. Jeebee's new role might well mean new barriers as well as new liberties. Jeebee devoted his hands and attention to Wolf.

"So you brought a girlfriend home for dinner, did you, boy? Too bad I've nothing on the stove to offer the two of you."

The female wagged her tail vigorously at the sound of his voice. Watching her now, out of the corner of his eye, Jeebee decided that her fur was really not yellow but of such a light brown that the sunlight seemed to give her an overall yellowish cast. She tried to worm her way past Wolf, but he deftly twisted his body and blocked her with his hip. She gave up and trotted off into the wood. Wolf immediately detached himself from Jeebee and ran after her. Jeebee waited a few minutes, but they did not return, and he went back to his watching of the highway.

No one had shown up so far this day and it was past midafternoon. His eyes were getting tired of squinting through the lenses of the opera glasses. He scanned as far as he could see with his small binoculars toward both the east and west ends of the highway, where they disappeared against the line of the horizon. At the eastern end, to his left, he thought after a bit that he made out something. He could not be sure, even with the binoculars. It was merely a dot, as far off as anything on the roadway could be seen clearly—if indeed it was there at all.

He continued to study it; and the more he did so, the more sure he became that there actually was something there. If so, it should not be more than half an hour away from him. But if it was, it would have to be moving toward him at the slowest walking pace he could imagine anyone traveling.

He set himself to wait. But the hours passed and nothing changed. Yet, when he examined that end of the road, he was still sure he saw something there.

In the end, and since it had been a day of no travelers anyway, he decided to take the unusual step of moving toward that end of the highway, in hopes he could get a better view of whatever was there, if indeed it was not all in his imagination.

He began by going back away from the highway. Even to satisfy his curiosity, he was not going to take any chances. The route he followed went from the back of his observation point, on a long slant under a fold of land to where he was once more under the cover of a good-sized patch of trees set in an old watercourse, to the east of his starting point, and up toward the roadway again.

He repeated a number of these traverses between areas of good cover, until he had moved perhaps as much as half a mile eastward from his regular position. The clump of brush he was now in overlooked the highway. He moved to its outer edge, lay down, and tried his opera glasses once again on the vanishing point of the freeway.

Now he saw that he had not been imagining anything. It was definitely a vehicle of some sort—apparently quite a large vehicle, but with no horses attached to it. This was all wrong. Motorized transport of any kind had never before appeared on the road below him; nor had he expected it. Publicly available supplies of gasoline for motors had effectively dried up a little more than a year before, nearly eight months before he had left Stoketon.

The drying up of all supplies of fuel for motorized vehicles, he remembered, had been the signal for most of the last members left of the study group to try to get out. It had also marked the beginnings of Jeebee's efforts to accumulate necessary items for his own escape. Prescription drugs for his emergency medical pack, the electric bike, and the solar-cell blanket, which recharged the bike battery, were all things he had acquired at this time. The bike itself had been an experimental vehicle that he had located, left or forgotten in a commercial research-and-development center.

Only a heavy transport truck or possibly a mobile home, he thought, could be the size of what he now saw. But the thought of either was ridiculous. Such a vehicle would be an obvious target for any human predators along the way, and totally incapable of escaping off the road. It would, in short, be nothing more than a traveling death trap for its owners.

Now he was intrigued. Moreover, he was extremely puzzled by the fact that whatever it was, it did not seem to have moved since he had first spotted it. The only possible explanation was that it was in fact a motored truck that had somehow gotten hold of enough fuel to drive this far, but had finally run dry at the spot where he saw it.

That explanation involved so many coincidences that he found it hard to accept. Finally, he decided to get even closer so that he could make sure of what he thought he was seeing.

But it would be too risky to try that in daylight. He was all right in the brush; but moving from patch to patch of it while the sun was up would leave him too exposed and vulnerable as he got closer to the vehicle.

He had picked up some of Wolf's almost excessive caution where the unknown was concerned. It was now getting on to late afternoon. He could go back to his camp and eat something, then come back and work down the highway at night to get a look at the object. He was tempted to just stay where he was until dark and then reconnoiter, but common sense disagreed.

It would be safer to approach anything he wanted to look at closely after sunset in any case. But not at first dark. With the first approach of night they would instinctively become more aware and cautious. He had time, and a full belly was always a wise precaution against the unexpected.

So he went back to the camp, ate, put three extra cans of food in his backpack, and refilled his water flask. He hid the .22 safely out of reach in the branches of a tree at some distance from his camp, taking only the loaded .30/06, with extra cartridges. As soon as the sun set he started out on his nighttime trip of exploration.

Under these conditions, he went more openly and easily than he would have in full light. Twilight, even nighttime, had become for him a much more secure time for travel than day. At night he could go directly to his goal, down the strip of highway, staying in one of the shallow drainage ditches along either side of both concrete strips so as not to be outlined against the stars.

He would come toward them from a direction which any people there would probably not be watching. It would be most natural for them to expect any attack to be from the dark, open country on either side of them, out of which enemies could approach under the cover of trees and deeper folds of landscape.

Accordingly, he worked down the road until he had covered what he estimated to be at least a couple of miles. To his surprise, whoever was with the vehicle had lit a fire in the open beside it, which could only mean either that they felt unusually secure or that they were unusually foolish.

Just on the chance that they were unusually secure, he abandoned his roadside approach for a small woods that was fairly close to them, less than a hundred yards away. He was upwind, so no animals that might be with them should be able to catch his scent on the relatively light night breeze.

Under cover of the trees, he took out the binoculars again and tried to find out what he could with their help. They were not night glasses; and with the restriction looking through them placed on his field of vision, he had some trouble locating the spot of light that was the blazing fire. But eventually he zeroed in on it. By its illumination he was finally able to make out the shapes of at least two people. One was a good-sized adult, and the other was either a small adult, or perhaps a teenage youngster, wearing a red shirt.

There were also what looked like dogs. At his best count, there were at least five of them. This probably meant that there were more, for he had lost sight of some that moved out of the circle of firelight as he counted, and possibly missed others that had come in without him spotting their entrance. Borne on that same light, night breeze, he faintly heard the distant whicker of horses.

So, they had horses along with them, too. He had been right to be cautious. He could not hope to escape on foot in country like this from a mounted pursuer who could see him.

With the idea of dogs and horses as cotravelers with the two human shapes he had seen, he began to reassess what he could see of the vehicle. This was not easy because the firelight lit only one side of it, and the rest of it was in darkness. But gradually, studying it, he came to the conclusion that it was some kind of large covered wagon, with a boxlike body having high sides and a curving roof. It apparently ran on large wheels with truck tires on them.

It was too large to be drawn by just a couple of horses, but a team of perhaps four or six should be able to move it handily. If those wheels rolled as easily as they looked to, four horses should pull it easily on level, well-paved roads.

The more he examined the situation, the more he became convinced of two things. One, that it was indeed a horse-drawn wagon modeled on the old prairie, or "Conestoga," type that had been common in the wagon trains of the nineteenth century, during the migration of settlers westward. The rounded, canvas-style top and the rectangular body made something like that almost certain. The second was that he must have a still closer look at it, in daylight.

He decided he would stay where he was until almost dawn. If the wind did not change so as to carry the message of his presence to the noses of those dogs, he should be fairly secure here. With the moon down, in the darkness just before the sun rose, he could get closer, look it over in the predawn light, and be safely gone before full light.

He dozed, accordingly, through the night; lying where he was, waking occasionally to drink from his water flask or empty his bladder. He woke before first light, and realizing from the utter darkness about him that the dawn was close, he began to decide how he would make his approach.

The difficulty was that he was not closely acquainted with the area where he was lying, although he had passed by it in his searches for abandoned farms that might have buildings that would yield things he could use. In the darkness, the wind was still in his favor, and he thought he remembered from his earlier trips up and down along the highway that there was another small stand of trees closer to where the wagon was now. If he could reach those further woods in good time, he could look the outfit over in the first predawn illumination and still be able to get clear away before sunrise.

Accordingly, he began to move. It was almost a matter of feeling his way. But his night running on the first weeks out of Michigan had taught him how to do just that over unfamiliar territory. Necessarily he went slowly, but also directly, down alongside the highway and only about twenty yards off it. Eventually, he reached what he thought was the patch of trees he remembered. He worked slowly through these until he was at their edge, where the open ground to the highway began. He lay down to wait.

His waiting was no more than a matter of minutes. The extreme darkness of predawn had begun to lighten as he entered this final patch of woods, and very shortly along the eastern edge of the sky a paling began, which trumpeted the eventual sunrise.

He looked down in the direction of the freeway at the point where he believed he should see the wagon emerge from the darkness. The fire had died out completely, so there was no help there. He lay utterly still, and—blessedly—the wind stayed in his favor.

Slowly around him the predawn brightened. Slowly the shape of the wagon emerged out of the darkness like a sketch in black and white. It was a little farther down the freeway than he had expected it to be when he finally saw it.

He waited. The light got stronger and soon he could use the opera glasses. The vehicle was as he had thought; an oversized wagon, of the Conestoga type, rolling on eight pairs of large, rubber-tired wheels.

Behind it, enclosed in a sort of stake-and-rope corral, was a herd of perhaps as many as fifteen or twenty horses. Both of the riding and pulling variety. Three other horses were unaccountably together close to the back of the wagon. There was something strange about the shape of those three horses. But the light was not yet strong enough for Jeebee to tell what.

The dogs were sleeping shapes on the ground around the wagon and the ashes of the fire. The wagon, he thought, studying it with the glasses, was really oversized. The top of its roof could be no less than twelve feet above the road surface. Also, its front behind the wagon seat was not open, but closed by a wooden wall. Forward of this, a tongue projected only far enough for a first pair of horses. But Jeebee was confirmed in his guess that it would take at least four to pull it handily.

No people were in evidence this early. They must all be in the wagon; and again he thought that they must be very secure, or else they would have had someone posted on guard. He had been wrong about the number of dogs. He counted eight—no, nine—shapes sleeping around where the fire had been.

As the day brightened, the black and gray of the wagon began to acquire colors and he could see words on the side that faced him. A little more light confirmed that the words had been made in black or red paint against the white surface of the side, which formed a continuous curve up and over the roof.

Perhaps the white was cloth after all. Cloth over an open wooden box. The letters of the words spelled out PAUL SANDERSON AND COMPANY, PEDDLER.

The letters were a good three feet high, painted in what, as the morning brightened broadly, he saw to be a very brilliant red indeed, upon the white cloth. They looked almost as if they had been freshly painted. Overall, there was an air of unusual cleanliness and competence about the wagon and everything connected with it. It seemed stoutly built, well maintained, and strangely businesslike in this newly disorderly and dirty age.

Just then one of the dogs stirred, got to its feet, and shook itself. It was time to go; but Jeebee wanted one more look at those three horses by the back of the wagon. He swung the binoculars on them and saw they were tethered to the wagon; each one saddled and bridled with a full pack behind each saddle, and a rifle in a scabbard at the right front of each one. This was something to think about. Jeebee began his retreat.

In the brightening light he made it back quickly to the trees where he had spent the night before. From there, he took a longer, and much clearer, observation of the wagon, now aided by the daylight.

Now that the sun had risen, the inhabitants of the wagon evidently began to stir. Smoke rose from a metal flue through the wagon's roof. Following that first dog on its feet, all the others had roused. Now they began to move around and congregate closely near the front of the wagon. After some time, Jeebee thought he smelled cooking on the breeze that was still toward him from them. Eventually, the smaller—and Jeebee now saw— beardless figure came out and threw a panful of scraps of some kind to the dogs. They dived hungrily at them and gobbled them down.

While they were still eating, another dog burst from the trees in the same patch that Jeebee had been in earlier, and raced down to the wagon. It was the yellow dog Jeebee had seen with Wolf. She jumped up on the slight figure, greeting the human effusively, and receiving a vigorous scratching and petting in return.

With the morning formalities concluded, the human turned toward the front of the wagon. Jeebee could not hear anything, but he got the impression that the person he saw had called out. Within moments two more figures appeared. One was the larger person Jeebee had seen in outline by the fire the night before, clearly a large, somewhat blocky man of middle age, with a short, square beard. He was followed almost immediately by a smaller man, clean shaven and carrying something that turned out to be more scraps, which were fed to the yellow dog.

After a consultation among the three figures, the smaller man went back inside the wagon, the one who had met the yellow dog as she returned went back to the rope corral. This person ducked through the rope and selected six of the heavier of the horses, who allowed themselves to be caught with no protest whatsoever. They had halter ropes loosely about their necks. They were led out of the rope corral and toward the front of the wagon.

They were met halfway by the larger man, who took the horses over, led them to the front of the wagon, and began the process of harnessing them two by two to the wagon tongue. Meanwhile the one that brought the horses to him was now back, bringing three fresh riding horses up to replace the ones who had been tied to the wagon back.

The replacement horses were tied to the end of the wagon, and the handler transferred saddles, bridles, guns, and all gear from the ones who had stood there during the night to the three just brought up. Halter ropes with short, loose ends were put around the necks of the ones just stripped of their gear and they were turned loose. They followed like dogs as the handler returned to the corral and began to take it apart. The horses released from the wagon joined the others, but they all stayed in a close group.

It was plain that the wagon was at last preparing to move on. Whether the decision to start going had anything to do with the return of the yellow dog or not, Jeebee did not know. But he knew that he wanted to start getting away from where he was and back into familiar territory. He crawled backward, stood up, and went off at a slow jog, keeping a fold of land between him and the wagon.

Now that he understood more about the vehicle and those with it, he was less concerned about keeping out of sight as he returned. Simply going back from the highway, he went west in a straight line, shielded by the land between him and the wagon, until he was back among his familiar trees.

As he went, he made some mental computations of the time it might take for the wagon to get under way and to get up level with where he was now. He decided that there would be time to circle back around his own camping place. He could make sure everything there was all right and the .22 was still safely hidden in the tree, as well as the bag of food he had hung up separately.

He did so. All was as he had left it. He took the .22 with him when he returned to his observation point. The .30/06 was still in the rope sling on his back.

Lying down at his usual observation point, he used the opera glasses to study the wagon's three people as it got closer. There was just a chance these were the kind he could risk approaching.

The legend "Paul Sanderson and Company, Peddler," was in itself reassuring. It implied that those with the wagon were used to meeting people at all times and in all places. Consequently, they should not be startled into defensive action by someone showing up along the roadside. On the other hand, they had looked like a very efficient outfit. And if they had survived with that kind of a rig to get this far, they must be in a better state to take offensive action, if they wanted to, than they appeared.

With the advantage of the angle from which he viewed their approach, and the small but definite added height from which he viewed them, he began to see not only the wagon, but what was behind it.

The extra horses he had seen earlier were following the wagon in a herd, apparently keeping station there pretty much of their own will. The man who had greeted the yellow dog was now mounted on horseback, and riding gracefully back and forth between the herd and the front of the wagon, where the large man sat driving the team of six horses that pulled it.

The little man had been sitting with him on the wagon seat earlier, but now there was nothing to be seen. Obviously he was inside the wagon. The three new horses that had been tied to the back of the wagon and furnished with bridles and saddles, packs and rifles, came along pretty much at the length of their tethers, but without putting any strain on them. Apparently they, too, were used to following the wagon under certain conditions, and in a certain pattern. All in all the wagon gave the curious impression of being a self-contained community; highly organized and time-tested, to a high pitch of efficiency.

Jeebee found himself still of two minds about approaching it. The very order and discipline he saw was a factor in urging him to make contact here. On the other hand, he remembered the wagon train with the several wagons, all of their drivers chained to their seats. In a way, what he saw was too neat and reassuring to be true, just as the wagon train had seemed at first glance. There was always the danger that there could be something unobvious in the situation now approaching him down the road that he would find out, too late, that he did not like, at all.

On the other hand, he had to take a chance sometime. This was by far the most promising and attractive set of travelers he had seen since he first started his watch on the interstate.

The wagon was only about a hundred and fifty yards down the road now, and coming along with the horses pulling it at a slow trot. Evidently those horses must be changed frequently, for they could not keep up this pace for too long. Then Jeebee found his attention suddenly attracted away from the horses to the dogs alongside the wagon.

The other dogs were pestering the yellow one. None of them was as large as she was. But five of them were attempting to get close enough to mount her. She kept turning back her head over her shoulder to snap at them, and occasionally stopped and literally drove them back before she turned on again, but they came after her once more. Her rather lean, short-haired tail was tucked protectively down between her hind legs. She was female and must be in heat. That would explain Wolf trying to keep her and Jeebee apart, particularly if he had designs of his own on her. Clearly, the other dogs were males; and it was becoming more and more obvious they were pestering her to the limits of her patience.

They and the wagon were almost within a hundred yards or so of the first edge of Jeebee's protective trees when the female, apparently at last completely out of patience, turned and made a bolt. All at once she was in a flat run, away from the other dogs, the wagon, and everything else, toward Jeebee and the woods itself.

The other dogs raced out after her, but were shouted back by the man driving the wagon. Only the female herself ignored his voice and continued her flight toward the woods.

The rider on horseback abandoned the following equine herd and galloped after her. But the female vanished into the woods some twenty yards to the left of where Jeebee lay, before the rider could catch up with her. Another shout from the wagon train made the rider pull slowly to a halt and turn back before entering the trees. The slim figure in the saddle was apparently unhappy about doing so, but obeyed. Jeebee guessed that the rider might be a son, or some younger relative of the wagon driver.

The driver pulled to a stop as the rider came up to him. What appeared to be an argument ensued. Little snatches of it reached Jeebee; but what he was able to hear was too fragmentary for him to make out more than a few of the words, even though they were speaking in fairly high-pitched and somewhat angry tones at each other. Clearly the wagon driver was forbidding any attempt by the rider to follow the dog into the woods.

The wagon stayed stopped, however, and the argument continued. From what little Jeebee could catch of the argument, the driver was claiming that the rider would only be safe staying with the wagon. The rider, on the other hand, was arguing that the woods were perfectly safe.

Then a snatch of the conversation came clearly to Jeebee's ears. They were only about a hundred feet away from him. He did not catch all the words but what the rider said, in a high-pitched voice, was that they were definitely not going on again until they had Greta safely back with them.

Just then the voices were drowned out by the yelping of a dog in the woods to his right. Jeebee swung his opera glasses swiftly in that direction, but the trunks of the trees and the stands of bush hid whatever was going on. Then the yelping moved past him, out toward the highway again, and he saw that the yellow dog had emerged from the woods, tied to Wolf, who was now breeding her.

Greta headed back toward the wagon, and Wolf had little choice but to follow since she weighed at least as much as he did. The wagon driver reached back and drew a rifle from the wagon. He was putting it to his shoulder before Jeebee finally recognized his intention was to shoot Wolf, who was now being towed to within about fifty feet of the wagon.

Reacting completely without thought, Jeebee scrambled to his feet. He had taken the .30/06 off his back earlier and laid it up in a tree behind him. Grabbing it, he dashed out of the woods toward the wagon, himself.

"Stop!" he shouted. "Don't shoot! He's mine! It's all right!"

He continued on at a run toward the wagon.

The rifle in the driver's hands swung to cover Jeebee himself, and a revolver was suddenly in the hands of the rider, also aimed at him. Jeebee threw the rifle away and continued to run toward the wagon, calling out to them not to shoot.

But before he reached there, Wolf came loose, and was immediately set upon by the other dogs. To Jeebee's surprise, the yellow female immediately wheeled about to his defense and began snapping and snarling at the others.

They fell back before her. Apparently she had rank among them, as well as being the largest. Jeebee, panting for breath, had just reached the wagon.

He caught hold of one edge of the wagon seat to hold himself upright, panting. Looking up, he saw the face of a broad-shouldered, stocky man with a salt-and-pepper beard trimmed short, and hair of the same color; and the nearby round, young face of the rider, whom he now saw was unmistakably a woman rather than a man. Blue eyes looked at him from under a light brown hat.

"Don't shoot!" Jeebee cried in one last, breathless gasp.

CHAPTER 7

The wagon driver slowly lowered his rifle as Wolf disappeared among the trees.

"All right," he said. "He's gone anyway." The driver's voice was a slight, reedy baritone. His eyes turned to look down into Jeebee's face. "What is he, a coyote? He's big."

They stared at each other wordlessly for a couple of minutes. Finally, Jeebee got both his wind and his wits back together at the same time.

"He's a wolf," he answered. "You're Paul Sanderson?"

The other nodded.

"I'm Jeebee," Jeebee said. "Jeeris Belamy Walthar. Your wagon says you're a peddler. I might be able to do some business with you."

Sanderson's eyes flicked up for a moment to the edge of the trees into which Wolf had disappeared.

"Maybe," he said in a noncommittal voice. His rifle had not ceased to point at Jeebee, and there was a revolver holstered at his hip. "How many more of you up there in the trees?"

"I'm alone!" said Jeebee. "Except for Wolf, that is. Completely alone. Look, I threw my gun away, I just want to buy some things from you, if you've got them to sell."

"We'll see." Sanderson nodded at the rider. "Check him out."

Jeebee had noticed that she was female, but it hadn't really registered; so now there was some shock as she—a young woman, if not literally a girl—approached him from behind. He felt businesslike fingers inserted into his boot tops and then hands run lightly up and around his legs; patting his hips, searching his back pockets, then feeling about his shirt, up under his armpits, and across his chest from behind. At last the woman ended by even digging for a moment into his long hair and beard. Then the hands went away.

"Nothing on him, Dad." The voice was unmistakably feminine.

She came around to stand facing him. She had a healthy-looking round young face that would have looked cheerful, except for the moment just now, it wore an expression of suspicion. He caught a glimpse of short, clean, light brown hair showing under the wide brim of her dusty brown hat, and a light, dark-colored leather vest, unbuttoned over a regular tan workshirt and blue jeans. About the only concession to her femininity was the fact that the heavy work clothes had been tailored to fit her rather better than Sanderson's fit him and the single touch of brightness that was the turquoise bandanna knotted around the column of her throat.

She was now wiping the fingers with which she had searched him on the legs of her jeans. He was offended, then suddenly embarrassed. Sanderson was getting down from the wagon seat, leaving his rifle up there, and the girl, for she could not be much more than that, Jeebee thought, had already reholstered her revolver in order to search him.

"All right," said Sanderson, now standing on the ground in front of Jeebee, "what do you need?"

"A couple of horses," said Jeebee. "Supplies and tools."

Sanderson laughed.

"For someone just standing there with nothing on you," the wagon owner said, "you want a lot. What are you going to offer for all that?"

"Oh, I've something to pay with," said Jeebee.

He reached in between the buttons of his shirt to the money

belt underneath. With three fingers he reached inside and gathered three of the heavy coins. He brought them out and displayed them on his open palm for the wagon driver to see.

"So that's what you had in that hideout belt," said the girl's voice behind him. "I felt them there, Dad, but I figured they couldn't be anything dangerous, so I didn't say anything."

Jeebee looked back at Sanderson and was surprised to find the man silently laughing.

"And you were right enough, Mary," Jeebee thought he heard him say. After a quick glance at his daughter, Sanderson's eyes fastened on Jeebee, again.

"Gold," he said, and shook his head.

"But it actually is gold!" Jeebee said urgently. "These are gold coins! I collected them over about a two-year period. I belonged to a Gold Coin of the Month mail-order club." He offered his laden palm to the wagon driver.

"Go on," he said. "Check them out for yourself. They're almost pure gold. You can bite into them easily. Besides, somebody like you ought to know gold when you see it."

"Oh, I believe you. They're gold. Those are Krugerrands, all right," said Sanderson. "It's just that they aren't going to buy you a lot. I couldn't offer you much for them. Too risky to try trading with most people, too hard to find a buyer you can trust. The safe things to trade now are low-bulk, everyday necessities people nowadays can't find or make easily."

After he finished, there was a long moment of silence and then Sanderson spoke again.

"Just what did you figure on buying besides horses?" he asked Jeebee.

"What I need to survive with," Jeebee said. "I'm headed for my brother's ranch in Montana. I figure once I get there, I'll be safe. I'd hoped to buy just a couple of horses from you, one to ride and one to pack; and for the packhorse, say, a spade, an ax, some blankets, some basics like flour and sugar and maybe bacon. I need a sidearm of some kind. A revolver, if you've got one to spare, and ammunition for that and the rifle I threw down back there, plus another one I've got up in the trees. I've been waiting a couple of weeks now for somebody to come by who looked like they might be safe for me to try to buy from. I might not even have come out for you if it hadn't been for Wolf."

"How much of that gold have you got?" Sanderson asked.

"Twenty-three coins," said Jeebee. "All practically pure gold."

"Well, I'll tell you right now," said Sanderson, "that much gold wouldn't even begin to buy you a packhorse. Maybe a shovel, an ax, and a sidearm—maybe."

He looked at Jeebee awhile longer.

"Got anything else to trade?" he asked.

"Nothing I can spare," said Jeebee.

Sanderson stood for a minute as if thinking. For all that Jeebee overtopped him by about an inch or so, and the fact that he must be twenty years older than Jeebee, Sanderson was square-shouldered, thickly built, and strong looking. He passed his rifle to the young woman. She took it without a word.

"Come on," Sanderson said to Jeebee, "we'll go pick up that rifle you threw away, and look at what you've got."

"Dad—" began the girl.

"You just stay here," Sanderson told her. "I'll be all right. You're the one could be made use of by someone hiding up in those woods. If they've got me, they've got nothing. Everything that's valuable is down here; and you've got Nick."

Jeebee blinked a little. "Nick" must be the third person he had seen by the light of the fire beside the wagon the night before. He assumed that this Nick, whoever he was, was in the wagon. In any case, Sanderson had already started toward the trees and Jeebee turned and caught up with him. They found the rifle—in fact Sanderson found it before Jeebee did, picked it up, hefted it in his hand, turned it about, and worked its action.

"Nothing great," he said, "but you've kept it in pretty good shape."

He had ejected the cartridge that Jeebee had automatically jacked into the chamber the moment the wagon appeared in his binoculars, and removed the clip. Now Sanderson picked up the shell and gave it back to Jeebee, along with the clip.

"Put that in your pocket," he said. Jeebee took them wordlessly. He and Sanderson went on up into the woods and Jeebee found the .22, which he also handed to Sanderson. The .22 was a single-shot and Sanderson jacked the cartridge out of it as well and handed it to Jeebee to pocket, then gave him the rifle. Neither one of them said anything and they went on through the trees back away from the road and the wagon.

"Where's your camp?" Sanderson asked as they stepped into the dappled shade of the woods.

"It's in another grove behind this one," Jeebee answered. "We can go there if you like, but there's nothing there. Nothing at all. It's just a place where I light a fire at night and sleep."

"Let's look anyway," said Sanderson.

They went on through the little patch of woods, across the open space behind and into the further trees. When they reached the campsite, Sanderson swept his eyes around and immediately focused on the bag Jeebee had made out of the canvas and hung up in the tree, bulging with canned goods from the root cellar.

"What's that?"

"Cans of food I got from a root cellar," Jeebee answered. "Do you want me to climb up and get one to show you or would you like to climb up and see?"

"I've got a better idea," said Sanderson. "You climb up and bring the whole thing down."

Jeebee shrugged, climbed up the tree, and with some effort brought the container down. He opened it up.

"By God, you weren't kidding!" Sanderson poked with his boot toe among the cans. "Any of them make you sick?"

"Not so far," Jeebee answered. "They're all still short of the expiration date stamped on them."

"All the same." Sanderson stopped poking at the cans. "It's no good for trade with me. We're not short of food back at the wagon, and I wouldn't dare trade it to someone else just in case they got sick from it in spite of the date."

He glanced around the campsite.

"You were right enough," he said, "there's nothing here but the ashes of your fire, covered over."

"I told you," Jeebee answered.

"Call that wolf of yours in," said Sanderson. "I'd feel more comfortable with him in sight."

"He won't come just because I call," Jeebee answered. "He comes and goes as he likes."

Sanderson stared at him. "Then why do you say he's your wolf?"

"I didn't want you to shoot him." Jeebee searched for a word that would explain his connection with a wolf. "He's my partner."

The last word sounded strangely on the still air of the little patch of forest. Sanderson smiled. It was just the slightest quirk at the corner of his lips. But his eyes looked back around the empty space of the campsite.

"Maybe," he said. "In that case how do you know he's not gone for good?"

"I can try if he'll answer. He may not," Jeebee replied.

He cupped his hands around his mouth, put his head back, and howled. They waited but there was no answer. Jeebee shrugged at Sanderson and howled again. Again, no answer.

"He may not be hearing me," Jeebee said, "or he may just not feel like answering. Let me try it once more." He turned more toward the interstate and howled a third time. There was a very long moment of silence. Jeebee shook his head, but just as he did so, from a great distance came the long, train-whistle-like howl. Jeebee smiled at Sanderson.

Sanderson nodded. His face still gave nothing away, but Jeebee got the impression from the way he stood that a great deal of the distant element in his manner had gone out of him. It was almost as if Wolf's answering howl had struck a strange chord of understanding and friendship in the man toward Jeebee.

"Come on back to the wagon," he said.

They turned and started back together.

"Tell me about yourself," Sanderson said as they headed back. "Where are you from, and what brings you here?"

"I'm trying to reach my brother's ranch in Montana," Jeebee

said. "I ought to be welcome there—and safe. I'm not all that safe by myself."

Sanderson laughed shortly.

"Not these days, right? Even with the wolf for a partner," said Sanderson. "But go on. What were you before you started coming west? And how did you get that way?"

He kicked at the site of Jeebee's fire, uncovering the ashes.

"No. We're none of us safe these days," he went on before Jeebee could answer. "I was lucky. I saw it coming about five years ago and started getting ready for it. We're not safe, either, at the wagon. But we're safer than most. People've got use for a peddler."

Jeebee did not dare ask why. He wanted to know more about this man he might have to deal with. But he did not feel that a direct question about the other's background would be welcome. He decided to answer Sanderson's question about his own.

"I was on the staff of a university," Jeebee said, "part of a special study group from the University of Michigan. A little over a year ago when things started to get bad, the other people in the group began to leave, looking for safer places to be. Most of us felt pretty safe in the smaller place we were in."

"And that was—where?" Sanderson asked.

"Stoketon, its name was," Jeebee said. "Small town. Nice. But things began to go bad, even there, after the electricity and water shut off. And of course any long-distance phoning had been out a long time before that. At any rate, the others began to leave, looking for some place safer. I was the last to go, and I just got away with my life. That was some months ago, early this spring. I've been trying to make it to Montana ever since."

Taking a chance, he added, "You make pretty good time with those horses on the interstate."

"When we move," said Sanderson, "but we stop for customers. Tell me how you got this far."

Sanderson listened with what Jeebee found to be a surprising amount of interest for somebody who was simply a passerby on the highway, and who, by the very nature of his business, must be meeting new people all the time. Jeebee had not really finished talking about his background when they emerged from the set of trees over the highway and came down to the wagon. The girl's horse was tied to the wagon and she herself was on the wagon seat. She jumped down as they came into sight and came partway to meet them.

"I'm glad you're back, Dad," she said. "I was just starting to think about leaving Nick here and going after you after all!"

"That wouldn't have been smart, Mary," Sanderson said, shaking his head. "You know I've always told you—stick with the wagon. That's your strong point. Stick with it. You're like somebody who's got a fort and runs outside it where they can be picked off, if you leave it."

He turned to Jeebee. "Jeebee," he said, "this is my daughter—" Again Jeebee thought he heard the name "Mary."

"M-e-r-r-y," spelled the girl, looking hard at him. "Merry!"

"I'll remember," said Jeebee, to his own surprise, flushing a little under his beard.

"Merry," said Sanderson, "this is Jeebee—what did you say that full name of yours was?" he added, turning to Jeebee.

"Jeeris Belamy Walthar," Jeebee answered.

"Glad to meet you, Jeebee," Merry said levelly. She glanced at the two rifles Jeebee now carried, one in each hand.

"That's right, Merry," Sanderson said. "That's all our friend here owns, except that wolf of his, and he doesn't even own that. But I've been learning about him."

Swiftly, and briefly, he sketched in Jeebee's background for her.

"What I'm thinking, Merry," Sanderson wound up, "is we might offer Jeebee, here, a chance to earn what he needs."

He turned to Jeebee.

"How would you like to work with us for a couple of months before we turn south? You might just be able to pay for at least part of what extra you need."

CHAPTER 8

"Dad?" Merry said, and gave him a long look. "You're sure?"

"He's alone," Sanderson answered. "I think he'll do all right for us."

Merry said nothing more. It had not been a father-daughter interchange. It had been a statement made by a leader to a subordinate.

"Still and all," said Sanderson to Jeebee, "why don't you tell Merry something more about yourself, the way you told me."

Feeling more than a little awkward, Jeebee tried to explain some of the statistical exploration of the world economy he had been engaged in when the world itself collapsed. He got tangled up in his own explanations and finally gave up. But Merry's tense animosity toward him, surprisingly, seemed to have relaxed. It was oddly as if both father and daughter looked for understandings outside and beyond normal verbal explanations.

"But this wolf of yours," said Merry, after a moment when he finally fell silent, "how do you know he's a wolf, and not just a dog that looks a lot like a wolf?"

This, too, was too complicated to explain. It was hard to explain a conviction born from experience in the hard logic of words. But long since Jeebee himself had given up all doubt.

"He's not a dog," said Jeebee.

"Could be a mix," Sanderson put in, "Dog-wolf. But what difference does it make? Merry, why don't you show Jeebee around everything."

"Everything?" Merry frowned at her father.

"Well," said Sanderson, "you don't need to take him into our own rooms. But let him look inside the rest of the wagon, see the horses, and everything else."

"How about having him bring that wolf of his in here first?" Merry asked.

"He won't come," said Jeebee. "Not with the rest of you here. You're strange and he doesn't trust you."

"Been shot at, has he?" said Merry.

"Something like that," said Sanderson, a touch of impatience in his voice. "Give him a quick look around, Merry. Then we can get going again."

"Come on," Merry said to Jeebee.

She wheeled her horse around and went back down alongside the wagon at a walk. Jeebee hurried to catch up with her. They were back at the end of the wagon in a few steps. Jeebee had expected to find the horses scattered all over, but they had simply stopped where they were and were peacefully cropping the grass of the median.

"Can you ride?" he heard Merry asking bluntly.

He turned to look up at her. With the shadow of that hat brim of hers over her blue eyes—it was a large, Stetson-like hat—she looked severe.

"Not really," said Jeebee, uncertain what level of horseback skill she meant by "ride."

"Well, you're going to have to learn, then," she said. "I'll pick out the most easygoing riding horse we have for you to start learning on, but you better be prepared for something a little more than they'd have given you once at a for-hire riding stable."

She lifted off a coil of rope that was fastened to her saddle, shook it out, and he saw that it was a lasso. Gathering it up again, she rode into the midst of the horses, dropped the loop expertly over the neck of a slim gray animal, and led it, plodding gently, back to Jeebee.

"Here, hold her," she said, handing the rope of the lasso to Jeebee, so that his hands closed about it only some six inches from the neck of the horse. She dismounted and dropped her reins onto the ground. Her horse stood where it was. The gray mare Jeebee held looked at him with calm eyes.

"I'll get some gear," Merry said.

He watched her go and saw that the rear of the wagon was closed with a wooden back wall just like its front, with a regular door inset in it. A boxed-in single step below the door made it easy to reach the entrance from the ground. She went through the door and was gone only a little time before coming back with another saddle and a set of reins, the saddle riding on her forearm with the stirrup leathers dangling down on either side, and the metal stirrups themselves chiming together as she moved.

She put the bridle and saddle on, drew the cinch strap tight, and buckled it under the belly of the gray mare.

"All right now," she said. "Mount up."

Jeebee put down his two rifles, took hold of the saddle horn, found the stirrup with the toe of his boot, then stopped himself. He was on the horse's right side instead of its left, the customary side for mounting.

"It's all right," said Merry as he started to go around the animal, with a touch of exasperation very like her father's in her voice, "any of my horses you can mount from either side. They'll stand if you drop the reins to the ground and lie down so you can lie between their legs and fire a rifle across their body, if you have to. But we'll get to that later. Now, mount up!"

Jeebee hoisted himself clumsily into the saddle. His left toe searched for and found the other stirrup. He had a moment's feeling almost of triumph.

"All right now," said Merry, "walk her around a bit."

Jeebee struck with both heels at the side of the horse under him. The mare leaped forward with a suddenness that almost unseated him and in panic he hauled back hard on the reins. The mare skidded to a stop and then began to back up.

"Loose those reins!" the voice of Merry shouted.

Jeebee fumbled with the reins and dropped them on the

horse's neck. The mare came to a standstill. Jeebee looked over at Merry and saw her glaring at him. However, as she continued to look at him, the glare softened and disappeared.

"Well, you can't help it. You just don't know," she said. "Now, to make her walk forward, just lift the reins off her neck. That's all. Hold them loosely in your hand."

Gingerly, Jeebee obeyed. To his relief and joy, the mare began to walk slowly but steadily forward. Merry remounted.

"That's right. Now, guide her around in a circle," Merry said behind him. "You do that by laying the opposite rein against the side of her neck. Lay the left rein against her neck and she'll walk to the right."

Jeebee obeyed; and the mare obeyed. It made the complete circle; and then Merry had him walk the mare around it again in the opposite direction. After that Merry directed him into a trot, and he bounced uncomfortably in the saddle for a bit before she advanced the trot into a canter, her own horse now moving alongside his. After a little distance, she brought them both to a stop, turned them around, and led Jeebee back to the other horses.

Once there, she ordered him down from the saddle and got down with him, dropping the reins of her own horse to the ground so that it stood as if she had tied it in place. She showed him how to loosen the cinch strap under the belly of the mare and take off both the saddle and the bridle. Then she had him carry both items in the back, through the back door of the wagon into a tiny cubicle with a further, closed door. There the saddle was put to rest, hanging on a hook, and the bridle with some other bridles on a projecting dowel.

He took a moment to pick up his rifles again as she led him back out of the door into the sunlight, ignoring another door that seemed to lead further into the wagon. They walked around to the front of the vehicle, mounted the steps by the wagon seat, and entered the vehicle from its front. Following her, Jeebee stepped into an area dimly lit by the bulb in an old-fashioned auto headlight, glowing with what, to Jeebee's astonishment, had to be electricity. Merry pointed briefly at it.

"Car battery," she said briefly, "generator-driven by the wheels."

The place was crammed and packed to the arching roof with boxes, tightly filled bags of all sizes, and what looked like ranks of tall wooden chests filled vertically with wide, narrow drawers. The room had a mild, pleasant, health-food-store aroma about it.

"Don't come in here," Merry told him, "unless Dad, Nick, or myself has said you can."

There was a narrow aisle down through the center of the close-stacked contents of the place, and she led the way along it to another door. Staying close behind her, Jeebee stepped through into a second, crammed-full area that was barely long enough to allow two net hammocks to hang at full length against its walls, under the arching roof overhead. Both hammocks hung on their further hook at the moment, neatly rolled up.

Down below the roof now, a short, deeply tanned old man with a triangular face sat in a straight, wooden chair behind one of two large firearms, across the room from each other, which Jeebee recognized as heavy, air-cooled machine guns. The guns faced apertures in the steel beyond which was again what looked like white canvas. Something like a periscope tube angled up from the base of the wall to end in a wide, oval lens just above the breech of the machine guns.

A number of other weapons hung on the walls and filled the room, including four tubes that Jeebee was pleased to discover he could identify as rocket launchers. The ammunition for the rocket launchers was stacked beside them, and the launch tubes were clipped upright to a pole that rose to the center of the arch of roof overhead.

"You can put your rifles with the others in that rack on the side there." Merry's voice woke him out of his study of the room. She turned to the old man, who seemed not to have moved, but now held a revolver, loosely. "Nick, this is . . ." Merry turned again to Jeebee. "What did you say your name was?"

"Jeeris Belamy Walthar," Jeebee answered. "Call me Jeebee. Everybody does."

"Nick Gage," said the old man. He put the revolver casually

away again under the seat of his chair, where it disappeared, apparently supported there somehow.

Jeebee extended his hand to the other, whose blunt, dry fingers closed around it, and who shook it a couple of times formally before letting go, without getting up from his seat at the machine gun.

"I had you in the sights on this from the moment you left the woods," Nick said, patting the breech of the machine gun.

"Nick can do anything," Merry said. "He'll teach you all about the weapons. I'll get you to riding, eventually, so you can take your shift of riding herd on the spare stock. I don't suppose you can cook?"

"Not really . . ." said Jeebee, embarrassed once more.

"Well, both Nick and I'll have to teach you about that then, too."

Merry turned to Nick.

"Dad says we're going to take him on to replace Willie."

"Willie knew a few things," said Nick. His voice had a matter-of-factness that made everything he said come out almost as a monotone. "But maybe we can make even more of this one. Leave him to me."

"Merry!" came Sanderson's voice from the front of the wagon. "Can we get under way now?"

"Have you got anything else to pick up?" Merry asked Jeebee. Jeebee shook his head. He had his two rifles, even if they were in the rack some feet from him, and in the backpack he was wearing was everything else he owned.

"All right, Dad!" Merry called back. "We're all set. I'll be right out!"

She turned and went, leaving Jeebee alone with Nick Gage. There was a moment of silence as they looked at each other.

"Did she or Paul tell you much?" said Nick.

"No," said Jeebee, suddenly thoughtful.

"Thought not. That's right, too," said Nick. "It's my job to tell you. Take a good look at me."

Jeebee had of course been looking at him all this time. He kept on looking. He did not see anything he had not seen before.

"You see a little old man, right?" said Nick.

"If you want to call yourself that," said Jeebee. It was a strange conversation and he felt awkward about how to handle it. "I guess I'd have to say you're right."

"Right," said Nick. He held out his left hand, palm up. The skin of the palm was remarkably pink, contrasted to the leathery brownness of the back of the hand and all the rest of the skin surface of Nick that was visible. It was not so much a broad hand as a hand that seemed to have been stretched wide. There were large gaps at the base of the fingers between them. A hand that looked stubby and strong, not overly callused, but used.

"What do you see?" Nick asked.

"Your hand," Jeebee answered.

"Right," Nick said again. He closed his hand and magically it now held a knife with about a six-inch blade pointing right at Jeebee. "Now what do you see?"

Jeebee drew in his breath. His stomach muscles had tightened, and he found he was standing closer to Nick than he had thought. The knife point was less than its own length from those same stomach muscles.

"A knife," he said after a moment, keeping his voice level.

"And that's right," said Nick. He put the knife back into one of the capacious pockets of the leather vest he wore over a red shirt and jeans, very like those worn by Merry and her father. "Figure it out if you can and tell me how it was done. When you do, we'll talk about knives some."

"I don't know how you did it," said Jeebee. "But it had to come from some place. The only place that could be is up your sleeve."

"Good guess," said Nick. "We'll talk about knives then, but not today. Today I've got to show you around. Meanwhile . . ."

He unbuttoned his left sleeve and pulled it up. A harness with what looked like a leather tube was attached to his forearm.

"That's what did it," said Nick. "Take a good look at that. That's a rig. It's also damn useless; all rigs are. Rigs will be just what you need one in a thousand times, but one in ten times they'll get in the way of what you're doing and get you killed."

He reached up, unbuttoned something, and the whole contraption slid off his arm. He put it on a tablelike surface hinged to the wall next to his chair. "Meanwhile, remember that's a trick. I know lots more besides that. Since I know tricks you don't know, I'm not old and I'm not little. I'm bigger than you are. So you do what I say and I do what Paul says. All right?"

"All right," said Jeebee, "for the moment, anyway."

"That's good enough for me," Nick said as he got to his feet. "Come on with me now and I'll begin to teach you what you've got to know about everything to do with the wagon here and what you'll have to do."

Nick reached into a drawer under the table surface beside his chair and brought out a typed list about three pages long. He handed this to Jeebee.

"This is a checklist of things you're to do, or check on," he said. "You'll go clear through the list every twenty-four hours. The part of the list under Quiet Room is this room here. We call this the Quiet Room so we can mention it with other people around and not advertise we're armed. After a while you'll know the list by heart and be able to do the things automatically. Whenever one of us doesn't have you doing something else like washing dishes or changing a tire or anything at all, fetching and carrying, you go to the next thing on the list and check that out. Now come along with me."

He led Jeebee all through, around, and underneath the wagon. Jeebee learned that the vehicle was heavily armored inside, everywhere—though Jeebee was not taken everywhere. The two areas into which Nick did not take him were the bedrooms of Paul Sanderson and Merry. Otherwise, Jeebee was introduced to weapons, innumerable storage places, the equipment of the wagon itself, and everything about it.

There was one odd little room with all its inner surfaces covered with metal. It held an anvil on a sturdy support and a large black-metal dish on a tripod of three spread legs. The dish held what looked like the remnants of black chunks surrounded by gray ashes.

"This is where I blacksmith." He gestured at a couple of

large vents, one in one wall near the floor and another in the ceiling. "Battery drives fans behind those. I'll show you that sometime when I'm working. Gets hot in here, then."

Jeebee could believe it. There was barely room for both of them in the small room as it was. But he was intrigued by the idea of blacksmithing. It had been one of his dreams as a child, to hammer together pieces of white-hot metal and make things with them.

They left and Jeebee was turned loose to study his list. It included a number of car batteries. Two of these were up and working at any given time, two were live and ready to be put to use, and eight others were brand new, had no acid in them, and were waiting to act as replacements for the present working batteries.

These on-duty batteries were charged by a generator hooked to the wheels, as Merry had said, and produced light when the bulbs were turned on, in each of the rooms of the wagon.

Later on they stopped for lunch and Nick took him around the outside of the wagon. On the far side of it, which was why Jeebee had not seen it before, there was a long pipe built into the body of the wagon, so from outside it showed merely as a slight bulge at the base of the box body, its outside painted black so that it resembled a decoration strip about eight inches wide. The pipe held water, which was purified after it was put in by being run through what was essentially a distilling apparatus. It was warmed by the heat of the sun absorbed by the black paint, to the point where it was hot enough that it came to the boil almost immediately, if put in a pot over the stove that was built into the wagon. That stove could cook things either with electricity or with ordinary fuel like wood.

"The only things you don't have to worry about," Nick said as they finished the tour of inspection, "are the wagons and the driving. The driving's Paul's responsibility—and he'll be teaching you how to do that, because you'll take your turn at that eventually, although he likes doing most of the driving himself. Then there's the horses, and the horses are all Merry's responsibility. How well can you shoot?"

Jeebee had gotten a little tired of being deprecating about what he could do.

"I'm not the world's best marksman—" he began.

"That's all I need to hear," Nick cut him off. "Anyone who tells me he's not the world's best marksman can't hit a barrel at five feet. Well, Merry will teach you shooting as well as how to ride. She's a natural shot; even better than I am—and that's saying a lot."

"Oh?" said Jeebee.

"That's right. You'll see," said Nick. "Now, that's enough of that. It's time for the wagon to quit pretty soon for the day. We always stop well short of sunset, so anybody around where we are will have a chance to see us in place for a while and spread the word. Brings customers. I'll be cooking tonight. You can come help me."

CHAPTER 9

The dinner Nick put together was essentially a stew made of beef and vegetables. To Jeebee's surprise, the other man opened an apparently heavily insulated and tightly fitting locker in the room containing trade goods, in which there was a good deal of bacon and smoked meat, as well as what looked to Jeebee like a quarter from an obviously recently butchered, cow-sized animal.

He puzzled silently to himself as he watched and helped Nick in the preparation of the meal, as to how they could have fresh meat like this when they showed no signs of taking time out to hunt for it. Then it woke in him that of course the meat had come from the same place the vegetables had. Paul would have customers with such things to trade along their route. At a guess, the smoked meats and the bacon were for a time when such fresh meat was not available.

The wagon had a small metal stove, ingeniously designed to be easily detached from its flue and carried outside by insulated handles.

Nick carried it outside this evening after the wagon stopped and did the cooking. It had a firebox underneath its solid metal top that was fed with chunks of already burning wood from the fire he had lit immediately beside the wagon when they had finished moving for the day.

With the stew they had bread, produced from another locker, and which also must have been traded for. Both foods were served up on a sort of compartmental tray like those Jeebee had occasionally seen in school lunchrooms. Folding lawn chairs were brought out from the wagon and they all ate with their trays on their knees, sitting around the fire. After they were done, everybody gave their trays and utensils to Jeebee, and Nick took him around to show him how to get hot water from the solar-heated tank on the far side of the wagon. The water flowed from a spigot at one end of the tank, into a washbasin that opened out like a swinging compartment table from the side of the wagon, forward of the tank.

"Wash your hands before you wash the dishes," said Merry.

Jeebee felt a moment's irritation at the tone of her voice. However, he was surprised to notice, it was not as much irritation as he might once have felt; and it went away in a moment. There was something about these new times that allowed for peremptory orders, and for a lack of resentment on the part of those who had to take them.

He was at the bottom of the chain of command, here at this wagon. It seemed natural, therefore, that everybody should give him orders. Besides, he realized, looking at his hands, they were indeed dirty. He used the basin's soap and some water from the tank to wash at the spigot. The water was, remarkably, not merely warm, but hot. He wet his hands, then turned the water off while he soaped up. It was a shipboard trick to conserve water, which he had read about. When he had scrubbed his soapy hands together thoroughly, he turned the spigot on again, briefly, and rinsed them clean.

He was slightly ashamed to realize he had forgotten to notice how dirty they were. Now, with clean hands, he filled the pan with water and washed the dishes.

Nick appeared in time to show him where to put them away, then led him back to the fire, where they found Paul and Merry simply sitting, talking and enjoying the colors and heat of the fire as the sunset faded and the day cooled. Nick took one of the two empty chairs. Jeebee hesitated, not taking the other one.

He turned to Paul, and waited until he and Merry paused in their conversation. Paul looked at him questioningly.

"Wolf won't come down to the wagon," Jeebee said, "but he's used to getting together with me most nights just at twilight and at dawn. If you don't mind, I'm going up into the woods where he can come up to me and feel safe."

Paul nodded. He got to his feet and went into the wagon, coming out a few minutes later with something that looked like a very large fishing reel loaded with line. Its base was welded to a block of metal, so that it could be set upright. He carried this back to his chair, sat back down with it beside him and pulled the end of the line out, handing it to Jeebee.

"Just hang on to that when you go up into the woods," Paul said. "Have you got a watch?"

Jeebee nodded and pulled back the cuff of his leather jacket to show the digital watch he had strapped to his right wrist.

"Right here," he said to Paul. Consciously, he lied to them. The fact was that the watch was an experimental model with a hundred-year battery, the first and only one of its kind. It had no more been available on the market at the time when the world had fallen apart than the electric bike. But, since the others were not going out of their way to give him any unnecessary information about themselves and their possessions, Jeebee felt no need to give them information it was not immediately necessary for them to know.

"As I say, hang on to the line then," said Paul, "and give a yank on it every five minutes or so. If you don't feel a yank back, wait a bit then yank again. When you feel a single yank back, you're good to stay up there for another five minutes. If you get three quick yanks, then stop whatever you're doing and come back. If you don't feel anything, use your own judgment about what you want to do. On that basis, go ahead."

"Fine," said Jeebee. He took the end of the fishing line in his grasp, wrapped it several times around his left hand and then started across the fairly level land toward some trees that here were only about fifty yards away.

The line was light, and the reel ran freely. He was hardly

conscious of the pull of it against his hand as he walked into the trees. He went into the trees about fifteen yards, found a little open space that was actually no more than a wide spot between the tree trunks, and sat down.

The light was fading slowly but inexorably. He remembered that when he stopped at night, he normally built a fire. Wolf might be expecting that. He tied the string to a nearby tree trunk and scraped together some twigs and fallen branches so that he would have dry wood. He used the fireplace starter that he carried, folded up like a jackknife in his pants pocket. It gave off a spark that caught on the dry leaves and other tinder he had placed under a little pyramid of twigs.

A tiny flame flickered up. Delicately and carefully, he fed it to greater life with slightly heavier pieces of dry branches, and in a matter of minutes he had a small but cheerful fire going.

He waited by it but Wolf did not show up. He waited, in fact, until it was full dark, tugging on the line every time the silent alarm of his watch sent a vibration into the skin of his wrist at the five-minute intervals for which he had set it. At last he faced the fact that Wolf would not come, tonight at least. He put out the fire, feeling a little empty inside, and made his way back out of the woods, the string taking up its slack as the reel evidently rewound.

Once again in the open he saw the wagon clearly, like a lantern lit from inside. The thick red paint of the sign was now black against the yellow-lit outer body canvas, in a night that had already seen the sun down and the moon not yet up. The sky, moonless, was thickly sprinkled with stars above him. But these did not give enough light to do more than announce their own presence.

The lantern-lit letters spelled out PAUL SANDERSON AND COMPANY, PEDDLER, almost as plainly as they had in sunshine. It was as good an advertisement and beacon at night, lit up this way, as it had been in the daytime. He went toward it.

As he got close, he saw the other three still by their fire. An L-shaped, black, metal rod had its long end vertically driven into the earth beside the fire and its short, horizontal end bent into a hook from which a coffeepot hung over the flames. The three had cups in their hands.

"Didn't find him?" Paul said as Jeebee got close. "Help yourself to the coffee cup on your chair seat, there."

"He didn't come. That's right," Jeebee said flatly, filling his cup at the pot. He tasted the dark liquid. It was real coffee.

"Thought so." Paul nodded. "The dogs would've sounded off if he had."

Jeebee looked around for the dogs but saw only the yellow female, Greta. She lay with her head on the boots of Merry, who sat, coffee cup in hand, on the far side of the fire.

"Where are the rest?" Jeebee asked.

"They're posted," Nick answered. "Out beyond the horses and around us."

"Why do you think we have them?" said Paul. "If anyone comes close, they'll sound the alarm. So will the horses for that matter, but they're not as quick to pick up someone moving in on us as the dogs are."

"All except Greta," Jeebee said. "Is she posted?"

"Greta," said Paul, looking at his daughter. "Greta's Merry's special pet. She found us and took to Merry right from the start."

Jeebee sat down on his chair, holding his cup, and looked almost directly through the flames at Merry. She looked back at him. For such a cheerful face it was not an unfriendly stare, but there was nothing warming about it either. She had hardly said a kind, or even a semikind word, to him since they had met, he thought. Then he relented, within. Times were different now. It was natural to suspect a stranger and he was still that to those here—as they were to him.

His mind wandered as he sipped the hot black coffee. He wondered how Wolf was doing. The sudden awareness of a shape beside him brought him abruptly out of his thoughts. He turned his head to find his nose almost inches from the muzzle of Greta. She was standing beside him, leaning toward him, wagging her tail and with her ears laid back and a smile on her face. When he looked at her, she fawned upon him and sniffed eagerly over his pants legs and on up to examine his jacket. Eventually, she completed her survey and came back to manage a brief but successful lick at his face before he could dodge her tongue. Wiping his face, he fended off another tongue swipe. He petted her and she crouched down beside him. In fact, she curled up beside him, almost, but not quite, with her head on his boots as she had on Merry's.

The thought of Merry made Jeebee look across through the flames at her once more. There was an expression on her face now. And he thought it was an even less friendly expression than before. For the first time it struck Jeebee that she might resent her dog paying this much attention so soon to Jeebee. She would have good cause to, with a dog that was particularly her own taking up like this with a stranger. Almost ashamed to admit it himself, Jeebee identified his guess of a possible resentment in her with a sneaky feeling of triumph inside himself. He might not be able to ride a horse like her, or do half a dozen other things, he thought, but dogs liked him—or at least this dog seemed to.

It was only then that it occurred to him that what might have attracted Greta was not him, but the smell of Wolf on his clothes.

They continued to sit around the fire for some little time, drinking coffee. Very little was said. It seemed to Jeebee that the other three did not talk much simply because they knew each other so well that there was very little to say. In his own case he had nothing to say to them and it could be they said nothing to him because they knew so little about him.

Eventually Paul threw the dregs of his cup into the fire, stood up, and stretched.

"We'll need to get going with daylight," he said. "If we want to reach the Borgstrom place by late midmorning, tomorrow."

Merry had risen at almost the same moment. She whistled sharply and Greta jerked her head up from Jeebee's legs, got to her feet, and trotted over to Merry.

"Guard," Merry said to the dog, and turned toward the wagon. Greta walked off a few steps with her back to the rest of them and dropped down on the grass, her paws crossed in front of her, her gaze outward into the darkness. Paul, followed by Merry, disappeared into the wagon.

"Well," said Nick after they had been gone a few moments. "Guess we'd better turn in, too. You're going to take that hammock on the south side, Jeebee."

Jeebee felt a strange reluctance to go inside. He had been sleeping so many nights under the stars that the thought of trying to rest in the wagon struck him almost like entering a prison cell.

"I can bed down out here," he said.

"No," Nick answered, calmly, "you sleep inside where I can keep an eye on you until we get to know you better. You'll like that hammock, once you get used to it."

He dumped his own cup's small amount of remaining liquid on the fire.

Looking past Jeebee, he said, almost conversationally, "You got any idea how strong you stink?"

Jeebee started.

He had not thought. Of course, that would be one reason Merry would take the attitude toward him she had. How long had it been since he had taken off the clothes he was wearing? How long since he had been ordinarily clean? He could not remember. It was a matter of months, anyway. At least since he had run away from Stoketon. These people here probably could smell him ten yards off.

"I'd forgotten. . . ." he said.

Nick's eyes came back to meet Jeebee's.

"We've got a large metal tub inside," Nick said. "Big enough to get into. You can fill it and the water in the pipe's just about right for a bath now. Also, I can let you have some soap, scissors, and razor, if you want them. Might be I could even find you some fresh clothes."

Gratitude warmed Jeebee.

"Thank you," he said. "I could use all of that. You don't know what it means—"

"Yes, I do," said Nick. "I've been there myself. Besides I've got to share the Quiet Room with you as well as the guns, tonight."

Nick went into the wagon and came out again with the washtub. As he had predicted, it was a big one—almost three feet across on the bottom and a foot and a half high on the sides, made of galvanized iron. With Jeebee's help he half filled it with hot water from the tank on the wagon's side and brought it around to set near the fire. Then he went back inside to come out again with a heavy bar of yellow soap that looked homemade. The clothes were jeans and a shirt, the scissors were large, and the razor was a straight-edged one. Nick had also brought a towel. He threw them all down beside Jeebee.

"You're going to have to wash out your own shirt, socks, and underwear," he said. "Use the bathwater after you've cleaned yourself. Wring the clothes out afterward and bring them in the wagon. You'll find some hooks by your hammock. Hang them on those to dry. Sleep in the fresh shirt. It and the jeans are new. Paul'll be charging you for those, later on."

"Thanks," said Jeebee. "I mean that. It'll be good to be in clean clothes—new clothes at that."

Reflexively, he felt his beard and hair.

"I'll shave the beard," he said, "but the hair, I think I'll just cut—some."

Nick turned to the wagon.

"Good night," he said. "I'll turn down the lantern in the Quiet Room. You turn it all the way off after you've slung the hammock. By the way, the safe way to get into a hammock is sit down first in the middle of it. I mean, not just in the middle between the two ends, but in the middle of it, crosswise too. Then lay down and swing your legs up, holding on to the hammock edges. If you do it right, it won't turn over and dump you on the ground. The mosquito netting's pinned up; and you might as well leave it that way. No mosquitoes this early in the year."

He went into the wagon and this time did not come out.

Jeebee cut his beard down as close as he could with the scissors; then wet the stubble down thoroughly with bathwater and soap, and gingerly shaved with the straightedge—blind. He had not thought to ask Nick for some kind of mirror.

Done at last, with only five small nicks, he cleaned the razor, peeled off his old clothes, and settled himself slowly into the still-hot water. He sighed, leaning back against the curved metal edge of the big tub. The heat soaked slowly through him.

He thought of Wolf and of the people in the wagon. It was foolish of him, he knew, but he could not help feeling a bit bothered by Merry's attitude toward him. He told himself that it was simply a weakness in him that wanted everyone to like him. It was also, of course, the fact she was a woman, and he had not seen a woman—barring the monstrous lady in the long black dress at the railroad whistle stop where he had acquired Wolf—for a long time. There had been nothing sexually attractive about the store woman. But Merry was different.

It was not that he lusted strongly after her. It was simply that she was female. He was male, and conscious of her accordingly—he told himself. It seemed to him, now, watching the stars, that she could have at least smiled once at him. It would not have been too much for her to do, and it would have meant a great deal to him.

He shoved the thought from his mind. He was dangerously close to self-pity again. He made himself think once more of Wolf.

Wolf was a free person. Perhaps he was already gone for good. Even if he was not, something that had been between him and Jeebee would be destroyed if Jeebee should ever try to trap him or bring him to someplace like this wagon by force.

But, otherwise, how was he ever going to get Wolf to join them? Well, at least he could keep going from the wagon out into whatever woods were close at twilight, howling and waiting. Perhaps he should have howled from the woods, this evening. But he had been afraid, he faced it now, of getting no answer.

Possibly, somehow, eventually, Wolf might show up and be enticed to come closer to the wagon.

Possibly . . .

The water was cooling. He washed himself and stepped out. The night breeze was almost instantly at him, robbing him of the water's warmth, encasing him into a chill that felt as if he was being buried in ice. He toweled himself dry and quickly put on

his new pants and shirt. Then he washed the socks and underwear he had been wearing in the bathwater—carefully. He also
washed the extra, long-dirty shorts and T-shirt he had carried in
his pockets against the day he could clean them. Somehow, the
day had never come. Both sets of underwear threatened to come
apart in his hands.

After washing his outer clothes, he emptied and rinsed out
the washtub.

Picking up the tub with his wet clothing inside it, he went,
the night air cool on his naked face. He climbed up and into the
wagon, going back past the goods into the weapons room. Nick
was in the right-hand hammock and evidently already asleep. He
slept silently, without snoring. Jeebee found some empty floor
space to put the tub until morning, draping his wet things on
hooks and over the tub to dry. He then slung his hammock and
found it was not as difficult as Nick had given him to think. It
was merely a matter of finding a balance point. Once in, he
stretched out, carefully. It was surprisingly comfortable. There
had been a blanket rolled with the hammock, and he pulled this
over himself now.

He felt the walls and roof and floor close about him, and
thought once more of Wolf.

"I'll never sleep," he told himself.

But even as he thought this he was falling into a dreamless
slumber.

CHAPTER 10

Three nights later at twilight in a little patch of woods near where the wagon had stopped, Wolf came to greet him.

Wolf put his paws on his shoulders, licked his face with an undodgeable tongue, and frisked around Jeebee before stopping to sniff Jeebee carefully all over. He concluded by going back into greeting behavior, ending by rolling on his back and inviting a stomach scratching. Jeebee obliged.

Jeebee had been all but sure within himself that Wolf had left him for good. The return of his partner filled him with warmth and gratitude. He wrestled exuberantly with Wolf and scratched the furry belly with satisfaction. Finally, things calmed down for both of them. The sun had set but there was still light in the sky. Jeebee got up and moved back out of the woods and toward the wagon, some fifty feet away, in the open grassland of the old superhighway.

Wolf followed him to the edge of the trees, but stopped there. Jeebee tried to play with him to entice him further. But Wolf refused to be drawn. He stood watching Jeebee, but not advancing any further into the open, and gradually the dark came upon them.

At last, it was clear that nothing was going to bring Wolf out beyond the trees.

"Good night, Wolf," Jeebee said softly at last. "Tomorrow night at this same time, maybe?"

Wolf looked back at him agreeably but otherwise, as usual, paid little attention to the sound of Jeebee's voice. He was very unlike a dog in this. Body attitudes had always seemed to be the basis of his communication rather than sounds. But Jeebee was accustomed to this fact by now. He turned and went down toward the wagon, once more lit from within. Several times he stopped and looked back, but until the darkness hid Wolf completely, he could still be seen just barely inside the woods.

Jeebee went around the wagon to find the others sitting by the fire that was kindled every night. They had clearly already finished eating. Tonight, Paul and Merry were talking over the possibility of getting rid of some of their horses and buying other, younger stock to replace them. Merry wanted to hold off until they had recruited at least one more person. Jeebee had learned in these last few days that the wagon usually carried not merely four, but five people. In other words, besides himself, one more pair of feet and hands were needed.

He turned to Nick, but Nick seemed in no mood for talk. His mind was on something else. He did not reject Jeebee's attempt to make conversation, but his answers were brief and he kept his eyes on the fire.

Left to himself, Jeebee went about the business of heating what remained in the cooking pot and filling his tray.

He sat down in his folding chair to eat, his mind still busily searching for some way to bring Wolf down to join the wagon group. But that was a search he had been at ever since he himself had joined it. Paul had not yet trusted him to have his weapons back again. But as far as Jeebee could tell, he was getting along well with all of them, except that Merry still held herself at a distance, refusing to commit to any kind of sociability.

Jeebee's mind went off on a different tangent. He could not tell himself that he had done well, except in a few instances, but certainly he could not have done badly, for someone the three others all knew had never had any experience with this kind of work before.

One of the few times he had earned at least some approval had been from Nick. This had been in the process of the lessons that Merry—and Nick as well—had given him about the various weapons of the wagon, ranging from short-barreled revolvers small enough to fit into the top of one of Jeebee's boots to the .30-caliber machine gun and the rocket launchers with their ammunition.

"You're sure you never kept guns around and worked with them before?" Nick asked, after Jeebee, following several trial efforts, had successfully stripped down one of the air-cooled machine guns for cleaning and put it back together again.

"That's right. I never did," Jeebee answered. "But my father liked working with his hands. I picked up something of that when I was a kid. Also, I like knowing why things work. When I was young, I used to take apart clocks, and things like that, to see if I could get them back together again and working."

"Well, you certainly got a knack for it," said Nick.

"I wish I had the same kind of knack for riding the horses and driving the team," Jeebee said wistfully.

"That'll come," said Nick. "You just have to remember that with a horse you stay in charge all the time."

"Merry doesn't seem to have to work at it," Jeebee said.

"Well, she likes horses," said Nick, "like you liked knowing how things work. Besides, she's done so much of it the horses are ready to do what she wants the minute she slaps a saddle on their back. Most of them, that is. There's always a few hardheads. Did you know that back when there were rodeos, there were some horses nobody could ride?"

"No," answered Jeebee.

"Well, there were," said Nick. "I've seen some myself. Some of them had prices on them for anybody who could ride them. But those horses not only wanted to get people off, they knew how to do it. If a horse really wants to get you off, he'll get you off. That is—if he knows how, like I said."

"I can see the sense of having to keep the team under control," Jeebee said.

In spite of being warned both by Nick and by Paul, Jeebee's

first attempt to hold the reins of the six horses pulling the wagon had been a shock to him. To begin with, he had thought of them as automatically pulling together. They could and did do that, but the driver had to make sure that they did it.

Each horse had ideas of its own, left to itself. Almost as shocking had been the fact that the six of them were easily capable of falling completely out of control if one of them stumbled for a moment for any reason. Paul taught him to hold the reins separately between the first, second, and third fingers of each hand, while maintaining a strong grip on them with the rest of the hand. It seemed to Jeebee that there was no way he could keep a strong grip, with the thick leather straps between his fingers, that way, but Paul insisted that in time the necessary strength would come to him.

"For now," he said, "if your hands get tired enough to loosen, pass the reins back to me. Never—even if you're alone up here—wrap them around anything to take the strain off. You'll end up with the team running away, or half of them breaking a leg apiece."

He looked hard at Jeebee.

"Right," said Jeebee.

They changed horses several times a day. Jeebee had come to learn that with its metal armor inside, its load of goods, and its oversize build, the wagon was a heavy pull, even for six fresh horses. Since Paul did not want strangers to know what kind of defenses the wagon had, he changed horses frequently so that the ones pulling were always rested.

Changing teams normally took the efforts of both the driver and at least one other person. At first, Jeebee had been more afraid of being kicked than he wanted to admit.

He gradually lost that fear as he came to understand that a horse could not kick you unless he first shifted his weight onto the nonkicking leg, opposite. If you watched how the horse stood, you could tell whether he was getting ready to try to kick or not.

Still, it took all his courage to dodge under the belly of one of the big, powerful wagon horses when hitching them, while this was something the other three people apparently did without thinking.

He also came gradually to understand that just as there could be a knack in assembling and disassembling weapons, so there could also be a knack in horse handling and driving. Once he understood this, he began to watch Paul closely as the peddler handled his team. Paul clearly preferred to do most of the driving himself. Particularly, for reasons of policy, he always made sure he was the one driving when the wagon came in sight of any inhabited place where they might do business.

Similarly Jeebee watched and studied Merry for the small things she might be doing that could pass unnoticed but that might be important in the business of handling the spare horses. But it was difficult to learn much from her, except when she deliberately set out to teach him something. Paul was much more open about explaining things than she was. Jeebee came to the conclusion, finally, that a lot of what she knew she had picked up unconsciously, by observation or by doing, so that she hardly realized she knew it herself.

The first hurdle had been his learning to ride. He finally faced the fact that he would never be able to sit easily in the saddle the way she did, moving with the horse as if the two had been welded together. Nonetheless, he did learn how to saddle a horse, to mount it, how to stay on it, and how to make it go where he wanted it to go. He also learned how to put on and take off saddle and bridle.

What had come more slowly were the tricks of rounding up the loose horses that followed the wagon. With Merry riding herd on them, they seemed to follow automatically and just as automatically stay bunched together. If the wagon stopped, they stopped; and they were apparently content just to crop the grass where they stood without straying too far. The dogs, Jeebee found, were quick to try to turn back any of them that made a serious attempt to stray.

But even with the help of the dogs, he himself had no real control over the loose horses. The minute he took his eyes off one, it seemed to drift away from the rest. Merry, on the other hand, appeared able to anticipate when a horse was going to try to move off on its own and to be in front of it when it did, blocking the way with her own riding animal.

"So. Did you get a look at that wolf of yours tonight?"

The words woke Jeebee suddenly out of his thoughts. He was once more back at the fire with his dinner tray on his knees and it was Paul speaking to him. He felt abruptly and reasonlessly guilty, as if he had been a student in a class who had not been paying attention and had been suddenly called upon by the instructor.

"Yes," said Jeebee.

"I thought that's what you'd been doing all these evenings," Paul went on, "but around here we don't ask. Have you been seeing him every night?"

"No," said Jeebee. "Tonight he came for the first time."

There was a moment of silence during which the fire crackled.

"I tried to get him to follow me down here. I wanted to bring him to the wagon and see if he'll travel with us at least a little bit of the time," said Jeebee. He was abruptly surprised at himself at speaking out so much to these people who were still in many ways holding themselves back from him. "He'd be gone most of the time anyway. But I'd like him to come up close. Have you got anything against that?"

He was speaking directly to Paul Sanderson. Paul frowned. "Hmm," he said.

He scratched with his left forefinger at the angle of his jaw close to his neck. The rasping of the fingernail on his beard was loud in the silence. Jeebee waited, listening for an answer, but his eyes were on Merry. However, Merry did not speak up.

"Most people got the wrong idea about wolves," Nick said, unexpectedly. "They think they're vicious because they kill game and livestock. It's not so. Truth is, they're shy. Gun-shy, trap-shy, people-shy. Good hunters, but shy. That wolf won't bother anything down here if he comes in."

Jeebee did not think it prudent to mention how thoroughly destructive Wolf's innocent but determined curiosity could be.

"Just as long as he doesn't get in the way of the team," Paul said thoughtfully, almost to himself.

"He'll stay well out of the way of that team, particularly when it's moving," said Nick. "Would you get in the way of a team that size coming right at you?"

"The other dogs will gang up on him if he comes," said Merry, unexpectedly. "Greta might help the wolf, if she likes him well enough."

Paul, unexpectedly, gave a little nod of his head.

"All right," he said, "if you can get him to come down to us—it's all right with me. He and the dogs will have to work things out amongst themselves. All right then, with all of us? Merry? Nick?"

"No reason why not if it doesn't make trouble," said Merry.

"I just told you how I felt," said Nick.

Jeebee felt a sudden increase of warmth in all their attitudes toward him. As with Paul, when he unexpectedly invited Jeebee to join them, Jeebee could not figure out what he might have done or said just now to change their feelings toward him for the better.

The others continued to give him no clue. A little after that, the campfire part of the evening broke up. As Jeebee had come to find was usual practice, Nick lingered a little around the fire after Merry and her father had gone into the wagon.

Jeebee cleaned up his plate and was about to gather up the others and take them to wash when Nick stood up suddenly.

"Let's take a little walk," he said abruptly.

Wondering, Jeebee joined him as the older and smaller man led the way out of the circle of firelight into the surrounding darkness. As usual, once they got away from the lighted area and their eyes adjusted, it was not too hard to see. The moon had come up since Jeebee had come back to the wagon and it was a three-quarters moon that shed a fair amount of light.

Nick stopped about thirty paces away from the wagon and spoke in a low, but conversational tone. "Look," he said, "maybe you've reached the point where you ought to begin to know some things."

He paused.

"I'm ready to learn whatever there is to be learned," Jeebee said, to start him up again.

"This is not exactly learning." Nick paused again. "There's something you ought to understand about Paul and Merry. Now, they don't look it, but this wagon and everything about it, the route and everything, is something Paul did only for Merry."

"I don't think I follow you," Jeebee said after a moment.

Nick sighed. It was almost a sigh of exasperation.

"I'm trying to tell you," he said. "Now, Merry's mother died about five years ago. Paul had been a salesman, but liked running a fix-it shop better than being a real-estate salesman—and he was a damn good real-estate salesman. He made a lot of money with it. But he liked fixing things, so he started the shop so that he and Merry could be together as much as possible. The shop was connected to their house, and he was home all the time."

"My mother died when I was sixteen," Jeebee said suddenly. He not only surprised himself by saying it; he realized he hadn't even thought of the fact for years.

"All right," said Nick, almost as if he hadn't spoken, "Paul did well with the fix-it shop, too—nowhere near as much money as he could have made selling real estate, but he'd made a lot of money at that already, that he still had. So they were well off enough. But he saw this coming, everything going bust the way it has. And he worried about keeping Merry safe through what he saw was coming. So he started this route five years ago. They spend their winters in the east and south. I won't tell you where. You don't need to know that, anyway. But they spend their winters, as I say, east and south; and with the first sign of spring down there, they start moving north and west. They follow this route Paul made with this wagon, he built for himself and had built for him. He began the route even back when cars were whizzing along these freeways, only then the wagon traveled on back roads, off to one side."

Nick paused again. This time Jeebee just waited.

"Paul's a good peddler. Bound to be, being the salesman he is. People like him, when he sets out to be liked," Nick said, "and gradually he's built up a bunch of regular customers. There's always danger, of course, but here with the wagon we're safer than most. People have got to know Paul and he follows the same route, so the locals aren't liable to be shooting at him. Otherwise—well, you've seen what we call the Quiet Room. We're armed well enough to stand off a pretty good-sized bunch. But that isn't what I wanted to talk to you about. What I wanted to tell you is, don't be taken in by the way they talk to each other. This wagon, this route, everything about this is something Paul built for Merry. He lives for Merry. And Merry, she wouldn't leave her father for anything, because she knows that there'd be nothing for him if she went."

Nick paused again.

"So, you should know that," he went on after a bit. "You're a young fellow, and Merry's young, too. But don't start getting any ideas, unless you want to stay with the wagon and her and her father for the rest of your life."

"I haven't—" Jeebee was beginning when Nick cut him short.

"You don't have to say anything," Nick said. "I just thought I'd tell you, that's all, so you'd understand."

He stopped talking. Jeebee stood, at a loss as to what to say.

"Well, I'm going to bed," said Nick.

He went off toward the fire. After a moment Jeebee followed him but Nick had already gone into the wagon by the time Jeebee reached the fire. Somberly, Jeebee washed the food trays, put out the fire with the wash water, and carried the trays into the wagon with him to put them in their usual place up in the storeroom, next to where he now knew the beef was kept in its locker. He went into the Quiet Room and saw Nick already in his hammock, turned with his face toward the side of the wagon and only his back showing. The lantern was already turned down, but not completely off. Jeebee slung his own hammock, put the blanket handy in it, got in, then reached up and turned down the little lever that extinguished the lamp completely.

He lay staring at the darkness overhead. He had not really thought much about Merry, he told himself defensively. Nick's warning was almost an insult. At the same time, he found that he could not really take offense at it. The truth of the matter was, Merry was a woman. She was young, and he could not help but respond to her, even if that response was annoyance at the way she treated him.

Still thinking about her, he fell asleep. Sometime in the night he dreamed of Wolf coming unexpectedly into the wagon to look for him.

The next day, rather unexpectedly, Nick began initiating Jeebee into the craft of blacksmithing. Jeebee found it fascinating, in spite of the almost intolerable temperatures of the tiny metal-walled room, after the forge was going. He listened eagerly as Nick described how a blacksmithing outfit could be set up anywhere, given a few starting tools. Necessary were an anvil, a pair of tongs, and what Nick called a hardy. This was something that looked like a small but stout chisel, made all of metal with a short end that fitted into a hole at one end of the anvil so that the hardy was fixed in place and faced upward with its cutting edge. That was, Nick explained, exactly what the hardy was to be used for. Its use was to cut the hot metal, once it had been heated to the proper malleability. The heated iron or steel was held in the tongs, laid against the up-facing edge of the hardy, and the strip hammered until the hardy cut through it.

The rest of the necessary things used in blacksmithing, Nick explained, could either be found easily lying about, or made, once the smithy was in operation. A forge with a firepit could be built out of any noncombustible materials. Rocks, mortared together with anything that would serve the purpose and was noncombustible. An air intake would have to be built into it and a bellows constructed to pump air up that intake. Also charcoal would have to be made, by burning hardwood in the absence of oxygen. The old-fashioned way of doing this was simply to set the wood afire and cover it with earth so that it burned slowly.

Besides the anvil, hardy, and tongs, a hammer would be necessary. But Nick said that this could probably be found in any abandoned farmstead—ideally it would be a short-handled six-pound hammer of the kind known as a maul.

He let Jeebee try his hand at doing some simple black-smithing tasks with the equipment in the small room, and Jeebee promised himself that somewhere along the line, he would have a smithy of his own. It was, he thought, in addition to everything else, something that would make him more useful to his brother's ranch—if he knew something about blacksmithing; and of course, the more he knew the better.

That evening, when Jeebee went looking in a nearby patch of woods, Wolf was waiting for him again. From then on they met almost steadily at twilight after the wagon had stopped for the day. But nothing Jeebee could do would persuade the other to follow him when he turned and went back down to the wagon.

The dogs around the wagon had not given tongue on any of Wolf's appearances. It was not until the third night that Jeebee realized that he had instinctively headed downwind to find his patch of trees. And it had been downwind that Wolf had been waiting for him. So much, already, of elementary woodcraft had rubbed off on Jeebee.

Jeebee wondered if perhaps it was the presence of the dogs that was keeping Wolf away from the wagon. He got to the point of actually considering that perhaps Wolf might feel safer if he put him on a leash and tried to bring him down to the wagon that way. Maybe being on a leash would give Wolf a feeling of security, as well as also keeping the other dogs away? Even as he thought this, he knew it was ridiculous. Neither the dogs nor Wolf were likely to cooperate under such conditions.

There was only, like a small nagging pain, the worry in Jeebee of how Merry really felt about Wolf showing up. The dogs and Wolf, as Paul had said, would have to sort things out with each other. Merry had agreed to Wolf's joining them—if he would—but, it seemed to Jeebee, with no great enthusiasm.

Merry was the one the dogs obviously liked best, and obeyed best, of all the humans around the wagon; though by now they had all gone so far as to approach Jeebee and make more or less polite friends with him. Only in the case of Greta, the yellow female, was this anything close to a warm friendship. When Greta was not on guard duty, she always sought out Merry first, unless Merry was on horseback. But if that was the case, and Jeebee was both outside the wagon and afoot, she would sometimes come to Jeebee, wagging her tail, sniffing him, and licking at his hands or face.

Greta also very clearly was dominant over all the other dogs as well as being larger than the rest of them. It was only later that something Nick had said one day made Jeebee realize that the other dogs were the results of litters she had had from contact with other, unknown dogs, at some of the places they had stopped.

Certainly the rest obeyed her, although usually not without protest if they were involved with something they wanted to keep or do. Watching the attitude of the other dogs to her, a wild thought came to Jeebee, a few days later. Perhaps he could take Greta with him on one of his twilight trips to the woods, and when the two of them came back, maybe Wolf would be reassured enough to follow them.

He actually tried this the next night, picking a moment when neither Nick, Merry, nor Paul was close or was within hearing.

"Come on, girl," he said to the yellow dog, "come on with me. We'll go for a walk."

The female came to him and went with him for a little distance. But at about fifty feet from the wagon, she stopped and would not go any farther. When he called her softly, she wagged her tail, flattened her ears and whimpered a little, but stayed put. Jeebee guessed that perhaps she had been trained not to go beyond a certain distance from the wagon, ordinarily. Certainly none of the other dogs usually did.

He turned and left her, continuing on into the trees and finding Wolf.

This time, including Wolf's usual greeting, the other, after sniffing around Jeebee's pant legs suddenly neck-rolled against one of them. Jeebee recognized suddenly that it was the same leg that Greta had pressed against when he had talked to her, just a few minutes earlier. It puzzled him, however, that Wolf would be interested in the scent of Greta now, since the female was no longer in heat.

He tucked the question away into the back of his mind and did not think anymore about it consciously until nearly evening, when Greta came up to him and sniffed with unusual interest at the pant leg against which Wolf had neck-rolled. A little later, when he started to leave the wagon, she trotted along with him almost as if she was now determined to go along with him.

But, again, she went only a little farther than she had before. At that point she hesitated, wagged her tail, put her ears back and whined loudly, but ceased to follow. Jeebee called her, but she would not come. He left her finally and went on, thinking that perhaps he might eventually be able to coax her all the way up, after all. The thought cheered him.

When he reached the woods, Wolf was waiting. He did not neck-roll as he had the day before, but subjected Jeebee to a very prolonged nose search. The demeaning thought struck Jeebee that he seemed to be a sort of human messenger service between the dog and the wolf. Possibly carrying love letters?

The thought made him chuckle, a sound Wolf ignored with complete indifference as he sniffed. The examination over—or the message received—Wolf reverted to his general greeting behavior, which ended up with his rolling over on his back and inviting a belly scratch.

That evening, as darkness settled around them and it came time for Jeebee to head back down to the wagon, he had a secret but strong hope that perhaps this time Wolf would follow him beyond the edge of the woods.

But once more it did not happen. Wolf came as far as he had come before, to the point where he could see into the open area, but that was all. Greta could be seen sitting, touched by the firelight and looking out. Jeebee left him behind and went back down to the wagon.

The next day just before noon, in clear daylight as Jeebee was both helping and learning how to herd the stock from Merry, a howl sounded from some nearby wood.

Jeebee's answering howl from the wagon was loud in the following stillness, and Merry whirled her horse about to confront Jeebee.

"What did you do that for?" she raged. "Look at them, they're all shook up and beginning to scatter."

But it was not Jeebee alone who had answered. So had Greta.

Merry stared increduously at the dog, then put her horse in motion.

"Help me!" she shouted over her shoulder at Jeebee. "We've got to get these horses back together again."

It was not until they two and the dogs had managed to get the stock bunched up once more in its usual pattern that Jeebee noticed that the yellow female was no longer with them.

"Look," he said to Merry, "she's gone. Greta's gone."

"Greta?" Merry reined in her horse and looked around. "I don't believe it!"

But Greta was indeed gone. Jeebee waited a little while for the fact to sink in, before he mildly offered a suggestion.

"I think she's gone up into the woods to meet Wolf," he said.

"She wouldn't do that—" Merry broke off. She stared angrily at Jeebee. "Hell! Watch the stock!"

She wheeled her horse about and galloped up to the front of the wagon. There were a few moments in which Jeebee could hear a conversation between Paul and his daughter, but could not make out exactly what they were saying. The voices ceased and the wagon came suddenly to a stop. Merry came back to the tail of the wagon again.

"You make sure the stock stays together," she said. "I'm going up after her and bring her back."

"I wouldn't do that if I were you," said Jeebee.

She literally glared at him.

"You know, this is all your fault!" she said. "You and that wolf! Why shouldn't I go?"

"Why?" Jeebee echoed. "Because if you start up there, Wolf is going to run away when he sees you coming. And Greta's already shown that she's going to follow him, so you're likely to lose them both. You'd be surprised how hard it is to find a couple of animals like that if they want to get away from you and hide."

He stopped. He felt sorry for her.

"It's all right, you know," he said. "As long as we leave them alone, she's going to meet Wolf just inside the woods there and they'll be together for a little while and then she'll come back to the wagon. Just as Wolf doesn't want to leave me, she doesn't want to leave the rest of you down here. She's simply being pulled two ways at the present moment."

The nearest patch of woods was up a gentle slope and about two hundred yards away. Merry looked past Jeebee at it, stared at it.

"How long will we have to wait?" she asked. Her own voice was suddenly, surprisingly calm.

"I don't know," Jeebee answered. "But I don't think it'll be long. What I'd suggest is that you stop for maybe half an hour—long enough to have lunch, say—and if Greta hasn't shown by that time, start to move off. She'll have been with Wolf long enough to get over her first impulse to go to him, and when she sees you leaving, she'll be afraid of losing you. I'm pretty sure then she'll come out and follow—in fact I'm pretty sure she'll catch up with us right away."

There was a long silence. Merry looked back at him.

"It makes sense," she said, more quietly. "Look, I'm sorry I snapped at you. You made it clear enough when you joined us that you couldn't control that animal. I don't mean to blame you for what he does, but maybe it'd been better all around if we'd shot him on first sight."

"If you had," said Jeebee, "I'd probably have shot at you. I mean that."

For a moment their eyes locked, and somewhat to Jeebee's surprise, Merry's face relaxed, relaxed a little more, and finally smiled.

"He does mean a lot to you, doesn't he?" she said. "I'm sorry. I spoke too fast. I wouldn't really have shot at him, even then. At least I don't think I would. Dad might've—but I doubt even that."

She lifted her reins and pressed with one knee.

"I'll go talk Dad into stopping for a bit," she said—and was gone.

CHAPTER 11

To Jeebee's surprise, Paul did not seem at all put out by the idea of a half hour or even an hour's delay. He was discovering something more about the man who had built and operated this whole peddler's scheme, and that was that he had a very lively curiosity about anything and everything.

There had been hints of this when he had been talking with Jeebee in the process of teaching Jeebee to drive the wagon team. Every now and then Paul would have a mild question about what Jeebee's life had been like before he had headed west to find his brother's ranch. At first these questions passed almost unnoticed by Jeebee as he answered them. Later, he began to realize that Paul was slowly and quite subtly drawing out of him his personal history. The questions invariably came after Paul had told Jeebee something about his own background, so that it was difficult not to reciprocate.

At first Jeebee thought that Paul was simply interested in what kind of man he'd picked up by the roadside. Then he began to discover that Paul was genuinely interested in the work of the study group. Jeebee tried to explain this in words that would be understandable to the other but Paul shook his head.

"Most of it I can't follow," he said finally, "but unless I'm wrong, what it all adds up to is that you saw this coming almost as early as I did and didn't do a thing about it. Particularly you didn't do anything to save yourself until you darn near got smoked out of your own home by neighbors that had set out to kill you."

Jeebee nodded.

"Why?" Paul had said. "Why, when you could see it coming, wait like that?"

Jeebee hesitated. It was not that he did not know the answer. It was just difficult to explain. Finally, he shrugged.

"If you're any good as a scientist," he had said, "you have to learn a certain detachment from what you're studying. If you don't, it's too easy to see what you want to see in the numbers. Anyone who studies social behavior has to learn to treat social processes and dynamics as pure abstractions that've got nothing to do with him personally. What happened in Stoketon was a truck that ran us down while we were still busy calculating, from its speed and weight, just how hard it could hit."

He could hear his own words and they sounded a little stiff and academic in his ears. But they were all true—all what had actually happened.

The day was bright and warm, so that the little air stir resulting from their passage was pleasant. Neither he nor Paul said anything for a moment.

"You and this brother of yours pretty close?" Paul asked.

"Yes," Jeebee said, and then hesitated.

He had never stopped to think about it, but he realized now that he had always thought of Martin as a sort of lesser and more distant father, lost somewhere behind the shadow of Carey, the actual father of both of them.

"That is," Jeebee went on, "when we were younger. There's eighteen years between us. He's the older. I used to visit up at the ranch and he'd visit us—my father, my mother, and me—sometimes. After my father died—well, actually, after my mother's death, when I was sixteen—we fell out of touch a bit; though we still wrote letters every so often. But I haven't seen him since I was about—oh, fourteen or fifteen years old."

"How come your father moved away from the ranch?" Paul asked.

"It really wasn't what he wanted," Jeebee said. "My grandfather did, and Martin did. But Dad really didn't care for it too much. He stuck with it until the Vietnam War came along. He'd already had Martin, but he joined up and went off to the war anyway. He told my grandfather that he was giving up all claim to the ranch so the way would be clear for Martin in case anything happened to him while he was gone."

There was another long pause as the wagon rolled and jolted on its way.

"Afterward," Jeebee said without prompting, finding a sudden relief—almost a pleasure in telling this to someone, finally—"there was the GI Bill. He always liked architecture. So he went to school to become an architect."

"Architecture," Paul said thoughtfully, "a far call from ranching."

"Oh, Dad was always a hands-on man," said Jeebee. "He liked to build with existing materials. If he saw a rocky hillside lot, he'd immediately be taken with the idea of building a house with the rock. A house that would seem to grow right out of the hillside, there. An interesting piece of wood could give him an idea for pegged, instead of nailed houses—even log houses."

"He try to push you toward architecture at all?" Paul asked.

Jeebee shook his head.

"No," he said thoughtfully. "Neither he nor my mother really pushed me anywhere. They loved me, all right. But they were a couple of strange people, in some ways. They didn't show much in the way of affection, to me or even to each other. My mother was an academic. She taught history on the university level. Usually she was stuck in her job someplace, and I moved around the country with Dad. It was that way most of the time I was going through grade school and high school."

He remembered it now, with a particular sharpness. He had been taller and skinnier than most boys his own age, and uncoordinated. Each new schoolroom had become an arena in which he knew in advance he would be tried, tested, and found wanting. Schoolmates his own age, but much smaller and better coordinated, were able to bully him, making him in his own eyes, as well as those of others, a weakling.

He had grown into adulthood coming to think of himself as that, to accept the fact he could not compete with the rest of the world physically. Then his mother had died suddenly of viral pneumonia when he was sixteen. And then, when he was away at college, his father was killed in a construction accident.

He told Paul something about this.

"Pretty much a loner, weren't you?" said Paul.

That was true enough, Jeebee thought. Among the study group at Stoketon he had been a maverick, more than slightly suspected as the recipient of special favor from Bill Bohl, the director, but respected nonetheless.

"I guess you could say so," he said to Paul. "I took sociology as an undergraduate. But there was always something lacking in it for me."

"How do you mean, lacking?"

"Well, I came to understand it later," said Jeebee, slipping unthinkingly into a more academic way of talking. "Sociology was really badly indifferent in some ways to the ecological factors in which social and cultural processes are rooted. Besides that, it was unsophisticated in the development of mathematical models of the kind that were revolutionizing other social sciences."

"So?" said Paul. "What did you do?"

"Well, I'd already decided that I wanted to be an academic," Jeebee said. "By the time I was ready to apply to graduate schools, economic geography seemed the best approach for me to the questions I was after."

"And where was this?" Paul asked.

"This was at the main campus of the University of Michigan at Ann Arbor," said Jeebee. "I was very lucky. I got Dr. Bill Bohl for an adviser."

"Bill Bohl?" echoed Paul. "Don't think I ever heard of him."

"Probably you wouldn't, unless you were an academic yourself, and working in the same area or a related area," Jeebee said, "but it was the best thing that ever happened to me. He was tremendous. He was fifty-two years old at the time I met him, and he was widely known and respected for his contributions to classical economics and innovative applications of general-systems problems in social ecology."

Jeebee laughed.

"You wouldn't think he carried all that clout to look at him," he said. "He was young looking for his years, but bald as an egg, and he had a face like a bulldog with a body like an undergraduate fullback. Meeting him, you probably wouldn't have liked him, first off. He was direct to the point of being almost brutal."

"Well, wasn't he what he seemed to be?" Paul asked.

Jeebee shook his head.

"I got to know him very well," he said. "Behind the way he talked and acted he was really very sensitive to the human realities underlying the abstractions with which we all worked. In fact, I still think he'd deliberately cultivated that tough appearance of his to hide his sensitivity toward the people he had to work with."

"So you liked him," Paul said.

"Yes," said Jeebee, "and he liked me—strangely enough."

"Why, strangely enough?" said Paul. "People like each other or they don't. You can't pin down reasons."

"Oh, he told me some reasons he liked me, from time to time," Jeebee said. "He thought I had a remarkable enthusiasm, and he told me I had a highly unusual, intuitive ability to represent social processes in the language of mathematics."

"Did you?" asked Paul.

"Yes," Jeebee said slowly. "At least as far as the mathematics went, I guess I did. At least compared with the people I worked with."

There was another stretch of silence. It was a comfortable silence during which Jeebee was thinking of his academic days and of Bill Bohl. He was brought back to the present by Paul.

"Well, there you were, studying for your doctorate with this Bill Bohl as an adviser," said Paul. "How did you get from there to Stoketon?"

"Stoketon was a real break for me," Jeebee said with enthusiasm, "and something I never would have got if Bill hadn't had such a high idea of me. You see, even before I'd finished my doctoral thesis, Bill had let me work with him on half a dozen articles that promised to open new avenues of approach to mathematical modeling. The articles got quite a bit of attention."

"That's important?" said Paul.

"That's very important," Jeebee answered, "particularly for someone at the stage I was at, then." He paused.

"Then, when I finished my doctoral thesis, Bill talked me into staying on at the university, on a postdoctoral fellowship. It paid next to nothing, but the main thing was it let me go on working with Bill; and this paid off handsomely later on, when Bill was awarded a founder's grant to establish the Center for the Study of Quantitative Sociodynamics—the Stoketon Group."

"He invited you in on that, did he?"

"He did more than just invite me," Jeebee answered. "He'd actually written me into the grant, with the grant paying my salary. All that was required after that was for the university to give me its blessing—award me a nominal academic title that made me eligible for fringe benefits and gave me access to their libraries; that went along with the faculty post. At Stoketon, I was a resident research fellow with a permanent position—as distinguished from the experts we had, who came, stayed for a while, and then left."

"I get the idea you liked it there," said Paul.

"I did," Jeebee said, remembering, "I really did. I was kind of a maverick, or at least, a lot of them thought of me as sort of an oddball. But it's great working with people who are good themselves; and we all got along very well. I think I really turned into something at Stoketon. Pity was, it was only along the lines of the academic work I was doing. As far as the outside world was concerned—the kind of thing I need to survive nowadays—I was just as much a loner and as much an innocent as I'd ever been. That was one of the reasons my neighbors chased me out, finally."

"You weren't going back to your brother's until that happened?" said Paul.

"Oh yes. Of course I was," said Jeebee. "The Collapse had

hit. We'd no connection with any of the cities around us anymore. The water was off. There was no more electricity. Stoketon was turning into a little, tight, armed community. The thing was, I wasn't really part of it. I'd almost been part of it, when a woman who lived there worked for me. But when she quit, it was a signal—even though I didn't know it at the time—that I was being cut off and labeled an outsider. Luckily, I'd already started accumulating some things to go west with—including an electric-driven bike. Anyway, when I finally did leave, it was with some of them shooting at me."

He hesitated.

"I lost the bike a couple of weeks back in a small town, where I stopped, thinking maybe I could do some trading. That was the same town where I picked up Wolf."

He fell silent again, remembering.

"Well," Paul said at last, his eyes on the ears of his horses, "I'd say you've done some growing since you left that Stoketon of yours."

After that they had driven on in silence for some little while before talking of something else.

Now, Jeebee found them pausing as he had recommended to Merry, and it turned their early lunch into something almost like a picnic. Normally lunches were eaten as they moved—sandwiches and hot coffee, and occasionally a piece of pie or cake baked the evening before. In this case, Nick, whose turn it was to cook, again set up a folding card table on the grass beside the wagon, with chairs at it for all of them, and served them soup, fried potatoes that had been roasted in the open fire the night before, and ham, covered with a homemade but very tasty gravy.

Jeebee did not require telling that part of all this, including the table outside on the grass, was intentional. The smells of the cooking were meant to reach up and tickle the noses of Greta and Wolf, back among the trees.

How much of what followed was due to this, or to other factors, was impossible to tell, but they were just finishing up their food when Greta showed herself at the edge of the trees. She came backing out of the woods with her tail wagging furiously.

She dropped to her elbows, her hindquarters still high, as though bowing to an unseen playmate, then darted in and out of the woods in a series of clownish dashes.

Jeebee went to get his binoculars and stood by the table, trying to focus on the darkness of the woods. He was positive that Wolf was in there, and that this behavior of Greta's was addressed to him. But the difference between light and shadow, particularly in the bright noonday, kept him from seeing very far in among the trees, even with the help of the binoculars—though they were little enough help at that.

After a moment, he felt the binoculars taken out of his hands and something round and a good deal heavier pushed into them. He looked down, and saw that Paul had handed him a pair of good binoculars, much larger and heavier than the opera glasses.

Jeebee put these to his eyes and eventually was able to make out a shadow that, as he studied it, resolved itself finally into Wolf. Just inside the shadow of the nearest trees, Wolf was standing, side on to Greta and the wagon beyond. He was the picture of canine perplexity. His near forepaw was slightly raised as though unwilling to advance one more step beyond the security of the tree line. His head, turned toward Greta and the rest of them, was held high and his ears were erect and forward, in an expression of extreme alertness.

It seemed to Jeebee that even at this distance, he could see the sharp brightness of Wolf's eyes, holding them all in tight focus. Jeebee thought he saw Wolf quiver as he stood. Nonetheless, he did not move toward the wagon.

Jeebee passed the binoculars back to Paul.

"It seems I'm not the only one who'd like to get Wolf down here for a bit," he said.

Paul put the binoculars to his eyes, adjusted them, and watched for a moment.

"He's coming out, I think," he said at last.

Indeed, in that moment, Wolf did move forward enough so that the sunlight revealed him clearly to the unaided eye at the edge of the trees. He stood, still in the sideways alert stance, looking down at Greta. After a moment he turned and took a few more steps toward them, then stopped and backed up.

"Greta!" Merry called. "Greta, come back here!"

Her call broke the tension between dog and wolf upon the hillside. Wolf turned at the first word and vanished into the darkness. Greta straightened up from her play pose and stood looking after him for a moment, then slowly turned and trotted back down to the wagon, stopping every so often to turn and look back at the woods. But Wolf did not reappear.

When she reached Merry, she fawned on her, crouching before her and clearly apologizing for whatever she had done that Merry had considered wrong.

"That's all right," Merry said, stooping over to pet her. "Good girl." Greta launched herself upward to lick at Merry's face in an ecstasy of joy at being forgiven.

Merry led the dog, still bounding and licking at her hands, back toward the horses.

"Looks like we're getting under way again," said Paul. "Nick, will you put things away—you might give him a hand, Jeebee. Then join me up on the wagon seat and we'll let you take the team again for a while."

They continued westward in the days that followed, stopping mainly at isolated farmhouses where Paul did business. The routine for these visits was always that Merry, with the horses, dropped back, and Jeebee moved into the Quiet Room of the wagon with Nick and the weapons. Then Paul would drive, apparently alone, up to the place he was planning to visit. Merry, with the extra horses, would have fallen far enough behind so that she was out of sight.

This procedure, Paul told Jeebee, was followed even when the people were old friends and knew that Merry would be along with Paul. The reason was that nobody could tell what might have happened to the particular family or group—many of these isolated farmsteads now contained up to forty or fifty people— since Paul had seen it last. If there was to be trouble, he wanted Merry at a distance, where she could get clear. For the same reason, Nick and Jeebee had weapons ready and were waiting in the weapons room.

If things proved to be unchanged since Paul's last visit, and the people still friendly, Paul usually called Merry in and let either Nick or Jeebee come out of the weapons room and also mingle with the customers.

The social scientist in Jeebee was aroused by what he saw at these isolated settlements. All of the communities they stopped at were ordered and disciplined, which did not surprise him, being precisely what his mathematical models predicted. But he felt a profound sense of discovery that his own off-the-cuff estimates of the varieties of their social systems should be as close to what he actually found.

They were all, like Paul Sanderson's small group, variations on a common social adaptational theme centered on cooperative daily efforts required for survival.

There were, of course, differences in matters of social power and authority, and marriage conventions had already begun to vary widely. Over the course of the weeks he was with the wagon, Jeebee encountered a good bit of monogamy—after all, one resource gatherer was adequate for the survival of a human infant only under a limited number of resource conditions. There was a fair amount of polygyny—again there were few species of mammal who were not polygynous—but also there was some polyandry, though these were rare and largely confined to regions where food resources were especially abundant.

Interestingly, there was less promiscuity than many of the people who had guessed at possible futures had envisioned. In fact, many of these small groups were almost puritanical in attitude; and Jeebee could understand why. Sexual permissiveness was simply not the best competitive reproductive strategy.

Jeebee found himself fascinated by all this, and a part of him all but reverted to the researcher he had been. It became even more interesting when it occurred to him to speculate that his own comradeship with Wolf might also be regarded as one of the variations in social order directly spawned by the general social collapse.

The fact was, Wolf was a person—an individual, with his own likes, dislikes, wishes, desires, and purposes. In this he was no different from the people of the communities Paul visited. But Wolf was also a product of a social order, not that different in many ways from the human ones, which had given rise in Wolf to certain instinctual patterns of behavior and response, and these patterns had found a congenial mesh with Jeebee's own, similarly derived patterns and responses.

It was likely, Jeebee thought, that the growing comfort he was finding in his relationship with Paul, Merry, and Nick were rooted in the same needs that had overcome Wolf's natural timidity and, eventually, could drive him to approach the wagon and its company.

The fact remained that in his relationship with Wolf he had found an emotional satisfaction that he did not find in his own kind—the three of the wagon.

From the beginning of their acquaintanceship, Jeebee had wanted to get closer to this companion of his; and for that a better understanding of what made Wolf "Wolf" was needed. If only Jeebee had looked deeper into what made wolves what they were, back before the world had fallen apart and both libraries and experts had vanished . . .

Well, there was no point in yearning for what was not available. So Jeebee watched Wolf's approaches to the wagon now with a fierce hunger for Wolf to come all the way in. Wolf was free in the most absolute sense of that word. There was no way to force him anywhere, short of wounding or trapping him, which would destroy the whole purpose of getting back together with him. Jeebee could only continue his watch and hope that Wolf would make the decision to join them by himself.

Gradually, it became apparent that he might.

He began to appear more often, a couple of hours before sundown, an hour or more before the wagon stopped for the day. At first he could only be seen occasionally, following and flanking the wagon at a distance. But eventually, his parallel movements became closer so that he was traveling within as much as fifty yards, where the terrain allowed.

As he got closer, Greta would often run out to join him. When she did so, the other dogs would often try to go with her— in which case, invariably, she would turn on them and drive them back to the wagon. Eventually, the other dogs became more used to his presence and no longer set up a chorus of barking at the very sight of him.

But, also, occasionally, when Greta was not around, one or more of them would charge out at him. In these cases, his behavior varied. If there were several of them running at him in a group, he usually turned and bolted.

The dogs of the wagon would follow him for a couple of hundred yards, and then would stop and come back, almost prancing in their pride and self-satisfaction at having driven off the intruder. Jeebee was secretly pleased to see that after all, Merry did not seem to like the dogs driving Wolf away in this manner any more than Jeebee did. But he recognized her quandary. If they were to remain effective guard dogs, she could hardly scold them for doing what they considered their duty.

If it was a single animal that rushed out at him, Wolf generally all but ignored it. No single dog of the wagon was any real threat to him. On occasion, his behavior was so indifferent that the dog, after sniffing him over, simply fell in beside him. Twice, the single dog was one of the males and actually tried to be aggressive. In each case, Wolf merely turned side on and twisted his body in a manner that threw the weight of it behind the impact of his left hip: and the other was sent tumbling. Only in the case of one other single attacker from the wagon was the dog persistent enough that Wolf turned on him suddenly and pinned him to the ground by the neck, clamping skin and neck alike in the vise of his powerful jaws so that it choked the other animal as well as locked it in place.

The dog ki-yied in fright and fled as soon as Wolf let him up. Back at the wagon, Merry's exploring fingers could find no sign of injury on the dog that had been neck-pinned.

Wolf, Jeebee concluded interestedly, must have a fine-tuned sense of possible responses to threats.

With time, however, the contacts between Wolf and the dogs of the wagon gradually built up patterns of tolerance between him and at least some of the males; and gradually Wolf came closer and closer, until one day he finally greeted Jeebee beside the wagon itself.

Meanwhile, as they got into the western part of South Dakota, to the north of the Badlands, the country became rougher and they left the route of the interstate more often to get to customers.

The wagon was stoutly built and could be taken across fairly open country when it was absolutely necessary, but there were definite limits to where it could go. Consequently, Paul normally chose to stick to roads. Or to the shoulders of old roads, where the road itself was too pockmarked and pitted. At other times, where it was impossible for the wagon to go to the customer, the customer came to Paul.

Usually this meant that Paul would stop the wagon in mid-afternoon and wait until the following morning before going on. If whoever had been used to trading with him at that point showed up, business was done. Otherwise, if no one appeared, Paul moved on the following morning. Those who dealt with him knew approximately when he was due in their area; and if they still existed or were interested in trade, it was up to them to show up.

If they did not, that particular stop was removed from Paul's customer list. Paul's practice was to travel along a road as far as he could, then stop and fire four spaced shots in the air; not from his usual rifle, but from a black-powder muzzle loader.

Almost always, within half an hour, one or more riders on horseback would appear and come to the wagon. These would later be followed by most of the whole clan or family. In a few cases Jeebee saw a small, temporary tent city set up for a day or two by the wagon while deals with Paul were made; and a certain amount of hospitality and celebration resulted.

Occasionally, where the wagon was able to go across country, they traveled where there were no roads at all; just as their forerunners, in the wagons of the nineteenth century, had traveled where there were no roads. Occasionally, they came to rivers, and Jeebee was surprised to discover that for all its weight of armor and goods, the wagon had been built to float. With the horses swimming, it could cross rivers in their path, provided the current was not too swift or the bottom too deep or rocky.

If it was either of these things, they sometimes forded. Otherwise, they turned either up the stream or down—depending upon Paul's knowledge of the best route—until they came to a place where it was possible either to float across or wheel over safely.

Altogether, as a result, their movement across country was not swift. There were pauses of as much as two days in some locations. Nonetheless, most of their time was spent covering distance by themselves. Little by little, Jeebee fell into the routine of the wagon, became competent with the weapons, able to handle the team for stretches of three to four hours at a time, and able to hold the following remounts of horses tightly bunched behind the wagon, moving along with it.

His knowledge of his traveling partners expanded. Paul he found to be an interesting, informed if not educated, and lively conversationalist; when he felt like talking. Nick talked very little and had periods during which he seemed not to want to talk at all and was best left alone. Merry, surprisingly, gradually emerged as the best company of the three for Jeebee.

By degrees her chilliness toward him, largely a surface protection in any case, thawed; and as she began to relax with him, naturally warm spirits bubbled to the surface. She reacted instinctively and emotionally to almost everything; with the result that she could change from summer sunshine to thunder and lightning in an instant, and back to sunshine again, almost before the first rain from the storm had begun to fall.

Jeebee was amused to notice that not merely Paul and Nick, but the dogs as well, did not take her sudden small explosions of anger seriously. The dogs, in particular, made a large display of acting repentant and apologetic, but it was perfectly obvious to Jeebee after a while that they were looking forward to being lavishly petted and forgiven within the next few moments, and would have been alarmed only if this had not happened.

Gradually he found himself beginning to look for, and delight in, her wholehearted, sudden enthusiasms, her suddenly revealed depths of sympathy and understanding. In the same gradual manner, he began to realize that he had fallen in love with her, entirely without planning to. It was something that must inevitably have an effect on his partnership with Wolf.

Meanwhile, full summer took them into its flow, and other interesting things were happening. They were now into country where there was a great deal more ground cover; not so much of trees but of hills and underbrush. The result was that Wolf had begun to stay closely with them in his visits; and, bit by bit, lured by Greta, but also simply because he was becoming used to the wagon, its horses and humans, and beginning to be less shy of them, he moved in closer and closer. Until he finally ended, for short periods at least, literally traveling with the wagon itself.

After a few snaps and snarls from Greta, the dogs simply accepted Wolf as they had accepted Jeebee.

Wolf, on the other hand, did not so much accept them as ignore them.

Jeebee had expected him also to more or less ignore the people with the wagon. To a large extent he did, since he was with them only for an hour or so at a time and he came and went unexpectedly. But he did treat the wagon area now as if he had a right to be there. His attitude was different with each of the humans.

Paul, he tended to avoid, but was invariably polite to. Nick was the only one he really ignored and generally avoided. Merry, to Jeebee's surprise, he greeted, if only occasionally. Clearly, he regarded Jeebee and himself as social outsiders.

However, at his first close meeting with Merry, Wolf was almost effusive toward her.

It was the last sort of behavior Jeebee had expected. Merry happened to be off her horse at the time, and the other dogs were within view, but not close to her, when Wolf first approached her. He went directly to her, with ears back, head low, tail wagging, and she squatted to meet him, talking to him as if he was one of the dogs. He licked at her face, squatted, and urinated a few drops, then fell on his side and rolled over on his back, as though inviting a belly scratch.

Jeebee could not repress a small feeling of jealousy. He had been with Wolf for weeks before Wolf had invited him to as

much familiarity. But here he seemed ready to make friends with
Merry with no further courtesies or introductions needed.

Feeling unwanted, Jeebee left them both to each other and
went up front to join Paul on the wagon seat.

"Good you came up," said Paul. "It's about time we had a
bit of a talk anyway."

"Oh," Jeebee replied. He was instantly alert.

"Yes," said Paul. "Do you know where we are now?"

Jeebee shook his head.

"We're a little beyond Weston," said Paul. "In Wyoming."

"Wyoming?" Jeebee stared at Paul. "You knew I was headed
north toward Montana."

"I know. I knew," said Paul. "You're still determined to go
find your brother's place?"

"I have to," said Jeebee. "I've got to find a safe place for
what I have in my head about the work I used to do. Someplace
to keep it alive against the time civilization can use it again."

"Right. I thought you still felt that way," said Paul. "That's
why I wanted to talk to you, now. A little beyond here—about
thirty miles or so—before we get to what used to be Buffalo, and
before we get into the Bighorns, I'll be turning south to start the
long swing down and back east again. So we're just about at the
point where we're going one way and you're going to be going
another."

Jeebee realized with a sudden shock that he had not expected their parting to come so soon. It had been well over a
month since he had joined them. He had fallen into the way of
life of the wagon, got used to it; and he was now almost more at
home here with Paul, Merry, and Nick, than he had been at any
place else in his life, except when he had been very young. He
suddenly realized that, unconsciously, he had been looking forward to this state of affairs going on almost indefinitely.

Even Wolf had fallen into the pattern. He now announced
his arrival at the wagon at dawn or twilight with a howl, and the
dogs had come to respond by howling back.

Also he had preempted the box-sided back steps of the
wagon as his own place when traveling with them. He was en-

closed and secure—and *above* any of the dogs who might approach him.

But now, all at once, Jeebee found himself face-to-face again with the prospect of pushing on alone. Particularly alone, that would be, if Wolf would not come with him after setting up his relationships with Merry, Greta, and the other wagon dogs. The thought of being alone once more was like having cold water dumped over him, just when he had grown accustomed to a warm and gentle shower, to waken his sleep-chilled body in the morning.

"Where did you say we were?"

"Just short of the Bighorns," said Paul. "Day after tomorrow, I turn south. I thought you'd want to make plans."

"Yes, I'll have to," said Jeebee, his mind lost in a welter of questions. He was trying to summon up a picture of the Wyoming–Montana border and how the geography of Montana was, farther north. It had been nearly fifteen years since he had visited his brother's ranch; and he had been only twelve years old. He had flown into Billings, his brother had met him at the airport, and driven for about an hour and a half to get to the ranch. They had driven north to Musselshell, which they had passed through just before they reached the edges of his brother's ranch.

"I wish I had a better idea of how the land lies around here," he said almost to himself.

Without a word, Paul reached behind the wagon seat and came up with a folded paper that he passed to Jeebee.

Jeebee took it and unfolded it. It was an AAA auto map showing Montana and sections of the bordering states of Wyoming, South and North Dakota. He spread it on his knees, studying it.

"Do you want some advice?" Paul asked.

"Yes." Jeebee looked up at the other man with the blue eyes and the gray beard. "I need all the help I can get. All the advice I can get."

"Well . . ." Paul passed the reins to Jeebee. "Here, you take the team."

He took the map off Jeebee's knees and, laying it on his own knees, began with one finger to trace a route.

"Here you are, approaching what's left of Buffalo from the east, on I-90. Now, you don't want to get into the mountains, particularly not the Bighorns. I'd suggest you start off straight north, going around Buffalo and Sheridan, and swing east when you get into Montana, to avoid the reservation, here. You might not get into any trouble trying to go straight through it, and it certainly takes you out of your way not to, but things are a little different in reservation territory—and who can blame them? No, I'd suggest you go around it, then hit back northwest—from what you've told me your brother's ranch is about midway up the state, pretty much in the middle?"

"The last town I can remember him taking me through on the way there, years ago when I was small, was Musselshell," Jeebee answered. He no longer felt any need to conceal his general destination from any of these people.

"All right, then," said Paul, his finger pushing up the paper. "You head roughly northwest after you swing around the eastern edge of the reservation; in fact after you've gone between it and the Custer National Forest, go straight north across old highway 94 and right on to here. Here's Musselshell, on highway 12. I mean the town of Musselshell."

Jeebee nodded.

"I'd give you this map to take with you," said Paul, "only it's one of those things that aren't easy to find nowadays—"

"It's all right," Jeebee interrupted, "one of the things I managed to hold on to in my backpack was my road maps for that part of the route—like this one."

"Then you're taken care of," said Paul. "Hand me back the reins."

CHAPTER 12

"Now," said Paul, "with the map business settled, we've got something else to talk about. Remember, we never settled on exactly what you'd get by way of pay?"

Jeebee, who had begun to leave the wagon seat, sat back down again.

"I forgot all about it," he said.

"You'd make a fine peddler," Paul said dryly. "Well, let's talk about it now. You put in well over a month with us—call it two months—so that'd be two months wages plus how many gold pieces did you say you had in that belt of yours?"

"Twenty-three," Jeebee answered unthinkingly.

"All right," said Paul. "What I can give you for that is essentially one riding horse, ammunition for those two rifles of yours, and some basic food supplies, flour, bacon, and maybe some other things like baking soda and salt and sugar. I can't give you winter clothes, but I've got blankets and three plastic tarpaulins that'll match well enough with the one you've got to let you set up something more than a pup tent; plus a saddle, rope, and packing gear. But that's about it."

"No packhorse?" said Jeebee.

"No packhorse," said Paul. "If you're smart, you'll use the horse I give you as a packhorse and travel on foot. Also, you'd better watch your wolf with a single horse. I'm sorry. But I'm stretching what your stuff's worth as it is. Oh, I'll get my money back in the long run when I find somebody who's really hoarding gold and is willing to pay a good price for those gold coins. But I'm going to have to hang on to them for some time—and that's just plain not good business. You need to turn over your goods and keep turning them over fast if you want to make enough profit to live on. This wagon has to be practically rebuilt after each year's trip. Did you realize that? New material for it costs. As it is, I'll have the equivalent of the worth of the one horse I give you tied up in those coins a year or more, and not likely to get it back until I find a buyer at the price I want."

"Well," said Jeebee, dispirited. "If you can't, you can't."

"I'm sorry," said Paul. "We've all ended up liking you, and we'd do what we could for you. But nowadays it just isn't practical for us to act as a charity. All sorts of things can happen, from me getting sick or killed on down, that could put Merry in a bind. There's no real cash going around anymore; but what used to be called 'cash flow' is still important. You need things that can be turned over fast and you need somebody who knows how to turn them that way. I'm responsible in both directions. We'd help you more if we could. But we can't."

"Even Merry?" Jeebee said, with a slight stab of emotion that made him speak before he thought.

"Now look here," said Paul, "there's something you've got to understand. Merry probably likes you better than anyone else we've ever taken on with us at the wagon. But she's known from the start that you're going to take off again. And her life is tied to this wagon. It's her security as well as mine. She couldn't leave and go with you, for instance. And you're determined to go. Wasn't that just what you said?"

Jeebee hesitated.

"If I didn't have to go, I'd really like to stay," he said. "I want you to know that."

"Well, there you are," said Paul. "It's self-defense on her part. She can't afford to get too attached to a young fellow like you, one she'll never see again, possibly."

"You mean 'probably,' don't you?" Jeebee said wryly.

"If you want the truth, yes," Paul answered. "Nick tells me you're good with weapons. Not the greatest shot, but good at handling and taking care of them. You've learned a lot with us about horses and trading and something of blacksmithing, plus a few other things. Count that learning as part of your pay. But there's something about you. You're a born innocent, Jeebee. You've got to understand that. The same thing that made you look right at your figures, or whatever they were, and see the world was going smash but still believe that somehow it wouldn't have anything to do with you—that's still with you. Until you learn this is a different world nowadays, that you're either top dog or bottom dog but there's no such thing as in-between dog, you're a walking risk to yourself."

"I wish I was Wolf," said Jeebee.

The words surprised himself. But Paul understood.

"He's just an animal, but he knows what it's about, better than you," Paul said. "That's because he listens to his instincts. Learn from him if you can, about the way life is, now. It's exactly the same for you and me now as it is for him."

"I have," Jeebee said glumly, "but I don't think I could ever see things the way he does."

"You've got instincts, too," Paul said. "Listen to them, and get this top-dog, bottom-dog idea clear in your head. You've got to understand that much of it. There's a reason I run this wagon and everybody in it. There's a reason my daughter's one of my hired hands first and my daughter afterwards, in spite of all she means to me. It's that way because it has to be that way if we're all going to survive. The same for you. You learn that much, and if you ever run into Merry again, it may be a different situation."

"No chance until next year." Jeebee looked at Paul. "Do you think I can last out the winter if I don't find my brother's ranch before then?"

"Up to you," Paul answered.

He flipped the reins.

"Get up there," he told the team.

Jeebee, knowing he was dismissed, began to leave the wagon seat once more to go back into the wagon interior.

"If you don't mind," he said, "I want to make some plans and there's some things about blacksmithing I want to ask Nick."

"Go ahead," Paul answered, without taking his attention off the team and the road, "we'll be stopping a little early tonight, anyway. Nick wants to have a special dinner to see you off right; even if it'll be some days before you actually go."

Jeebee went back into the Quiet Room, found Nick, and asked him where paper and either pens or pencils were to be found.

"What do you want it for?" Nick asked. "Don't tell me you're thinking of writing a letter?"

"Nothing like that," said Jeebee. "I just want to write down some notes and plans."

Nick got up and went into the forward compartment where the trade goods were kept, rummaged around, and came back with three sharpened lead pencils, a ballpoint pen, and some fairly thin typing paper.

"What notes and plans?" he asked as Jeebee sat down with the paper and pencils at the little table that hinged up against the Quiet Room wall.

"For one thing," said Jeebee, "I want to write down some of the things you've told me about building my own backwoods smithy."

"Paul told you we're turning south, then?"

Jeebee nodded.

"Well, all right then," said Nick. "What do you want to hear from me?"

"The whole process," said Jeebee.

"Let me tell you some other things first," said Nick. "Might be you'll find them more important."

Nick sat down at his seat behind the nearest machine gun, swiveled his chair to face Jeebee at the table, and looked out the window beyond the machine gun's muzzle, where a flap of the outer canvas shell of the wagon hid the firing slot for the weapon in the wagon's metal armor. Then he looked back at Jeebee.

"You know much about Montana?" he asked.

"No," Jeebee confessed. "I was there for a visit to my brother about fifteen years ago. But I don't remember much, really. My brother's eighteen years older than I am. In fact, I remember more about making the flight in by myself—it was my first plane trip alone—than I do about the drive up to the ranch. And most of what I remember about the ranch is just the main ranch house and the buildings around it. I know we had to drive more than an hour or so to get to it, from where I got off the plane in Billings. We went up- and down-hill a lot toward the end."

"It'll be cattle country. You want land below the pines," said Nick. "You need to understand something else, too. It's that a lot of these ranches made the switchover to the way things are now a lot easier and more natural than people closer to the cities. Particularly, easier than someone from farther east. They weren't that far different in lots of ways from the way things were there in their great-grandfolks' time. Like some of these farms you've seen us trade at, they were almost ready to operate on their own—maybe more so—even before they had to."

"I can understand that." Jeebee now knew Nick well enough to understand such a statement meant Nick had more than that to tell him. But Nick liked to be told that his listener was interested. "Why tell me this?"

"Just because you're going to be traveling through a lot of other people's country, other ranches owned by people besides your brother," said Nick. "You'll do best to just plain keep out of sight as much as possible. Remember, the sound of a gunshot carries a long ways. That's the bad part. The good part is that if there's high rock around, the echoes are going to help hide the place the sound came from to start off with. But it'll still be smart not to use your gun if you don't have to—and you're going to have to live off the land. Had you thought of that?"

"I'd thought about living off the land," said Jeebee. "But only as far as the fact that I thought that there might be more large game up there than I ran into earlier. Deer or something like that."

"There's going to be more game, more big game," said Nick.

"But that's where the sound of the gunshot comes in. Whatever you do, don't go shooting any cattle. They all belong to somebody; and it was always rough around there on anybody who killed somebody else's cows. It's not like you're a neighbor who needed meat in a hurry, or some such thing. They don't know you, so they don't need you, so they're not going to let you get away with killing what belongs to them."

"I see," said Jeebee. "All right, I'll watch that. Any other advice?"

"No." Nick's eyes went back to the canvas covering the slot outside the wagon. "Now, what was it you wanted to write down about smithing?"

Jeebee told him and got busy with his pencil, noting down the answers and making sketches.

This done, Nick returned to his own duties about the wagon, but Jeebee sat where he was, with his pencils and marked-up papers, thinking.

Paul, he knew, was being as generous as he could be. But what he was offering Jeebee, Jeebee now realized, would give him only a minimal chance of survival—let alone of finding Martin's ranch. If only there was some way he could justify getting more of what he needed from Paul . . .

Baffled, his mind went off on a tangent, in spite of himself. He thought of Wolf and wondered if Wolf would really continue to come with him when he went. It might be, seeing Wolf's occasional warmth toward Merry, plus his attachment to the dog Greta, that he would rather stay with the wagon than travel further, alone with Jeebee.

It would not be at all surprising, Jeebee thought bleakly, if Wolf decided to stay with them. His mind slipped back to a memory of the days before he had met the wagon and those on it, the period in which he and Wolf had been traveling together, isolated from the rest of the world. The emptiness of the land then, seemed to move in on him now. He would be stepping back into that emptiness when he left these others and the wagon.

That thought brought him back to his earlier problem. There must be some way he could justify getting more of what the wagon had to supply; in particular, a second horse for packing so he could ride the first one. Without a horse under him he would be at a serious disadvantage in a country where everyone rode. If there was only some way he could produce something of more value so as to get a second animal . . .

His mind roamed loosely over a field of wildly different possibilities. If it could only turn out that something he had been carrying all along was worth a great deal to Paul. If he could only think of something that he could point out to Paul, something from which the other man could make an immediate profit—on the rest of this trip—

An idea suddenly jolted him more profoundly than any of the highway's potholes, in and out of which their wheels would periodically bounce, shaking all the wagon. He went up front and sat down by Paul again.

"You sell mostly to farmers, don't you?" Jeebee asked.

"Pretty much so." Paul glanced sideways at him for a moment. "A few other people. But nearly everyone farms some, now. What about it?"

"Farmers plant crops," said Jeebee. "One of those crops—one of those most important crops—is wheat. Wheat makes bread, wheat is useful in all sorts of ways. But what if the wheat seeds are attacked by some plant disease and the crops become useless?"

Paul laughed.

"The last supply outfits making chemicals to control plant diseases went out of business over a year ago," he answered, "far as I can find out."

"I thought so," said Jeebee, "so when people plant nowadays, they merely plant their seeds and pray that the crop will come up all right without, say, mildew attacking it?"

"Of course," said Paul, "but what can they do about it now? There's no way of controlling those diseases if you can't get the chemicals."

"As a matter of fact," said Jeebee, "maybe there is something—"

Paul looked sharply at him.

"So," Jeebee went on, "I suppose you could find a good market anywhere for a wheat seed that would resist mildew, the seed of each crop could go on, year after year, resisting mildew? Am I right?"

Paul's look had become more curious than sharp.

"Of course I could," he said. "What are you getting at?"

Jeebee went on as if Paul had not spoken.

"And something like that would be worth something to you—enough so that if I could bring you some, or show you where you could get some, maybe not right away but eventually, it would be worth something to you?"

Paul nodded slowly.

"What's on your mind?" Paul said.

"I just thought of something," said Jeebee. "I think I know where some might be found. The people there were just in the process of experimenting with genetically altered wheat that would have a natural resistance, particularly to wilt, but also to some of the other diseases that attack wheat. I might be able to locate a source of it. If I could do that, what else would you be able to pay me in the way of an extra horse and supplies?"

Paul kept looking at him for a moment, glanced back to check on the horses, and then returned to rest his eyes on Jeebee's face. He was plainly thinking.

"If you could really lead me to something like that—it would depend on whether you actually produced some seed, or just were able to tell me where it could be found somewhere along the line—it would be worth quite a bit to me," he answered at last, thoughtfully. "I couldn't say exactly until I see what you come up with. But there's a good chance I could give you that extra horse and some other things you'd find useful. Maybe even some things you wouldn't think of for yourself. Now, do you actually know where some of this genetically changed wheat is? Or where some can be got?"

"I know where there ought to be some," Jeebee answered. "I won't know for sure if it's there until I actually go look for myself. But I don't know why it wouldn't be there. If it is, there might be more than you can carry. If that's the case, I can bring back as much as I can packload on the horses you let me take. If it turns out it's just a place where the seed's going to be available—say later this fall sometime—maybe next year you can arrange to swing around here at a time when you can harvest some for yourself."

"Whoa," Paul called, pulling back hard on the reins in his fingers. The wagon rolled to a stop, the horses tossed their heads and looked backward and fidgeted, as if they were annoyed to be interrupted at their work by such a sudden and unexplained halt.

"There," said Paul, looping the reins around the brake post to the left of the seat to set his hands free, "now I can give my mind to it without worrying about the team or the road. Where is this grain you're talking about, now?"

"I think I can find it," said Jeebee. "But it's the location I'm selling you. Once you know where it is—once anybody knows where it is, they can just help themselves. In fact, people around it may have been helping themselves already; but there ought to be enough of it, if I'm right, so that you could pick what you want."

"Are we close to it?" Paul asked, gazing steadily at Jeebee.

"We've passed it, actually," said Jeebee. "It's behind us and to the north a ways; in fact, just at a guess, it'd be about five days back by wagon. Then on foot, maybe a three-day walk to the north. Then a day or two to hunt around and gather the grain, and three days coming back."

"Well"—Paul sat thinking for a minute—"it'd take a couple of people, with packhorses, to make that trip properly. That means, of course, that whoever goes is going to have to cover those five days it took the wagon to get this far, in about a day or two of reasonable riding with the horses, because of all the stops we've made. Leg to the north would probably be . . . maybe two days by horseback?"

"I don't know," said Jeebee. "I've done all my traveling by myself on foot, I tend to think that way. I know where it was or is, from being told about it, about three years ago. But I've never been there, and finding it now that things have changed may take a little time. Exactly where it is, that is. But I definitely remember it was outside a little town called Wayne, north of here."

Nick stuck his head curiously out the front entrance to the wagon behind them, just as Merry rode up, looking as annoyed as one of the horses.

"What's going on?" she demanded. "What are we stopping here for?"

"Jeebee may've come up with something very good for us," Paul said briefly.

The look of annoyance disappeared from Merry's face. She looked at Jeebee curiously and said nothing.

"Go on," Paul said to Jeebee. "Tell them."

He did; and they listened.

CHAPTER 13

It was just a few minutes to noon, four days later. Jeebee and Merry reined their riding horses to a stop on the top of a small, open rise that gave them the advantage of a little altitude from which to survey the countryside. Behind them, the packhorses on the lead rope that connected them, the end of which was tied to Merry's saddle, stopped patiently where they were, dropped their heads, and started to crop at the sparse ground cover on the sandy soil of the hill.

They got out their binoculars and began to scan the surrounding territory. What Jeebee was now using was a superb pair of Bausch and Lomb Elite, eight-by-forty glasses that had been lent him by Paul for the trip. Merry, with another pair of glasses just like his, scanned the left half of the visible landscape while he scanned the right.

"We'll stand out like a bright light up here, if anybody's watching," Jeebee grumbled. His months of travel before he had met the wagon had trained him to stay undercover, avoiding places where he might be outlined against the sky; and he felt uneasy in any place as open as this.

"Can't be helped," Merry replied, without taking the glasses from her eyes. "All I see on this side is clumps of woods and a few fields. No sign of State Highway 37. But it has to be there, somewhere."

She lowered her glasses.

"We can see for miles," she said, "and you didn't argue when I suggested coming up here."

"No," said Jeebee.

He lowered his glasses and saw her putting her own down. They both tucked them back into the binocular cases that were strapped to the side of their saddles, and Merry got out a map, which she unfolded against her saddle horn.

She stopped as she saw Jeebee fumbling for something inside his backpack, which was now secured behind his saddle.

"What's that?" she asked as he brought it out.

"This is one of my maps," said Jeebee. "It covers this area, too."

He unfolded the map. It showed slanting, parallel lines drawn clear across the face of it from top to bottom. "Time to get out the compass."

As Merry stared, he unbuttoned his shirt and withdrew the compass that hung around his neck. His unfolded map lay on the flat surface of the pack behind his saddle and he turned to lay his compass upon it.

"There!" he said. "You see that bend of the river just beyond those trees about five miles off. Now that's got to be, according to this map, part of Cross River, and let's see, the azimuth on that would be . . . about thirty-seven degrees off of magnetic north and figure about five miles on a back azimuth and that would put us right about here."

He used the base plate of the compass to draw another line on the map and then made a small dot.

"Now the road we're after is here. . . ." He laid the compass on the map once more and rotated the capsule that housed the needle. "About sixty-eight degrees and I'd figure less than two miles before the river takes a bend and runs away from us."

He folded up the map, put it away, and put the compass—it was a Finnish Suunto on its cord—back around his neck and inside his shirt. He tucked the map away and turned to Merry, who had been watching him intently all this time.

"We go that way," he said. "It shouldn't take us much time at all."

She was still staring at him.

"It's called orienteering, in simple form," he said. "If you draw lines on your map parallel to magnetic north, you don't need to bother with all the fussy little calculations that adjust for the difference between true north and magnetic north. You just use the compass to measure angles—like a protractor."

He mounted and led off. He did not look back, but he could hear her moving after him, along with the packhorses, as he rode down the hill and off in the direction he had indicated. A pleasant glow of accomplishment encompassed him, but he was too wise by this time to show it to her in any obvious manner.

"Was that," Merry asked, moving her horse up to ride level with him, "the reason you didn't object when I first suggested going up there?"

"Partly," said Jeebee. "We might just have sighted the road, of course."

"But you hoped we wouldn't," said Merry, "so you could show off this orienteering business."

It was true, of course, but he was not about to admit it. Not when he had at last found something he could do better than she could. "It always pays to check the general area occasionally," he answered.

Nothing more was said until they were among the trees of a patch of woods along the road they had been seeking.

Meanwhile, Jeebee had been busy thinking. It would not only be quicker but safer to cut straight across to their destination; or at least to the area of their destination, since Jeebee knew only the general location of the former seed farm. It would save them at least a day's travel time if they went directly. On the other hand, he was hesitant about trying to force his point of view on Merry.

All his weeks of working westward alone, using orienteering as a check to make sure he was traveling in the right direction, had him uneasy now at having to depend on her way of finding their destination. At the same time, he did not want to challenge her methods without strong reason.

She had taken for granted from the start that she would be in command of the expedition. All Jeebee was supposed to supply were directions. This had also been taken for granted by her father and Nick. None of them thought too highly of him as someone who could take care of himself, let alone one other person and a string of valuable horses, while traveling through territory that was unknown and could well contain at least some hostile people.

He had been a little surprised at first that Merry should be the one Paul had chosen to go with him; particularly after Paul's earlier objections to her going up into the trees by the highway, alone. But this was plainly a decision that required that some risks be taken. In the end, the decision had been obvious. The wagon remained the anchor point for father, daughter, and Nick. Paul himself could not quit it any more easily than a ship captain could abandon his vessel to go off on a side trip or a venture.

Also, if Paul should be lost, Nick and Merry would not be able to carry on the peddling route as well without him. He was the man that the customers along the way were used to dealing with. Even though they might know Merry and Nick, they would not have as much faith in them and some might even try to take advantage of them—which might end in a shoot-out.

No, Paul had to stay with the wagon. Nick was not a good choice for Jeebee's companion, being a follower by nature. That left Merry. Merry was not only capable of command, she was used to it; since in all things but the overall direction of the wagon, she controlled a great many matters. The horses, the dogs, and apparently a good deal of the internal management of the wagon, aside from most of their personal supply of food-stuffs, were her daily responsibilities.

Jeebee had realized from the first planning of the trip that his orienteering skills, and any suggestion that he plot a straight line course for them to the area that was their destination, would probably be unwelcome—to Paul and Nick as much as to Merry. They had little understanding of his knowledge and skills. His suggestions could only raise suspicions that he was proposing that he lead instead of her. Merry was too valuable to the other two men to be entrusted to the care of a latecomer to the wagon's people. Only the belief that she would be firmly in command had made her going with Jeebee practical in the eyes of Paul and Nick.

That was why, for a long time, Jeebee had avoided even producing the compass and map. But time was as critical for him as it was for them; and her methods of hunting for roadways to point their route involved too much daylight lost in guesswork and an unnecessary waste of hours in blind searchings for landmarks.

He and Merry rode along now, therefore, in mutual silence, with Jeebee not knowing quite what to do about it. He had not seen any sign of Wolf, but he had a feeling that Wolf was with them, or at least traveling in the same direction and keeping in touch with them. He had been tempted to howl and see if Wolf answered. But since Merry would know why he was howling, he was afraid that that, too, might offend her. He had found himself trapped by a singular feeling of helplessness.

Unexpectedly, Merry spoke.

"How did you happen to learn this orienteering?" Her tone was as calmly conversational as if they had been merely making idle conversation, all along.

"Oh, that," Jeebee answered, a little embarrassed, "actually, I learned it in the Boy Scouts. I always wanted to do some exploring; but I never really seemed to have time. Also, what I was doing usually didn't give me the freedom to take off and go hunting around unknown territory."

He hesitated, uncomfortable talking so much about himself. He made an effort and went on.

"I told myself that anyone—" He broke off. "What I mean is, I thought that I ought to be able, at least, to fly a light plane, and navigate a small, but ocean-going boat by myself. In fact, I tried to take lessons in both things, several times, but other matters always seemed to interrupt. I did get some flying lessons on three separate occasions, but something always seemed to come up each time, and I had to go back and start all over again. After doing that several times, I gave up. The same thing with handling a sailing boat on the ocean. I wasn't anywhere near the ocean. But orienteering you can do anywhere."

"Is your family alive? I mean are your parents alive?" Merry asked.

Jeebee shook his head.

"Only my brother," he said, "and, as I maybe said, he's eighteen years older than I am. I was an unexpected baby when my mother was in her midforties; and by that time my father had become an architect. You see, my grandfather had the ranch my older brother has now. But Dad and he never got together. I don't mean they fought. I just mean they saw things differently."

He paused. "So my father went off to Vietnam. Afterwards he went back to school on the GI Bill and became an architect. He never wanted the ranch, and my brother and grandfather got along real well. So my brother got it when my grandfather died."

He hesitated again, not sure but what he was saying too much. "My father was killed in a construction accident," he said, "while I was in college. My mother had died of pneumonia when I was sixteen."

They rode along in silence for a moment or two.

"It must have been hard for you," Merry murmured at last. It was hard for Jeebee to tell whether the words were really addressed to him, or only to herself.

"Not really," said Jeebee. "We were a family of individuals. The three of us all went our own way more or less. My father was wrapped up in his architecture and my mother taught at a number of colleges. Her life was the academic world she was in."

"Did you ever have a pet? A dog?" Merry asked.

"No," said Jeebee. "I just read a lot—and experimented with things. I always wanted to know things. For example the grandfather of a friend of mine told me once that the lumberjacks back in the timbering days used to sharpen the two blades of a double-bladed ax differently."

He steepled his fingers in the air before him to make two sharp sides of a "V," the fingertips touching in front of his nose.

"One edge was sharpened like that," he said. He bowed his fingers out. "The other was beveled to an edge—like this. I tried looking it up, but I couldn't find out anything or anyone that backed him up. So I bought a double-bladed ax head and built a sort of small guillotine. I had the ax head falling down between two uprights into a piece of wood, first with one edge of the ax head, then the other, and comparing the cuts the different edges made. I found out there was a real difference; and later on I found out why that difference was useful. When you chop down a tree, you know, you first chop across horizontally, on a level. Then you chop down at an angle through the tree trunk above your first cut, so that you take out chunks at a time."

"Yes," said Merry. "I've seen trees chopped down."

"As it turns out," said Jeebee, "the flat 'V' shape leading to an edge is best for cutting across horizontally. The beveled one pries a chip of wood outward as you chop down into the horizontal cut, so it's best for that. It really didn't matter whether I found this out for myself or not, but I liked doing it. It's always been that way with me. My head's full of all sorts of bits and things I picked up because they were interesting; and I wanted to test them out for myself. It was that way with learning orienteering."

Having said so much, he felt foolish. There was a strong impression in him that he had overexplained himself. Merry was probably not the least bit interested in so much personal detail. On the other hand, she had started it, by asking about his folks.

"So what you mean," Merry said, "is that you didn't have time for pets."

"I suppose so," said Jeebee.

"I just wondered," Merry said, "the way you picked up Wolf, and the way you feel about him. I'd have expected you to have a long history of having pets."

"Wolf's not a pet!" said Jeebee, and the words came out more sharply than he intended. "He's my partner."

"You really believe that, don't you?" Merry said thoughtfully. "Dad said you told him the same thing. You talk about Wolf as if he were a person. Do you really feel that way?"

Jeebee answered slowly. "I guess it depends on what you mean by 'person.' Pets are a lot like children. If you stop and think about it, adults don't really think of children as 'persons.' When we say 'persons,' we really mean 'grown-ups.' In that sense, Wolf really is a 'person'—not a human person, maybe, but a self-sufficient individual with his own way of looking at the world. If a dog is going to survive, he's got to behave as though he looked at the world through his master's eyes. The same thing's true of children—teaching them to do that is what psychologists call 'socialization.' Maybe that's why children—and dogs—are so dependent on us, so eager to please us. Their survival depends on it. Not Wolf. He survives just fine looking at the world through his own eyes—just like any other grown-up person. He's not dependent on me—in any way. He stays with me because he likes me. He's with me the same way another adult human being would be with me; and he can leave at any time he wants. We both know that."

"Still . . ." said Merry, "is there really any difference between him and the dogs, except that they're tame and he's wild?"

"Yes, there is," said Jeebee. "Oh, I know they can interbreed. We saw that. But there's more to it. I may not have had a dog, or dogs, but I got to know them, growing up. Some of them were a lot more 'wild' than Wolf—but they thought like children. Take a toy away from a dog and hide it, and he'll act like it never existed. If I hide something Wolf wants, I'd better use a padlock—and then hide the key."

Merry was watching him closely.

"You seem to understand him awfully well," she said.

He shook his head.

"I've only begun to understand a little bit about him. They told me where I found him that he was a wolf, but I didn't really believe that. I thought he might be at best a wolf-dog. But the difference runs too deep. That's why I'm sure now he's a real wolf. I've been hoping someday to run across a place, say a library somewhere, and find out more about wolves. Because even if the library's been broken into, the people who broke into it probably weren't very interested in most of the books there. I might just be able to find some informative books on wolves and read up on them. But you know, it's like the sharpening of those two edges of that doubled-bladed ax head. There hasn't been any place where I could find information about wolves—yet."

"I think Dad might be able to tell you something," Merry said thoughtfully. "We used to stop at a customer a little farther west and south of here, before we stopped going over the mountains, who owned some wolves. I never saw them myself. But Dad saw them."

"Why didn't you?" Jeebee asked.

"The man was a little crazy, I think," Merry answered. "He didn't want me on his place. He was even a little slow to trust Dad in his house and on his grounds. But he did let Dad in eventually; and Dad got to know him. Then he began leaning on Dad to stay a day or two with him. Evidently he was hungry for company but didn't trust anyone."

"I'm not surprised," Jeebee murmured.

"Dad humored him," Merry went on, "because he bought a lot of things and needed a lot of things. When Dad came back from one visit, he told me about the wolves. The man had them all separated, each one to a cage. Three of them, or something like that. Dad said he was trying to breed back for what he said were the original breed of wolves. I remember because the man had a whole library of books on wolves. Dad knew something about them and I remember he told me he argued with this man about keeping them like dogs in a boarding kennel. Dad knows a lot more about things than most people realize, you know."

She looked over at Jeebee.

"And he told me he knew this much about wolves, that they were pack animals and needed company."

"What did the man say?" Jeebee asked.

"Oh, the man said that he'd tried keeping them together but that they fought too much and he got tired of having the local vet sew them up. I know Dad said that he went and hunted through this man's books, some of which he recognized—and actually found one study where wolf puppies that were isolated from other members of the litter began to show symptoms of stress. One even died."

"Doesn't really surprise me," Jeebee said thoughtfully. "As independent as Wolf is, he seems to need company from time to time more than he needs food. One night when we were camped above the interstate—where I first saw your wagon—he came back to camp and was expecting our usual romp. I was preoccupied and ignored him. He acted more desperate than I've ever seen him act when he's gone hungry for a couple of days. Whoever that was Paul talked to does sound crazy. How far from where the wagon is now, would you say that this wolf-man's place is?"

"About two and a half weeks as the wagon travels," Merry answered. "You could ride it probably in a week if you don't want to push your horse; and you shouldn't, of course."

"I'd like to have a look at those books of his," Jeebee said wistfully.

"I don't know if he'd be the kind of person who'd lend them to you. Or even whether he'd let you in," said Merry. "On the other hand, he may have been raided by this time by somebody or other. If they just robbed and ransacked the house but didn't necessarily burn it down, maybe the books would still be there. We haven't seen him for a while, of course."

"I've got to see those books," Jeebee said.

Merry frowned at him for a second, then the frown went.

"Rein up," she said abruptly, checking her horse. Jeebee stopped beside her; and behind them the train of packhorses on the lead rope stopped also.

"Let me see the map."

Jeebee produced the map and handed it over, wordlessly. She unfolded it completely.

"Can you show me where we left the wagon?" she asked.

He leaned over and tapped a faintly marked dot on the map with the pencil. Merry took the pencil from him, studied the map for a moment, and marked a point that looked about a hundred miles southwest by west from where they were now.

"His place is at the end of a box canyon about an hour's ride north of Glamorgan," she said.

He looked at it, like a miser might look at a treasure map.

"That's great," he said to Merry, "thank you!"

She smiled, her whole face lighting up. But then her expression sobered suddenly. She lifted the reins of her mount and rode on a little ahead of him.

CHAPTER 14

Perhaps, thought Jeebee, traveling with Wolf might have made him a better observer and more sensitive to the little signs of body language. But there was something about this business with the map that gave him a definite feeling that Merry had, for a second at least, offered a sort of truce between them. Or if not a truce, at least the signal of willingness to their having a closer association.

He spoke to her back.

"This'll make all the difference, your telling me about this man with the wolves," he said. "When I get back, I'll ask Paul about him. Even if I can't go there now, now that I know where his place is, I can find my way to it later and see if any of his books are there to look at."

Merry reined her horse back until they were side by side.

"It really means a lot to you to know more about wolves—and Wolf?" she said, looking at him.

"It does," Jeebee answered. "As I say, he's a person. And there're as many possibilities in him as there might be in any human being you might know—only one whose language you couldn't quite speak or understand. Also wolves are more like us, socially and in individual character, than I ever realized. It could be that understanding them better could help us understand our own species. The matter of instinct, now—"

He broke off with a feeling he was talking too much.

"Dad'll be glad to tell you about this character, I think," Merry said, after waiting a moment for him to continue. "As I say, people don't understand. Dad's done a lot more studying and knows a lot more about a lot of things than people realize."

"I'd about come to that conclusion on my own." Jeebee was half-afraid of saying the wrong thing and frightening her off, but at the same time he desperately wanted to build some kind of bridge more solidly between them, before they had to go their separate ways.

"You really have?" Merry looked at him and her very bright blue eyes were even brighter with searching. "Hardly anybody does. I didn't expect you would."

"All my life I've been used to having people to talk to who are full of information about things I don't know," said Jeebee. "Actually, a lot of them know, but can't talk. Not their fault, actually. They'd like to communicate but just don't know how. Your father does. I found that out almost from the start."

"You did?" Merry was looking at him, warily.

"Yes," said Jeebee.

"How?" she demanded. When he was slow about answering, she went on. "I mean how did you find out? You say you saw this for yourself. But what showed it to you—before I mentioned it just now, that is?"

Jeebee shrugged.

"Experience," he said. "A number of things. As I said, I'm used to talking to people who know a lot, and a lot of what they know I don't. You get to know the signs. Your father shows them."

"But what signs?"

"I can't tell you," said Jeebee. "In Paul's case, it's the way he answers questions. What he tells. What he decides not to tell. The way he thinks before he speaks sometimes . . . a number of things; but, believe me, I know what I'm talking about. Your father's not only very capable and intelligent, but a very well-read man. Self-educated, I'd think. But he has knowledge."

Merry continued to look at him almost suspiciously.

"No one else that I know of ever picked that up," she said. "That is, not counting a few people who used to know him years ago. But those are all gone, or dead now. What's different about you that you'd understand that?"

Jeebee felt a strange weariness.

"It's part of—" He broke off. "My whole working life, actually—maybe beginning with my parents—I've lived with people who live by and with what they know. It marks them. It's the same sort of marking that makes a teacher look like a teacher after forty years and a doctor look like a doctor and so on and so forth. The signs show, the way they talk and act shows."

"He didn't know about this seed farm," said Merry.

"I only know about it by chance," said Jeebee. "My work put me in contact with somebody who worked for one of the large seed companies, and he offered to show me what such a place looked like. I was in Denver on a sort of vacation at the time, and this place we're going to had a few things he particularly wanted to show me, in the way of crops they were experimenting with. So he took me to it. That's the only reason I know."

"Why did you go?"

"The seed farm was a commercial enterprise, but the social dynamics models I was working on had to consider any factors that might affect distribution of resources, especially food resources."

They rode in silence for a little bit. Merry was no longer looking at Jeebee but thoughtfully forward into the next stand of trees beyond the bit of open country they were now covering.

"Do you know where Dad's heading in the long run?" she said at last, without turning her head.

"I think so," Jeebee answered.

She looked at him quickly.

"Do you? Where's he heading now, then?"

"If he can keep going another twenty years," Jeebee said, "I figure he plans to set up what you might call stations, along the way of this route of his. Places where goods can be safely stockpiled, with already-established, reliable people there. With, say, one person or more to watch over them. Eventually the stations can grow into local outlets for the merchandise he's been carrying himself about the country; and the deliveries of goods will be direct from where he gets them to the stations, instead of to him so he can carry them along the peddling route. The country is going to grow back and he wants to grow back with it.

"By that time," he went on, "Paul'll be in a position of sitting tight somewhere, probably back farther east, getting information from the stations on what they need and arranging to buy it so that it can be sent out to them. Again, he'll have picked the strongest possible place for his headquarters, some community that's growing in strength and beginning to form the nucleus of a new city."

She drew in a deep breath.

"So that's what you think," she said.

"That's what I'm almost certain of," Jeebee answered quietly. He still did not want to scare her off or make her angry. "Your father's operation is a microsystem of resource distribution. In its present form it's pretty much an optimal adaptation to the current state of social organization. In the next twenty years the isolated farmsteads you've been visiting are going to become extended communities—"

"All the better for us," she interrupted.

He held up his hand for a second to check her, and went on.

"Resource demands will change. Your father's enough of a salesman to know that distribution systems will have to change accordingly. Besides, he has to want something better; not only for you but for himself. Particularly as he ages, and it'll not be as easy for him to be on the road like this."

She looked ahead again without responding, and they rode on in silence until the trees closed about them with no more words said.

But the ice had been broken. After a little while she asked him more about his childhood; and he told her, then asked her in turn about hers. It turned out that they both had been isolated children, with people but not of them, because of the movements of their parents or some other situation beyond their control.

They continued to talk more steadily as the day wore on. By the time they stopped, close to sunset, and pegged out the packhorses before starting a fire and settling down for the night, they had come to know a great deal about each other. They were talking like people who had known each other for years.

When the fire had caught strongly on a couple of short ends of wood, Jeebee got down the portable stove from one of the loads the packhorses had been carrying before they unloaded them for the night.

The stove was a smaller duplicate of the one on which they cooked at the wagon. It was metal and consisted of only two compartments; like a miniature chest of drawers with two drawers, one above the other. In the bottom one went the burning coals from the wood of a fire that had been going awhile. Then a lid was lifted to get at the top compartment; and on the sheet of metal that was its bottom, you could heat or cook food as the burning coals below continued to draw draft through the slots cut on either side of the stove, venting them through a higher grilled opening, and heating the metal surface above them.

On this particular evening, they merely reheated the ingredients of a stew, mixed with water from the containers they carried, to make a hot meal. Just before this was ready to eat, Jeebee put in to heat four of the biscuits that had already been cooked back at the wagon and sent along with them. They were Nick's biscuits and they were good.

They had eaten everything but two of the biscuits when Wolf appeared out of the darkness like a magician out of an apparently empty box. One moment he was not there, the next he was coming around the fire smiling, head down, tail wagging. He had learned to avoid the hot metal of the stove; and he came first to Merry, who was closest, and licked at her face when she squatted down. He accepted her petting, and then after a little bit moved on to Jeebee, where he crouched and rolled over on his back.

Jeebee scratched his belly for him.

Wolf got to his feet again and invited them to play, crouching down over his forepaws with his hindquarters in the air. He dodged away as Jeebee reached for him, and tried to get Jeebee to

chase him. Jeebee squatted and sat and Wolf came back to him
for a moment, then romped over to Merry and made play invitations to her.

"He'll wear you out if you try to chase him," Jeebee said.

"I can believe that," said Merry. She talked to Wolf in a low,
soft voice, mainly nonsense words. Wolf whimpered and licked at
her face.

After some minutes of this, going back and forth between
the two humans, Wolf's path brought him right beside the stove.
With a suddenness that was almost too fast for the eye to follow,
he suddenly turned his head, snatched up the two biscuits from
the still-hot top of the stove, where they were keeping warm, and
bolted them down—practically choking in his efforts to growl at
the same time to warn Jeebee and Merry against any attempt to
take the biscuits from him.

Having done this, he wandered over to investigate the packs
from the horses, but they were already on the ground in the
midst of the four horses, who were picketed in a rough circle
around them. The horses drew together at his approach and
looked anything but welcoming. With an air of indifference, he
turned and wandered back to the fire, flopping down on his side,
with his belly toward the heat of it. His eyes watched Merry and
Jeebee sleepily.

"Will he stay now?" Merry asked. There was a gentle look
on her face that Jeebee had never seen there before.

"Overnight, probably," said Jeebee.

They settled down again to their talking by the fire.

It was astonishing, thought Jeebee, how much there was to
know about her. How much he wanted to know about her. He
had not talked at extended lengths like this for a long, long time.
He had had long discussions back at the study group, but they
had not been like what was going on here and now, a close,
warm thing. Not only intellectually, but emotionally, he wanted
it to go on forever. Somewhere along in the talk, Jeebee looked
over and saw there were only the two of them here now. The fire
had died down and darkness now hid the location of the horses.

"Wolf's gone," he said, reaching for a torch made of dry

twigs bound together. "We'd better check the packs. We don't want him tearing them apart."

"Are you sure he'd do that?" Merry asked.

Jeebee nodded. "I think it's instinctive for him to chew things up. That's something else those wolf books might be able to tell me."

He pushed the far end of his torch into the glowing coals of the fire and they blazed up almost immediately. By its light they went back together to examine the packs and horses. The horses were alert and all facing in another direction. But nothing seemed to have been touched.

They were about halfway back to the fire when Jeebee's torch reached the water-soaked end that made its handle and burned itself out. Merry stumbled in the abrupt darkness and blundered against Jeebee, who reached out to catch her automatically.

He was suddenly holding her, and without thought, without any conscious plan of any kind, he found himself tightening his arms around her; and a moment later finding her lips in the darkness and kissing them.

She shoved against him, in an attempt to break away, but the effort did not last. It died before her full strength tore her loose.

She stood for a long second, merely letting herself be kissed. Then, slowly, Jeebee felt her arms closing around his own back and holding him to her. Then she was kissing back.

For a long moment they held together. Abruptly, with a furious push, she broke loose completely from his arms, turned, and stumbled rapidly over the night-hidden ground toward the fire. He followed slowly.

When he stepped once more into the open firelight of the little clearing where they had settled for the night, she was standing on the other side of the dying fire with her back to him. He stopped, not knowing what to do or what to say.

Neither one of them spoke. The fire crackled and sparks flew up between them, toward the stars.

"Well," said Merry in a thick voice, "now you know!"

"Know what?" Jeebee said dazedly. What he had done was not like him. But her reaction had been equally unexpected.

"That I'm just as human as you are!" Merry said, still without turning around. "Damn you, stay away from me, or I'll kill you."

Jeebee was lost in his own inexperience and bewilderment. He did not understand her and he did not understand himself. He was lost. Only, he realized he had wanted to give in to his own impulsive action of a moment before for a long time now.

"If that's what you want," he said numbly.

"That's what I want!" said Merry, still talking to the dark woods in front of her. "You're leaving us in a few days!"

"You could come with me," said Jeebee, in spite of himself and all Nick had said, suddenly reckless.

"I can't leave the wagon," she said fiercely. "You know that! Just like you know I don't have a chance to stay anywhere or meet anyone. You know!"

"It isn't that," said Jeebee, not exactly sure himself what he was talking about, but protesting against the emotion in her voice rather than the words she was saying. "I just—"

"You just go your way and I'll go mine!" Merry turned around and looked at him through the firelight. "I mean that. I mean every word of it!"

Jeebee shook his head, not in denial but simply because he could think of nothing else to do. He sat down cross-legged on his side of the fire, as if to appease her by not seeming to stand over her, in spite of the space and fire between them. She turned aside without a word, went to their supplies, and put a fresh, homemade, and traded-for candle into the lantern she had brought with her, then set it aside and went to her sleeping bag on its air mattress. She sat down, took off her boots but nothing else, and lay down on her side in the sleeping bag, zipping it up tightly.

Jeebee was left sitting on the ground and staring into the fire. He sat staring for a long time, finding no answer to anything there—or anyplace else for that matter.

CHAPTER 15

In the next five days it took them to find the experimental seed farm, Merry never came within six feet of Jeebee. On his part, he was careful to make no move that would seem as if he was trying to intrude into that zone of privacy she had established around herself. In all other ways she acted as if the moment with Jeebee had never taken place. She ignored it so successfully and completely that Jeebee found himself at times almost doubting that it had happened. Only the continuing space between them testified to the fact that it had.

They avoided the small town of Wayne itself, when they came close at last to their destination, just as they had avoided all other dwellings or evidence of human habitation on the rest of the trip. Jeebee's map included enough landscape features to plot a point-to-point course that intersected the major east-west highway through Wayne several miles west of the town. Merry had wondered why they hadn't headed directly for Wayne, and Jeebee explained that since they were most likely to miss it in any event, it would save time if they knew for certain whether they'd erred to the east or to the west. Comfortably west of the town and its possible inhabitants, they could circle north and zigzag until they hit the seed farm.

They circled the invisible location of Wayne accordingly, and their zigzagging eventually brought them to the seed farm. They almost walked through a corner of its land without realizing it. Only the fact that it was open territory made them stop and look more closely. Some young bushes and immature saplings masked even this openness to a certain extent; but when they checked, it became clear that between and around this heavier vegetation were what had been organized plantings.

Working around it, they came to identify plots that had been planted with one kind of seed or another—areas in which the rowed stalks of plants even now towered above the weeds of late spring. The plots varied from something like ten to eighty acres in size and were separated one from another by open areas where only weeds flourished.

"I was told these were buffer zones," Jeebee explained to Merry. "They marked off one experimental area from another, and they also acted as roads, in effect, on which harvesting and other machinery could get at the plots."

Eventually they came to what seemed to be the only building on the property. It had been visible from some distance, because it was not a small structure. But like Wolf, like all people nowadays, they made any approach to a strange structure cautiously.

It was a large building of iron, with a corrugated metal roof and metal siding. It was about a hundred and fifty feet long and as high as the average barn. From a distance it looked untouched; and after examining it through their binoculars with as much wariness as Wolf, himself, might have shown, they decided to wait a night. It would be wise to see if there was any light or movement around it after dark.

So they camped in some trees at the edge of the open land, and during the night hours took turns keeping a watch on it. But nothing showed to indicate that anyone was there, so with the first predawn light to aid them, they went up to it and found it deserted. The heavy metal doors of a loading dock stood slightly ajar, indicating that the place had been left alone for some time; leaves and other windblown trash had piled up at the bottom of the opening.

The doors had evidently not been moved in some time and

were hard to move. But they got them apart enough so that they could squeeze through to the inside.

Windows high in the wall, most of them still unbroken, let light into the interior.

It was a dusty, dusky sort of light. But as their eyes adjusted, it became as useful as full daylight for their purposes. They found sacks full of seed stacked near the further end of the building, which held another loading dock. Before this, inside, was a large hopper through which Jeebee remembered the already-gathered seed had been moved to be winnowed and cleaned. The sacks bore tags with dates in late August of the previous year. But the only identification of the seed itself seemed to be a letter followed by four numbers, followed by a date of the previous year.

One-year-old seed could be used; but how to tell which kind to take?

Jeebee and Merry looked about some more. There was a large, empty area in front of huge metal doors on rollers at one end of the building. Jeebee thought he remembered large machinery having been parked there, harvesters and planters. But there were no machines here now. Possibly they had been taken away somewhere back when the world had first started to fall apart. Maybe they had never been kept here on a regular basis.

There was also one dusty room, a cubicle built into a corner near the docks. It contained a couple of large metal desks, four filing cabinets, and a number of shelves with labeled glass specimen cases of seeds upon them and arranged in no particular order. The labels were marked in some form of symbols that neither Merry nor Jeebee could interpret. But on one wall there was a large map showing an area divided into rectangular sections, which drew Jeebee's attention immediately.

As he stepped closer to it he saw that the map was actually a paper or plastic sheet about eight feet long and four feet from top to bottom. Over it there was a pane of glass, on which lines had been drawn and notations had been made, possibly by some type of crayon. Like the letter and number on the tags, they were indecipherable.

"I think the best thing we can do," Jeebee said at last, "is head out into the fields themselves and simply go looking for a plot or field of healthy volunteers."

"Volunteers?" Merry echoed.

"That's what I was told they call domesticated plants like these that're left alone and simply reseed themselves, and come up in a second crop without any human attention."

Accordingly, they went out and began their search. Jeebee was grateful for the horses, because they had a good deal of area to cover. Luckily the markers about the seed farm were still in place, not only those identifying the various fields of a certain experimental type of plant, but the ones marking the corridors of ground that spaced these fields apart. They started with corridor number one and went progressively through the rest, beginning at the end where the building was and going to the very edge of the farm itself.

Jeebee had half counted on his memory to point him toward the fields of wheat where genetic experiments were being tried out. It did not.

"Are you sure they actually were still experimenting with disease-resistant winter wheat?" Merry asked, after they had been up and down between the fields for several hours.

"I can't be sure, of course," said Jeebee, "but it doesn't seem to make sense that they'd give up on it." He waved his hand at the field on their left that they were just passing. It was a field of thin, green stalks, already at some height, but powdered with what looked like a gray dust. "That's what we don't want to get," he told her, "powdery mildew. If we can just find a stand of healthy, green volunteers, we'll know we're home free. It's too bad we aren't here a little later in the year when we could actually harvest some of the seeds ourselves. But there's a good chance, if we find a healthy field that's reseeded itself and doing well, we'll just take its code number. Any sacks back there in the building with the same code on their tags ought to be good bets to hold healthy, genetically resistant seeds."

It was well past noon when at last they found a field of thick-standing green wheat stalks about knee-high.

Jeebee reined in at a corner of the field. The stalks were

feathery, green, and almost happy looking in comparison to the stunted gray-dusted stems they had found until now.

"Look at that!" Jeebee waved at the healthy young plants. "That's what we've been looking for. Now, if we can just find the signboard for this field and get the code number off it."

"That shouldn't be too much trouble, as long as the sign's still standing," said Merry. "We just have to ride around the edge until we come to it."

And so they did; and so, finally, they located the signboard.

"G-4370A," Jeebee read off the sign. "I think I can remember that. Do you think we ought to write it down?"

"I am," Merry answered. Jeebee looked over at her and saw her using a pencil in a small, pocket notebook. "Let's get back to that building and start looking for the sacks with matching tags."

They went. Once back in the building, the hunt through the sacks, through the dust and the dimmed light, was almost as frustrating as their hunt had been through the fields. But eventually Merry found what they were after.

"G-4370A!" she said. "Jeebee, they're here!"

He had been examining the tags on sacks about fifteen feet away. He hurried to her side and studied the tag.

"Looks beautiful, doesn't it?" Merry said with a grin.

Jeebee grinned back.

"All we have to do now," he said, "is load the packhorses and head back. Not all of this grain will sprout, probably. It's a full year old. But most ought to do very well for whoever plants it."

So they did. They had six packhorses to load; and when the job was done, they were dusty and itchy, as well as worn out from their work. But they were infinitely cheerful—and more than this had happened to them. The distance Merry had been maintaining from Jeebee had evaporated. They had worked closer and closer, until effectively all barriers had dissolved between them.

The first three nights out they both slept like the dead, each in their separate sleeping bags. The fourth night Jeebee found himself slow to fall asleep, although Merry had dropped right off. He found himself lying by the fire and watching her unmoving sleeping bag molded by her figure within it. A great deal of understanding had made itself manifest in him these last few days. He realized that more than the work had brought them together. Tacitly they had both acknowledged what they shared. He knew that now if he went over to Merry in her sleeping bag, she would not push him away.

That much of the battle was over. They were both ready to belong to each other and they both knew it. Nonetheless he lay still where he was. Because she had been right.

It was the time of iron years that had descended upon the world, binding people to paths they must follow whether or not they wished to do so. Just as Wolf had been bound by the instinctive part of him, which had told him not to go down into an unknown place like the root cellar. Come what might, they must be what they were. They must do what they had to do. And what must be borne must be borne whether they liked it or not. The only control they had over the situation was the manner in which they bore it.

Merry had been right. Jeebee must leave and she must go on. Theoretically, there was no reason why they could not meet again next year. But practically, the chances were slim. In this different world, two people who parted had much less chance of coming back together again than formerly. Many things could happen to either one of them or both to prevent their meeting again.

The situation came down at last to their making what they had to bear as easy as possible. Better they stayed apart, forgot each other, and looked elsewhere. Things would be easiest in the long run if they had a minimum of memories to forget.

So, he would stay here. He would fall asleep here, as she had fallen asleep over there; and they would go back to the wagon, separate but apart, knowing that there was no help for it, no way of having it any different. Like Wolf, they had choice only within limits.

In some strange way their silent mutual understanding that they both wanted each other and could not have each other had brought them closer together than Jeebee could remember being with anyone else in his life. In those days in which they rode back to the wagon with the collected seed, they rode side by side in silence for most of the time, simply because there was no need to talk. It was as if some invisible current flowed back and forth between them and they were joined by that beyond the need for words.

They reached the wagon at last just at twilight and were welcomed by both Paul and Nick, standing just outside it to watch them ride up.

Wolf, who had not been visible to them all day, came trotting in almost on their heels. The dogs of the wagon came out to meet Wolf, and for the first time Jeebee saw him acting almost apologetic toward them, with his ears back and his tail low.

The dogs swarmed all over him. For a moment, as Jeebee and Merry came finally up to Nick and Paul, Jeebee thought that the dogs were likewise being welcoming. They were, but almost in a negative sense. They were swarming around Wolf in a generally antagonistic manner, none of them seemingly giving him a direct challenge, but all of them barking at him and nipping at him from the side or behind. Surprisingly, Greta also joined in this.

Wolf endured this more than objected to it. Only when one or two got too obtrusive did he show any sign of threatening back. Eventually the dogs slowed down their unwelcome attentions, and one by one dropped out of the group that were effectively, it seemed, punishing Wolf for having been away for such a length of time, without touching base with the rest of them.

Later on, quiet was established, the packhorses were unloaded, and the seed grain tucked into storage spaces that had already been made for it, clearly by Paul and Nick rearranging what was already kept in the storeroom.

Both Paul and Nick examined the grain, found it good, and listened with interest through dinner and into the twilight to the story of the going, the coming, and the gathering of the grain.

"I think by next year," Paul said thoughtfully, "we can simply swing that far north and load directly into the wagon."

Merry had done most of the relating, Jeebee only coming in when it got to be a matter of explaining the business of the difference between hybrid and genetic grains and the reason behind the various patterning of the plots and the experimental farms as a whole.

Merry seemed content to let him do this and was quite warm to him in front of her father and Nick; at the same time Jeebee thought that she showed a certain amount of relief at being back at the wagon, with her familiar environment around her. The next day they all, including Jeebee, fell automatically back into their old routines.

The wagon itself moved on, while Jeebee took his turn to be in charge of the horses. Merry, with Nick, worked in the wagon to separate the grain from the chaff with which it had been sacked. Jeebee felt himself caught in a timeless moment in which he could not think about either the future or the past, and right now did not particularly want to think about either.

Eventually, after they had stopped briefly for lunch, which as usual when they were in transit consisted of sandwiches and coffee, Merry took over with the horses and Jeebee went up to take his turn at handling the wagon, while Paul took advantage of the one luxury he allowed himself, which was a brief midday nap while the wagon moved.

Following this nap, Paul came forward and sat down beside Jeebee. However, he made no immediate move to take the reins back out of Jeebee's hands. After a moment he spoke.

"Tomorrow," he said, "we'll turn south. You'll be leaving us then."

"Yes," said Jeebee. There was nothing much else to say.

"We'll stop a little early tonight and have a sort of going-away party," Paul said. "I'll pay you off, and I think you'll be pretty well supplied with what I can give you. Also, we've each one of us got a small, personal gift for you. You'll get those while we're sitting around the fire after dinner, this evening."

Jeebee was startled into glancing at the older man for a moment. Only for a moment, because he could not take his eyes off the road and the horses for longer than that, but his glance was a sharp and questioning one.

"Gifts?" he said. "I haven't been with you . . ." His voice trailed off.

"You've been with us long enough," said Paul. "Anyway, we can do what we want, can't we?"

"Oh. Of course," said Jeebee. "It's just, I wasn't expecting gifts."

"Well," said Paul, producing his pipe, packing it, and lighting it up, "you'll be getting them." He struck a wooden match and held the flame to the tobacco in his pipe, drawing long and hard until the packed shreds were alight.

After a second he spoke again.

"I see you and Merry worked things out," he said.

Jeebee glanced at him again, this time only out of the corner of his eyes, and saw that Paul's gaze was fixed ahead on the horses pulling the wagon.

"Yes," Jeebee said after a moment, unable to think of what else to say.

"I hoped as much," Paul said, still to all appearances talking to the team ahead. "That's one reason I wanted her to go with you."

This time Jeebee didn't glance at him.

"I thought there was no choice," he said. "You couldn't leave the wagon, and Nick—"

"Oh, I could have left." Paul took his pipe out of his mouth, blew a jet of smoke, and glanced up at the few clouds dotting the blue sky ahead of them. "It wouldn't have been as smart as you two going. But Merry could have handled this wagon by herself if she'd ended up having to. She knows all there is to know about it. She still can't handle customers like I can, but most of them know her, and she knows how she ought to deal with them. Nick would work for her. No, if I'd thought it was really best, I could have been the one to go with you. I just thought it was better she did."

Jeebee drove in silence for a few seconds, letting these last words sink into him. Plainly, the silent understanding he and Merry had come to was obvious; at least to her father, and probably to Nick as well.

Jeebee decided to accept the fact.

"It wasn't easy," he said.

"Didn't figure it would be," Paul said, puffing on his pipe. "Most important things aren't."

Jeebee laughed unhappily.

"You're right about that." He glanced ahead and up at the clouds, himself. They seemed to be moving, following the way along with the wagon, although he knew that this was only an illusion. Still, for the moment, seeing them seem to move, it was as if the wagon was holding its place while the earth turned underneath it, so that once he left it and those riding it, the rotating world itself would carry him away from them.

CHAPTER 16

It was both strange and hard for Jeebee to admit to himself that he had come to feel so close, not merely to Merry, but to Paul and Nick. Close enough so that he was torn at the thought of parting with them. It was even harder and stranger yet to accept the fact that they might have become fond of him in reciprocal measure.

But evidently that was the way it was. His whole life had taught Jeebee to trust his perceptions. Faced with a problem—physical, mental, or emotional—his instinctive reaction was to take it apart and find out why it was the way it was, as he might have done with an unfamiliar mechanism that was not working, like the nonworking alarm clocks of his childhood.

This need to dismantle and understand was instinctive in him. As a result, he faced the fact that the present times were simply those in which friendships could come more strongly and more suddenly than they had in the earlier, more technological years.

At the same time it was part of what they all had to do for survival's sake. He and Merry could not stay together. Paul could not give him in trade anything he had not earned or paid for, no matter how much the other had come to like him. There was a point now at which charity became unnecessary sacrifice, and unnecessary sacrifice became self-destruction.

Still, as they rode now through the hours before stopping, he and Paul discussed what Jeebee would take by way of payment for his gold and the seed he had brought back. Jeebee had not realized that he would have to make choices. He could have a horse to ride and a packhorse. Beyond that Paul strongly suggested that he take traps to support an appearance as a trapper, if nothing else. That would at least identify him as someone other than a raider.

"No," Jeebee had said, "there'd be too much risk for Wolf if I started setting traps around."

He had seen the twin jaws of the metal traps, with their offset teeth and stiff springs, and the part of him that was likely to feel for anyone and anything had imagined itself as an animal with a leg caught by those jaws.

"Suit yourself," Paul told him, "but I'll tell you one thing. I haven't got any cold-weather clothing to trade you. I don't visit my customers during the winter season, and the room I have for goods is limited, so I just don't carry that sort of thing. That means you're going to have to make your own warm clothing. I can give you heavy needles and thread, and instructions on how to tan and use hides. You think you can take it from there?"

Jeebee nodded.

"The thing is," said Paul, "it's you, yourself, who's going to have to produce them when it comes time for them, when the snow and ice season comes. One of the best ways to fit yourself with winter clothes is to use animal pelts, fur and all, and there's only two ways to get them. One is shooting, the other's trapping. Trapping's more practical for you."

"I'll still take my chances shooting," said Jeebee. "What else can you give me?"

It turned out that what Paul was able to give him, not only for the seeds he had gathered with Merry but for the valuable knowledge of the location of the seed farm, were the two horses complete with saddle and packsaddle, bridles, halter ropes, and saddle blankets. Also ammunition, for Jeebee's two rifles, cooking utensils, some light clothing, salt, and bacon. Also, Paul had thrown in a variety of lesser camp supplies.

"Now," Paul wound up, "some of these seeds can be yours. If

they're really designed for northern crops, you'll want to plant a seed source for yourself. If so, and you can meet me along about here, this time each year, with some sacks of clean, good seed, we can make a regular business out of trading for it. Or if it turns out I can get rid of either the seeds or gold for more than I think, I'll make up the difference to you next time we trade. Fair enough?"

"Fair enough," Jeebee said.

They pulled into camping position by the side of the road while there was still a good two hours of daylight left. Jeebee unharnessed the team and put the horses from it back with the rest of the string that Merry was settling for the night. Then, with both Merry and Nick in attendance as well as Paul, both his saddle and packhorse were picked out.

Jeebee had known nothing about horseflesh three months before. He knew only a little bit more now; but he had picked up enough to appreciate that he was getting two good animals. His riding horse was a large bay, and his packhorse was a small but sturdy-legged black-and-white-splashed mare, calm and agreeable. She had been one of the packhorses on their seed trip.

Jeebee knew of, if not all about her. Her name was Sally. The bay, Brute, was one of the wagon's horses he had never ridden. He saddled Brute now with the saddle that Paul produced, to try both of them out. It was a good saddle, he thought. But Brute clearly had a mind of his own and a somewhat uncertain temper. However, he, too, was good in all the essential ways. Jeebee rode him around for some five minutes, ending up putting him into a full gallop back along the roadside for a hundred yards or so before turning around and coming back to the wagon. Brute was both fast and strong, and his wind was good.

"I like him," said Jeebee. "In fact, I like them both."

"They're good horses!" said Merry.

"I figured so," Jeebee said hastily. "I just thought you'd like to know that I liked them."

"Always good to hear that," Paul answered.

They unsaddled Brute, gathered all of Jeebee's goods and possessions together in one spot near the front of the wagon, and Nick got started on planning dinner.

Meanwhile Paul dug back in among his trade goods and came up unexpectedly with a bottle of sour-mash bourbon and four glasses.

"Where did you get this?" Jeebee asked. He knew that Paul did not like to be questioned about where his goods came from. He had picked up that much almost by osmosis, in the time he had been with the wagon. But the words were out before he could stop them.

He added, a little lamely, "Liquor seemed to be the first thing everybody was tearing places apart for when things started to go to pieces."

Paul climbed down from the wagon with the bottle and began to mix drinks in the glasses, roughly half whiskey and half water, from the evaporation-cooled water bag hanging to one side of the front seat.

"I've got homemade stuff back there, if you'd like it better," he said. "I just figured since this was a special occasion, it needed something special in the way of a drink."

Jeebee had not known that Paul drank alcohol. But it turned out that he did, with moderation. Jeebee and Nick took a couple of glasses. Merry took a small one.

Jeebee had never thought of alcohol in the past unless he suddenly found himself in a situation where he was expected to drink it, and had never really enjoyed the taste of it. But for some reason, now it tasted good to him. Somehow, standing out by the side of the road in the late-afternoon sun, with the ruined freeway stretching in both directions and at the end of a day in the open, the combination of whiskey and the evaporation-cooled water from the bag combined in a sensation that was pleasant and memorable in his mouth.

Nick came out of the wagon, evidently having decided to do his cooking inside. He was carrying the usual four metal folding chairs, and he set them up on the shoulder of the road. The four of them sat there, enjoying their drinks and watching the afternoon wane, like four people in a backyard before civilization had vanished as the Roman Empire and others like it had done.

Every so often Nick would get up and leave them, to go

back inside the wagon to his cooking. But he was never gone long.

It was a curious, almost golden time. Jeebee found himself thinking that if Wolf had been there and lying silent close by, then everything that was worthwhile in his present existence would be caught in this one temporary but timeless moment. He smiled a little ruefully at his own perfect fantasy of a scene. If Wolf had indeed been there, he would not have been lying quietly—not with all the new and uninvestigated things around. He would have been shredding the folding chairs, leaving irreparable tooth scars on Jeebee's new possessions, and generally disrupting the serenity of the evening. Sometimes the best thing about companioning with Wolf was his absence.

But Wolf had left again during the night just past, and not come back yet. Eventually, the sun set, and they started their evening fire close to the wagon, but safely enough away so that there was no danger of setting anything on fire. Nick brought out the dinner.

It was a remarkable surprise. Nick had made a soup, followed by a small roasted chicken and skinned roast potatoes.

"Where did the chicken come from?" Jeebee asked when they were all at the table beginning to eat it.

"Came from a can," said Nick, smiling. The smile was a sly one. "Not many of them got sealed up whole like that, in cans. I mean, sealed up, cooked whole, and after you get them out, you can recook them. They were restaurant goods, mostly. I've had this one tucked away for a while, now. I had some wine, too, but it went sour. You can't keep wine in a wagon that jolts around like this."

"It doesn't matter," said Jeebee. They were all drinking plain water now, one after another having ceased to add the whiskey to their glasses. "It couldn't be better than this."

"He's right, Nick," Merry said to the older man.

Nick's V-shaped face creased in an even deeper smile.

"Special occasion," he said again. "There's dessert, too."

The dessert turned out to be a sort of rich pudding, very black and crumbly, with a thick, buttery-tasting white sauce or icing on it—it was impossible to say which class the topping fell into. At any rate it was very sweet and filling. To Jeebee, who weeks before had lived with hunger, it seemed to be the best dessert he had ever tasted.

After dinner Nick cleared the dinner trays without handing them to Jeebee to wash.

They sat at the table by the fire, drinking coffee, with Paul, in addition, puffing on his pipe. On the open air the smell of the tobacco was fragrant in Jeebee's nostrils. It was only after a while longer than Jeebee would have thought it necessary for Nick to wash and store the dinner dishes that the smaller man appeared back out at the fire, carrying something wrapped in cloth and looking a little like a board close to two feet long and four or five inches wide.

He sat down and laid it on Jeebee's knees. Paul produced a small similarly cloth-wrapped package from his pocket and Merry produced apparently from nowhere a fairly bulky object about eight to ten inches by six, also cloth-wrapped and neatly tied with ribbon.

"Gift time," said Merry.

Jeebee stared at the three packages.

"*Little* gifts?" he said.

"A bit larger maybe than little," said Paul, complacently puffing smoke.

The three packages had been laid out, apparently for him to pick up himself. Now it became a question of who he might offend if he picked them up in the wrong order.

After a moment's thought he came to the conclusion that the only safe thing was to open Merry's package first.

"Merry," he said as he started to carefully try to untie the ribbon, "I don't know what I can say—"

He interrupted himself. The ribbon that he had tried to untie had slid itself down into a knot.

"Oh, just break it," said Merry.

It seemed like a brutal way to handle a package so carefully wrapped, but he pulled on the ribbon and it snapped. After that, the cloth came off, revealing a pair of Bausch and Lomb Elite eight-by-forty binoculars, under an inner wrapping of cardboard that had disguised their shape. The packaging had been deliberately deceptive.

Paul frowned a little.

"Those are your binoculars, Merry," he said.

She looked at him.

"And I'm giving them to Jeebee," she replied evenly.

Paul puffed on his pipe and said nothing.

Wonderingly, Jeebee picked up the binoculars and put them to his eyes, looking off at the horizon where the moon had just risen. They were, indeed, a perfect match for the binoculars Paul had lent him and taken back again. A magnificent gift.

"You shouldn't give me these," he said to Merry.

"Well, I have," Merry said. "Open the other gifts."

Jeebee reached for the small package that Paul had laid on the table. In this case the cloth wrapping had not disguised it and merely snapping the string about it and unfolding the cloth revealed to Jeebee what his finger had told him he might—which was a very small revolver.

"It's a Smith and Wesson .38 Bodyguard Airweight," said Paul. "I'll fit you out with ammunition for it before you leave."

It was a revolver that would fit into the palm of his hand. Jeebee had heard of very small automatics, but never of revolvers, this size. It had a shroud over the hammer to keep it from catching on clothing. It looked, in fact, almost like a toy. But very plainly, it was not.

"It's a boot gun. Stick it down inside the top of your boot and it ought to be out of sight, as well as easy to get at," Paul said around his pipe stem. "It's good for up to about twenty feet. You'd better practice a bit with it—as I say, I'll give you the shells—so that you can get some idea of how it throws. We can do that tomorrow morning before you leave."

Jeebee had been trying not to think that it was tomorrow Paul turned the wagon southward. It was as if a corner of emptiness entered him. As if the wagon was taking everything he knew away from him. He had never thought he would feel like this when the time came.

"And now," said Merry, "Nick's going to pop if you don't get around to opening his gift."

Jeebee came to with a start.

Something about the size and overall shape of Nick's gift had made him feel hesitant—he did not know exactly why. That was at least one of the reasons he had left it until the last, although opening Merry's gift first, because she was the woman, and Paul's second because he was the leader, was only natural.

But now he picked up the small man's gift, which his knees had told him was a little heavier than he would have expected. As heavy in proportion to its large size as the handgun Paul had given him had been light for its smallness.

He opened the last package and found it was two packages inside, one large and one smaller. He opened the smaller and found three items. An ordinary carpenter's hammer, a large pair of pliers, and what looked like a small, iron chisel, but with only a short, thick handle; the whole thing less than five inches in length.

"A hardy!" he said, recognizing the chisellike object from seeing the one like it, stuck chisel-edge-up through a hole in one end of Nick's anvil.

"Right," said Nick, "that, and the hammer are what you can use to start blacksmithing from scratch. Any good solid piece of steel will do for an anvil. You can find that yourself; and you can build your own forge and bellows. But you need the hammer to beat the metal with, the hardy to cut it with when it's heated enough, and the pliers to hold it until you can forge yourself a regular pair of tongs. Also, the pliers can be used as pliers. Lots of times a pair of pliers can come in handy—open the other package."

The last words came out abruptly, cutting off Jeebee's attempt to thank the smaller man. Jeebee took the hint and opened the larger package.

What tumbled out onto the tabletop, inside a newly sewn leather sheath, was a knife almost large enough to be a small sword. It had the general shape of a bowie knife; and when he pulled it from its scabbard, it was indeed a bowie.

It had a five-inch handle made from disks of leather impregnated with some sort of glue that left them as hard as the plastic he remembered from the world, now lost behind them all in time, and tightly compressed between the cross guard and a heavy brass pommel that screwed to the end of the tang and counterbalanced the massive, twelve-inch steel blade. It had been carefully and evenly honed from the hilt to the upswept tip and then back along the recurved top edge to a thick strip of brass that had been silver-soldered to the back of the blade. It caught the firelight and flashed in his eyes as he turned it over, feeling the weight of it. It was a precious and lethal gift intended for only one purpose, and that was to do damage to any living thing at which it was directed, just like the pistol Paul had given him.

It was curious, he thought, how natural these warlike gifts seemed, and this strangely different scene, from his surroundings even a year ago. He now sat by an open fire in the open air surrounded by darkness with two deadly weapons and a pair of binoculars. These were not the sort of things anyone would have gifted him with before, except perhaps the binoculars, and even these were far more powerful and expensive than any pair even his closest friend might have given him in that earlier time.

"Feel the edge," said Nick, directing Jeebee's attention back to the knife. "No, use the ball of your thumb, very lightly, and just stroke it over the edge, away from you."

Jeebee did so. The edge had been feathered to a razor sharpness.

"You want to keep it like that," said Nick. "You'll probably never use it, but just in case. Meanwhile, go right on carrying that other knife you've got hanging at your belt, and use that for any ordinary need you've got. Except for practicing with it—and I'll show you how to practice before you leave tomorrow—this new knife of yours, you'll hope it'll never leave its sheath. I'll tell you about that, too, tomorrow."

"Thank you, Nick. Thank you all," Jeebee said, looking around at them. "I don't know how to thank you. But Nick—"

He turned back to the little man.

"Where did you get this?"

"I traded for it quite a time back," Nick said. "It wasn't in the shape you see it now when I got it. It had been made as part of a collection set. It's supposed to be a pretty fair replica of the knife Jim Bowie gave his name to, but near as I could ever find out, nobody knows exactly what the 'original' Bowie knife really looked like. For that matter he probably had half a dozen knives like this of different sizes and each one made some different from the others.

"Anyway, it was a collection piece, but it had been used for everything under the sun, including to chop kindling. It'll do that, too, but I don't want you to use it for that. I've put a fighting edge on it, instead of the chisel edge it had when I got it. So it may look sturdy as hell, but don't cut branches with it, don't sharpen sticks with it, and above all don't drop it on anything hard. I've got a sharpening stone for you to take along with it, and I'll teach you how to use it. With some practice you'll be able to touch up the edge, but if you nick it or have to rebevel it, you'll spend half a lifetime looking for a stone that's long enough to do the job."

"Believe me," said Jeebee sincerely, "I'll take good care of it."

"You don't know anything about using a knife, do you?" Nick stared across the table at him.

Jeebee shook his head.

"Good," said Nick, "better that way. If you don't know how, you're not as likely to try to use it and get yourself killed."

Jeebee stared at him.

"What're you giving it to me for, then?" he asked.

"Tell you tomorrow. Well—one thing I will tell you today. If you ever do have to use it, remember just one thing only. Forget everything else. Just remember to let the weight and the edge work for you. Go up through the belly. Aim for the balls—excuse me, Merry, the crotch—and you've got your best chance of ending in the belly. You got that?"

Jeebee nodded.

"What you really want to do is go up under the breastbone. If you go in deep enough there, you'll hit the heart; or you'll cut a main artery. The blade's long enough, but you want to be up underneath the ribs. You've got to be good—and lucky—to go between the ribs. Never try that. I'll show you in the morning."

CHAPTER 17

Shortly after dawn—and before breakfast, since Nick had said that Jeebee would learn faster on an empty stomach—and even if he didn't learn faster, be lighter on his feet—the two men stood outside the wagon parallel with and facing each other. They stood about five feet apart, Jeebee just having finished some target practice with the little handgun Paul had given him. As Paul had predicted, it threw high and to the left, but it pointed naturally, and by the end of the session Jeebee was grouping his shots with satisfying consistency.

"Stick it down into your boot," said Paul, after.

"You'll just have to do a lot of practicing and get used to it," he said. "Do a lot of dry firing, but always have it loaded with empty cartridge casings when you do. Saves wear on the firing pin. If it didn't have a shroud, I'd probably suggest that you let the hammer rest on an empty chamber, but with only five rounds you'll probably want all the firepower it's got to offer. Now, reload it and put it down in your boot—no, in the boot with the bowie strapped outside it."

Wondering a little, Jeebee obeyed. He was now wearing calf-high horseman boots that had been given him and that came up within about four inches of his knee. The sheath holding the big knife was strapped to the outside of the boot.

"Now, maybe you're beginning to understand?" said Nick. "You reach down and everybody's going to think you're going for that big knife when you're really going for the pistol in your boot. You might even be lucky, with somebody holding another gun on you, and a second person tries to take the bowie from you—because it's so big and it attracts so much attention—but never thinks to look inside the boot for a holdout gun."

Jeebee nodded.

"All right," Nick said to him, "now, you can untie those thongs holding the bowie handle to your leg, pull the knife out, and let me see how you stand with it."

Jeebee untied the thongs, pulled the knife, and stood up with it, feeling a little foolish with the huge weapon in his hand.

Nick looked at him and nodded. "Just as I thought," he said, "you don't even know how to stand, do you?"

"No," Jeebee answered.

"All right," said Nick, "we'll start at the very beginning, then. To begin with, remember this big knife is there mainly for camouflage. Your real weapon is that little revolver down in your boot. But it just might happen that for some reason a revolver won't do it for you, or isn't there, or something like that. So you have to use a knife. If that's the case, here are the rules."

A knife considerably smaller than Jeebee's suddenly appeared in Nick's hand.

"The first rule of knife fighting," said Nick, "is—don't. If you think there's any possibility of somebody pulling a knife on you, get out of there—wherever there is. Best way to avoid something like that is to make sure it doesn't start in the first place.

"The second rule is," he went on, "if you see someone standing the way I'm standing, run. Or get out any way you can if you haven't already. That's because the man you'll be looking at knows something about how to use his blade. Look at how I'm standing."

Jeebee looked. Nick was standing full face on to him with his feet almost parallel. The left foot was a little behind the right and the stance had the feet slightly spread. Nick's left arm that was not carrying a knife was bent at the elbow up and out in front of him, and almost mimicking its position was his right arm and fist that held the knife, blade up and with the point forward toward Jeebee.

"Now," said Nick, "if there's no way you can get away from someone who stands like this or this"—Nick suddenly reversed his grip and held it like an icepick with the blade lying along his wrist—"and is forcing a fight on you, the only advantage you're likely to have is the length of your knife. Most good knife fighters like the quickness of a short blade, but a long blade gives you reach. Make it work for you. Stand back and make him come to you. Don't wait for a vital spot; attack whatever part of his body comes into range. If you cut his knife hand, the fight's half-won, but if he's standing like I am, chances are he'll try to draw your attack or tangle up your knife with his empty hand. You can limit his options by circling to his right—that is, the side that's holding the knife. But if his empty hand gets too close, cut it. Do whatever you have to do to keep him away from you. If a man with a small knife gets in close, range is on his side. He could cut you three, maybe four or five times before you could get that big bowie moving. So use the pommel. It's not just for decoration and balance. It's a weapon. Hit him in the face, the temple, even his knife hand.

"If you cut him up enough, he'll slow down. Cuts kill, but they don't kill quickly. That's why a knife has a point. So remember what I told you last night. Go for the belly—but aim low and angle up. If you go straight in and he scoots his hips back, you'll either miss or catch his breastbone on the upsweep. If you aim low, you'll be under the breastbone—which is where you want to be. If he's wearing a lot of clothes, try to go in at a point where the clothes button together, because thick cloth, and especially, thick layers of cloth, can stop a knife blade better than you ever dreamed. So if someone comes at you with a jacket or belt or even a shirt wrapped around his left arm, don't count on being able to cut it.

"All right. Then there's a whole list of other don'ts. Even if you figure you're as good as the man opposite—if you ever get that way, which I hope you don't, for your sake—don't fight the people I'm going to tell you about. One, don't fight anyone my size or smaller, particularly if he's as young or younger than you are, unless of course he's a kid. Even then, even if he's a kid, you could be in trouble. The reason is, if he's smaller, chances are his reflexes are faster than yours.

"Second, for the same sort of reason, don't try to take on anyone a lot bigger than you. He just maybe could be enough bigger and heavier so that he can absorb enough punishment to get to you. And if he can get to you, chances are he can either kill you or do real damage to you even if he dies for it. Don't get into a fight at all if you think the other man's got friends around. They don't even have to step in and help him. You could just be backing up and find a chair in your way where there wasn't a chair before, to say nothing of being actually tripped. Carry the big knife in all kinds of weather, so it looks like you're used to using it, but try to forget you've got it, except for cleaning and sharpening it when you think it needs it. Otherwise, just put it out of your mind. It's like a life preserver on a luxury liner; it's there, but ninety-nine-point-nine percent of the time you don't even need to think about it. Just so you shouldn't never think about using this knife until there's no other way than that. Remember that forearm knife rig I showed you, your first day at the wagon? Well, this bowie's just another rig. Remember that."

"I will," said Jeebee.

The knife disappeared from Nick's hand as magically as it had appeared.

"Now," he said, "if you'll forget all about the revolver and the Bowie, I've got some sticks here; and I'll run you through just a few things that might help you with real knife trouble. Take one of the longer sticks. We'll use them like knives."

The sticks were about as thick and round as broomstick handles. Jeebee picked one that was about sixteen inches long and, standing at a little more than arm's length from Nick, tried to imitate the other's stance.

"If you want to make best use of the longer blade," said Nick, "you probably shouldn't stand like me. Let your right foot lead. You won't be able to make much use of your empty hand, but it'll give you another six inches of reach. All right, that's better. Come at me, then."

"No," Jeebee said cautiously, "you come at me first."

"Good. You remembered," said Nick, "let the other man make the first move." He was still talking when suddenly Jeebee found himself tripped by something hooked behind his right ankle. He fell heavily on his back, and a moment later one of Nick's boots was pinning down his arm that held the stick, while the other one rested lightly with its boot edge against his Adam's apple.

"I thought you were going to show me about knife fighting!" Jeebee said.

"That is part of knife fighting," said Nick. "It's your 'third' hand. I find people remember that part of it better if I simply show them before I tell them about it. Do you remember what I did just now?"

Jeebee had to stop and remember, as if he was rerunning a memory tape in his head. He remembered Nick suddenly dropping toward the ground, then he had been tripped—that was all that came to mind.

He said as much. Nick laughed.

"Watch," he said, "I'll do it slowly for you."

He took the weight of his one boot off Jeebee's arm and the touch of his other boot off Jeebee's throat and stood back.

"I did this," he said.

He dropped vertically suddenly until he was squatting on one leg. The other leg snaked out and swung in an arc at full length before him, the toe of the boot turned inward.

"That tripped you up," Nick said. "Then it was simply a matter of stepping on your arm and on your throat. If I'd wanted to, I could have crushed your throat and everything would've been over right then and there."

"I'm going to have to practice getting down and doing that leg swing," Jeebee said ruefully.

"Practice all you want," said Nick, "but remember that that's just one thing you can do. When you're fighting, a knife is just one of the things you fight with. Most people forget that, just like most people think that if you point a gun at them, it's all over and you might as well give up. Not necessarily. Now, if you're interested, we will work with the actual sticks themselves while we're on our feet."

They practiced for a while with the sticks. Jeebee tried desperately to use his longer arms and stick to keep the stick Nick held from touching him, but he was a constant failure. If they had actually been holding knives, Nick would have killed him a dozen times over.

At the same time, Jeebee's mind was reacting in its usual manner by trying to remember what he was going through and to see some pattern in it. He was just beginning to see what he thought of as that pattern when Nick called a halt.

"Enough for now." Nick reached out with his left hand to take the stick from Jeebee's hand. "You're beginning to get jumpy and poke out blindly. After you leave us, try it the same way you'd try shadowboxing. Just imagine me or somebody coming at you with a knife and imagine what you'd have to do to block him. Let's go to breakfast."

This morning Merry was making the breakfast, and Nick would be washing up afterwards, now that Jeebee was leaving. They ate pancakes and bacon, and after they were done, Merry took off her apron and put her hand on Jeebee's arm.

"Come along," she said, "come on back with me to the horses."

Jeebee swallowed a final syrup-drenched piece of pancake, gulped the last of his coffee from its cup, and got up. The two of them went out of the wagon, climbed down to the ground, and walked together toward the back of it, behind which the horses were picketed.

Merry went briskly, so that he had to stretch his legs to keep up with her. It was almost as if she brought him along with an invisible grip on his ear with her fingers. Behind the wagon, Jeebee saw that tied directly to it was one horse already saddled, and tied to that saddle with a lead rope, another horse, which must be his packhorse, which had only a blanket on its back secured by a strap around its belly.

On the ground next to this horse was a pile of gear ready to travel. Merry took him to it.

"Here you go," she said over her shoulder, "and here's something I particularly wanted you to have."

From a sack, the drawstring of which she had untied, she brought out a ball of dark blue yarn, thick strands, and a couple of long knitting needles stuck through the ball.

"There's a book here, too," she said, rummaging in a small box, and produced it. It was not so much a book as a thick pamphlet, with paper covers. The title *How to Knit* was printed plainly on the cover. She shoved it into his hands.

"You study this now," she said sternly, "and you work with the needles and the yarn. Learn how to knit things for yourself. You'll need them more than you think, and they can be more use to you than anything you can imagine. You'll have all winter long someplace where you've nothing to do but knit, so you might as well start learning now. You'll need socks, sweaters, everything else. Look here!"

From the same box she produced a pair of socks knitted of bright red yarn. They looked enormous, and Jeebee estimated that they would come well up to his knee, if not over it. The feet were very large and the legs were wide. He felt slightly embarrassed, since clearly she had guessed at his feet and leg sizes and had got them wrong.

"I don't think you understand," she said, looking at his face. "When winter comes, you're going to need to wear layers of all kinds of clothes, including three or four pairs of socks. This is the pair that goes outside everything else, that's why I made them so big. I made it exactly according to the diagram and directions on page forty-nine. The first thing you do is try to make another pair of socks just like it; and you can look at this pair to see how close you're coming. Do you understand that?"

"Oh, I see!" said Jeebee. "I . . . thank you. I never thought of anything like this. I'll do just what you say. I'll learn how to knit."

"You'll make a lot of mistakes while you're learning, and there's going to be no one around to help. It'll be you and the book," said Merry. "But if you keep on trying, you'll get to where you can make socks, sweaters—all sorts of things. Mittens too. Don't forget mittens!"

She passed him the pamphlet and dug back into the box, coming up with another paper-bound volume. She shoved it into his hands.

"This," she said. "This will give you instructions on how to skin animals, how to tan the hide, and how to use it making clothing and shoes. Study that, too!"

"I will," he said. The gear that was to go on the back of Sally, the packhorse, was piled on the green plastic groundsheet that could have its edges tied together to protect its contents from rain. He stooped to put what she had just given him into one of the loading bags that had room to take it.

Pushing it into one of the bags, he stopped, staring at what was laid out on the groundsheet before him.

"Now," said Merry's voice crisply, "let's see you load Sally and see if you do it right."

He straightened up and looked at her.

"I wasn't supposed to get all this stuff," he said, waving a hand at the items on the groundsheet. "Paul said—"

"He changed his mind," Merry said, still crisply. She looked straight at him. He stared back, his mind fumbling for words he wanted to say to her and finding none.

"Paul only promised . . ." he began at last, unsurely.

"It's that gold of yours," she said, still looking him in the eye as if daring him to argue. "He'd been valuing it at the minimum he could get for it. Instead, he decided to value it for the maximum. There can be a big difference; particularly if he can sell those coins in one of the southern cities that didn't burn itself to the ground, or have everyone in it shoot each other trying to stay alive after the power, water, and food stopped coming in."

"He didn't say anything about changing his mind to me." Even to Jeebee's ears, his own words sounded weak and unconvincing. It was hardly Paul's way to announce his reasons for anything he did, even for a change as enormous as this.

He looked again at what lay on the groundsheet. Besides the

flour, ammunition, blankets, clothes, and other things of relatively small value that Paul had promised him, there were both a
double-bladed and a single-bladed ax, a small wall-supported
tent with a frame of aluminum poles, and a large number of
other kinds of gear that were—from the viewpoint of Jeebee's
survival—unexpected luxuries.

He raised his eyes again to Merry.

"You had something to do with this," he said.

"What makes you think so?"

"I just know you did," he told her. "Paul wouldn't do it on
his own and Nick couldn't make Paul change his mind, even if
Nick wanted to. It had to be you."

For the first time, her direct glance yielded a little. There was
no real change in her expression, but having said what he had
and seeing her standing there, for the moment silent, he was suddenly sure of what he had merely suspected before saying it.

"What did you give—what did you promise to get me all
this?" Jeebee demanded. "I'm not going to take—"

"Nothing!" she said, almost violently. "I didn't give up or
promise anything. Dad understands me. I told him you had to
have these things if you were going to have any chance of staying
alive until we come back next year."

"And he went along with you—just like that?"

"All right!" she said. "I told him I'd give you my own things
if he wouldn't, and he said in that case he didn't have a choice,
because he'd just have to replace them so I'd still have them. Yes,
I know it was a hard thing to do to him. He loves me, Jeebee. All
this—"

She waved her hand at the wagon.

"—all this, he did for me. I didn't give him any choice in this
case, no. But I'd do what I did again in a minute. I tell you, I
want you to stay alive."

They stood staring into each other's eyes for a long, painful
minute. Then Jeebee stooped to the pile on the groundsheet and
began the process of loading the packhorse. Merry had always
taken charge of packing the horses when the two of them had

gone after the seed. Even when she had allowed Jeebee to help, it had been strictly under her supervision.

Merry had explained that not only was each horse best off loaded with the optimum amount the animal could carry, some carried their loads best when those loads were arranged in a way that suited the particular horse. Jeebee had followed orders, listened, and to his surprise, ended up knowing more than he had ever suspected there was to know about loading a packhorse.

In this case, he could take it for granted that Merry had not supplied him with too heavy a load for Sally to carry comfortably, and he remembered that Sally had a ticklish spot high on her left side, which was best off without having anything pressing directly on it.

As he worked, he waited to hear Merry correcting him in what he was doing. But she said nothing. When at last he had put everything on the horse's back, covered the load completely with the groundsheet, and secured it all with rope in a diamond hitch, he heard something that was almost a small sigh behind him.

He turned and stood facing Merry once more.

"It's all right," Merry said, after a moment. "You'll do all right. Just remember, she can carry perhaps another fifty pounds comfortably for a full day, at a walking pace—but no more, for day-in, day-out travel."

They were once more looking unhappily into each other's eyes.

"You don't have to go," Merry said, finally. The words came almost as if forced from her.

"Yes," Jeebee said with a tight throat, "you know I do. And there's no hope at all. . . ."

His voice ran out.

"I can't leave Dad," she said. "You know that. But you'd be as safe with us as with anybody else."

"It's not just safety," he said. "It's a place where I can work I need."

"What work?"

"Maybe someday figuring out how all this happened to us. How maybe it could be kept from ever happening again."

She shook her head slowly.

"Why you?" she asked. "And what difference does it make now?"

"It makes a difference because a civilized world's going to grow back together again," he said. "You know that. Paul knows it. He even plans on it—for your future. You know that, too. As for why it has to be me who finds it, maybe it doesn't, but I don't know of anyone else who's trying, with what I know."

He had never told her as much of his personal history as he would have liked, and the meanings of it to him—even though they had talked at length on the seed-farm trip. She had not, perhaps, asked the right questions to get him going, and he was not yet beyond the reticence that had simply been his habit for a lifetime. So now, even as the words left him, he felt suddenly sure she would not understand what he was talking about.

Perhaps she did not, but in any case, she seemed to take them at face value.

"We'll be coming by here again next year at this time, give or take a week or so," she said.

"I'll be here," he said.

They stood for a moment more. Then, since nothing more came to him to say, he turned, put his foot in the stirrup of Brute's saddle, and himself up onto the back of the riding horse.

He looked down at her from horseback.

"Well," he said, "I guess I'll get going."

He could not bring himself to say good-bye. Apparently, neither could she. But as he lifted the reins and Brute stirred to make his first step, she caught hold of Jeebee's knee with one hand, stopping the horse.

"I love you!" she said.

He looked down at her, feeling the pressure of her hand on his knee. It was out in the open now. Like a naked, twin-edged sword between them, he remembered, as if it had been only a moment ago, the pressure of her body against his when he had held her for that moment on the seed trip.

He knew now that she had no more defenses left. If he should get back down from the horse now and put his arms around her and hold her and kiss her, she would go with him. Or would he stay? The strength of the emotion between them was almost overwhelming. They could gamble either way—that it would work out if she came with him, that it would work out if he stayed with her.

But this was not a gamblers' world anymore. The last few months and weeks, especially the weeks before, had taught him that. That in his near starvation, they dared not kiss.

"And God knows—" he said, sitting still in the saddle where he was. The words were pulling from him, after a moment's struggle to find his voice. *"God knows I love you!"*

He shook up the reins and Brute led off, Sally trailing obediently at the end of the length of rope that attached her to Brute and Jeebee. Wolf, who had been lying all this time, watching them from the step to the back door of the wagon, leaped down and trotted to catch up with him.

Halfway to the trees beyond the cleared side of the road he half turned in the saddle, looking back, and saw her still standing where he had left her, gazing after him. He lifted his left hand from the elbow in a single wave. Her hand went up in answer.

He turned, rode on into the trees, and the wagon behind him, with all about it, was lost to sight.

CHAPTER 18

"**D**amn!"

The sound of his own voice, within the silence of the lodgepole pines, startled him. Mountains stood on his left hand, the side of the western horizon. He was riding through the north of Wyoming, toward the Montana border.

He reined in Brute; and the packhorse, Sally, feeling the sudden slackening of the line tying her to Jeebee's saddle, stopped also—Brute being no respecter of sex or familiarity in the case of any other horse crowding his heels. Like a professional boxer reacting to a thrown punch, his two iron-shod hooves would lash out in automatic reflex.

So they all halted, even Wolf, who at the moment was traveling with them. He looked up at Jeebee.

"What's wrong with me?" Jeebee said to him. "It's only the end of June! I've got plenty of time to find that customer of Paul's who kept wolves, and maybe get a look at what books on people like you he might have!"

Wolf merely watched him. The only readable expression on his furry mask of a face was one of mild curiosity. Jeebee had not known whether the other would leave with him or not. True, Wolf had gone with him and Merry on their trip to get the seeds, but Jeebee had become more than half convinced that the golden-eyed individual had come to like Merry better than himself, and would choose instead to stay with the wagon.

There were so many questions in Jeebee's mind about Wolf and his kind—which brought him back to why he had just sworn at himself and pulled up.

It was less than a day and a half since he had parted from Merry, Paul, and Nick. The wagon had turned off Interstate Highway 90 a safe number of miles before reaching the ruins of Buffalo. From there it had swung downward to meet and head south on U.S. Highway 87, on Paul's customary path to Texas. From Texas it would turn east and go back along a route through the southern states, during the late-summer and fall months, to Paul's headquarters somewhere in the Carolinas.

Jeebee had headed north since leaving the wagon, planning to follow the route of U.S. Interstate 90 north and west across the Montana border toward Billings. His plan had been to circle Buffalo to the east and follow up on the eastern side of 90.

He was still short of Buffalo and east of highway 87. Both horses were behaving well and his way seemed clear. Except that, suddenly, just now the thought of a change of route had come to him. He reached into his backpack, fastened just behind his saddle.

By feel his fingers identified the case holding his own marked and ruled maps. He found the brown plastic map case, took it out, and located the map he needed.

Instead of heading straight north and crossing I-90 to be on its eastern side as it headed north, it would be very simple for him to turn west, cross 87, and swing northwest until he hit U.S. 16, the road leading out of Buffalo and through the Bighorn Mountains by way of the Powder River Pass and Ten Sleep Canyon.

On the other side of the mountains was Worland, from which a day's travel northward would bring him to Glamorgan, the small town near which Walter Neiskamp, the man who raised wolves, had his place. Paul had located the position of Neiskamp's house with a small neat cross in red ink.

Once Jeebee had found Glamorgan, he hoped to be able to talk the man into either selling him some of his wolf books or letting him read them. After that, he would head north into Montana, roughly following U.S. 310, which crossed the border just above Frannie and below Warren, and from there on continue up and around Billings.

Above the Billings area, he could follow the general routes of either State Highway 3 or U.S. 87 up toward the Musselshell River and highway 12, which led eastward toward the town of Musselshell. It was all ranch country there, east of the Little Snowy Mountains, with the Big Snowy Mountains behind them.

It was still early in the day. Only ten miles or less separated him from a point beyond which highway 16, which went through the Powder River Pass, split off from I-90. He could make highway 16 by noon.

He sat in his saddle, torn two ways, while Brute stirred restlessly beneath him.

The strong desire to reach Neiskamp's, and at least get a look at the wolf books, was almost like a compulsion on him. Balancing it was what could only be described as a fear of making the crossing of the pass.

It was unlikely that the pickings, which travelers such as he and his two loaded horses could offer, would be worth anyone's lying in wait along the pass in country like this. But on the other hand, he would undoubtedly be reaching points where the only available path for him would be the road itself, as long as he had the horses.

The cool finger of fear touched him once again, inside. Once committed to the pass, he would be a sitting duck for anyone lying in wait with a rifle along the way. There was nothing to be done about that. But in any case, he would be safer traveling at night, as he had in his early period before he had gotten into South Dakota and met the wagon.

It was remarkable, but for the first time in his life, he was experiencing two interlocked sensations, neither of which he would have believed was possible to him. The fear—it was almost a superstitious fear—of crossing the pass, was there. Irrationally, something inside him seemed to say that if he tried to cross the pass, he would never make it through alive, and as a result, he would never see Merry again. It was the latter possibility, not the former, that now left him hollow inside.

It was a real, if reasonless, apprehension. But strangely, woven with it at the same time—and remarkable after all these months that had taught him the value of taking no chances, of playing safe, of always taking the most protected route—he felt an almost fierce desire to tempt the very fear itself. He had never felt anything like that desire in his life before. It was as if to cross through the pass was something he had to do, a test he must pass for his own sake.

He had always wondered how people could want to dare ridiculous dangers. This danger was not necessarily ridiculous, but he found a grim desire in him to dare it anyway. It was as if the crossing of the pass was an enemy he was required to seek out and cross swords with, when all his life he had avoided crossing swords with anyone.

After a long moment of sitting undecided where he was, it was that last, unreasonable need that won out.

"Well, Wolf, it looks like we turn west," he said—and suddenly realized that Wolf had already disappeared into the little patch of trees surrounding them.

He turned the horses. The possibility of death lying in wait for him in the pass went before him still, like a wraith in his path. But his desire to go brushed that wraith aside. Something new was stirring in him. A fatalism, an almost physical desire to gamble. The challenge was attractive in a way he had never felt before. He wished that Wolf was with him. It was as if Wolf would be a catalyst of some sort to test his decision. Still riding, he howled.

Brute and Sally, used now to his making such noises, stolidly ignored him and continued walking.

He howled twice, but there was no answer. It was unlikely that Wolf had gotten too far away to hear him in the short time they had been parted, although sounds sometimes played tricks, particularly with mountains nearby. But then there was no guarantee that Wolf would answer a howl, in any case. Jeebee shrugged. There was nothing he could do about it. It would be up to Wolf, just as he had thought earlier, to find them and go along, if he wanted to.

The decision was then to be Jeebee's, alone, unhelped. The fatalism held him. He lifted his reins again, rode across the road, and turned north.

He and the horses reached the woods just above a patch of highway 16 near noon. He stopped well out of sight of the road and unloaded both saddle and pack from the two horses, then tethered the horses about ten feet apart.

For himself he laid out the groundsheet covering the gear and unrolled the foam mattress on top of it. Wolf was used to the packload, he hoped, and had lost interest in it. But even if his destructive urges were triggered while Jeebee slept, any tugging on the groundsheet by Wolf trying to get at the gear below him would wake Jeebee instantly. The arrangement did not make the most comfortable of beds, however.

But it would do for a nap. He lay down on it, accordingly, deliberately leaving himself uncovered so that the coolness of the afternoon shadows would wake him. The last few months had developed an internal clock in him that could be preset for the time he wanted to awake. Lying on the packload, he closed his eyes, turned on his side, and almost instantly dropped into slumber.

He woke feeling stiff and chilly. But the feeling did not bother him. Like an animal, he knew that getting up and moving about would warm him quickly.

He had chosen a spot not far from a small stream, and he took the horses there to water before splitting Sally's load between her and Brute. They would both be packhorses on the slopes ahead, and he would cross the pass on foot, himself.

Above, the sky was still bright with late afternoon. The chill that had woken Jeebee had come from the treed slope behind him, falling into shadow from the rise of the mountain behind it. Even when he had finished watering and loading the horses, sections of the road opening eastward below him were still in sunlight.

Nonetheless, the day was aging.

Without warning, his fear came back on him. It made no sense that anyone would bother to lie in wait for the infrequent travelers who would use such a pass.

On the other hand, if someone did—with the mountain rising on one side of the road and the slope falling precipitously on the other—the traveler had no chance of passing safely.

Now, in the large shadow of the mountains and the indirect light overhead, a thought crept into Jeebee's mind. He had scrupulously shaved himself all the time he had been at the wagon after that first night. He had kept himself clean shaven because he knew Merry preferred him that way. Now, since he had left the wagon, he had paid no attention, and dark stubble had begun to reconstruct the beard on his face.

The impulse came upon him strongly and suddenly to shave. It was as if his being shaved clean would be a sort of talisman protecting him against anything that would keep him from being reunited with Merry again, eventually. It was a feeling even stronger than the one that had challenged him to cross the pass in spite of his reasonless fear of doing so. But in this moment he found himself believing in it utterly.

He stopped the horses, got his shaving materials out of his pack behind the saddle, and used some of the water from the water bag to make a lather with the soap he carried. Carefully he put to use the straight-edged razor that had been one of Merry's gifts to him, through Nick—although he had not found that out until a couple of weeks after the first day on which Nick had given it to him. With it, he scraped his face clean.

His face now feeling raw and naked to the cooling evening breeze, he put away the shaving things and went on.

The day aged quickly. But shortly after this Wolf reappeared. He had been gone only a few hours, but his homecoming was as enthusiastic and elaborate as if they'd been separated for weeks. Jeebee remembered how the wagon dogs had mobbed Wolf on his return from the seed farm, and it suddenly occurred to him that Wolf's greeting might actually be an instinctive act of appeasement. He filed the thought away as something else to check on when—and if—he found the books. Formalities satisfied, Wolf dropped to all fours, gave a wet-dog shake, and stood with a quiet air of expectancy, apparently waiting for Jeebee to mount Brute. He seemed puzzled when Jeebee led off up the road into the pass, the lead ropes of both the now-haltered horses in hand. Once convinced that they were indeed on the trail again, Wolf rejoined them, but about twenty minutes later Jeebee noticed that he had disappeared once more.

Jeebee continued, finding himself held to a slow, if steady pace by the upward angle of the road. It was only beginning to climb, but already on occasion the land on one side of it dipped into a deep valley, thick with stands of pines, where the horses could not have made their way. The road surface was only slightly broken up by weather and lack of care, but the air grew cooler.

Meanwhile, overhead the blue and cloudless sky was beginning to pale in the west while it darkened in the east, and the shadows of the depths beyond the left edge of the road were becoming impenetrable.

Still, it was the time of month near the full moon, and the weather had been clear recently. Jeebee had hopes of moonlight to help most of his crossing.

But it would be a while yet before the moon would rise. Now, in the depths to his left and the rising slopes to his right, lodgepole pines covered the ground as thickly as soldiers standing on parade. Tall and straight as the masts of nineteenth-century sailing ships, as a result of struggling with each other to reach the sunlight above this angular pitched ground, they grew more closely together than seemed possible, with branches only near their tops.

Weighing the fading of the daylight against the darkness already between the trees, Jeebee concentrated on the road surface itself as a guide. There was no sign of any kind of habitation, or of other, recent travelers on the route. In the gathering darkness the asphalt looked more and more as if it had been abandoned for years. It was cracked, with potholes here and there, and a litter of branches and pine needles fallen, or blown across it.

His map had shown a distance of fifty-odd miles from Buffalo to Ten Sleep on the other side of the mountains. He had joined the road at a good distance out of Buffalo and did not have to reach Ten Sleep itself, but still, to reach the lower levels at the far side of the pass in one night's trek would be a long, hard walk.

It would be particularly hard on the loaded horses, but there was little to be done about that.

They plodded forward and upward. At least, he told himself, he had taken the greater burden off at least one of the animals, since Sally's load weighed little more than a hundred pounds, and he himself was packing nearly twenty-five with his own pack, weapons, and gear. He had been surprised to discover, when he had weighed himself at the wagon before leaving, that he was now up to one hundred and eighty-four pounds, most of it muscle—a weight and condition he had never expected to achieve in his earlier, adult life. Nevertheless, breathing was becoming more difficult, and despite the high-altitude chill, he could feel the sweat plastering his shirt to his back beneath the pack straps.

After a while the moon did, indeed, come up, and they speeded their progress; at least until Wolf rejoined them, and took Jeebee's traveling on foot as an opportunity to play games, snatching with his teeth at the flapping cuffs of Jeebee's heavy work pants or his jacket or trying to catch the reins with which Jeebee was leading Brute.

Jeebee, however, was becoming wiser in his companion's ways. He had more than a small suspicion that Wolf was trying to distract him from the idea of traveling further. He put the reins over his shoulder. Wolf could easily have jumped high enough to catch them and indeed did so a couple of times, but when Jeebee persisted in recovering the reins, they slid rather easily through the gap behind Wolf's canine teeth. Jeebee knew that if Wolf had been seriously interested in the reins—and not merely enticing him to play—he'd have gripped them with his massive shearing molars, and even Brute would have been hard pressed to get them loose. When it became obvious that Jeebee would not be drawn in, Wolf abandoned the ploy with the wolfish equivalent of a good-natured shrug.

However, the road had been steepening steadily, and though Wolf still took short side excursions from time to time, from then on he was generally with them.

In the time since they had left the wagon, with the dogs no longer around to inhibit him, Wolf had made a few experimental rushes at Sally, possibly sensing that the load she carried made her more vulnerable. But Sally had long ago learned to discourage the unwanted attentions of three or four unruly wagon dogs. A single dog—or wolf—was more of a nuisance than a threat. And the first time that Wolf made a grab for her tail Jeebee had been relieved to discover that the kick he'd received for his efforts had resulted in no broken bones. Brute, on the other hand, had merely rolled his ears back the first time Wolf approached, and Wolf had given him wide berth after that. But Jeebee knew how persistent Wolf could be and had taken to tethering the horses far enough apart so that they would not be tempted to kick each other, but close enough that they could, if necessary, support each other in holding off any approach by Wolf.

The moon had already moved well up from the mountain peaks to their left when they reached a wide spot in the road. It was a lookout point with a plaque on a post notifying travelers that this was the high point of the pass. He could not read it in the darkness, but Jeebee stopped at this point to rest the horses.

He had been giving them short rest stops in any case, roughly every half hour by his watch, so that they would have at least five minutes merely standing, even though still loaded. Their breath steamed a bit, and he let them cool before pouring them some water into his hat. He also made an effort to see if there was anything more in Sally's load that could be shifted to Brute's back; but short of completely undoing the loads and spreading everything out, with the resultant turmoil that would occur when Wolf saw all these things on the ground to play with, there was little to be done. So far, both horses seemed to be facing up to the climb at a walking pace, pretty well. The steep road had not winded them too badly.

For the moment, Wolf was not around again. Jeebee suspected the other might have simply lain down, hoping that Jeebee would come to his senses and give up this nighttime trek. The moon was fully overhead now and its light gleamed off rock, road, and sky. But in spite of that brightness, the stands of pine trees all around merged into a solid black mass at a very short distance. Jeebee reached the high point of the pass and started the horses on the road down the far side of it.

He had planned on going back to riding Brute once they were headed downhill. But now that they were actually at the point where he had meant to swing again into the saddle, he used his own fatigue as a measure and judged that the more he could spare the horses the better. Also, as he found out when they started down the slope in the opposite direction, after a small semilevel bit, he might be tired, but he had a lot of walking left in him.

Nonetheless, he estimated that they had already covered more than twenty miles from their starting point. If he could make another twenty—if they all could make another twenty—he calculated that they should be into Ten Sleep Canyon and be able to pull off the road and find a place where they could camp and rest up.

Shortly thereafter, Wolf was suddenly back with them again, moving out ahead of Jeebee in his customary position when they traveled together.

They slogged along. The moon was now descending to the dark rim of the canyon as they plunged down into the depths beyond the pass. Slowly the hours went by. Jeebee dared not stop except for the short rests, for fear of putting ideas into the heads of the three with him. Once Wolf abruptly fell back, and Jeebee turned and saw the dark furry shape lying on its side on the road behind him. The meaning of the action could not have been more obvious. Wolf was calling an end to his share in the trip.

Jeebee turned his head forward again and kept on going. There was an emptiness inside him. For the first time in a long time he seriously considered the chance that he had driven Wolf away from him, permanently.

But what drove him from within gave him no choice, and the two horses following him were given no choice. They went on.

But they went on alone for a good fifteen minutes and more before Jeebee's ears caught, once again between the soft beat of the horses' hooves on asphalt, the scratch of claws on that same surface. He kept on going without looking back, and a moment later Wolf caught up with them once more, passed them, and assumed his usual position in the lead.

From under his eyelids, as he focused on the road immediately before him, Jeebee saw Wolf glancing back over his shoulder at him. But Jeebee refused to meet those glances. He merely kept going with his gaze on the road surface just ahead of him. So they went on, with only the sounds of their feet on the road, and the moon sank lower and lower to the dark line of the rock topping the canyon wall. Just before it disappeared completely, Wolf whined, once.

Jeebee looked up at him, then, and for a long second gazed into Wolf's night-hidden face, with the color of its eyes now lost in the darkness. Jeebee said nothing. He did not even change his own expression, but looked away again and continued, leaning into the halter ropes to pull the weary horses along with him.

The four of them continued. Now that the moon had disappeared, the road had become only a dark blur, visible for no more than a half-dozen feet before them, in the starshine overhead. Jeebee was too worn out now to be grateful for the fact that the night was cloudless, so that there could be at least enough light to keep them from walking off the cliff edge of the road.

They went on. The moon had been down so long, Jeebee had almost forgotten what the road had looked like in its light. He and the horses stumbled from time to time, unable to see the breaks in the road surface. But his feet were able to tell by themselves if he wandered off the asphalt, and they kept him on the road.

The time seemed endless. Finally, the sky began to pale slightly from its utter blackness between the points of starlight. Certainly, the slope of the road was less now, even if only slightly so. At his most optimistic guess they had been descending now for somewhere close to fifteen miles, since they had left behind the highest point of the pass.

They were still among the rock walls and precipitous slopes, and even as the sky lightened above, the darkness pooled below. Still, soon they should be moving into territory where it would be safe to try to leave the road and find a place to camp. It might have to be a dry camp; but at least the horses, Wolf, and he would be able to rest. But there was not yet enough light to see if their surroundings were improving in this way.

It seemed that the sky overhead would never brighten, day would never come. Jeebee's pack felt as if it was stuffed with bricks as he forced one foot in front of another. He was conscious that the horses, and even Wolf, moving ahead of him still, would be equally tired, but he could find no energy left over in him to sympathize with them.

All his attention now was concentrated on keeping his legs moving. They seemed to weigh a ton, each of them. Still, as he kept them going, one step at a time, all the rest of him moved with them.

A fury rose in him that his body was not more capable of going farther and faster and so covering more ground. He tempted and encouraged that fury to make him forget his sore feet and weary body. Surprising himself, he cursed at Wolf, unexpectedly, when it seemed the other would get in the way of his own moving legs.

The words were hardly out of his mouth before reaction set in. He stared at Wolf, braced for whatever reaction Wolf might show. But the other's eyes, golden again now in the beginnings of the dawn light as the sky whitened overhead, merely looked back at him briefly, and away again. They went on.

Suddenly, without warning it seemed, he became aware that it was day. The sun was not yet above the rock walls about them. But the sky was bright now with morning, and the day star itself would be clearing the mountain rock very soon. Around Jeebee everything was fully visible. It seemed to have become so all at once. Either that, or else he had simply been walking without noticing while things brightened about him, tired as he was. He remembered once reading about World War I and how whole regiments of men had marched into towns in France on forced march after forced march, all in column all together and all asleep on their feet as they walked.

At the time of reading that, he had found it impossible to believe. But could he have fallen asleep, just now, walking? Possibly. Or, maybe he just had not been noticing—too out on his feet to be aware of the moment-by-moment change in illumination around him. At any rate, day had come and now they could find a stop, a place to camp and rest.

He raised his head and looked about. The canyon walls had opened out, and ahead they began to spread far apart. He had become used to the two overtowering walls of vertical rock, seemingly only a couple of hundred yards apart, with a plunging depth between them that descended so steeply he could not see to the bottom of it. Only occasionally had he been able to hear the rush of river water far below. Now, this had suddenly become the same two walls opening out into a wide area, between them. An area in which the land rolled in gigantic waves, like a wild sea of tidal waves gone mad and working against each other, in every direction.

But the waves were unmoving, solid slopes of earth, largely covered by lodgepole pines.

He was through the pass and into the Ten Sleep Canyon, at last.

Their own road still clung to the side of the vertical rock that had been on his right. At his left, however, he could now look out on the vista of black-treed slopes brightening in the new daylight. Into this more open space, the morning sun was reaching brightly here and there, although as yet it had not reached as far as the four of them.

But now, the road was on another small, momentary rise. It had tended generally downward since they had crossed the highest point of the pass, with little rises like this only now and then, as if the road itself was about to change its mind. This, like the earlier rises, would ordinarily hardly have been noticeable, but now they were all close to exhaustion from the night's trek. The extra effort of going upslope, even for a short distance, seemed like a heavy burden. Jeebee's legs were like rubber, and they gave as he leaned into the upslope of the road.

This rise was large enough to block out sight of the further road beyond it. The horses were still behind Jeebee at the length of their halter ropes. Ahead of him was Wolf, still moving lightly if perhaps a little gingerly, on feet that must be sore.

As he watched, Wolf reached the crest of the rise and moved all at once into the full illumination of the advancing sunlight, and there was a second that became a picture frozen in Jeebee's memory forever.

It was of Wolf, leading them upward into the sunlight, with the rest of them still toiling in darkness, but mounting also, steadily behind him.

Jeebee's heart bounded with a new burst of happiness within him. Suddenly he remembered what he had forgotten. Somewhere during the dark hours he had lost it, his apprehension about crossing the pass, and his superstitious fear that if he did, he would never see Merry again.

Now both things together were swept away in the sunlight that suddenly spread golden fire around Wolf. It was over. Jeebee had made the crossing. He had won.

True enough, he had won over nothing more than shadows within him. Still, there was that same feeling that he had had after he had come successfully up through the cellar and past Wolf with the canned food in his arms, and the feeling following that evening in which Wolf had come to him in a new, strangely submissive manner. In both cases, he had known a feeling that he had passed some kind of watershed in his life. That feeling was in him now, very strongly.

He had made another step up the ladder. He was different in this moment than he had ever been before. He had faced the pass and its shadows, had gone through them and left them behind.

Now at last, morning was here. The land between the widening walls of the canyon was no longer too steep for the horses to negotiate. They could find a place to stop, to camp and rest.

"Come on," he said to the horses.

He turned and led them down the road and at last off among the trees. There was no way that the horses could have known that the night's trek was at last over. But it seemed that their heads came up, and they moved more willingly.

Down at the bottom of the fold he found a stream that had probably cut its way there over the centuries. It was a remarkably small stream. Only by a little was it too broad for him to jump across, and it varied from mere inches to perhaps a couple of feet in depth, purling softly among the close, branchless lower trunks of the pines. He saw the darkly pale shadows of fish for a moment flickering out toward the middle of the stream, before they lost themselves from sight.

There was no clearing among the trees ideal for a camp. But that did not matter. Wolf ran forward and began to lap from the stream and the horses literally pushed him aside to get past and put their heads down to suck up the water. He himself watched for a second, then turned and walked a little upstream before dropping flat on the ground himself with his head over the edge of the bank, to drink. The water was icy cold. Later, he thought of giardia, of the danger of parasitic infection from the clearest of running streams. But that was only later.

Once he had drunk, it seemed to take a tremendous effort merely to lift his tired body back to its feet. But there were things to be done, even now, before he could dare rest. Wolf had already flopped down in a little natural hollow beneath one of the pines and seemed already asleep.

It was a great temptation for Jeebee to follow his example. But the horses had to be unsaddled and unloaded, and all the gear that had been on them made safe from Wolf's tendency to tear them apart as soon as he had had sufficient rest to feel frisky. On their trip to gather the seeds, he and Merry had placed their loads in the center of a rope corral that had contained all the horses running loose. Wolf would not have ventured into that corral, because the horses would have taken alarm and attacked him on the assumption that he was after them. One wolf was not going to argue with half a dozen horses.

Now, with only two horses, a rope corral was not the answer. However, back at the wagon with the help of Paul and Nick he had come up with a way, several ways of dealing with this problem, one of them to be used among trees of about this diameter.

The horses had finished drinking. He led them to trees and tied them up temporarily—tied them on short hitches so that they would not be tempted to lie down until he was ready to leave them to their extended rest.

Then, from Sally's packload he took a hatchet, a block and tackle with rope, and a pair of lineman spurs Nick had made for him in the forge aboard the wagon. He strapped these last to the heels of his boots. He added a wide, long belt, that Nick had also helped him make, which he fastened around his waist and the lower, eight-inch-thick trunk of one of the pines.

It fitted loosely enough so that there were several inches of space between him and the tree trunk. Then, digging in his spurs and hitching the belt up as he went to support his upper body, he climbed some fifteen feet up the trunk.

With spurs dug in, leaning back against the support of the belt, he hacked two deep notches on either side of the tree trunk and anchored the block and tackle by firmly tying it strongly with rope around the tree and in the notches he had made. He climbed back down, bringing with him one end of the rope reeved through the blocks.

Tying that end loosely to the tree, he went to get Sally and retie her to the tree he had just climbed. He loosed the rope of the diamond hitch holding the pack on her back, then brought up from underneath the load the gather ropes of a loose net that had been laid between the blankets padding her back. Now he pulled its ropes out and around to hold the load in a rough sort of bag. The net ends had metal eyes firmly fixed to them and through all of these he ran the loose end of rope from the block and tackle he now carried with him.

Tying it tightly, he switched to the far end of the rope that now ran from the load, up through the double block tied to the tree overhead and back down and up again through the single climbing block he had fixed to the net. He began to pull down on his end of the rope from the ground.

The rope running through the blocks took up the slack between it and the load, and then slowly, jerkily, began to lift the load toward the blocks themselves. Sally heaved a deep breath as the weight of the load came off her. The load itself rose slowly, moving upward with each jerk a fourth of the distance Jeebee had just pulled down on the end of the rope he held. It was slow, but it was certain. The distance lifted was proportionately less, but the amount of force with which Jeebee pulled down was lifting four times its weight at the load end.

So, eventually, he wound the load in its nettinglike sack up to the notches on the tree, high above where even a leaping Wolf could reach it. He then drove his weary body to duplicate the climb and the lifting off of the load Brute had carried, and put it, also, in safety.

This done, he retied both horses on long tethers, fastening them securely to separate trees, but close enough together so that they could reinforce each other against any undue interest shown in them later by Wolf. Right now Wolf was flat on his side by the stream, looking as if dynamite could not wake him.

Both horses lay down almost immediately, a strong indication of their exhaustion after the long march. He himself spread the groundsheet from the gear he had taken off Brute when unsaddling the riding horse, and unrolled his mattress on it, covering himself with the two free horse blankets. Rolling himself up in this, he fell immediately, deeply, asleep.

CHAPTER 19

Jeebee came out of sleep like a fired bullet out of the muzzle of a gun.

It was a habit he had picked up on those first few weeks of his lonely flight out of Michigan. He had gotten away from it while sleeping in the wagon. But it had returned when he and Merry had gone after the seed—and it was back with him now again. Plainly, sleeping in the open had become the trigger of a reflex.

He woke to find Wolf with his teeth set in a corner of the groundsheet, trying to tug it from underneath him.

"No!" Jeebee shouted instinctively—and, as instinctively, sat up and drove his fist at Wolf's head.

His knuckles jarred on hard bone. Wolf let go and backed a step, his eyes on Jeebee's without animosity, his head cocked slightly to one side.

"No! Leave it alone!" said Jeebee.

He lay down again, ready at any minute to feel again the tugging that had woken him. But it did not come, and when he lifted his head to look, Wolf had disappeared. Still too steeped in the need for sleep to worry further about it, Jeebee closed his eyes and was instantly in slumber again.

When he woke for the second time, there was still no sign of Wolf. The two horses were on their feet and looking at him. The sun was high overhead. But so thick together were the branched tops of the lodgepole pines, in their fierce competition for daylight, that down here on the thick carpet of dead brown pine needles all was in pleasant shadow. Brute lifted his head and neighed.

Jeebee struggled out of the confines of his bedding. Of course, the horses needed to drink from the stream from which their tethers kept them, and what little fodder they had been able to find in the needles underfoot was now cropped close.

He threw the last of the entangling blanket aside and staggered to his feet. He was suddenly aware that with the warming of the day, he had become drenched in sweat under the blankets. He stumped over to the horses, untied them, coiled up the now-loose ends of the ropes that had held them to their trees, and led them down to the stream.

They drank thirstily, and reminded of his own dryness of mouth, he stepped upstream to drink, himself, then remembered the danger of parasitical infection. He paused only to empty his bladder, then retied the horses, lowered the load with the water bags, and drank from the disinfected contents of one of these.

These primary needs taken care of, he reloaded the horses, gave them nose bags supplied with some of the grain in the loads, and let them eat.

For himself, he got from his saddle pack the last of the short-bread Nick had made for him before he had parted with the wagon. These hard, floury little cakes, rich with fat and sugar, tasted delicious in his mouth after the long, almost mealless day and night preceding. His conscience troubled him a little for eating them now. He could, he told himself, have saved them for a day or two and hoped to either pick up some game, or find an abandoned farmstead with the latest generation of crops run wild, to fill his empty stomach instead.

Instead, he finished off all the cakes, even licking the crumbs from the palms of his hands. He went back to the water bag, drank as much more as he could hold, then emptied what little was left. He refilled it from the stream, adding one of the disinfecting tablets he had gotten from Paul. In a couple of hours it, too, would be safe for him to drink. With Sally now carrying the full packload and Brute once more saddled, he led both horses down to the stream to give them also a chance at a final drink—which both took.

The trees about him were still too thick and the ground underfoot too sloping for easy travel off the road. He mounted Brute and headed them all back up onto the cracked pavement, heading downhill toward Ten Sleep.

It took him eight days, traveling north at an easy pace, to reach the neighborhood of Glamorgan, where Walter Neiskamp, the man who had kept wolves and been Paul Sanderson's customer, lived.

The little town—it was barely more than a couple of blocks on either side of the main street, with no more than three rows of houses behind the stores—was close below the border of Montana. He approached the town just as night was coming down and made camp in the closest patch of trees to it, which was about a half mile distant. The next day and night, he spent observing it. Caution had come to be second nature with him now. However, he saw no signs of life about it. No movement of people in the daytime, no smallest flicker of light from a window after dark.

Finally, gingerly, he approached it. Wolf, who had caught up with him again, followed him perhaps a hundred feet out from the trees and then stopped, leaving him to go on alone. It was all open country, but he had picked the time just before twilight to make his approach. If it turned out that for some reason he had to run from it, after all, at least he could count on darkness closing down around him to aid his escape. He approached in a series of zigzags, keeping below the crests of the open but rolling land that surrounded it. He was puzzled by the lack of appearance of life around it. The cities, even the larger towns, had effectively destroyed themselves once their power, water, and communication with the outside world had been cut off, as the people in them had fallen to fighting among themselves for the necessities of life that were still available where they were.

But tiny towns like this had normally survived. For one

thing, they were close to the country, which meant that they could draw upon or trade with their rural neighbors. For another thing, they were country people themselves, and more accustomed to being self-sufficient. Finally, there would be very little at a place like this for people to fight over.

So he thought. But, as the shadows deepened and he ventured at last around the houses and the stores into the main street, he had to face the fact that the town was entirely dead, and several of the houses at the far end had caught fire and burned down to shells. The stores themselves had their windows smashed and inside each of them things were strewn around as if a hunt had gone on for anything that might be useful or valuable.

For the first time the complete silence of the town impressed itself on him. He had been moving with extreme caution, out of the habits ingrained in him these last few months and the possibility that someone might be hidden in this otherwise deserted-appearing place. Now an absolute certainty settled in him that there was no one here. A faint breeze whistled softly through some of the broken doors and windows, but that was all that reached his ears, and for the first time he accepted that he was utterly, completely alone.

The place had been raided by some considerable armed force and was presently no more than a ghost town.

Without bothering to continue being particularly silent or trying to stay in the shadows, he ventured into several of the stores and buildings along the street. But they were all empty. There were no signs either of living people or dead bodies.

He worked his way down the street and at the very end he came across a small cemetery. In one corner of it a large area had evidently been dug up, at one end of which a rough wooden cross had been driven into the spaded earth, but with no sign or message upon it.

So, somebody at least had either escaped and come back, or come along, found the dead here, and buried them. It could not be otherwise. As for who had sacked the place, it had probably been raiders, a good-sized group to take even a small town like this so completely.

He shivered. He had been lucky so far not to encounter any such post-Collapse gang.

The further end of the tiny town reached into the fold of the foothills below which the town was set. A gravel road, already beginning to be overgrown with small plants of the spring, led off up into the fold. He followed it. Walter Neiskamp, the customer of Paul Sanderson who had kept wolves, had lived out just such a road at some little distance from this town—perhaps half a mile.

Jeebee had gone only a couple of hundred yards, however, before the turn to the road put hillside between him and the dead town. It was at this point that Wolf came out of the shadows and rejoined him. Together, they moved on. A small night wind whispered and muttered about them in the dark shapes of the trees flanking the road as the last of the daylight faded, and little patches of moonlight showed them enough to keep Jeebee from losing his way.

The road ceased even to be gravel and became simply a rutted path, now thick with small ground-covering vegetation. This narrow way ended finally in an open, bowl-shaped area, clear of trees and, as Merry had described, completely surrounded by the close slopes of the foothills, an area barely large enough to contain the house and grounds the hillsides enclosed.

A little stream chuckled in the moonlight, down along the far side of the house and out of sight into the trees on Jeebee's right. This place had also clearly been visited by the raiders. Jeebee went forward to examine the house, Wolf following more cautiously, a little behind him, but showing—Jeebee noted—an unusual willingness to investigate this unknown, in contrast to his usual caution.

However, well short of the point at which he would have entered the dead house before them, Wolf balked. Jeebee himself had paused for a moment before the entrance, the door of which had been reduced to nothing more than a few shreds of wood hanging from the hinges, evidently as a result of some interior explosion. Then he stepped through, himself.

He would have been stepping into utter darkness if it had not been for the fact of the same explosion—perhaps the raiders had thrown a grenade, or something with more than the destructive power of a grenade, perhaps a stick or two of dynamite taped together, through the windows beside the door. Certainly the windows were all broken. Likewise, the roof overhead had been blown half off the room into which he stepped, and the light of the now-rising moon shone down brightly through this, to reveal, in shades of black and gray, a scene of utter devastation.

Apparently there had only been one piece of furniture in the room, which was itself rather large. This one piece of furniture was a sofa, with its cushions now torn apart and its underframe broken. It lay in two halves at about a thirty-degree angle to each other against a further wall.

The floor also had holes in it, but none large enough to fall through. Jeebee made a decision and reached into his backpack, took the risk of lighting a candle.

The wavering light from the candle flame showed him a slightly smaller door in the shadows of a further wall. He went through it. It led him into a hallway, which in turn took him into two bedrooms, or at least one had been a bedroom, for it held a bed apparently completely untouched, except that there were no blankets or covers upon it, and the other had been some kind of storeroom full of papers. He passed a couple of other rooms full of what seemed to be odds and ends of leather and metal junk and came at last to a room with shelves all around its four sides. Shelves that were filled with books, none of which seemed to have been touched or taken.

Jeebee's breath shortened. If this had been the library of Walter Neiskamp, then there was a good chance that the books he wanted would still be here. They would have been of no interest to the raiders. But the sensible thing was to go through them in daylight.

He was about to turn around and leave the house again, but he was out in the corridor and only one door was left. He yielded to curiosity and stepped through it, to find himself in the kitchen.

The windows of it had been smashed, and it, too, had been blown apart, though apparently with somewhat lesser force than that which had torn apart the living room. More importantly, on the floor of this room lay the remains of a human being. Small scavengers at least had been at it, for it was barely more than a skeleton, but the clothes seemed to indicate that it had been a man rather than a woman.

Suddenly glad that Wolf had not come in with him, since Wolf was attracted to carrion of any kind, Jeebee turned about and retraced his steps back through the house. He stepped out into the open, blowing out his candle and returning it to his backpack. Wolf was waiting there and greeted him like a long-lost comrade. Turning, Jeebee headed toward the area behind the former house.

Surprisingly, out here, Wolf showed far less hesitation. Behind the house there had been an arrangement of wire pens, a number of small ones individually capable of being locked; those led by further doors within them into a larger pen that seemed to have been some sort of runway. If the man, Neiskamp, kept wolves, here was undoubtedly where he had kept them; and, in fact, Jeebee could catch in the moonlight here and there a glint of white bone on the nearer dark ground of a couple of the wolf pens.

He found the doors that had let him into them. Lock had been too strong a word for what he had assumed kept them closed against the animals inside. Opening them was merely a matter of pulling a wooden peg from a latch that secured each door. The first door he so opened moved with a screech of metal that was surprisingly loud in the silent night. He went inside; Wolf pushed past him, went ahead, and began to sniff immediately at where Jeebee had seen the glint of white.

Catching up with Wolf, Jeebee found the bones of an animal about Wolf's size. It was not possible to tell for sure in the moonlight, but it seemed to be the bones of a wolf, with some bits of fur still attached and possibly even some scraps of decayed flesh, although that was hard to tell in the darkness.

As best he could in the moonlight, Jeebee examined the skull of the carcass. It was shattered in front, broken by a large hole as if the animal had been shot. Wolf pushed past Jeebee, put his nose down on the remains, sniffed, then turned and began to explore the pen.

Jeebee left him to it and went to the next pen. It, too, held its bones. All in all, he found six cages, all with remnants of a carcass in each, and each carcass with a hole in the head.

It was fairly clear that the animals had been deliberately destroyed. Whether Neiskamp had destroyed them himself, for reasons of his own, triggered into action by the arrival of the raiders, or—more likely—the raiders had killed them, was an unsolved question, and its solution was probably unimportant. Jeebee let himself back out of the pens, leaving the door ajar so Wolf could join him, and, after a little while, Wolf did so.

That library, Jeebee thought, would have to be examined in daylight. There was no reason not to shelter inside the semi-destroyed house, but Wolf was still unwilling to enter it and Jeebee felt a certain sense of distaste at the thought of doing it himself.

In the end, he camped just outside the house, after fetching the horses, on the east side, where the sunlight would wake him early.

A brightening sky woke him some hours later. He got up and fixed himself some breakfast, taking the horses to drink at the little stream. There was plenty of ground cover for them to feed on here. In fact, around the house there was no lack of grass and the horses had been quietly cropping most of the night. After watering them, he tied them up once more, fed himself, and turned back toward the house. Wolf had taken off and was nowhere to be seen.

As daylight flooded down the rounded sides of the foothills enclosing them and the sun itself rose into clear view, the house was revealed as more damaged than it had appeared by moonlight. Apparently the raiders had wasted little time after tossing explosives into it.

Considering the damage, Jeebee became even more sure that it had been dynamite that had been used, rather than something essentially as antipersonnel as grenades. Going in by the back door to the kitchen, he found some confirmation for this in the fact that the single body there had several firearms scattered around it, one shotgun and two rifles as well as a couple of pistols. All had been too damaged by the explosion to be workable—undoubtedly that was why they had been left where they lay.

Jeebee's best guess was that Neiskamp-had been trying to hold the raiders off from here with enfilading fire. Possibly he had hoped to discourage them from trying to obtain whatever the house might hold. In any case his defense had not worked.

Jeebee went on into the library section. There, the room was half-full of collapsed roof parts as a result of the explosion that must have stressed it to the point where it collapsed inward.

The bright light of day streamed in and revealed a room even more bare of furniture than the living room with its single couch. In fact, the couch, the bed in the bedroom, a small table by the bed, and two chairs and the table in the kitchen were the total sum of furniture that the house had apparently owned. But the bookshelves were full. Now, needing neither candle nor any other type of illumination but the daylight coming through the broken roof, Jeebee began to brush the dust from the spines of the books he took from the shelves to examine.

It was a slow and dusty process, since he had to clean each book before he could identify it by the printing on its spine. There were a remarkable number of issues of magazines, like the *National Geographic*, bound in homemade covers. There was also a plentiful supply of books about the west in particular, particularly histories of the rise of the cattle industry.

But also, there were a fair amount of histories of the plains and mountain Indians of the west. Halfway around the room, he found what he was looking for, a respectably small number of books on wolves. He took these out, identified them one by one, and made a pile of them on the floor. It did not look like there were too many of them to be added to the load Sally was already carrying without putting her under too heavy a burden.

Eighteen books in all. He took them and left.

CHAPTER 20

Jeebee had time for reading in the days that followed for he continued to travel by night and lie up during the day. The first part of the daylit hours would necessarily be given to sleep, but after that there were always three to four hours before he felt safe to move again with the sundown.

In those few hours he first attended to whatever needed attention about packs and mounts and the welfare of the horses themselves, and refilled the emergency water bag that he carried fastened to his saddle from whatever fresh-water source was handy. He had gotten a large supply of the sterilization tablets from Paul, but realized that he was going through them fast.

Counting them now and looking at the rest of the days of the summer and possibly through the fall, he could see the point was coming where he would be reduced to boiling his drinking water as the only way left to be sure of its safety.

Still, for now at any rate, the time he had left over was at least a couple of hours a day, and in that time he absorbed as much as he could of the books from the library shelves in Neiskamp's ruined house.

Academic habit made him begin by reading the reference lists, which all but one of the books provided, and then checking them against each other to see which of the volumes he had taken from Neiskamp's house were most mentioned.

Only two of the titles had rung any kind of bell with him, though he had read neither book. One was *Never Cry Wolf* by Farley Mowat, for which he found only two citations, both of which referred to it as "semifictional"—which he knew to be academic shorthand for, "Don't bother reading. Not a serious work." The other was *Wolf and Man: Evolution in Parallel* by Roberta L. Hall and Henry S. Sharp, about which he remembered something. It might have been that a review had attracted his attention because of the idea put forth in the title, which intrigued him.

He read through the lot, beginning with the most-referenced works, L. David Mech's *The Wolf* and a similarly titled volume by a Swedish-German biologist, Erik Zimen, and so working his way down his list.

When he finally did get to *Never Cry Wolf*, he recognized it as evidently the source of a movie he had seen once. Its authenticity may have been questionable, but he realized that besides being a fine work of writing, the author had produced a first-rate piece of prowolf propaganda. He tucked it away against some future day when Wolf's survival in the cattle country of Montana might require a good bit of public relations.

Though Mech's *The Wolf* was obviously—and from what he could see, deservedly—regarded by other authors as something of a Bible, there were several others that offered insights he could apply more directly to what he had observed in his personal relationship with Wolf. One was a volume edited by Harry Frank and published as recently as 1987, entitled *Man and Wolf: Advances, Issues, and Problems in Captive Wolf Research*. These, and Zimen's excellent book, really began to supply him with the background his academically trained mind was reaching for, to give him a context into which he could fit his half-formulated speculations.

All but about three of the books he had gathered helped him enormously. It was a curious process, as if a patch of desert, suddenly supplied with water, had begun to sprout in all directions and develop into a green and growing place. He had had absolutely no idea that so much work had been done toward understanding Wolf and his kind.

At the same time it was frustrating. Most of the more scholarly writing left him vastly more informed, but irritatingly much more conscious of how much there was he did not know about the wolf. His limited experience with one member of the species was not enough even to let him make full use of the data that he found in the books, he told himself.

He had been observing Wolf closely all these weeks. But from what he read, Wolf would be a different sort of character if he was an established member of a pack. A lot seemed to turn upon Wolf's age. He remembered the bulky, scruffy look of Wolf when he had first seen him. If he was understanding what he was reading at all well, this thick, untidy coat and appearance of bulk fitted a wolf still in his youth, possibly no more than a year old, for all his adult size.

If that were the case, Wolf was now much closer to being the sort of person who could partner with him. From those readings that compared wolves with dogs, he gathered that the social behavior of the adult dog was similar in many ways to that of the immature wolf, still agreeable and not yet prepared to challenge adult authority for a place in the status order. Apparently, it was quite common for adults of a domesticated species to retain characteristics found only in juvenile members of their wild ancestors. The books called it "neotenization." The contrast he had drawn for Merry between childlike dogs and Wolf as an adult person was closer to the mark than he had imagined.

He thrust firmly aside, for the moment, a desire he felt budding within him to speculate on the human race in this light. He had enough to do.

Jeebee knew almost nothing about Wolf's early history, but some of what he read for the first time helped him make some educated deductions. There was nothing wrong with Wolf's eyesight, so it was unlikely that he had been orphaned or taken from his mother before he was about ten days or two weeks old. Wolf pups deprived of mothers' milk before that age apparently tended to develop cataracts.

Of course, Wolf might have been fostered into a litter of nursing dog pups, but the dog owner would probably have left him with the mother until he was weaned at five or six weeks of age. But in that case, Wolf would not have taken to Jeebee the way he had.

Wolf pups who remained with their mothers more than about three weeks after birth apparently lost the capacity to form lasting attachments to human beings and soon began to react to humans much like any feral wolf would. This was documented, even in cases where the mother was herself completely tame. Jeebee reasoned that the same thing would happen if a wolf pup were fostered on a mother dog. So Wolf had probably been hand-raised by the cattleman called Callahan, beginning no earlier than two weeks of age and no later than three.

The books also taught Jeebee that wolves who were raised only among humans were afterward seldom able to establish normal associations with other canines. So Wolf's relationship with Greta was strong evidence he had been allowed at least periodic contact with other dogs, beginning shortly after he was weaned. Thinking back to Wolf's behavior with the dogs at the whistle stop, Jeebee now considered it altogether likely that some of the older dogs—possibly including the collie type Wolf had killed as they escaped—had also been residents of the small ranch where Jeebee acquired the jacket that had first attracted Wolf's attention.

In contrast to wolves, said the books, dog pups apparently passed through two such sensitive periods, or "windows"—one of which allowed them to develop normal social bonds with other dogs, and the second of which allowed them to form attachments to humans.

Dogs were therefore capable of forming "dual identities" and, in this respect, were more flexible than wolves, living quite happily in two worlds. Unlike a dog, even a hand-raised wolf never really lived in a human world.

As one writer had explained it, wolves raised by humans—or in very early association with humans—treated humans as wolves. That is, they seemed to expect humans to honor the same instinctive conventions that governed the social life of wolves. Jeebee guessed that this might be the root of the popular myth that any wolf would eventually "turn on its owner" or "revert" to wild behavior. It also went a long way toward explaining a number of things about Wolf's actions and general behavior.

But while the books explained much, they did not explain enough, at least to Jeebee, to provide the handle he needed for an overall understanding of Wolf's character.

There was so frustratingly much in these pages that he knew he was not getting. Information that seemed to lie below the surface of the words, invisible and sensed, but not seen. He asked himself if this was his imagination, and answered himself that it was not. There was knowledge there—his years of searching for answers on the academic level had trained a sensitivity into him, a nose that told him when there was information to be discovered.

His problem, Jeebee thought, riding northward under the stars as he moved into the middle of July under the nearly always clear sky, was mostly that same lack of experience on his part.

The problem was that the people writing the books knew what they were talking about, and they were writing mainly for readers who in most cases also knew what they were writing about. Jeebee did not. He had no context into which to fit much of his new information, and as a result, individual facts wandered loosely in his mind trying to partner with other individual facts and finding holes in every fabric his mind attempted to fit them into, as a pattern to explain Wolf.

He crossed Montana's southern border to the west of Warren, and moved on northward, crossing highway 310 again and passing to the east of Bridger. The country now was either hills and mountains or open, rising range, with very little tree cover. As Paul had advised, he avoided the Crow Indian reservation, now east of him, and swung in fairly close to Silesia. He also passed close to Laurel, but went unusually wide once more around Billings—or what had once been Billings.

There was an uneasy feeling in him that in this part of the country even cities as large as Billings might have survived the crises that had destroyed the cities further east. Billings might still be dangerous at some distance out. To be on the safe side, he headed generally north toward Broadview and Slayton, swinging around the western side of Molt and up through the Halfbreed and Hailstone Wildlife Refuges.

By this time a lot of what he had come to read had had time to soak and work in the back of his mind. As a result, one conclusion was obvious. He would have to work with whatever the books had been able to tell him, and try to apply as much of that as he could to what he had only half understood, by more and closer observation of Wolf.

Happily, Wolf was not spending so much time away from him now. The other showed up frequently during the day and often for short periods traveled along with Jeebee himself. It was the difference in their speed of travel that caused him to veer off as much as he did, Jeebee guessed. Wolf's normal traveling pace was a trot that was perhaps a mile to two miles an hour faster than the walking speed of the two horses. The horses traveled at roughly three miles an hour, which was also a human's normal walking speed. But it was not sensible for Jeebee to push them at any faster rate.

The thoughts that had been growing in him from his first acquaintance with Wolf, however, continued to grow. The books, specifically the writings of Harry Frank, had also told him one other remarkably fascinating thing, that the "mind" of the wolf seemed to be sharply divided into two separate systems.

The higher and—to Jeebee—more interesting system harbored a humanlike intelligence. The sorts of tasks wolves had performed under laboratory conditions suggested capacities comparable to the abilities of dolphins, which had stirred so much popular interest in the 1970's. Compared to their domesticated cousin the dog, for example, their abilities to solve complex problems were truly remarkable. Jeebee himself had seen Wolf use what he could only think of as deception, by "pretending" to play so that he could work close to, or attract the curiosity of, some small animal he hoped to catch.

He had also seen Wolf puzzle out the problem of crossing a small but very fast-running river. A tree had fallen across the river and was partly supported by a rock in midstream with its further end high in the air above the turbulent water and rocks.

Wolf had apparently realized that if he ran out on it and added his own weight to the end, it would tilt down enough so that he could jump to the further bank. Jeebee had observed this while slipping and sliding over the rocks of the same stream bed twenty-five yards downstream, feeling the fast water tugging at his lower legs and threatening to pull him off his feet—while Wolf lay down dry and comfortable, grinning at him from the opposite bank.

A corner of his mind was still busy puzzling over the problem of why understanding Wolf should be so important to him. Part of the reason was obvious, of course. Wolf had come into his life at a time when he felt desperately lonely, at the culmination, in fact, of a life that had been, in many ways, always lonely. He loved Wolf. He could not really assume that this affection was returned, and for purely human emotional reasons he wanted it to be. At least in one sense he was searching for a way to read into Wolf's behavior the fact that a real, personal affection for his human associate could exist.

But there was something else. There was also some elusive connection between understanding Wolf and the personal dark shadow and nightmare that had pursued him out of Stoketon. Wolf, once understood, might in the similarity of social instincts between his kind and human, offer a deeper understanding of what Jeebee had been working at with the study group in Michigan.

Certainly, what had happened to the world was something that would have been better off not happening. From the creation of the study group, Jeebee had felt that it had been on the track that would lead to some better understanding of the human race and why things happened to it. Possibly it could even have turned out to be a basis for foreseeing and preventing disasters, such as the Collapse itself had triggered.

Certainly, even now, the world ought to be able to pull itself up by its bootstraps again in no more than a couple of centuries, at most—and possibly in much less time. There was too much twentieth-century technology now in existence for the knowledge of it to be lost completely. People like Paul Sanderson would be finding ways to use it, keep it alive, and build it back toward what it was before everything fell apart.

Somehow, he felt, an understanding of the Collapse and why it happened could be tied in with the understanding he needed of Wolf and of what he was. It was an elusive connection, a ghost of a connection, but he had learned to trust such little tickles of queries in his mind.

He had also learned how to deal with them. Which was to put each of them consciously out of mind as much as possible, push ahead, and wait for the back of his head to make connections that the front had been unable to do.

This reaching out for understanding of Wolf had some tie-in to an understanding of why the human race should commit this sort of partial suicide. That was the other element in his need to understand. *Forget it for now,* he told himself. But it was not easy to forget it.

They were beyond the large cities now that Billings had been passed. They traveled either in open range or in foothills. It was full summer and the days were often hot. But these passed, and in between them the weather was very pleasant, particularly at night. Jeebee had fallen back into the habit of being the same sort of outdoor creature he had developed into, coming west.

Again he fell into the habit of wearing the same amount of clothing no matter what the temperature was, and being more or less indifferent to whether he needed warmth or was too hot—except that he stowed the leather jacket away. Also, the daily habit of shaving he had resumed briefly at the pass was forgotten. His beard once more was full and black. It was almost as if his clothing had become his pelt, as Wolf's pelt was his; and there was no reason to think of making changes in it simply to adapt to small changes in temperature.

So he let his beard grow and lived in his clothes. These things were unimportant. Important, was the fact that he was now in territory where he would be more visible and more conspicuous. Consequently his concerns were with the precautions of traveling within the cover of trees, in folds of land, or along river bottoms, as much as possible.

The rivers in these parts, particularly in these midsummer months, were small and not fast flowing. But they tended to have cut their path below the level of the surrounding ground. Also, they were commonly bordered and hidden by thick clumps of willow, occasionally so close-stemmed that passage was difficult.

These willow stands, however, offered a place for him to hide, if he suspected someone else might be about. He could vanish into them, horses and all, and simply stay still until whoever it was had passed, animal or human.

Traveling as he did, any sight of other humans was unusual, even though this was an area that seemed to be almost untouched by the change that had come upon the world. Most of the buildings he saw, he passed at a distance, and many of them had lights showing at night, if it was early, or gave other evidence of being actively lived in at the present time.

But one night he did finally come across a group of ranch buildings that had been burned almost to the ground—and not too long ago, because the smell of burnt wood was still about them—and when he rubbed a finger on the remains of a burned-out window frame, his skin came away black in the moonlight with soot from the wood.

It was true that this was not the season for rain, and in fact there had been remarkably little rain in the last few weeks, so that he was accustomed to finding the cattle clustering around what water was available and grazing as close to it as possible. But still the building must have burned sometime since last winter's snows, and possibly within the last month or so, for there was little sign of weathering of surfaces in rooms now exposed to the elements.

But the discovery of the dead building alarmed him. A place like this could attract scavengers. He moved further into the foothills, still following stream beds and willow clumps as much as possible. He came at last into an area in which there was a certain amount of tree cover, but willows still clustered by the running water.

Here, up in the hills, he began to let himself travel more into the daylight hours, because the area was so free of people. He got into the habit of going on foot, leading Brute by the reins, with Sally still patiently tethered to the saddle on Brute's back. This was as much to spare the horses as because he had become more and more able to read the ground before him; at the same time he felt himself to be less visible than he would be sitting up on the back of a horse, even down here in the hollow of the creek bed.

The sky was lightening one morning when Brute suddenly balked—stopping, pushing hard and back with all four feet. Jeebee stiffened and looked swiftly around him. It was just before dawn, all but full day. He could see clearly, except for what was hidden from view by the willow clumps, just ahead and around him and also clustered on the far side of a stream that could be no more than twenty or thirty feet wide. There was no sign of anything to alarm the horse, but Sally was also pulling back on the rope with which she was tied to Jeebee's saddle.

Jeebee pulled hard on the reins but Brute resisted him with all his equine muscle and did not move an inch.

"What the fuck's wrong with you?" Jeebee snarled—and was astonished at the sound of his own words in his ears. It was not merely that he had sworn at the horses. It was the fact that even a year ago, it would never have occurred to him to do so.

It was a shock to realize that he had changed so much. The restraint that had been second nature in him as far back as he could remember, had been scoured off by what had happened to him in the last few months. He was uncomfortably reminded of how he had been equally startled to discover in himself a readiness to kill Wolf, if necessary, to keep for himself the food he had found in that root cellar.

Then, suddenly more thoughtful, Jeebee forgot his momentary temper. He had learned to trust the awarenesses of the animals beyond his own. And if horses' noses were not the superb instruments Wolf's was, they were still far better than his human one. He was suddenly aware that the breeze was blowing toward them from upstream, in the direction they were going.

He turned, led the horses back until the tension began to go out of them, then tethered them in a small open spot on the riverbank. They might as well browse and drink while waiting for him. Jeebee looked around for Wolf. The other had been with them just a short while ago. Where was he now?

Jeebee cupped his hands around his mouth and howled. He waited. No answer came back. He howled again.

Still no answer. Wolf should not have been able to go beyond hearing range in the short time since Jeebee had last seen him. Jeebee had trusted the other's natural curiosity to bring him back to investigate what was causing Jeebee to do all the calling. But when no response came to a third howl after a good three-minute wait, Jeebee gave up. He pulled the .30/06 from its scabbard at Brute's saddle, checked to make sure it was fully loaded, and started upstream once more, by himself.

He went cautiously, on principle. The willow clumps here were thick enough to hide anything as large as a steer or a range bull.

He was carrying the rifle balanced in his right hand, his fore-finger on the trigger guard so that the knuckle of that forefinger controlled the grip. His left hand was free to push willow branches out of his way—but quietly, as quietly as possible. A large animal alerted to the point of having already begun an attack on him might not even be slowed by a bullet from a rifle of this caliber.

A willow clump barred his path, followed by a little open space, then another clump and another open spot, more earth than grass. He was down on what was called the false levee. Now, at July, the river had shrunk from its spring volume of water, which would have filled this ground to over his head, in-undating the lower halves of the willow stems with rushing, brown, foamy water, clear up to the top of the true banks on either side.

He went a little further and passed a gap in the willows on his left, so that for a moment, out of a corner of his eye, he saw clear to the bank top. In that moment he thought he glimpsed the gray, now lean-looking body of Wolf slipping past, moving paral-lel to him. But when he turned his head to look squarely, the gap was empty.

Wishful thinking, he told himself. Not that he had any great hope of Wolf coming to his assistance in case of trouble. The other was not one to come rushing to the defense of a human companion, movie-dog style. Wolf's actions were governed by the practical self-interest of his wild instincts.

But if Wolf had indeed been with him, the lupine sense of smell might have been able to tell him more of whatever had alarmed the horses, and from Wolf's actions Jeebee might have been able to read a fuller warning of any animal danger ahead.

Jeebee pushed through the last of a clump of willows and stepped into one more clearing. This was the largest so far. It narrowed toward the true bank, but stayed open enough so that at the very top of it he now saw Wolf plainly, after all, looking down at him with interest—but only looking.

Jeebee turned to go forward again. With no sound by way of warning, what seemed to be a couple of black dogs—one as large or larger than Wolf, and one looking very much like a half-grown pup—erupted from the willows ahead and came rushing toward him, the smaller one trailing behind.

He had time to think, *Oh no! Some rancher's dogs!* and that, whether they were friendly or not, he must not shoot. Because if they were, their owner might be riding just a little distance off, perfectly able to hear the sound of a rifle.

He poked out with the hand that held the rifle, as anyone might use a stick to hold off an animal that was either threatening, or trying to be too friendly by jumping up on him. Suddenly the larger black creature stood up on its hind legs, and things began to move very swiftly, though he saw everything quite clearly and his mind was quite calm and alert. Only his body seemed to move slowly in obedience to his wishes.

Upright, what he had thought to be a dog had become a night-dark monster with shaggy head and unbelievably toothed jaws. It was as tall as he was. He had a glimpse of deep-set eyes and felt a puff of hot breath on his face.

Now, at the last possible moment, he recognized it as a female black bear, although he would never have imagined an adult bear so lean, and the smaller animal as its cub.

A powerful blow on the rifle sent it spinning out of his hand toward the stream. He had no time to see where it fell, because another heavy blow glanced off the right side of his head and yet one more struck his upper arm on the left side.

Time had suddenly slowed. Jeebee was abruptly aware of Wolf, appearing as if by a magician's trick, and joining them with impossible swiftness. He registered first, not with the high, bounding leaps with which he had attacked the collie at the station, but as a gray blur, running close to the ground. In the second in which he reached Jeebee and the bear, Jeebee's memory also registered a momentary still snapshot of Wolf's tail low behind him, his ears down and jaws slightly open, as he came up behind the bear. Jeebee caught a glimpse of those powerful jaws, closing for a split second on the bear's left leg, the canine teeth sinking deeply in toward the bone, before Wolf almost immediately let go and leaped backward.

The bear turned, swiftly, but too late to catch Wolf.

Jeebee's mind, working in what seemed no time at all, but with unusual clarity and calmness, drove him like an impersonal engine. He bent down, reaching for the pistol in his boot. Even as his hands stretched out he realized how useless its light slugs would be in stopping such an enemy. His fingers closed instead on the oversized knife in its sheath on the outside of his right boot.

He gripped the handle and pulled the knife loose, snapping the leather cord holding it from falling out, as if that cord had been thread. As he did so he felt the breath of air above his head from another blow of the bear's paw that had missed him as he stooped. Coming upright, he was nearly felled by another solid blow, this time on his upper left thigh.

Straightening, he instinctively drove the point of the knife forward as he had been taught by Nick, toward the crotch of the bear; and felt the blade go in and up. Another blow just grazed his left shoulder lightly. Then the black body fell backward away from him. He stared down at it, unbelieving. As Nick had warned, his blade point had gone high. It had entered near the top of the soft stomach area. Somehow, he must have been lucky enough to hit a vital spot—maybe the heart was reachable, up in there behind the breastbone. . . .

The cub had disappeared. Jeebee's left leg suddenly gave under him and he sat down. Something was obscuring his left eye. He put his hand up and brought it away wet with redness. Reaching higher, he found something ragged hanging down, which turned out to be part of his scalp.

He pushed it back up. Wolf, having attacked again, had just leaped clear when the bear fell, then watchfully circled around toward its hindquarters. Now, with the bear down, he was making cautious approaches, pausing every step or two as he drew closer, and as Jeebee pushed his scalp back in place, Wolf took one last step and stretched his neck until his nose almost touched the black furred hind leg. His ears flagged up and down as he sniffed. Finally, he gave the leg a sharp prod with the top of his nose and leaped back. Then he stood watching, his ears now pricked, his eyes bright.

There was no reaction from the dead bear. Wolf moved forward confidently and began a more thorough inspection of the carcass.

Jeebee forgot about Wolf. His knife was still standing upright in the upper belly of the now plainly dead animal. Instinctively he retrieved it and wiped it on his pants leg before returning it to its sheath.

Surprisingly, he felt no hurt. He would, undoubtedly, any minute now. His mind still held that amazing clarity and calmness. The bear's claws could have infected him with the bacteria in the dirt on them, he told himself with no emotion whatever. He would need the antibiotics in his pack sack behind Brute's saddle, as soon as possible. He should get back to the horses while he could still move.

He tried to climb once more onto his feet and found his left leg reluctant to lift him. Looking down at his thigh where he had felt the blow, he saw the trouser leg torn and bloody. Almost enough of his blood available to paint with. The thought was funny, but he did not laugh.

With his fingertips he felt among the redness on his thigh.

Torn cloth, furrows in the flesh, and . . . holes where the claws had first struck. Surface wounds, then, but the bruising would immobilize him in hours. He would have to reach those horses. Undoubtedly there was internal bleeding under the bruised areas. Cold compresses for that, once back at the horses. The river water would be cold.

He felt his upper left arm and felt wetness there. More blood on his fingers. Happily, nowhere else did he seem to be bleeding. He looked around. His rifle was only about six feet away, teetering, half over the edge of the water. Rolling over on his good right side, he crabbed along the ground to the rifle, and when he got it, used it as a prop to get him up on his one good leg.

He began to hobble along the riverbank, downstream, back toward the horses.

CHAPTER 21

Ⅰt was hard going through the willows. His wounds still did not hurt, though he was conscious of them.

Possessing him still was that same clarity and clearheadedness. Now, like mental tunnel vision, it was concentrating all his attention only on the seriousness of the moment, and what must be done right away. Time was now moving at its normal pace.

He must get back to his medical supplies, at the horses. From what he had read in the books on wolves, as well as in first-aid texts, with large-animal-created wounds, his greatest danger was probably that both arm and leg were deeply and massively bruised by the paw blows of the mother bear. The flesh, where it had been hammered by those paws, would flood with blood from broken internal blood vessels under the skin.

He would probably not lose much blood—he was not even losing much now, except from his scalp—which seemed the least important. But the real damage was the inside damage, below the skin. That would mean swelling, which would take about twenty-four hours in which to reach its peak.

Treatment for swelling? His mind searched his memories of first-aid manuals. Cold compresses. He had no compresses or material for them at the moment. But the water in the stream close beside him was mountain-fed. It would be icy cold and he had, back at the horses, clothes he could tear up and wrap tightly around both the lower and upper wound. Also his scalp—which was still doing most of the bleeding.

The sooner the cold was put to work the better. At his present hobble, it would be a while yet before he could cover what he estimated to be about a hundred and fifty feet back to the horses. Thank God he had tied them up where there was water and grazing before leaving them.

It was the willows in their clumps that was slowing him down. Sometimes he could push his way through or go around, but they slowed his progress. He glanced at the stream. It was no wider anywhere than about thirty feet and had looked no more than about three feet at the deepest. There were no willows in it, and he would get the double benefit of immersing the hurt leg in its coldness and at least begin washing the leg wound clean.

For that matter, he could also keep splashing water up on his arm as he went. Both actions would help to clean the worst of the dirt undoubtedly there from the bear's claws and pads. At the same time, he could get to his destination in half the time it would take him, limping around these willows or forcing his way through them. And the water would slow him no more than the willows.

He veered toward the stream and checked himself at its bank, suddenly remembering that the water might carry toxic organisms. There was one—a parasite named giardia—that came from the excreta of beaver, and other wild animals, and was supposed to be found in western mountain streams like this.

But there was no real choice. It was a gamble of possible illness against the near certainty of being immobilized by his wounds, possibly dangerously so. Unable to walk, unable to get up, he would have trouble getting food or water as well as being helpless in the face of any predator or human enemy who found him. As he stepped down into the water that came almost to his waist, feeling the jar of his good foot against the stream bed, he remembered just in time to take the revolver out of his boot and stick it under his belt.

It was common, the books he had taken from the ruins of

Walter Neiskamp's home told him, for wolves that showed signs of weakness or disability to be harassed or mobbed by other members of the pack. An injured wolf that stood high in the ranking order was an especially inviting target of attack. True, the latter was usually supposed to happen only when the attacking wolf was old enough to become "political"—concerned with its ranking in the pack. This could happen, he had gathered, anytime after the wolf's second year of life, when wolves in packs typically reached sexual maturity.

Wolf best fit the description, Jeebee now guessed, of being only a year or so old, when Jeebee had first met him; too young, theoretically, to be "political" yet. But what all of the books had agreed on—both the formal academic works and the first-person narratives by amateur wolf enthusiasts—was that wolves didn't read the books that told how they were "supposed" to behave; the only thing predictable about them was their unpredictability. Wolves as decision makers were individual persons, as Jeebee himself had seen at first hand, with Wolf.

And prediction was even more problematic if there was validity in Frank's claim that some aspects of wolf behavior were governed not by the animal's own highly developed cognitive system, but by a separate instinctual system—which operated largely independently of the conscious, thinking system. Instinctive behavior patterns, triggered by cues a human might not even recognize, could cause a wolf to act in a manner its own mind could not control. Predatory reactions could be triggered by the awkward, uncoordinated movements of a crippled pack mate as easily as by the thrashing about of an injured deer. Whatever companionable feeling Wolf had for Jeebee, the man's injuries could provoke an attack. That Wolf might later experience something akin to regret was little consolation; Jeebee must either move as normally as possible when Wolf was around or remain immobile—as sick and injured wolves do.

All the time he was thinking this, he was feeling his way upstream next to the bank, the barrel end of the rifle in his right hand, the rifle butt below the water, tapping the bottom ahead of his feet like a blind person's cane for potholes or obstacles.

So far he had been lucky, encountering neither. Nor had any roots, projecting from the bank beside him into the water, tripped him up. It was not far to the horses now. Still his mind was glass clear and diamond sharp, concentrating on searching for whatever might need to be done or endured.

Perhaps, he thought, it was his own, human instinctive system, triggered by the need to survive, that was helping him now.

But finally, he was wading around a last bend in the stream and seeing the horses where he had tethered them. It was time to look for a place where he could climb, crippled as he was, out of the stream up onto the bank. There was waist-deep water and two feet of vertical light brown earthen bank to surmount. He solved the problem at last by laying his upper body down on the bank, still holding his rifle, and then rolling his body away from the stream to pull his legs after him out of the water. He rolled over the pistol in his belt, bruising himself.

He hauled himself to his feet with the help of the rifle and limped toward the horses. Wolf was nowhere around, he was glad to see. Perhaps his fear of an instinctive attack was foolish; but he would rather not test the chance.

It was fortunate his left arm rather than his right had been damaged by the bear. He was right-handed. Nick Gage had made him practice with the pistol in his left hand, but he was just not accurate as a lefty marksman.

He bound his wounds with wet compresses made from cut and torn strips of blanket, and swallowed his first dose of antibiotic. It was Augmentin, which he had carried in his backpack from Michigan for just such a moment as this. He washed the pill down with the bag of disinfected water he had always carried at his saddle. Only then did he take time to empty his boots of water and take off the soggy socks beneath them.

He was beginning to feel his wounds now. It was not real pain he felt from them as yet. But he was conscious of them being there. But there were still things to be done before he could give in to them. It seemed that almost as soon as he had stepped out of the cold water, the swelling in his leg and arm had begun to develop and stiffen those limbs. If he was going to lose the ability to move, soon, there were things that had to be taken care of, first.

He might become unable to unload the horses. If so, he would have to leave Sally with her pack and Brute with his saddle for several days, and that was unthinkable. There were no trees here large enough so that he could rope Sally's pack up out of Wolf's reach—even if he had been up to climbing a tree at the moment. Even the thought of climbing a tree was ridiculous, now, hurt as he was.

The best he would be able to do would be to dump both the pack and the saddle off their backs, and leave both horses where they could reach water, as well as whatever grass was within reach.

Once the packload was lying flat on the ground, there was no way he could think of to protect its contents from Wolf. Then it occurred to him that he could drop it between the two horses; and lie on it himself. Hopefully, in that case, Wolf would not try to get at it.

It was a gamble, but he had to gamble now. For the first time he realized how even a minor wound could cripple a wolf enough to threaten its ability to survive.

Difficult as it was with one hand, he managed to untie and throw off the rope of the hitch from Sally's load, and then, with even more difficulty, single-handed, to loosen the cinch strap holding the blanket underneath it. Crowding Sally against some willows so that the slim stems pressed the cinch strap against her far side as it slipped loose, he managed to slow the descent of the pack as he pulled it to the ground with his one good arm.

He was able to do no more than break its fall with that single arm. But he ended up with it in a not too untidy pile, which he was able to rake together so that the groundsheet would cover him and it, once he lay down upon it.

That left several things yet to do. The arm and leg were definitely beginning to hurt now, and he thought of the Dilaudid, the painkiller that was also in his pack.

But it was not that bad yet—in fact probably far from as bad as it was going to get—and also he had to get the saddle off

Brute and the backpack under the groundsheet with him so that he had his drugs at hand if he ended up so that he could barely move.

He undid the cinch strap on Brute and got the saddle, backpack, and saddle blanket off him. By bad luck they all went off on the other side of Brute, but he was able to reach an end of the cinch strap and pull all three things to him underneath Brute's belly. Brute was either in unusual good humor or indifferent, for he made no attempt to step on either item, or protest at something being done underneath him.

Jeebee hauled to him both saddle and pack, detached the pack, took out from it the drugs, and stowed all of this under the groundsheet, but with the pouch holding the drugs separate and close to his hand once he would be lying down.

There was still a final job to do, but now he was beginning to come out from the strange state of intensive clearheadedness he had been in up until this time. For the first time he was beginning to feel a weakness take over his legs and pain spread out in his leg, arm, and head.

He pushed himself to keep rummaging under the groundsheet until he came up with a spare water bag. He put in it the proper disinfectant pills and limped to the stream to fill it with water, taking advantage of the opportunity to thoroughly soak once more his three clumsy bandages, on leg, arm, and head.

For a moment he thought resoaking the bandage around his head had disturbed the broken scalp to the point where a heavy flow of blood had started again. But it was merely diluting what had already dried up there. He wiped the reddish wetness out of his eyes with his good hand and took the filled bag, hobbling along with the rifle still to support him, to the groundsheet pile between the two horses. Gratefully, at last, he sat down on it.

Seated, he took the half-full and disinfected water bag he had already had hanging from the saddle, so that he now had a full bag and a half-full one within arm's reach. He pulled the bags with him under the tarp and moved the softer materials beneath him into something that would do as a bed. He piled these high at the foot end to elevate his legs; and stripped off his wet clothes. He was fortunate enough to find dry underwear, pants, and shirt with the blankets under the packload tarp.

He pulled his wet clothing off and toweled himself dry with a dry shirt. The air temperature of the growing day around him must already be at fifty degrees, but he was beginning to shiver uncontrollably as hypothermia set in. He cursed weakly when he found he could not pull on the dry clothes over his compresses; throwing them down for him to lie upon, he settled for undershorts and socks. Then he cocooned himself in his blankets and wedged himself under the groundsheet, shivering while his face flushed. He was panting heavily. His eyes hurt and he was beginning to feel very weak indeed, and the pain was coming more fiercely from the wounded areas.

He lay there, thinking that he would put off taking one of the Dilaudids as long as he could. But with nothing else to occupy his mind but the consciousness of it, the pain seemed to grow swiftly toward the point of being unbearable. Meanwhile, he was already feeling so weak that the thought of getting up from where he lay was something to be contemplated only in an emergency.

He warmed finally and tried to doze in the sunlight. He woke in midafternoon, however, shivering again. There were no more blankets to add to his pile. In desperation, he pulled at the groundsheet, feebly struggling for more blanketing. Then he pushed it back to make sure that it still also covered all of the load.

It was time. He fumbled in the drug pouch and brought out the container of Dilaudid. He awkwardly shook one of the small, orange, two-milligram pills from the bottle that held it into the palm of his right hand, and washed it down with a swallow of water from the half-filled water bag.

He held the bottle up to read the prescription directions and they were for one to two of the pills four times a day with a one week limit, but less if possible. He knew that while effective, they were addictive, and the last thing he wanted to happen to him, out here alone, was to become hooked on some medicine. Once it was gone, he would have no way at all of getting more, even if it were safe for him to have more.

He relaxed and closed his eyes. His wounds were alive now, and the pain in them seemed to throb with his heartbeat. But gradually the Dilaudid took effect and he slept.

He woke to the daylight of a young morning and to find Wolf's large, sticky tongue stropping across his forehead and scalp.

"Get away!" he shouted—or tried to shout—but what should have been a stern roar came out weakly and hoarsely. A moment later, the pain hit him.

It was hard to imagine that he could hurt so much. He looked at his arm and leg and saw them swollen to what seemed gargantuan, unnatural proportions.

With his shaking right hand he scrambled among the gear at his right and underneath him to find the medicine pouch. The groundsheet was now only partially over him and the bandages had been pulled off both arm and leg—and from the feel of the breeze on his head the head bandage had been pulled off, too. But nothing mattered at the moment but the Dilaudid.

He found the pouch, he found the bottle holding the Dilaudid. Clumsily, he shook a pill onto his chest from the bottle. Awkwardly, one-handedly, he screwed the top of the bottle back on and put it away. Then there was another scramble to find the water bag—any water bag. He found it and swallowed a sip, washing the pill down.

He sighed with relief. The pain, of course, had not abated a jot, but he knew now that it would, eventually.

He looked down at the groundsheet that should have been covering him. It had been rooted under and pushed back until both his left arm and leg were exposed, the bandages pulled away, and the wounds themselves licked clean. He lifted his right hand to his head and found his scalp wound lacking any crustiness of dried blood, but covered with the kind of film that a thin, dried solution of sugar syrup might have left on it. From past experience he knew it was the dried remains of Wolf's saliva.

Wolf must have licked the wounds as he would lick such wounds on himself, or a pack mate.

Now that he was beginning to wake fully, and the Dilaudid was on its way to relieving the pain, fuzzy memories returned of being waked at least once before by Wolf licking him. Jeebee remembered now; he had yelled and snarled at Wolf to make him stop—he also remembered a first frantic fumbling for the pistol before he realized Wolf was only trying to help; and he remembered taking other doses of Dilaudid.

How much had he taken in that confused time? He could not remember, but since he had remembered hurting badly each time he woke, he probably had not exceeded the permissible dose by too much. . . .

"Mhrmmp. . . ? Mhrmmp. . . ? Mhrmmp. . . ?"

Wolf was still by him, now making small, inquiring sounds in the back of his throat. Jeebee half rose on his good elbow, looking at him, and Wolf hastily backed off several steps. He was watching Jeebee now, ears folded far back in a strong signal of peaceful intentions, tail awag. His head was cocked a little on one side, with what, from long experience during their months together, Jeebee recognized as an interested, worried look on his face.

"Sorry," Jeebee said hoarsely, looking at Wolf. "I'm not mad. . . ."

He tried to lift himself higher—but pain stopped him and his elbow gave way beneath him. Wolf came forward a step. Literally, Jeebee realized, he could not get up. He reached out with his hand toward Wolf, and Wolf came forward another step and licked at it. Jeebee reached up into the thick hair under Wolf's neck and scratched there.

Wolf licked at his hand again. Then—as suddenly as if a switch had been turned off—all appearance of interest or concern vanished from him. He turned and trotted off into the surrounding willows, leaving Jeebee suddenly alone.

Jeebee lay where he was. Slowly, the Dilaudid began to take effect and the pain to recede. As it did so he was aware of the fact that a full bladder was bothering him.

He found himself in a quandary. He literally could not move. Even with the pain reduced, the left arm and leg were stiff as wood. However, with some effort he was able to roll slightly over on his right side again to the extent that he could urinate beyond the edge of the goods piled underneath him. A suffusing rush of warmth as well as relief spread through him. He remembered then that Dilaudid, like codeine, morphine, and all other opiates, increased parasympathetic activity—which meant that it would be slowing down his normal bowel action and causing constipation. If he was to be confined to the packload for several days, this side effect would be a help. Also, if he remembered correctly, Dilaudid caused nausea, which would lessen his normal hunger for the next day or two.

The physical relief was tremendous.

He lay back, relaxing. He was in shade right now, this early in the day, but the sun would be up and shining directly on him in a couple of hours. Well, there was nothing to be done about that except possibly use something he could reach, either underneath or beside him, to shade his eyes from the direct glare.

He was becoming relatively comfortable with the Dilaudid in him and he was slept out. His mind was much calmer than he had expected. Some of Wolf's pragmatism had apparently rubbed off on him. He was in danger here by the little river and among the willows. A rancher, a rancher's dog, even another bear could stumble across him. He must get able to ride, or at least to sit a horse long enough so that he could move out of this grazing land and up into the country of the foothills, where the cattle would be unlikely to go, and consequently the ranch people as well.

The real problem would be getting the gear below him packed back onto Sally. He might be able to pull himself around after a fashion in a day or two, but it was almost inconceivable that he would be able to repack and resaddle.

On the other hand, there was nothing he could do about that right now. What his body needed was rest. What his wounds needed were cold compresses and to continue to be elevated.

Right now, the cold compresses were out of the question. He could not even pull himself to the edge of the bank so that he could dip into the water the cloths that had been wrapped around the damaged parts of his body. On the other hand, he could after a fashion keep his hurt arm, leg, and head elevated.

Just before he'd fallen asleep, he had evidently built up part of what was beneath him to make the mounds on which both the wounded arm and wounded leg could lie. With Dilaudid reducing the pain, he clumsily pulled them up on these mounds again. Anything beyond this would have to wait until he was stronger.

He remembered now, from the wolf books, that the saliva of wolves was very acidic, and therefore destructive to bacteria. Wolf had probably done him a favor by licking the wounds clean. There was no real bleeding; but if he craned his neck so that he could see arm and leg, he could see, exposed from where the bandages had been pulled away, a certain amount of suppuration from the torn areas. Wolf's nose would pick up the smell of that, and perhaps he would automatically clean them with his tongue again.

His mind went away on a slight tangent. He was still amazed at Wolf's concern for him. The thought that had been uppermost in his mind had been of Wolf as a danger, not as an aid. At first thought, his partner's behavior seemed to run against what he had read in a number of different places in the books.

It was too easy simply to assume that a depth of affection he had not noticed in Wolf before was suddenly operating within the other. He remembered the small noises, somewhere between a whimper and a grunt, that Wolf had made, watching him just before he had left. Certainly, Wolf had sounded concerned.

But there must be a more reasonable explanation than that. Jeebee's mind sorted through his memory of what he had read in the wolf books. His memory was good, but it was not an eidetic memory, a photographic one. However, any fact he ran across that could find a way to hook onto knowledge that was already in his mind had a tendency to do so and thereafter hang on as if it was glued in place.

But nowhere, specifically, in the books, was an explanation for a deeper concern in Wolf than he had expected, or a sudden change of attitude in the other. Jeebee lay musing as the sun climbed in the sky and the shadows about him shortened. He was still in shade now, but just barely from his feet up. Another hour—another half hour—would see him in need of a sunshade for his eyes.

Abruptly, an answer came to him. He had been making a mistake, thinking of the situation only from the viewpoint of the complete amateur he was in all matters dealing with wolves. The wolf was a social animal, and he was a social scientist. Now, thinking about what he had read of the pack behavior of wolves from the standpoint of a social scientist, he realized abruptly that the behavior of a wolf in a pack might not necessarily be the behavior of a wolf in a situation such as existed between himself and Wolf right now.

A wolf pack was evidently rather like an Italian court of the early Renaissance, in which everyone smiled at each other while carefully guarding their own back and keeping their eyes open for any opportunity that would expose the back of another, particularly a superior, to their dagger.

Among wolves, ranking was important, but that was only under pack conditions. The situation he enjoyed with Wolf did not embody pack conditions.

Now that he stopped to think of it, there had been a great deal of study of wolves in packs, but he'd read almost nothing of nomadic wolves traveling either alone or in pairs. But what operated in the case of the pack was a delicate balancing act between the advantages of belonging to a cooperative social group and competition for the privileges of high rank—especially the privilege of reproduction. He and Wolf, traveling as they did, were a pair of bachelors with no contest for reproductive rights to make rank an issue and all the natural gregariousness of their species to hold the partnership together.

Certainly the gregariousness—the need for company on both their parts—was there.

He had been overjoyed to have in Wolf someone who could share his life with him. He also remembered telling Merry of Wolf's first full submissive approach to him, which had come after he had seen the people chained to the wagons. It had come when he had essentially ignored Wolf, at a time when they were usually close.

Wolf clearly valued such social sharing as much as Jeebee did. It would make little sense, accordingly, to destroy the source of a comfort and a pleasure merely for the sake of relative ranking. Besides, if you did, there was then no point in being one up in the hierarchy because the hierarchy would be reduced to a single individual and cease to exist.

The sun climbed steadily up the sky until he was fully in sunlight. He pulled the corner of one light blanket, which was partially underneath him, over the top part of his head to shield his eyes. It would not have to be there more than an hour or so, because by that time the sun would have moved to the point where he would be getting shade from a clump of willows in a slightly different direction. Lying with his eyes hooded, but just able to look out from underneath them, and with the growing comfort of the narcotic pill within him, he dozed off.

He slept lightly and woke easily, this time to Wolf sniffing him all over. He opened his eyes and found Wolf now directing his attention to the wounded leg, which he proceeded to lick with a steady movement of the tongue. After which, essentially ignoring Jeebee in all other respects, as if he was busy at some business of his own, he moved up to lick the arm wound and then the head.

This time Jeebee lay still and let him work, only closing his eyes again when the wide tongue approached them. When the tongue ceased, he opened his eyes again. Wolf was in the process of backing off. He lay down on his stomach with forepaws extended, back legs angled out to one side, and his head on the crossed paws at the end of his front legs. His eyes seemed out of focus, as if he was watching nothing. But Jeebee had learned that any move he might make would be followed by a slight movement of one ear. Actually, he had come to understand that in moments like this Wolf was watching everything.

As it was, however, he could not move—or at least he could move only a tiny amount, and then with great pain and difficulty. The Dilaudid had not taken the pain away, but had reduced it to a level where his mind could operate. It was now early to mid-afternoon, as well as he could tell from the light and shadow around him. Possibly it might be time for another painkiller soon, but certainly not yet. Besides that, the less opiate, the better.

He was suddenly shocked to remember that when he had woken earlier he had scrambled around for the Dilaudid but could not remember taking the antibiotic. He wondered if he had taken it at all, after that first moment of his reaching the horses on his return. Painfully, with the hand of his usable right arm, he fumbled around for the drug pouch and found it. He got out the pill bottle that held the Augmentin, and by the process of spilling it carefully onto his chest so that none would roll off and away and be lost on the ground, he got the pills in position to be counted, if he craned his neck upward and separated them in bunches of five with his fingers.

There had been sixty of them originally, gotten on prescription through the doctor who had been on call for the study group. Now Jeebee only counted fifty-seven.

He had taken the first one yesterday morning. That meant he must have taken the other two during the blurry waking periods he could vaguely remember. The prescription called for three a day for at least a week, for up to ten days in a severe case.

The doctor had given it high marks, very high marks indeed, for effectiveness. It was supposed to be, he had said, effective against gram-negative bacteria and gram-positive bacteria as well as against staphylococci and against anaerobic bacteria.

Laboriously, he got the pills—all except one—back into their bottle, the bottle safely closed again and put away. Then, with a minimum of movement, he managed to wash down the remaining pill with water from the lighter of the two water bags.

Gingerly, for every movement was jarring to the sore side of his body, he tried lifting both bags to estimate how much water remained in them. The one from which he had drunk was nearly empty. The other was down somewhat but was at least three quarters full. He estimated he should be able to last until tomorrow without feeling any serious shortage of water.

For a short while he thought about rationing the water that remained. He decided against it. He was unclear, in cases of severe bruising, whether an adequate intake of water was needed for healing. Probably it was better to drink whenever he felt thirsty and let his body tell him how much and when.

Surely, by tomorrow, with Dilaudid freshly in him and the urgency of empty water bags facing him, he would be able to pull himself along the ground to the stream and refill both bags.

Once more he struggled to delve into his backpack, checking that the large, yellow, water-disinfectant pills were available and that there were plenty of them left. He had taken as many of these from the wagon stores as he thought would see him through a year. He must have several hundred left. Once those were gone—well, he could always boil for five minutes any water he wanted to drink or use in cooking. He wished now he had not lost the drinking tube with the ceramic filter he had carried from Stoketon in his backpack. With that, he could have risked drinking directly from the stream. But about two weeks ago he had looked for it and been unable to find it.

His semidrugged mind went off to other things that needed to be done. Wolf was still lying, apparently oblivious but actually alert. The big problem, Jeebee thought once more, would be loading Sally before he took off. An alternative, of course, would be to cache his supplies, to dig a place to hide it and cover it up so that neither Wolf nor any other wild animal would dig it up.

But he was in no better physical condition to do that than he was to load the horses, right now. A final solution would be to take what was absolutely necessary from it that Brute could carry and simply abandon the rest. Bringing Sally herself, of course, along for future use. That, and hope that he would be able to go back and find at least part of what he had owned.

But knowing the open country as he now did, he knew how unlikely it was that he could come back, even after a single day away, and find a pile of goods and food undisturbed. Humans might not find it, but the wild creatures would, and in less than a week, even if he did come back, there would be nothing worth picking up—probably.

Well, he would wait and see how much, if at all, he had improved by tomorrow. In any case, tomorrow he would be faced with the crawl to the stream. To a certain extent it all depended upon the effectiveness of the antibiotic and whatever aid in recovering he would get from the fact that he was in fairly good physical shape from the last few months of living an active physical life.

His mind went off on another tangent, triggered perhaps by Wolf's presence. The trouble was, the focus of his interest in his four-legged partner had been sharpened, rather than satisfied, by the wolf books. He had begun just by wanting to understand Wolf because of his own emotional bond with this four-legged partner. Then that had developed into a genuine scientific curiosity about Wolf and his species. Now it had gone even one step further. He could see now that it was not going to be merely satisfying to understand Wolf better, but perhaps vitally necessary—perhaps a matter of life or death somewhere along the line.

For example, Wolf had turned out to astonish him by attacking the bear when Jeebee himself was attacked. A wolf's instinct for self-preservation should have kept him prudently out of a battle with any predator larger than himself. What had overridden that prudence? It was only in the movies that Jeebee had ever seen one normally wild animal come doglike to the rescue of the human being with which it was familiar. Doglike—maybe that was the answer. Dog behavior had its roots in wolf behavior, and the evolutionary linchpin of wolf survival was social organization and cooperation.

Sharp's chapter in the parallel evolution book had highlighted the similarities between wolf packs and human hunting bands. Was Wolf's intervention the instinctive act of a cooperative hunter? Hell! Speculation was a useless self-indulgence. For all he knew, wolves—or some wolves, like some people—were just disposed to help their friends.

The scientist in Jeebee shied away from conclusions based on insufficient data. And the survivor in Jeebee realized that if he were wrong about situations in which Wolf might turn out to aid him, he might be wrong about other situations. Situations in which Wolf might turn out to be an actual threat to him—not merely standing aside in the face of some outside threat, but even attacking him suddenly without warning, because of some unthinking cue Jeebee did not even realize he had given.

What he had to do was read the books again, looking at their contents with different eyes, and do a great deal of comparing and searching to separate the elements that were basic to wolf character from those that were imposed by their social relationship, man and wolf associated as free individuals.

There could be advantages to their being together. If they could work as a team, they could tackle larger animals than either could take on alone. But then they would no longer be independent, and the problems that might arise between two individuals who saw the world through such different eyes were infinitely more difficult to anticipate than those that might arise between human partners.

He thought he could exclude reproductive competition from his worries, but what about competition for food? Did pack mates or nonterritorial pairs quarrel over division of the kill? Probably not, or the lowest-ranking members of a pack would be better off on their own, and the group would soon collapse. But were there other, less obvious sources of tension he ought to consider? Was social ranking, which was evidently so vital to a wolf in a pack, important to a traveling pair such as he and Wolf were . . . his thoughts abandoned the question of Wolf. The pain was really getting quite bad again; and the idea of more Dilaudid was tempting.

He found suddenly he was weary of speculation. He tried to remember just when he had first been brought fully awake by Wolf licking him.

He looked at the sun now, then suddenly cursed to himself internally for being so stupid.

He lifted his right wrist and looked at the watch upon it. He had completely forgotten that watch with its valuable battery, hoped to have a hundred-year lifetime. It was a digital watch with several modes to it. Countdown, stopwatch, and alarm were the three extra modes. The regular clock mode could show the hour and minutes in either A.M./P.M. fashion or in so-called "military time," where 1:00 P.M. became 1300 hours.

With this, from now on, he would keep track of his doses of medication. Also, tomorrow, one way or another, he would drag himself to the river, fill his water bags, and get to work on plans to move out of here. He had had enough of playing invalid; and thinking.

CHAPTER 22

The third day after meeting the bear, to his infinite joy, the swelling of his arm and leg had decreased. It still looked like about a third more than normal size. Definitely, however, the wooden stiffness that had come into both the damaged leg and arm from the engorgement of the blood vessels had relaxed somewhat. His torn scalp also felt better under its stiff cap of dried blood and hair.

It was too painful to attempt much flexing of either arm or leg, but he experimented to the point of convincing himself that the improvement was actual, and not just a product of his imagination.

Buoyed up by this and his latest dose of Dilaudid, he was able to creep off his erstwhile bed and drag the unusable parts of his body, with the two depleted water bags, to the river. There, he refilled them one by one and put in each a couple of sterilizing tablets.

It would be half an hour before the water so medicated would be safe for him to drink. But he had drunk most of what had remained in them before he made the attempt to reach the bank and he could easily wait out those thirty minutes or even a bit longer if necessary.

He also had brought along the rough bandages from his leg and arm, by the expedient of tucking them into his belt. He now soaked them in water and wrapped them again in place. The icy touch of the liquid was welcome upon the wounds.

He realized suddenly that while he had remembered the Dilaudid, his mind, occupied with the business of attempting the journey to the riverside, had made him forget his Augmentin.

But a delay of half an hour in taking the antibiotic would not be so desperate a matter to endure.

He had aimed at a slight dip in the bank, which gave him a rise to his left where he could sit down and elevate both the left arm and the left foot. With these up, the wet cloths around them, and the water bags beside him, he relaxed. Having gotten through the difficult journey to the river, there was no point in going back until he had to.

Luckily Wolf had been gone when he started the trip, otherwise Jeebee could imagine the other objecting to the arm and leg being covered again. Jeebee had made up his mind that if Wolf did, he would simply unwrap the limbs himself and let Wolf get at them. The idea of Wolf tugging at the cloth wrapped around his left leg, in the sensitive state it was in at this moment, was something he did not even want to think about.

He would in any case, he thought, unwrap the limbs the moment he saw Wolf, and leave them open. If Wolf went through his process of licking them, no harm should be done. If not, he would simply fold the cloths into a pack and lay them directly on the torn areas of skin so that they could be pulled off by him or lifted off by Wolf's nose easily.

The current Dilaudid was just beginning to take full effect. He was beginning to approach comfort to an extent that he had hardly thought possible for the last thirty-six hours when he suddenly realized that he had reached the point where he could no longer avoid evacuating his bowels.

With a great deal of discomfort and awkward crab crawling on the ground, he managed to get away from the place where he was lying to a spot at the edge of the riverbank just down from him, and satisfy the natural requirement.

Having done this, he re-dressed the lower part of his body

and got back to his riverside hollow, with the arm and leg elevated again.

The awkward movements had done the two damaged limbs no good. It was some time, even with the Dilaudid in him, before the pain started to abate again. He lay full in the sunlight, and—particularly with the cold cloths on him—the heat was welcome. He half dozed; and later on, when Wolf did come back, he uncovered the wounds. But Wolf merely sniffed at them without licking. Jeebee dozed off again, and woke to find himself once more in shadow, chilled by the absence of the sun, and with Wolf also gone.

He made the slow pilgrimage back to the stack of bedding that was the load and settled himself there for the night.

The next day he was a great deal better. He had less pain, and the arm and leg had definitely gone down in their swelling to the point where he could bend knee and elbow perceptibly. There would be one more day at least before he could think of trying to move out. To leave at all meant at the very least he would have to saddle Brute, and that would require his standing, lifting, and doing a number of other things that were still beyond him.

The next day, however, he had improved to the point where he decided to at least experiment by trying to saddle Brute.

It would be necessary for him to make a crutch, first. The trouble was that not even the thickest of the willow stems growing around the stream was strong enough to hold him up. Happily, however, he had some folding tent-pole props. He was able to unfold one of these and tightly wrap it with leather cord so that it was not too likely to buckle under him.

The crutch he ended up with as a result was shorter than he would have liked. But used with care, it did not give underneath him. He also had nothing that could be easily fixed at the top to make a crosspiece to go under his armpit. He ended by making a tight wad of cloth at the top of the prop, which fitted into his armpit. It worked, but cut off the circulation in his arm after a few minutes use.

His first attempt to stand on his feet with this support was comic. But he did get up; and he was supported. He propped the saddle ready so that by still leaning on the staff and holding to it with what strength there was in his left hand, he could reach down with his right and lift it.

It was a heavy load for one arm to lift, let alone for one arm to throw over the back of the horse.

Luckily, Brute was still in an agreeable mood, apparently, and did not sidle around or try to avoid the saddle as Jeebee made an effort to put it on. To Jeebee's surprise, he still had more strength in his right arm than he had realized.

The way he had been living—and eating at the wagon—had evidently wrought a more permanent physical improvement than he had thought. Also, a certain amount of desperation was at work inside him. If nothing else, even if he had to abandon everything else to escape some danger here, he had to be able to get that saddle on Brute and cinched tight.

It took him nearly two hours to do it. Most of this time was spent in working out a method, using knee and single hand to pull the cinch tight enough so that the saddle would not slip around under Brute's belly and dump him off the horse when he was mounted. A fall like that, now, would not only be painful but could put him back out of action for several more days.

Finally he got the saddle on and cinched properly. He tried mounting, but that was too much for him, as yet. He unbuckled the cinch strap and dropped the saddle to the ground, again.

With the excitement of working over, he began to realize acutely that it was time for another painkiller. So far he had stuck to three tablets of Dilaudid a day. He was determined not to exceed that so he could be sure to be able to give up the medication at the end of seven days.

However, at the end of forty minutes of rest on his makeshift bed, the pains had eased off. So much so that he thought he might perhaps try getting the saddle blanket on Sally, and at least some of the more necessary items. The blanket was light, he had worked out ways of pulling the cinch tight with his good hand and bracing knee, and Sally was much more likely than Brute to stand still while he put stuff on her.

Accordingly, he struggled back up on his crutch. But to be-

gin with, there was the problem of tying an anchor knot to a ring
on the cinch strap one-handed when he had been used to tying it
with two. He tried various ways, using not only his knee but as
much of the hand on his hurt arm as possible, to hold the rope
still while he threaded the end of the rope around and through
the metal ring. Finally, eventually, he found a way to get it tied.
Then came the relatively easy job of looping the rope back and
forth through the other iron rings that secured it to the cinch
strap; then finally the almost impossible-seeming problem of pulling it tight and tying the final notch.

This last defeated him. As the sun was sinking, he got the
knot tied, but the rope was not pulled anywhere as tight as
it should have been, and there was no telling whether the load
might not shift under the movement of the mare as she tried to
carry it.

He was worn out, and the pains had come back with re-
doubled force. It was finally time for him to allow himself another Dilaudid. He took it and collapsed on his bed. He fell
abruptly into sleep, but woke up after a short while, hungry.

He had been surviving on the trail mix and some dried beef
that Merry had supplied him with when he left. There was
enough left of this for two or three meals yet, if he made them
very light ones. He compromised by eating only a handful of the
trail mix and drinking a good amount from the water bags.

He fell asleep again, still ravenous. He came awake suddenly, feeling alarmed, but not knowing why. The sun was just
up. Light was just beginning to flood the landscape.

After a few minutes he heard the sound of a single, distant
rifle shot.

He waited, gripped by fear. The sound was not repeated. He
guessed, however, that there had been another before it, and that
this was what had wakened him earlier.

At all costs, fit to travel or not, he must get away from his
present exposed position. Even if it meant taking his next Dilaudid ahead of time.

He struggled to his feet again and began trying to saddle and
load the two horses in earnest.

Whether it was the new Dilaudid or what he had learned earlier that made it possible, or whether it was the necessity of leaving nothing behind to signal his presence here, piece by piece he managed to get all the load on Sally and tied down, and Brute saddled.

The sun was high, and he did not like to move in daylight. But the horses were now ready to travel, and he must move with them. He could not risk waiting around here much longer.

Leaning heavily on his makeshift crutch, he got his foot in the stirrup, a firm grasp on the saddle horn, and tried valiantly to swing his bad leg over the back of Brute so that he sat in the saddle. It was a tremendous struggle, but he failed.

He told himself he would not give up. He leaned against the side of Brute, panting, his wet forehead pressed against the leather of the saddle horn. Wolf had meanwhile come back and was standing a dozen feet off, watching.

He made three more efforts before he finally, by some miracle of rage at himself, got the leg over and his rump into the saddle. Dismounting, he realized now, would be almost as painful. But that did not matter now. Now he could travel. He lifted the reins and spoke to Brute.

"Get on, you bastard," he said—and Brute moved off among the willows. Sally trailed obediently behind at the end of the rope that tied her to Brute's saddle. Jeebee could no longer see Wolf. He did not know if the other was with him now or not. But he no longer had any doubt that Wolf, if alive, would be likely to catch up with him somewhere. In any case, it did not matter. Jeebee was moving, and he was traveling upstream toward the foothills.

By midday, he was exhausted and called a halt. He left the horses, having no choice, with their gear on, and slept on the ground beside them until nearly dark. With nightfall he went on, taking a chance and leaving the willow bottoms of the stream for a more direct route overland to the foothills, as he had seen them at the end of the day.

Later on, he was never able to recall this part of his trip with any clarity until he saw the burning buildings. In the saddle at last, he had begun to have hopes of making it into the foothills in one night's ride.

It was true it was a night placed on top of a day that had asked the most from him. But he had given that much before and assumed that he could do it now. However, to a certain extent he was still worried about the painkillers he might have to take to help him reach his goal. It seemed to him he had heard of army surgeons in field hospitals during the war in Vietnam becoming hooked on Dilaudid because they had had to operate twenty-four hours around the clock and taking the drug was the only way they could do it.

But the Dilaudid was the only thing that could get him through. As it turned out, it did; but it was not easy. He was still holding off on his first pain pill of the trip, now that he was mounted and moving. But even with the horses going at a walk, he found riding hard. It was not so much that he could not deal with the pain on a minute-to-minute basis. It was the problem that the tension in him from his defiance of it was wearing him out. It was a matter of bracing himself against a new surge of pain each time Brute's hooves struck the ground, jolting his hurt body. But there were things even beyond that to deal with.

One of these was the question of how to place his hurt left leg. Both in the stirrup and out of the stirrup it was uncomfortable. He had deliberately shortened the stirrup on that side and he was grateful now he had. But even that position was not good. In the end he put his toe, only, in it, and tried to forget his leg was there.

As the meager moonlight appeared with the rising of the moon to help him on his way—thank God the sky was clear and also that the horses were good at picking their own way in the sense of knowing where to put their feet—it became impossible to ignore the fact that riding in this position with his left leg hanging down was asking for trouble. He took a Dilaudid. Once it had gone to work to make him more comfortable, with great effort he pulled his left leg up with his hand until his knee was partly crooked around the pommel and the leg itself was held mostly near the horizontal.

This was a dangerously loose way to sit the saddle, even with Brute at a walk. He was not sure how long he could go on with it, without doing some kind of further damage to the leg. Thank God the knee would bend at least that much.

Normally, even at a walk like this, three to five hours of traveling should have brought them safely into the hills. They needed to find a place well above any of the ranch houses, a place where both he and the horses could hide overnight.

The fact was, he thought suddenly, he was standing up to the ride better than he had expected. Along with the action of the Dilaudid, there seemed to have come to his aid a sort of semi-hysteric state of determination to make the ride.

It was a state not too different from the shock he had gone into during his encounter with the bear. In this condition, the early hours of the night passed something like a bad dream, in which he was partly insulated from the physical cost of what he was doing and against any tendency to feel so exhausted he had to stop.

He ended by not getting down from the saddle at all, after one or two attempts, simply because he was afraid of getting down and not being able to make the climb back up. If that happened, he would be caught out here in the open, for around him there was nothing but sagebrush and open ground that should have had a certain amount of grass. It was bare partly from the drought of the last few years but would have been treeless even in a wet year. Somehow, he must keep moving until he got to a place where he could hide, both himself and the two horses with their burdens.

In the end he passed into an almost completely dreamlike state in which only a corner of his senses and vision kept watch normally. His vision, even, seemed to adjust unnaturally well to the reduced light of the partial moon, so that he felt he could see where they were going and the ground ahead of them as well as if it were daylight. But the small, sane corner of his mind kept insisting this could not be true.

Still, it was in this condition that, somewhere after midnight, the sane part of him noticed a glow on the horizon. It had to be after midnight because the moon was already starting its descent, which would leave him feeling his way in a nearly complete dark, with nothing but stars to light him along.

The glow came from directly ahead of him. It waxed and waned in curious fashion. He rode directly toward it, fascinated, for some distance, before realizing he was seeing the light of a large fire up ahead of him somewhere.

The hallucination of daylight vision in his present state did not completely shut out a sense of caution. As soon as it sank in on him that the light ahead was that of an unlikely large fire—the kind of fire that a ranch house and buildings might make—he began immediately to circle away from the direct line he had been taking toward it. It was a move as instinctive as that which had pulled him toward it.

He circled to his left, going wide but not so wide that he would not be able to get a view of whatever it was that was burning, when he got closer to it.

With the Dilaudid inside him, his mind was still clear as the minds of those surgeons in Vietnam must have been. A burning ranch house might well have attracted help from neighbors, which meant that there could be a number of people around the blaze.

On the other hand, if a lot of people were there, they still were most likely to be occupied with trying to put the fire out. Moreover, he knew how deceptive light like this could be. After staring into such flames for a little while, even a short distance away from it, everything would seem lost in utter blackness.

He should be able to pass fairly close with some safety from being observed.

Perhaps.

CHAPTER 23

Jeebee had moved out to his left in his circling movement to the point where he estimated he would pass the fire at better than a hundred yards to its left.

Accordingly, he now altered his course back toward the foothills, heading toward the high blackness ahead where the stars speckling the night sky ceased at an undulating horizon of blackness. The moon was already down.

There was only the slightest of night winds cooling Jeebee's right cheek, but the flames ahead burned brightly. As he got closer he could see that outbuildings, including the tall barn, were being fiercely consumed by flame. The ranch house at first had looked almost untouched. But now he began to see a little tongue of flame that appeared and disappeared, running flickeringly along the eaves on the closer edge of the roof, on the side of it he would be passing.

Also, as he got closer, he began to hear the sounds of voices—voices raised in yips and yells, like the voices of those at some wild revel. He also began to make out the black silhouettes of figures dancing and running about. Occasionally he saw a figure of a riderless horse among them.

The first thought of his weary brain was that he must be looking at the home of some unfortunate rancher who had incurred the enmity of his neighbors. The way Jeebee himself had unconsciously done back in Stoketon, Michigan.

Then he rejected this idea, along with another, that perhaps the figures he saw were neighbors who had come to try and help. He could hear shots now, though whether they were being fired into the air, from the ranch house, or at the house, was impossible to tell.

He realized at last, with a cold clutching at his guts, that what was happening to the ranch house was most likely to be an attack and destruction by one of the large, semimilitarily organized bunches of nomadic raiders. If so, these were the kind of people Nick Gage had spoken of as the only real danger to Paul's wagon.

Such gangs lived from moment to moment and had no interests in leaving even a peddler alive because they might want to trade with him again next year. By next year these later-day Comancheros might well be dead, or hundreds of miles away.

They literally lived off the land, and off what still remained on it. They survived by staying away from cities and moving continually, fast enough so that no local group could be mustered in time to oppose them successfully.

When he was level with the burning buildings—all burning now, because the roof of the ranch house was also on fire—he stopped. Awkwardly, he turned in the saddle enough to reach behind him with his good hand and fumble out the binoculars that had been Merry's special gift to him.

He put the heavy pair of glasses to his eyes, then had to take them down again to readjust their focusing knob. After several adjustments and subsequent trying of the binoculars, he got the scene around the burning ranch in sharp focus.

There was a strange ludicrous effect to what he watched. The silhouettes of figures running or riding back and forth between him and the flames had an unnatural appearance, like black marionettes of heavy cardboard dancing to invisible strings before the fire. It was as if they held some wild celebration that had now gotten out of hand, so that something frenetic drove them to their antics before the leaping red light.

As he watched, one of the black figures fell, ignored by the rest. Apparently there were those still alive in the ranch house who were firing back at their attackers. But none of the defenders could last long. A good piece of the roof over their heads was now a-flicker in several places. Soon the house itself would become an inferno. He put the glasses away and rode on. The memory of what he had just seen—the lurid red flames, the black figures, and the air of orgy—was painted in his mind even as he himself passed, unseen. His own pains and discomforts took him back into them, and away from what he had just seen. He kept moving.

Almost immediately, he was away from the ranch and into sloped ground. Brute grunted and leaned to the slope, and Jeebee himself leaned forward in the saddle. He was empty with fatigue. After a while he stopped the horses for a moment and turned Brute's head back so that he could look down at where he had traveled.

There was a ridge now between him and the ranch, so that he could no longer see the fire. But against the starry sky the glow of flames was much less. He knew he had not gone so much farther that with the glasses and on the ridge top behind him, he would not be able to see whether the raiders were still there when the sun rose. But he wanted only to go forward to personal safety. He started the horses moving again. Shortly, he was into trees, pine country.

The trees closed around him after a while. He told himself that if he could only find a stream to water the horses, he would stop at last. Luck was with him. He crossed a wide-open slope, slippery with shale rock, where the horses went gingerly, and came out through a fold to a little open spot among trees where he could hear water running. A few yards further brought him to a small flow of water that headed generally in the direction of the ranch buildings below.

With great and painful effort he dismounted, tied the horses to trees, and left them with some grass around them at the edge of the small stream.

He did not even have strength to unpack or unsaddle. It was hard on the horses but he had reached his limits. He slid down from the saddle, took the water bag from his saddle, and the crutch. He then worried a blanket out of Sally's packload. Rolling himself in this, at the foot of one of the pines, he curled up in the blanket and took the Dilaudid he had held off from taking—for so many hours that his exhaustion-dulled mind could not remember their number.

He was instantly asleep.

When he woke, it was dawn of the next day. The sun slanted through the green branches over him.

For a moment he felt perfectly ordinary. Then with a rush, pain and exhaustion closed in on him once more. He was still weak and hungry for rest. For a moment he thought he could not even get to his feet.

The pain in his damaged left leg reminded him of how it had been crooked across the saddle through most of the long ride.

He dragged up his left pants leg as far as he could, to look at the wound. But he could not pull it up far enough. In fact, it was too uncomfortable to pull further, since at this point the cloth of the lower leg was tight against the swollen limb. It seemed to him, however, that the leg was more swollen than it had been twenty-four hours before, and fear of infection passed briefly through him. But at that point the pain registered on him.

He glanced at his watch. Certainly it had been over eight hours since he had gone to sleep.

He turned to his backpack, got the pouch behind his saddle that held the medicine, took out the Dilaudid, and washed it down with water from the water bag. He lay for a little while clutching the bag, occasionally drinking a little bit more from it, waiting for the Dilaudid to take effect.

Slowly, it began to work. Slowly, the pain receded somewhat. He was able to think beyond his own body and look beyond himself. The first thing to catch his attention was the fact that Wolf was not there. Also the two horses were looking at him. Sally had a literally piteous look in her eyes, and even Brute's gaze held an unusual appeal.

He waited a little longer to get the most out of the Dilaudid. Then he got to his feet with the help of the crutch and went first to Sally, limping badly but being able to bear a little of his weight for a very short time on the hurt leg. He loosened the cinch strap that held the saddle blanket with the load above it, and the load itself fell with a thump to the ground.

Sally gave what was literally a sigh of relief. Jeebee held himself to her backbone for a few moments while he took the weight off his bad leg, then made his way around her body to within grabbing distance of Brute, who, for once, did not try to move away from him.

He had to go around Brute to get at the side where the cinch strap was fastened by the buckle. He did so, for once not thinking of Brute's heels, and, again, Brute did not try to take advantage of this to kick him. Slowly, under the difficulty of working with one hand, Jeebee loosened Brute's cinch strap as well and let the saddle slide off.

This much done, Jeebee went over to the little stream and sat down beside it. He unbuckled his belt, with difficulty, pulled off his pants and left boot and sock. He then immersed his left leg in the running water.

It was icy, but after the first shock it felt good on his leg. It was not as swollen from his ride as he had feared. Now he took the time to roll up his sleeve and put his hurt arm into the water, too.

He lay this way for some time. The stream here seemed clearer than the one among the willows, below, and eventually a pleasant numbness came to reinforce the effect of the Dilaudid in both limbs.

As the personal, physical side of his problems receded into the background, Jeebee's mind began to concern itself with larger matters. He had realized on waking that he was in no shape to travel any farther—today, at least.

Not only was he not up to it, the horses were not up to it. Both of them had already lain down, a sure sign that they were at their limits. It was to be expected. Particularly after their carrying saddle and packload for so many hours. They should be given a couple of days to rest and eat, anyway. There was a fair amount of graze in this little opening among the pines, here and around the stream.

Here, he should be fairly safe. For the moment, anyway, there was no need to search further for a resting place.

There was nothing in these hills to attract raiders, and any neighbors who came to investigate the results of the raid would hardly travel any distance into the hills to see if anyone was still lurking in the vicinity. Nor was there any reason for one of those who'd recently killed and burned to stay around.

So he and the horses were probably safe here for the present. He could have stumbled on worse spots.

Meanwhile, it was of vital importance that his wounds go on healing. Above all, it was important that he get physically able as soon as he could.

He lifted his left leg out of the stream and was certain that the swelling had gone down by more than a little since he had put it in. He made allowance for the fact that he was possibly letting himself be influenced too much by the fact that the skin was white and shrunken into ridges from being underwater as it had been. Still, he was sure the leg looked better.

Incredible that he could make such a ride and be so well. Perhaps the good food while he was with the wagon and the exercise of past months had not only strengthened him, but made him more fit to resist injuries than he had ever been before in his life.

How much fitter he actually was, he discovered when he put his pants back on and struggled back up on to his feet with the help of the crutch. There was more flexibility in his left leg than he thought.

He made his awkward and uncomfortable way back to the saddle he had dropped off Brute. There, he allowed himself a fair allowance of the trail mix that was all that was left in the backpack. He told himself that if he had to stay here at least another day, he would get the flour and salt out of the pack goods Sally had been carrying and make bannock. This was not quite bread, but baked on a stick slowly over the coals of a fire, it was the closest thing to bread, and it had food value. It would be some time yet before he could hope to do any hunting, even if he wanted to risk the sound of his rifle carrying perhaps to other people on the flatlands down below.

The .30/06 was really too heavy for small game like squirrels and rabbits.

Once back in the rugged and wooded part of these foothills, near the real beginnings of the mountains, he should be far enough away to shoot at anything that looked eatable with some safety. At least, he would have a reasonable certainty that the shot would not be heard.

Even if it was heard, with reflecting rock surfaces all around him, a single shot would probably not pinpoint his location. In Sally's pack there was also bacon, but he was saving that for real needs later on, when he could save the fat and use it as an extra part of his food.

As soon as he could set up a semipermanent camp in these hills he must go down and try to slaughter one of the ranch's range cattle for beef. The carcass would probably be blamed on the raiders if he was able to go in the next week or so. Even if he could not get it within that time limit, the body would soon be attacked by Wolf, or other predators, and it would look as if these had been responsible for its death.

Meanwhile, if his leg held up to it, it would probably be a good idea to ride Brute back to a place where he could take a look, with the binoculars Merry had given him, at the ranch that had been raided. Certainly, the raiders must be gone. But it would be wise to check.

His first idea of riding Brute, however, foundered on the fact that neither Brute nor Sally would be ready to be ridden for several days at least. Jeebee considered the distance to the highest ridge behind him. It was not more than about three hundred feet; if he took it in slow stages . . .

He remembered a first-aid training class, which was one of the things he had managed to take when he had first begun to have the sense to accumulate the electric bike, the watch with the one-hundred-year battery, and the other items he had carried out of Michigan with him. He could not see the page that it had been on in his mind's eye, but the orderly, academic part of his mind knew it had been on page one hundred and twenty-nine of the manual that had come with the course. It had been in the paragraph on bruises, particularly severe bruises.

Exercise, the manual had said, "is indicated as soon as the swelling is down enough and the patient feels capable of using the limb. Exercise at this point will hasten recovery, helping to pump the engorged blood out of the tissues and promote healing."

He looked down at his leg, remembering it as it had looked when he had taken it out of the water. He had no way of telling whether the swelling was "down enough." But certainly he was able to bend it further. It felt better—although probably that was because of the Dilaudid rather than any natural healing process. He felt a wild animal's need to be able to move. If he took the trip from where he was now to the top of the ridge, in easy stages, maybe he could do it and help the leg rather than hurt it further.

However, first he needed something more solid in the way of a crutch—something better than the stick with a wad of cloth at one end. He still had the Swiss army knife, and a somewhat larger folding, lock-bladed knife for ordinary work, in a button-down sheath on his belt. He got the latter out now and proceeded to see if he could spot any dry timber close by that looked capable of giving him the material he needed.

There was nothing close. However, some of the young trees, or larger saplings—it was hard to know which to call them—might still be stout enough. A piece of one of them might bend a little, as green wood might, but still support the weight he would want to put on it as the staff of a new crutch.

He found a likely sapling about an inch in diameter and cut a piece from it. He worked away at it with his knife until he got himself a length to fit comfortably under his left armpit.

He deliberately made it a little long, figuring he could always whittle it down if necessary. He put a point on the upper end of it and found another, shorter and thicker section in which he made a hole for the pointed end of the staff, using first, the point of his knife and then the leather punch of the Swiss army knife.

He pushed the hole in the crosspiece down on the pointed end of the staff as far as he could and bound it firmly with leather thongs. Then he put the lashed end under the water of the stream and held it there until it was thoroughly soaked.

It was hard to give it time to dry, but he waited a good hour. Finally, he put the still-damp end under his armpits and began his trip.

Wolf had not shown up at all since he had awakened, for which he was grateful. He was more certain now of Wolf's concern, if that was the right word for it, on the evidence of Wolf's licking of his wounds. But especially since he had read the books on wolves, Jeebee was wary of what the reaction of the other's instinctive system might be to the sight of Jeebee hobbling along in an obviously vulnerable condition. Disliking himself for doing it, but without any real hesitation, he stuck the revolver in his belt, where it would be easier to get at in his present crippled condition, and took the rifle as well as the binoculars. He was no longer sure he could bring himself to shoot at Wolf. Even months back, coming up from the root cellar, he had reversed the rifle to use its butt as a club.

But in any case, Wolf was far from being the only danger he might have to face. He felt better having the loaded weapons with him.

CHAPTER 24

But the trip turned out to be more than he had bargained for. He had counted on the leather thong holding the top of the crutch firmly in place. But it did not do so anywhere near as well as he had expected. Perhaps he should have been more patient about waiting for it to dry so that the cord could shrink itself tight in its wrapping—the way he had always understood leather did on drying out.

In any case, gradually his use worked the crosspiece more and more loose, so that it wobbled on the end of the vertical staff. His left leg, in spite of the Dilaudid, hurt and felt weak, and the heavy weight of the powerful binoculars swung back and forth with each step to bump his chest.

The latter was a minor thing, which he would have ordinarily scarcely noticed. But on top of the pain from his arm, leg, and scalp, it was an irritant. He found himself growing irrationally angry at anything and everything, and it was only by positive determination that he at last put the anger out of his mind.

He made the trek to the top of the ridge eventually, moving in small journeys, from point to point. He would pick out ahead a tree to which he could cling, and with which he could lower himself to a seated position on the ground, with his left leg out straight before him and the tree trunk also supporting his back, once he was down.

Then, after a short rest, he would pick out another tree farther on, haul himself upright with his good arm, and go forward once more.

The real problems came when he had to cross the stretch of loose shale on the slope he and the horses had walked over so gingerly on their way in.

He had picked the shortest possible crossing place. It was as far up near the top of the slope as he could go, before it became so steep he was afraid of slipping and falling. The very top of the slope rose at last into the vertical face of a small bluff.

Even where he chose to cross, it was a long stretch and he dared not sit down to rest partway over. With the crutch alone, and the loose rock under foot, he was not sure if he could get to his feet again. Also, even here, the pitch of the slope was steep enough so that if he fell, he might tumble for at least several hundred yards—for the shale spread out in a fanlike manner down the slope, until it brought up against a more level area, below.

He had known he must make this crossing. But he had not fully imagined what it would be like to go over it, crippled as he was. He rested, accordingly, for longer than usual before starting on the near side of the loose stone shards. Then he pulled himself up with the crutch and started out with determination, steadily inching his way across the open space.

He made most of the trip with his eyes on the ground, just ahead, examining the next few feet before him. It was necessary to pick a place between the loose stones to put down the tip of his staff. Also, he wanted firm, level spots on which to plant his good foot when he set it down.

Soon, again, he was enmeshed in a small world of sweating and straining, with his eyes almost hypnotized by the surface a few feet ahead, except when he raised his head to make sure of where he was going.

It was in a moment of such near ground-hypnosis that something dark became noticeable for a moment out of the corner of his right eye, upslope. For a second he ignored it. Only when he had found firm support for his crutch tip and his feet did he stop to turn his head for a better look.

Higher up, only about fifteen feet or so and under a natural outcropping of more solid rock among the shale, there was a good-sized dark hole that looked uncomfortably like the entrance to some animal's den. It would have been hidden from his sight on the trip in by the night darkness, even if he and the horses had passed close at all.

He had swung the muzzle of his rifle instinctively to cover the entrance the minute he recognized the dark circle for what it was. There were a few seconds in which he waited tensely; then he made himself relax.

The hole was big enough to take a fairly large beast. But anything large enough to den up there should not be likely to be shy about coming out to defend its property, as close as he had now come to it. At the same time, he now knew that all wild animals followed no rule book, but reacted in individual manners. The cougar, which was the most likely animal to be in there, would hardly be present in the middle of the day, since the big cats were daytime hunters.

Nonetheless . . . he kept the muzzle on the rifle on the opening as he began to move again, working his way on past.

But nothing emerged from the den. He heard no stir of movement inside it. Looking at it from a little distance, he became more and more convinced that the den—if indeed it was that at all . . . but what else would dig a hole that size into the soft earth under the shale?—was not and probably had not been in use for some time. It might be a bear den. But if so, it was summer now, when bears were out of their dens and, like most large animals, having their time fully taken up by their search for the food they needed to live.

He was worn out and traveling on a last burst of determination when he reached the far side of the shale slope and collapsed.

But he was now at the foot of a fairly short and steady, if steep, slope with no loose rock. As soon as he could catch his breath and get a little of his strength back, he made the last leg of his journey. On the way, a thought occurred to him that he should have had earlier. It was that, of course, the den was unoccupied; otherwise the horses would have reacted when they caught the scent of its owner on the way past, coming in last night.

At the top of the ridge he flopped down on his belly and put the powerful binoculars to his eyes. He focused on the ruins of the ranch house and its outbuildings.

It was clear that the raiders had gone; and they would have left no one behind. For one thing, there would be no reason for them to leave anyone behind, alive. For another, there was not a sign of life—even, when he swept the surrounding area with the binoculars, of any neighbor coming to investigate.

Either this ranch house was far enough removed from others that its neighbors did not know what had happened, or else these had seen the glow of the flames against the night sky, but prudently decided that they probably were not in numbers sufficient to take on a hundred or more of the horse nomads from an unfortified position. Certainly, none of them were in sight now.

Looking through the glasses, Jeebee was surprised to see how much of the ranch house still stood and how much of it and its outbuildings had survived the fire.

He had noticed before, in crossing the farmlands of northern Indiana, how often a house seemed to have been put on fire and yet the flames had died of their own accord before the building was consumed. Apparently, old and solid pieces of timber, large roof beams and such, had a fair resistance to fire.

It was not simply a matter of starting an edge of one smoldering and expecting the whole thing to continue until the whole thing burned up. Often, he had been able to see where the fire had begun on such a beam and given out. So that sections of the house often still stood, often with part or all of the roof immediately above them in place. He had sheltered in a number of such isolated ruins in his first dash out of Stoketon.

Now, as he looked down, he could see that nearly three quarters of the ranch-house roof seemed intact, although all the windows he could see through the binoculars were little more than blackened holes in the sides of a black and blistered building.

He lowered the binoculars to rest his eyes. It occurred to him that it would not be in the raiders' best interest to burn the ranch house to the ground, anyway. At least, not until they had a chance to search through it for things they wanted. The first flames to reach it might well have been accidental, blown over from one or more of the burning outbuildings. The raiders might well even have worked to put out the house fire, after resistance from those who lived there ceased, so that the flames would not destroy what they hoped to find within.

However, the more he thought about it, the more it seemed reasonable that there might well be many things still down below that would be useful to him; if and when he had the ability, time, and safety in which to search the ruins.

No live animals were visible about the place. Any horses, milk cattle, dogs or such, which might have once been there, were dead and gone. The bodies of several dead horses, beginning to bloat in the sun, were visible, but at some distance from the ranch house. Possibly they had belonged to the raiders and been killed by the gunfire from the ranch house.

In any case, they were now stripped of their saddles or whatever else they had carried, and simply left to rot.

Jeebee took the binoculars from his eyes and woke to the fact that Wolf was standing beside him. Wolf put his ears back and crouched down slightly as Jeebee's eyes came on him. He stretched forward to look at Jeebee's face, and Jeebee reached out reflexively to scratch in the fur under Wolf's neck and chin.

He was putting the binoculars to his eyes again when he realized he had responded to Wolf without a thought of the guns he had carried, and Wolf must have been beside him for at least several seconds.

Wolves, he remembered from the books he had picked up, never lied. Their intent was always signaled by their body language, and Wolf's greeting just now had been as friendly as ever.

It struck him that if Wolf was with him now, almost certainly the other had been close to him for most of his trip. It was Wolf's nature to tag along out of sight, from curiosity. So if Wolf had ever really been instinctively prompted to attack him, it would have happened before now . . . and his hand would never have had a chance to use any kind of weapon.

A vast, almost guilty sense of relief possessed him. Once more, he admitted to himself bluntly that he had come to love this four-footed companion of his, as he had admitted to himself earlier that he had fallen in love with Merry. Well, he was a human. He had a right to love, because he was capable of loving, whatever other imperatives might drive Wolf's kind.

A sudden shiver ran through him. He was also capable, he remembered, of killing, too. He had admitted that to himself a long time since, coming up from the root cellar, but he only faced it now as an abiding fact of his character, for the first time. He would kill. He would kill to stay alive, he would kill to get what he needed to survive. He would kill to protect Merry or Wolf.

He was a loving and a killing animal. It was so and there was nothing to be done about it.

His neck muscles were becoming weary from holding his head in a constant lifted position to look over the crest of the ridge. He inched forward slightly with his whole body and lowered his head so that his cheek rested on his good right hand as he stared sideways down at the burned buildings.

Everyone was dead down there. Everyone who could have been down there *had* to be dead. The ranch house was actually only a couple of hundred yards from him. But it was too far for him to hear anyone pinned under one of those half-burned beams who might still be calling for help, or a baby crying. Common sense said that if there had been any such, the raiders would undoubtedly have slaughtered them, for the sake of killing if for no other reason, just before they left. That kind of killer, he told himself now, he was not—not yet, anyway.

His thoughts went back to the people who had lived below. No, there could be no one alive down there.

He realized abruptly that he was trying to talk himself out of something.

It would be the worst sort of foolishness to go down there. As it was at this moment, the trail of the raiders would draw any attention, if and when the neighbors showed up after all; and if they brought in dogs. Should he go down now, his own trail would be freshest. Though, to be honest, if the books had been correct in telling him that a wolf had to be almost on top of a day-old footprint in order to pick up its scent, it was unlikely that domestic dogs could find or follow anything older.

No, again; it was mostly the thought of the long walk down that hill, the very hard climb back up again, and the possibility of what might result from his going, that made it foolish to go.

But if he did not, he would hear a hurt and abandoned child crying in the back of his mind for the rest of his life.

He got to his feet with the help of his crutch and began cautiously to descend the slope before him. The slope here was greater than the grade a few hundred yards to his right that he must have come up the night before. But straight down would be quicker and he must think about getting back to the horses.

He had gone only a few steps before he realized that Wolf was not with him. He looked back and saw Wolf still standing on the crest of the hill looking down at him.

"That's right," Jeebee said to him, "you're not a damn fool like me."

He turned his gaze and his attention back to the business of descending the slope. He went down with the end of his crutch dug in, and his feet dug in, sideways to the descent. The last thing he needed now was a fall. The pitch here was not so bad that he would slide or tumble any distance, but the very idea of a fall on the hurt leg and arm made him wince.

He reached the ranch and began his examination of what was left there. He checked all places under or behind which a body might be, and found seven of them. A grown woman, three men, two boys, and a girl—the oldest of the youngsters looking about sixteen. The youngest, which was the girl, looked as if she had been about twelve. They were all dead, and had been dead for some long hours. He did not touch them.

Leaving the ranch buildings, he once more attacked the hill behind it.

There were undoubtedly tools and other things the raiders would not have wanted but he could use, still in the house and outbuildings. Even while searching the house, he had seen a short-handled, three-pound hammer untouched by fire in one of the outbuildings. It was a one-handed sledge or maul, of the kind Nick Gage had described to him. Ideal for use with the sort of backwoods forge Nick had described and Jeebee had lusted to build for his own use someday. But he could not take it now. Even with the crutch, he would have all he could do to make it back to the horses. Besides, the afternoon was getting on.

He turned at last to retrace his way up the slope. The climb was difficult. When he came to the top at last, to relatively level ground, he sat and indulged in rest longer than he had planned. Wolf, he saw, had disappeared again and the day was moving on. Finally, he struggled to his feet and began the long, slow series of small journeys necessary to get back to the horses.

By the time he got there, his arm and leg had begun to hurt very badly indeed. He checked his watch and was relieved to see that somehow he had used up close to six hours since his last Dilaudid. He was entitled to another, although that put him back on the four-pill-a-day dosage he had started with right after the accident. This was the last of the seven days that he had accepted was the most he could risk taking the medication, without danger of addiction.

Beyond the safe limit for Dilaudid, he could fall back on the Tylenol and aspirin that he also carried. But he imagined now how weak a substitute these would be for the more potent drug.

Nonetheless, he took a Dilaudid, rested awhile until the pain had begun to recede, then set about finding dry wood for a fire.

He got the fire going and the horses tethered in areas of fresh graze, but still next to the small stream. He sat down to gaze into the fire with his back to a tree. The afternoon was fading and he drifted off into a doze.

A large, sticky tongue slathered his right cheek unexpectedly, and a paw landed on his right shoulder. He woke to twilight and the return of Wolf.

They went through the usual ceremony of greeting and Wolf lay down by the fire. Jeebee, thoroughly roused now, set about adding some heavy chunks of dry wood to the flames and getting some of his small remaining store of food from the backpack, which he had prudently tied on top of the cinch strap he had left tied around Brute.

Wolf was by now too accustomed to Jeebee's customary bed of tarpaulin-covered saddle and packload to indulge his instinctive urge to tear it apart. Jeebee ate, standing, then went to the load. He fished out another blanket and, rolling himself in the two he now had, lay looking at the fire and Wolf through half-closed eyes until he dozed again; and, dozing, dropped at last into solid sleep.

He slept long and hard, waking only briefly once or twice and going very quickly back to sleep again. Part of the night he dreamed that he and Merry were busily shopping to furnish a new house they had just bought.

When he woke a second time, the sun was well up in the sky, its light filtering through the upper parts of the trees near him. On first waking, his arm and leg hardly hurt, and his scalp not at all. But when he got up from his night's bed, the now-familiar pain started.

Still, it was not nearly as bad as it had been, even on the day before when he had first woken up. Also, his watch told him it was nearly fourteen hours since the last Dilaudid. He was tempted to try to see if he could get by on aspirin alone.

Creakily, he found the aspirin and swallowed two with water from a water bag. Then he went about the business of restarting the fire. It had died in the night, the last embers probably close to morning. In spite of the fact that he was now seasoned in sleeping out of doors, the chill had crept deep inside him, and he shivered as he waited for the first small flame to build into something that would throw some heat his way.

Wolf was already up and gone, of course.

Warmed after a bit by the growing flames, Jeebee rose from the fire and went to Brute. He allowed himself another meager handful of the trail mix from his dwindling food supply, telling himself he would try to cook something once he had gotten his body warmed to full life and ready to move.

His watch informed him it was twelve minutes past ten in

the morning. He was reproaching himself with having slept a good chunk of the day away when he realized suddenly that for some weeks now he must have been on Mountain, rather than Central Time, and set the digital display of the watch's clock mode back an hour.

The aspirin was proving itself useless against the pain. Like all hurts, his seemed to bite at him ever more viciously as he began to pay attention to them. He gave in and took a half Dilaudid, telling himself he would hold off for at least another six hours before taking the second half. After taking the half he waited expectantly. Finally, the pain began to back off somewhat. In half an hour it was ignorable.

He had been lying on his bed as he waited. Now he got to his feet, using the staff of his crutch simply as a staff. The crosspiece had come completely loose as the leather thongs failed. It struck him that probably it was only rawhide that shrank itself really tight if it was put on wet and allowed to dry. Or, perhaps, it had been stretched as it dried because of the wobbling it had done as he walked. In any case, once on his feet with the aid of the staff, he found he could limp around that way.

The horses were still finding graze where he had tied them. He went back to Sally's packload and routed out flour, bacon, and a frying pan. He hated to dig into the bacon this early, but he needed strength and that meant he had to have food, and this was the only reachable food left with the high caloric content and in quantities that would fill that need.

He made a bannock with the flour, water, and bacon fat and rolled the fried and rewarmed bacon inside it.

With the food inside him, he literally felt as if he had been given a new lease on life. He went through the complicated procedure of rigging up the block and tackle as high on the trunk of one of the lodgepole pines as he could reach to chop notches for its holding rope. With this, he finally lifted the packload, once more enclosed in the net, onto Sally's back again.

He saddled Brute with his one good arm and a knee in the horse's belly as he tightened the cinch strap.

He was ready to travel.

What he was looking for now was a site for a semipermanent camp. Someplace a little larger and more suitable than where he was. Water was the first requirement, and he already had that in this stream. The only question about where to look therefore was upstream or downstream? Upstream, then.

Curiously, although they were getting higher into the foothills, for a little while the slopes became gentler and the going easier, with even some spaces among the stands of trees that surrounded them on all sides.

They went slowly. Jeebee's leg still bothered him when it hung down in the stirrup, and was not really very comfortable pulled up and crooked around the pommel of the saddle. But the little stream led them at last to what could fairly be called a mountain meadow. Jeebee estimated it at something like three hundred yards in length and about half that in width.

Here the stream split off from a much wider one. In fact, the other was one that might even be called a small river. It was shallow, full of large boulders, but fast running. There would be no way, Jeebee thought, sitting Brute and looking through its clear water at its bed of large boulders, of leading the horses across it. Even if he was physically able to do so, which he still was not, the boulders were impassable. They were too large and unpredictable and would be too slippery for hooves. The chance of a broken leg for either animal was almost certain.

He tied Sally to a tree at the meadow's edge and rode Brute around the rest of the area to look it over more closely.

He went first to examine the point at which the little stream split off from the larger one. It was as he had suspected on first seeing the two streams. The smaller one showed clear evidence of having been deliberately man-made. He suspected it had been deliberately diverted to provide water directly to the ranch, the dead ranch now some distance behind and below them.

He continued with his survey of the meadow. It was more or less a wide aisle between the trees, with the end at which he had entered being fairly sparsely treed, and open; the trees gathered in closer beyond and were overshadowed by two rises of the hillside that began on either side and continued beyond the trees surrounding the meadow and up ahead, leaving only space for a narrow bed for the larger stream—so that the meadow was almost enclosed in a natural rampart of landscape, beyond its belt of trees.

The banks of the lower part of the stream were at present only a couple of feet above the water level, but farther up toward the end of the meadow that bank rose, almost abruptly, as the slope of the ground there itself rose, to a small bluff like that which had crowned the shale slope Jeebee had twice crossed the day before to take a look at the ranch.

The bluff became almost vertical in its last twenty or thirty feet, and here, as in the one above the shale slope, there was a hole, that might once have been the opening to some animal's den. Jeebee rode closer, and as he got close enough, the daylight was enough for him to see that while the hole was at least a couple of times larger than the one in the shale slope, it was only a shallow opening into what seemed soil that was nearly pure sand. He changed his mind about it possibly being a onetime den. It looked far more likely to be the result of some natural spill of the loose material of the bluff—possibly freezing and thawing of the earth.

Certainly, it was empty. There was no animal sign, and no vegetation inside it, or any indications that there had been, recently.

He was intrigued by the sight of it. With a little work and use of the tarpaulin and his other plastic cloths that he had gotten from Paul, it was the sort of place that he could make into a rain-proof, halfway comfortable chamber for himself to bed down.

As a matter of fact, that sandy earth he saw looked as if it would be easily diggable. Perhaps it had indeed been dug out by an animal at one time, after all, or at least the digging of it started by some animal. It would not be difficult to dig more deeply and make more space within. Then with something to cover the opening, Jeebee would have a den of his own for the first time since he had left the wagon.

CHAPTER 25

Three days later a large change had been accomplished. The horses were much better for the rest and the steady feeding. That trek from the stream by the willows up past the ranch had undeniably taken it out of them, but they were at last showing the signs of complete recovery. Now they were both almost frisky; even Sally, normally so staid and quiet, seemed impatient at being tethered.

As for himself, Jeebee considered both his arm and leg now almost as good as ever. He had even tried sleeping that second night in the cave of the meadow without even one Dilaudid, taking just aspirin instead, and found that, tired as he was, he had dropped off and slumbered without trouble.

Since then he had taken four doses of Tylenol in the last three days, and that was all. Now, while both leg and arm protested at being bumped against something or the muscles in them being used too abruptly, for the most part he could simply ignore the fact that they had been hurt. Both arm and leg still showed dark from the bruising, but the swelling in each was almost gone.

He had benefited from this improvement during the last couple of days by being able to ride Brute down at night into the flatlands. He had even gone out beyond the destroyed ranch, in hopes of finding a range cow and shooting it; and had actually done so.

The job he had done of butchering out the more eatable portions of meat had been clumsy. And packing them back on Brute to the meadow had been a problem. Brute had objected ardently to carrying the meat, which smelled to him very strongly of blood. But Jeebee limped back on foot, leading the horse firmly by the head, with a close grip on the reins just in front of his teeth. Brute's only option was to follow.

It was a long walk for Jeebee and a hard one. Particularly hard given that he had come tired to the first slopes behind the ranch house and had to lean into them to climb them. Of necessity, he ended up doing what he had done on his first venture back from his camping spot on foot with the crutch, going a small distance and stopping to rest, then going another short distance and stopping again, and so on.

He had started, out of eagerness, early that morning and had reason to be grateful for this, because it was still only midafternoon by the time he was well into the foothills. Up ahead of him was the one stretch he had been thinking of and dreading. This was the shale slope, where he did not think he would dare sit down and rest.

Theoretically, if he did sit down in the middle of the slope, he should be able to use Brute to help him climb to his feet, literally using the horse's leg and back and saddle as handholds to pull himself upright.

But that was only theoretically. He had noticed on the last few stops that he dared not rest too long, because the leg, in particular, was beginning to stiffen up when he did. That meant that taking a long rest before starting out across the slope would be dangerous.

He reached the nearer edge of the slope eventually. He sat down, keeping a steady tightness on the reins, while Brute stood over him and gazed at the slope itself.

At first glance it looked innocent enough. Merely an open space to be walked across with due care for the fact that it sloped very sharply away to his right. A closer look showed the points of reflection of sunlight from the sharp and loose pieces of bare rock covering it.

He looked almost longingly up to the top of its slope, past the hole that probably at one time had been some animal's den, to the short vertical bluff and the trees crowning it. It was tempting to try to go up and around it that way. But he had examined that possible route the first time he had crossed it with the crutch. Above the bluff the trees grew too closely and the slopes on both sides climbed at such a pitch that it would be both crowded and unsafe to lead Brute through there.

Moreover, he was eager to get back to the campsite. His leg in particular was paining him as it had not pained him for some days now. After a bit, he faced the fact that he dared not sit, with the leg stiffening, any longer. He got to his feet and started leading Brute carefully across the slope.

He could have used the crutch now, for Brute behind him went as gingerly as he did; clearly the horse's stance was no more firm on the slope among the loose rocks than his was. He sweated under the sunlight, working his way toward the far edge of the rocks.

But he made progress. The far edge came closer and closer, and in spite of the fact that his leg was complaining, he began to feel a sense of triumph. The edge was only about twenty yards away now. In a few moments he would be safe off the slope. He began to stride out more strongly.

His attention was all on the far edge he was trying to reach. So suddenly that it seemed to have happened before he realized it—though afterward he could remember the stone slipping and turning under his left leg and the leg sliding across in front of his right leg to trip him up—he fell.

Only his grip on the rein, and the fact that Brute's hooves were all on solid ground and the horse braced himself immediately, kept him from rolling free down the slope.

Panting with relief that he had not made the long fall, Jeebee turned his attention to getting back on his feet again. As he did so a spear shaft of pain lanced up through his left leg from the ankle below it. He woke to the fact that it had turned under him as he fell with his body partly on top of it.

Gasping, he straightened the leg and ankle out. The fierce

pain backed off slightly, but he was aware of something decidedly damaged in the ankle. He pulled himself up, hand over hand against the reins, in spite of Brute's protesting neighs.

Once upright and holding on to the saddle, he cautiously tried the experiment of putting some weight on the left leg.

The ankle gave almost immediately, and the pain lanced upward again, as if the limb above were a hollow tube through which it could strike. Quickly, he took the weight off again. He hung to the saddle with both hands, sweating. There was no way he was going to be able to walk the rest of the way back to the campsite, from here.

He would have to ride. That was the only possibility. To ride meant necessarily having to sit in the saddle, and that meant dumping all the meat he had gathered. He had tied the plastic-wrapped bundle of it on top of the saddle, since Brute had strongly objected to it being put anywhere he could feel its unfamiliar touch.

There was simply no choice in the matter. Jeebee undid the rope holding the bundle in place and let it fall to the ground. He would come back for the plastic later if there was anything of it to salvage. But he doubted that there would be. Wolf or other predators would have taken care of the meat. Then, taking a firm grip on the saddle horn, he hopped with his good leg upward, pulling with his arms as he did so, and managed to get the toe of his good foot into the stirrup and his bad leg, to the tune of an excruciating stab of pain, thrown over the saddle to the other side.

Then he urged Brute forward.

Brute was even unhappier now than he had been earlier. But he, too, saw the edge of the shale ahead of him and was eager to reach it. In a moment they were on solid ground.

The load of meat Brute had been carrying had been light. The horse was not the least bit tired, but the pain in Jeebee's leg at each jolt as Brute's hooves struck the ground kept him from putting the animal to any faster pace than walking; though he would have liked to have headed for his campsite with all possible speed. There turned out to be another three quarters of an hour of traveling before Jeebee at last slid out of the saddle—to the accompaniment of another silent scream of protest from his injured leg and ankle—and tethered Brute with his reins to a tree by the river, close enough so that the horse could drink.

Brute headed immediately to the water. Jeebee, holding on to the saddle and hopping along beside him, loosened the cinch strap while Brute drank, and then, pushing and tugging forward on the reins, got him back to where he could once again tie him to a tree and dropped the saddle off him. In taking off the saddle, he had also gotten his backpack and rifle, the saddle blanket, and a half-filled water bag.

These, his most necessary possessions, he kept always with him. He got down now on hands and knees and crawled, dragging all this, together with his rifle, behind him until he reached his sleeping spot by the water, upstream. Lying on the blanket, with the saddle under his head and the rifle beside him, he was able to dig out from it his medication pouch.

He had told himself he would not take another Dilaudid. But now he did, telling himself he would take this one and no more, just enough so that when it took effect he could get back down to the water, only about some twenty feet away.

In about twenty minutes it began to work. He crawled to the stream and began soaking the ankle in its cold water. With the Dilaudid and the numbing effect of the water, the pain dwindled to the point where he could begin to think of rigging some kind of a splint for the ankle to hold it unmoving. He already had a possibility in mind. It had been part of a ski rescue manual he had studied before he left Stoketon.

He made the crawl back with fair comfort, but taking every care to bend the ankle as little as possible in the process. Once there, he took Brute's saddle blanket, folded and refolded it until he had a thick, short length he could bend around under the instep of his foot with two sides extending up the sides of his lower leg. He took from a hip pocket the lengths of leather thongs left over from those he had taken to tie shut the plastic sheet in which he had bagged the raw meat.

With these he laced the blanket tightly in place around his

instep, ankle, and leg. He tied the thongs as tightly as he dared without running the risk of cutting off circulation in the leg. Then he rearranged the saddle and backpack so that he could sit with the leg propped up, his back against a tree trunk.

He was left with his thoughts. Uppermost in his mind was fury at himself for being so careless. A second's thoughtlessness and he was back to being almost helpless again. It was almost as if an inimical fate had deliberately chosen to kick him when he was most vulnerable.

He shook off the self-pity of that thought. He had simply failed to look, and what had happened was all his own doing. He should have been watching at each step, to make sure the foot was set down on something firm. It had been nothing more than his impatience to get off the slope that had led to this situation.

Not for the first time, he realized how even a small hurt—as small as a sore toe—could threaten the life of a wild animal by crippling its normal ability to escape its enemies and gather or capture its food. He was in exactly that position, simply because he had let himself get hurt again at the wrong time. Low on food, immobilized for at least several more days.

He made himself deliberately consider the brighter side of the situation. He was infinitely better off than any hurt animal. His weapons were still as effective, even though he might be crippled, personally. There was little likelihood anyone would stumble across him here, or that anyone would come hunting him. The slaughtered cow would almost undoubtedly be blamed on the horse nomads if anyone came looking. To his surprise, and as far as he could read sign around the burned ruins, no one had. There remained the fact that he could not climb up to his packload where his flour and bacon were. He had no food. Well, a few days without food would not hurt him. The Dilaudid had almost completely lulled the pain in his ankle. He gathered some nearby fallen branches for a fire, but did not light it. He would want it more after dark. He sat back against the tree. The afternoon was wearing on.

He slept.

He was wakened by Wolf licking at his face. It was twilight.

They had their usual greetings; differing only in that Wolf almost immediately appeared to take note of the fact that Jeebee, while being as comradely as ever, did not stir about as usual in the process.

In fact, Wolf made play invitations, and Jeebee, knowing the other better now, suspected they were at least partly a test to see if Jeebee had some reason for not moving.

To put an end to any further speculation, Jeebee lit the fire. Wolf gave up his attentions and settled down by it. Jeebee lay looking at the fire and thinking of how the delay from this turned ankle would affect his plans for travel.

Altogether he had lost more than a week with the bear, and it was into August. At the altitudes even of the flatlands of the ranch territories—here around three thousand feet—he could expect fall weather and even snow as early as late August.

He might be lucky. On the other hand he might not. But, since his memory of his boyhood drive to the ranch was all he had to go on, he probably would have to explore a considerable area to locate his brother's place. Luckily there was one thing that he had clearly in his memory. It was the brand on his brother's cattle, which was that of two overlapping triangles. If he saw any cattle with that brand on them, he would know he was close to his goal.

He had taken advantage of the camping period to get out his compass and maps and establish where he was.

At his best estimate, the territory in which his brother's ranch must lie was still some sixty miles northeast as the crow flew, from where he was now. Going back down to the flatlands, circling any possible habitations, and generally staying out of sight, could triple or quadruple that distance. In all, he figured it could take him at least a couple of weeks to reach the general territory he had to search, moving always at night, at a walk, and stopping to gather food where he could. Then no one could guess how much time for the search itself.

Events had cut his timetable dangerously short. The thought of being caught in a sudden blizzard on the open flatlands before he had found his brother's ranch was frightening. Under those conditions, he would simply not survive. If he had enough warning of the onset of winter to get off into the hills and den up like an animal in one of the holes in the earth like the one above the shale slope or the one here . . .

But even then, survival was unlikely.

His ankle was beginning to hurt again. He tried three aspirin to head off the pain. In any case he had some days now to do nothing else but think.

CHAPTER 26

Sometime in the night, pain woke Jeebee. Luckily, the night sky was as clear as the daytime sky had been for several weeks now. That could not last. They were getting to the end of summer and the good weather was bound to break.

He fumbled in the medicine container, found the Dilaudid container by feel, and brought it out, opening it with hands that trembled from pain and the urgency for relief. He stopped himself from taking it just in time. He reclosed the container with extra care and went searching for the Tylenol. Rationally, he knew that taking more than the recommended dose would not help cut the pain more; all the same, he counted out four. Then came a search for the water bag, which had evidently been moved by his body as he slept.

He located it less than an arm's length away under the flap of tarp, and swallowed water from it to get the pills down. He was shaking now from chill, awake enough again to feel the cold. He scraped together some of the dry wood he had saved and got the fire going. But it cast only feeble heat as the flames slowly caught.

Instinct drove him to movement to warm himself. He crawled around and managed to find more fuel for the fire. Finally, his shivering stopped.

Wolf, curled up beyond the flames, with his bushy tail over his nose tip, regarded Jeebee with drowsy eyes.

He could not go on like this, without some kind of cover to hold in his body heat. He would die of exposure as soon as he ran out of fallen branches close enough to find by firelight. But the blankets were all in the packload up out of his reach. There was no way for him to get his hands high enough even to pull one out—

Swearing at himself for being such an idiot, he started off on hands and knees toward the dark shapes of the horses. Even in the dark, Sally's silhouette and smaller size distinguished her from Brute.

Crawling to the side of her that was away from Brute, he literally climbed up her leg, pulling himself to his feet. Brute would not have put up with that for a moment, but Sally patiently let herself be used as a series of handholds.

"Good girl," he panted. Sally turned her head to look at him through the dark. He crouched, jumped upward mightily on his good foot, and twisted; somehow he managed to throw his hurt leg up and over her back. The pain of the movement almost blacked him out for a second. A fury in him helped to beat it back. He pulled himself up on her. She braced herself automatically against his off-center weight as he climbed.

Finally on her back, he pulled himself forward along her neck and urged her up to the tree to which her halter was attached. He untied it and, with knee pressures and heel touches, steered her to the tree holding the packload.

He halted her beside it. He could just make out the dark bulk of it, like an enormous morel mushroom, clinging to the dark tree trunk overhead.

"Steady now, girl," he said to Sally, "stand steady!"

Clinging to the tree trunk, he pulled himself up until he was kneeling on Sally's broad back. The bone of her spine bit, hard and uncomfortable, into the bones of his lower legs. He ignored the discomfort. Reaching up as high as he could in this position, he felt his hands grip and hold on the netted plastic that carried the packload.

It was too dark to see where the edges of the plastic tar-paulin came close together under the flap of the one corner of it he had draped over the edges as a rain roof. But he felt his way through its folds until his fingers recognized the tarp's edges, then worked his hands inside and felt for the rough-soft surface of his sleeping blankets.

And found them.

A few minutes later, triumphant, he was climbing down to a position back astride Sally, with three blankets wadded in his arms. Shortly after that, he was urging Sally back to the tree to which she had originally been tied.

He had been tempted to ride her to the fire and tether her to a tree beside it. But it would be unfair to tie her up where she could not drink. Once more he crossed the ground on hands and knees. Wolf had risen to his feet to stare at Jeebee as he ap-proached. Jeebee had tucked the blankets inside his jacket for fear Wolf would be impelled to grab any loose ends in his teeth.

But Wolf made no move. In fact, if anything, he seemed a little wary of Jeebee's shape, swollen by the blankets.

Jeebee made it back to his place by the fire, spread out the blankets, and gratefully rolled himself up in their double thick-ness. It was not until all this was done that Wolf lay down again. Thumped down, rather, with a grunt that sounded almost like a grumble.

Jeebee did not care. The Tylenol was taking hold. It touched the pain only lightly, but now that he had quit throwing it around, the leg seemed to recover a bit on its own. In moments Jeebee was warm; and shortly after that he was asleep once more.

When he woke the next day, Wolf was not to be seen. Jeebee found himself oddly worried by this. Since that evening Wolf had approached him with what Jeebee now knew to be submission behavior, Wolf had seldom left the campsite without touching base, first, with Jeebee, after the latter woke in the morning.

Did the leaving today signal changes in Wolf's attitude to-ward him? There could be drawbacks as well as advantages to being accepted by Wolf as a pack mate.

But Jeebee was in no state to ponder that question at the moment. It was full morning and the pain of his ankle was gnawing at him again. He took more Tylenol, only three this time.

They did not seem to help at all. He lay there, sweating, but finally decided that while it hurt badly, the discomfort was not insupportable—at least as long as he did not move the ankle.

He found himself very thirsty and drank deeply from his full water bag, until he remembered the difficulty he might have refilling either or both bags now that he had the bad ankle. He checked himself then and his body reminded him of other necessities. He badly needed to urinate, and he would at least have to move away from his bedding to do so.

He moved, therefore, crawling sideways off the rise of land he had lain on, trying to hold the bad ankle in the air so that it would not be dragged. A sudden increase in pain made him grunt as he jarred the ankle while dropping the several inches from his sleeping mound.

He had counted on the thick folds of the blanket splint to cushion the ankle at least to some extent in his movement. But the pain was so abrupt and fierce that it was as if there was no cloth between the injured body part and the ground.

He lay for some minutes, waiting for the hurt to subside before trying to move again.

The pain went down slightly—or perhaps it was only his swollen bladder, insistent, that started him moving again. At any rate, he pulled himself a little farther sideways, then swiveled until he lay along the edge of the slope to the river below. His hand shaking, he managed to unbutton the stiff metal buttons of the work pants he had gotten from the wagon, and at last allow himself relief.

It was only afterward that he realized he should have brought at least one of the water bags with him so that he could take advantage of having moved this far to fill it from the running water of the river, a body's length upstream.

At first he thought that once having made it back to his bed, he would never be able to face the thought of another trip, this time not only to the top of the bank, but down the sharp stones of it to the water's edge. But once he had made it back, he realized that he would do it. Whatever he must do to stay alive he would do, in the end, as long as his body held out. And if he would do it in the end, why not now, before the point of desperation set in?

So he went after his water, and got it.

He did not in any sense conquer the ankle pain. But after a fashion he came to terms with it.

As the day wore on, he discovered he could, indeed, move around, by dividing the work into short moments of effort, then resting until he felt ready to try again. A stubbornness that he had not realized he had, grew in him. Also an inventiveness. He took a stone from the earth near the fire and put it into the fire to sterilize it. Then, after it had cooled, he put it into the empty water bag, ran a light rope through the cloth carrying handle of the bag, and tied it in a slipknot around the neck of the bag.

With a sidearm motion he threw the bag from his bed place out into the stream, and after it had sunk and filled itself with water, he hauled it back with the rope.

In spite of the fact that the slipknot pulled itself tight around the neck of the bag, some of the water in it slopped out and was lost as it bumped its way back to him. But it was so much easier a way of renewing his water supply that the loss did not matter.

The success cleared his head. He began to look on himself as a great deal less helpless than he had assumed. By thinking out easy ways of doing things and by making large movements in small, slow steps, he began to get things done.

This way, bit by bit, he gathered enough fresh fuel through the day for his fire to last the night. He even managed to chop through a pine sapling, cut off its limbs, and make himself another crude crutch.

It did not stand up any better to use than his earlier crutch. But by using it he was able, after several days, to move the horses one by one to a series of new tethering spots, where fresh ground cover was available to replace the sparse grass they had cropped off completely within the earlier circle of their tethers.

But the ankle was remarkably slow to mend. It seemed unreasonable that all the bear had done should mend so quickly, while a simple turned ankle was so slow to improve. Jeebee worried over the possibility that he had done something more than merely sprain it. He knew sprains were stubborn to heal, but . . . He also fretted over the time he was losing when he should be on his way. Until he took himself firmly in hand and told himself that worrying over the fact that he could not move on would not put him on his way any faster.

To take his mind off matters he returned to the wolf books, reading the few he had not had time to finish and rereading all the others.

He was trained at this type of attention by his academic years, and it was not long before he became once more engrossed in wolf lore. As he read, his mind finally solved a puzzle that had stayed with him since the moment in the willows, when he had found himself fighting for his life against the bear.

The last thing he had expected then had been that Wolf would come to his aid, as a storybook faithful dog comes to the rescue of its master.

But Wolf had come. It had seemed to be against all the pragmatic reactions and instinct for self-preservation that Jeebee had seen Wolf show otherwise. Wolf had nothing personally to gain by putting his own life at risk in tackling the bear that was engaged with Jeebee; and much to lose.

It would have been far more wise, Jeebee had thought then and afterward, for Wolf to stay back and see whether Jeebee won or not. And only then come galloping in, once it was clear that the bear was defeated. Prudently, that way, he would have avoided getting involved in a situation in which it might have been Jeebee who was being defeated, and the bear would then have been free to turn on Wolf.

Now, not from what was on the pages before him, but out of some coming together of all he had read up until this moment, he found himself understanding why Wolf had done what he did.

The key—as he'd fleetingly surmised while he lay recovering from his wounds—was social evolution. Social organization allowed wolves to hunt animals many times their own size and made them the most effective predator in North America until the arrival of Man. But group hunting required foresight, planning, communication, and other forms of intelligent behavior found only in creatures like humans and chimpanzees, creatures that matured slowly and so remained helpless and dependent for much of their lives. For pups to survive so extended a period of immaturity had required the evolution of cooperative care of the young and an instinct for cooperative defense.

It was not Jeebee, the person, to whose rescue Wolf had come. It had been to the assistance of a *pack mate* under attack. For a wolf it would always be the pack that was of first importance, the individual only second.

In short, Wolf had simply joined in as he normally would if some other wolf of his pack had become involved with a bear.

The discovery was like a bright light in Jeebee's mind, illuminating a great deal of the rest of the material he had studied. He reminded himself again, out of his own scientific training, that there must always be an explanation.

Everything he had ever learned had always demanded that.

It did not mean that the explanation was always immediately available. But nothing happened without a reason; particularly as far as the actions of the higher mammals were concerned. There had to be a cause for every action.

That understanding brought his mind back to his latest concern about Wolf—that, against custom, Wolf had left without waiting for Jeebee to wake up.

Of course, Wolf had always come and gone as he wished. But his normal pattern lately had been almost exclusively to appear at twilight, stay through the night, and leave as soon as Jeebee had accepted his morning greetings.

Now, he was leaving before Jeebee was awake, but reappearing three or more times in the day—greeting Jeebee briefly, sniffing him over, and showing what Jeebee felt was a different sort of interest in him.

It was as if Wolf now was waiting for something to happen. However, invariably after he had been back for a little time, he would abruptly be gone again. Wolf never visibly came or went.

He was suddenly there, or he was as suddenly gone again. Except for the fact that Jeebee had long since become familiar with this behavior, it would have been a little like living with a ghost.

Jeebee found himself concentrating on the new puzzle of why Wolf was acting as he did. Again, there must be a reason. It was hard to think, because, although the pain was being controlled by Tylenol alone now, it had been days since he had eaten anything and he was becoming preoccupied with wanting food very much.

It was one thing to tell himself he could go without food for a few days. But now that the few days had stretched to nearly a week, the body began to send different and more urgent signals that nourishment was needed. It was not so much hunger as a sort of knowledge in brain and bones that it would be dangerous to go without food too long. And his body was telling him it was time he did something about the situation.

But, of course, there was nothing he could do. He was able to move around the clearing, but he could not even, as he would have to, *stand* on Sally's back to reach far enough up and into his packload to find the flour and bacon; which had been packed, from prudence, in the very middle of it. He had been lucky, in fact, to have found the ends of the blankets as close to the edges as he had been able to reach.

Lately, he had been debating with himself over using one of his knives to slash open the net and plastic wrapping of the packload so that everything inside it would fall to the ground. But to do that would be self-defeating. He might get food for a few days, but it would have meant damaging, and exposing to damage, everything he had, for perhaps three or four days' rations.

What was more, once his possessions were scattered on the ground, he would have no way of protecting them. Wolf, or other wild animals, would probably tear, chew up, or carry off a good deal of what he possessed.

Besides, the net itself would be irreparable. Theoretically, he had enough leather thongs to tie it back together again. But even if he could and did repair it, or could use another of the folded-up plastic tarps he carried in the packload—still, he would have to be able to climb the tree in order to reaffix it to the block and tackle and haul it up where it would be safe.

His own cleverness at tying the rope that secured both the blocks and the top of the packload to the tree trunk above the load itself now frustrated him from getting at what he needed.

Shortly after dawn one morning he was lying in his usual resting place on the blankets, straining his mind again for some way of getting at the packload, when Wolf made one of his visits back. By this time Jeebee was not only beginning to feel weak from lack of food, but also depressed. He hardly acknowledged Wolf as the other loomed suddenly above him and began to sniff at him. As Wolf sniffed up toward Jeebee's face, Jeebee smelled an odor, with a nose that had grown more sensitive by a life in the open. In the same moment he noticed what he had smelled.

There was a reddish dampness on the hair around Wolf's muzzle.

A sudden wild thought came to him. It was impossible, and under ordinary standards, unthinkable. But he had felt the fear of a weakness from lack of food that could keep him from surviving. He had nothing to lose by trying.

He pulled himself up on one elbow. Putting his face right up to Wolf's, he deliberately licked at the moist fur around Wolf's mouth.

The taste on his tongue was salty.

For a second nothing seemed to happen. Then Wolf seemed to cough, and as Jeebee pulled back his head, Wolf regurgitated onto the blankets some chunks of raw, red-gray meat, which steamed in the cool morning air.

Jeebee felt within him a leaping of ridiculous joy. It had been the craziest of possible chances. But he had taken advantage of the way wolves brought back food to their pups, and to the mother of pups when she was denned up with them. The regurgitation was reflexive—another of the social instincts that made it possible for wolf pups to enjoy an extended childhood and develop the intelligence they would need for group hunting. The wolf who had eaten could deliberately put himself in the position—as Wolf must have been doing these last few days—of giving up the food he had swallowed. But once he had been licked about the muzzle as pups of his species did instinctively, and Jeebee had just done, the reflex to regurgitate was uncontrollable.

It was a miracle out of nature itself. One of the writings on wolves had mentioned that an adult wolf would even bring food in this fashion to a den-bound mate—or even to another adult pack mate who might be too sick, or otherwise unable to get about, to travel or hunt.

The last seldom happened, Jeebee had gathered. But it could. It had happened now.

He realized suddenly that Wolf was looking at him, bright-eyed. Jeebee started to touch him in thanks, then realized that was not what Wolf was waiting for.

Jeebee changed his motion and bent down over the chunks of meat. Ordinarily the thought of eating something vomited up, whether by an animal or another human, would be nauseating. But Jeebee knew that Wolf gulped his food whole. There was no real chewing or digestion done in his mouth. His stomach acids would have begun to digest the meat only from the surface, and there could not have been time enough for that to work very much. At the most, the acids might have started to tenderize it; also, they would have effectively sterilized it, being very strong acids.

Acid would destroy any bacteria, even that which might be in the meat itself.

Jeebee put down his head and mumbled at the chunks with his mouth, pretending to eat.

Evidently, his act was good enough to satisfy Wolf. For when he lifted his head again, the other was gone. Jeebee took his water bag, which luckily was full, and washed off the meat, chunk by chunk, until it was thoroughly clean. Then, with fingers that shook with eagerness, he built a small fire, even though it was bright daylight. As soon as it was putting out anything like sufficient heat to cook, he threaded the chunks on a sharpened stick and held them over the flames.

His mouth was continually filling with saliva, which he alternately swallowed and spat out, as the chunks sizzled above the fire. He held out against the hunger in him as long as he could, then pulled the stick to him and began to eat the still-half-raw meat.

He had not tasted anything as wonderful since he had found the canned food in the root cellar, back before he had met Merry, Paul, and Nick. Fortunately, he remembered how the canned stew had made him sick, suddenly gulped down on a long-empty stomach. He was careful to eat slowly and with pauses; this time he avoided being ill.

From then on he licked Wolf's whiskers whenever the other came to sniff at him, and Wolf brought him meat at fairly frequent intervals. This way he survived another week. At the end of that time his ankle had improved to the point where he could hobble around on it, even without the crutch.

At last he felt able to stand on Sally and let down the packload long enough to get flour and bacon out of it.

Fortified by several days of this food, he finally ventured to saddle the smaller packhorse, as the calmer and more surefooted of the two, and take the rifle down into the lowlands by a route that avoided the shale slope. There, he had the good luck to find another midsummer calf and kill it. He butchered from it what he estimated to be about thirty pounds of its flesh, with none of that weight being bone.

It was a larger load than he had tried to bring back on Brute, simply because Brute would not endure carrying the raw and bloody meat in any way on the saddle. Sally was more complacent. She was not only willing to carry the extra thirty pounds, but also Jeebee, since he could never have walked that distance by himself.

It was an effort above and beyond the call of duty for the little mare. She had to climb slopes with nearly two hundred and twenty pounds of burden, counting Jeebee, the saddle, and meat, but she struggled back up through the hills to the campsite without protest.

He pegged her out by the stream in an area of fresh browse, with deep gratitude, and a resolution that she could stand idle for at least the next few days while she recovered.

He cooked the meat. During the process, Wolf appeared. Jeebee squatted over the pile of raw beef, guarding it, but threw what he estimated to be about ten pounds of it, piece by piece, to his partner while the rest finished cooking. He figured that Wolf had earned his share of the calf meat. Besides, it would have been impossible to protect all of the food from him, in any case, while Jeebee was cooking it.

Once the beef looked done, Jeebee took what he had been able to guard and wrapped this in one of his blankets, which he tied into a bag with some of his extra thongs.

With apologies, he pressed Sally once more into service after all so that he could kneel on her back. He tied the bundle of cooked meat as close as possible to three of the ropes holding up the net of the main packload. His new package hung down a little farther than the packload itself. But Jeebee had put it up at arm's length from a kneeling position on Sally's back, and the trunk was absolutely vertical.

Jeebee did not think that Wolf could leap high enough to get his teeth into it. Wolf watched from below.

The daylight was ending. Jeebee went back to his single blanket and the fire. Wolf lay down opposite him and regarded Jeebee somberly.

Jeebee knew how the other was feeling and did not blame him. By Wolf's standards, Jeebee should have eaten as much as he could hold of the meat, and then left it to Wolf to fill himself up with as much as he could hold.

In fact, Jeebee could have done so. But he knew that even with his stomach full, Wolf would still keep snatching up pieces of meat and running off with them to cache them someplace else, until all was gone.

He apologized to Wolf—not that it made any difference to the other, but it made Jeebee feel better—and then sat down with his back against the tree trunk, watching the fire and thinking deeply. He was on the verge of probably the most serious decision he had made since leaving Stoketon.

CHAPTER 27

The inescapable problem on his mind had been whether his ankle would be healed enough, soon enough, so that he could at least ride Brute. So that in a few days at most, he would be able to get the packload down from the tree and the horses ready to travel. But now that question had given way to one about whether he should go on at all, and try to find his brother's ranch this year.

It was already August. In mid-August, the traveling should be all right. But by late August, there would be the chance of a freakishly early snowstorm. By late September, snow would begin to be a certainty, even if it was not frequent and steady.

That gave him no more than two months in which to find his brother's ranch, and he had estimated it could be anywhere within over a thousand square miles of territory. Those thousand-plus square miles would be down in the flatlands. He would be moving across the property of other people who did not know him, and who might not even know, let alone like, his brother.

If he still had not found the ranch by the time the first heavy snowstorm, or series of snowstorms, caught him, he would not last long down below. Even if he was able to make it from where the snow caught him, up into nearby foothills, he would still face having to find or make some kind of winter-long shelter under the beginning of that season's conditions—an almost impossible task.

But—if he stayed where he was right now and started preparing a winter shelter, he would have those two months in which to work on it.

The odds were overwhelming against going on.

Actually, his only reason for doing so was that all his plans had been based upon reaching his brother's place before such weather set in.

Now that reason, set against the strong chance of disaster if he went on now, gave him no real choice.

He would stay here and make the best use of his time to build a place in which he could winter. Anything else would be not only foolish but dangerous.

He was surprised to find that finally making this decision seemed to lift an emotional burden from him. All the tension that had come from fretting about getting into physical shape to travel again was suddenly gone. It was only, slowly, that another, if more healthy, tension replaced it. When he began to think of the things he wanted to do, here in the meadow, the two short months he had just gained suddenly seemed to grow shorter.

On more than one occasion while he was lying around waiting for his ankle to mend, he had played with the thought of enlarging something like the hole in the sandy bluff at the end of the meadow. His mind had even ranged into the idea of making a sort of livable cave, with a wooden front on it. With a door in the wooden front, and perhaps even windows.

Now that he had faced his decision, he realized that it must have been a foregone conclusion in the back of his mind for some time. Thinking about what would need to be done, he began to see how much would be involved in building what his imagination had dreamed up so easily and cheerfully.

To begin with, the soil revealed by the hole was very sandy and crumbly. If he merely dug deeply into it, there was a real danger of the sandy roof and sides falling in on him. He knew how miners dealt with such things. They supported the roof and walled the sides with timbers to hold back the weight of the surrounding soil. There was timber, and even planks, available for him down at the ruined ranch. But to put these all together, he would need nails, and that would mean that he would either have to find some supply of unused nails down at the ranch—which he well might, since that was not the sort of thing the raiders would be interested in picking up—or pull nails from the outbuildings and the house itself.

He could do this, of course, while he was stripping the planks he needed to build his cave front. But it all meant a number of trips down to the ranch, a great deal of hauling material back up—it would be easier to drag it, come to think of it, than to carry it on the backs of the horses. Particularly the longer pieces of wood would not carry well on the back of a horse, but extend behind and drag on the ground, in any case.

Meanwhile, as he was doing all this, he would have to keep hunting at regular intervals, to shoot cattle for food.

Things would get easier as far as hunting went once the weather got colder. As soon as the nighttime temperature began to drop below freezing, a deep hole in the ground could act as a refrigerator, or even, later on, as a deep freeze.

Of course, until the ground froze solid, anything he buried, Wolf could dig up. Jeebee had read that wolves in one zoo had become so adept at burrowing under their fence that the zoo had spent thousands of dollars to pour a concrete apron around the inside perimeter of the enclosure. Facilities with tighter budgets—including, he had read with amusement, one connected with the University of Michigan—discovered that a three- or four-foot apron of wire fencing material was almost as effective. If it was securely anchored to the ground, wolves couldn't get an effective purchase on it with their jaws, and digging at it was evidently uncomfortable to their footpads or toenails.

At the ranch Jeebee had noted some wire fencing with a two-by-four-inch mesh, of the kind ordinarily used in rural areas. It had been put up around a rectangle of darker earth that had evidently been the family's personal vegetable patch. A section of that wire would do very well to cover a hole for meat storage in cold weather. Though he should probably find some way of either weighing, or staking, it down so that it could not be taken off of the hole by anyone but himself. Meanwhile, according to the books, wolves did not like to try to scramble over a thin barrier, even no higher than four feet.

While cold weather had some advantages for him, it would also make it increasingly hard to work outside. Cold rain could be expected, turning into sleet followed by snow. Work would not only be difficult, but more dangerous to his health—he couldn't afford to get sick, out here by himself.

Thinking of the weather reminded him that he would have to find some way of heating the cave's interior. Body heat would help to a certain extent, in such an enclosed, insulated space, but he would need more than that.

One of the first things to do would be to rig some kind of temporary cover for the cave entrance, to keep out rain and snow while he was working inside. The cover should be something heavier than the plastic sheets he had, which were called tarps but actually were not. Maybe some actual waterproof canvas could be found down at the ranch. Probably even a sheet of something that could be weighted along the bottom edge or otherwise secured to resist wind.

His mind ran on, thinking of a number of things. He was letting it freewheel at the moment without yet making it consider the practical problems involved in doing these things. But then, he reminded himself, it was always better to do the large thinking first and get down to the details afterward.

One of the things that had come immediately to mind the minute he had thought of staying was that now perhaps he could set up his backwoods forge.

He envisioned the cave—deepened, ceilinged, walled, and floored inside. It would have the wooden front—there was no reason why he could not extend that front off to one side to enclose a blacksmithy.

The nearly vertical face of the bluff itself curved backward slightly as it went away from the stream. So that if he extended the front, he would build out straight in front of that curve. The further part of that front would then have a space behind it, widening out like a slice of pie; he could dig further in to widen it, if necessary, and could further enclose it with a short end wall at right angles to the front section, to tie it back to the bluff face, and add a bit of roof.

He might wall it off from the interior, heated area of the

cave, since it would be strongly warmed by his forge, once he had it going. The important thing would be to keep out the rain and snow.

Building the forge, as well as the area for it, and the part of the cave he would live in, was going to keep him very busy in whatever time he had before the ground froze. All at once, he found himself desperately eager to get at it immediately. It was frustrating not to be able to ride Brute right now and use Sally as a packhorse.

Then it struck him that there were things he could do while he waited a few more days for the ankle to strengthen. One was to ride down to the ranch and spend some time examining it for things there he could use. Now that his decision was set, it was time for plans to be made, and careful planning was a part of his nature.

It was still early in the day. He saddled Sally. Now that he knew the area better, he knew a way down to the ranch that avoided the shale slope entirely. It took half again as long as going across the shale. But he still got to the ranch in a couple of hours; and he estimated he could spend at least three hours there before he had to head back to the campsite while there was still afternoon left.

He had brought his crutch along. Not because he could not do without it, but to ease the wear and tear on his weak ankle when he was on foot.

He was astonished at what he found when he got there. It was the first time he had looked at any place like this with the eye of a scavenger, rather than simply as a possible temporary shelter. In the outbuildings he located not only a keg of unused nails, but a large variety of hand tools, including some wire clippers with which he was able to cut loose and roll up a twelve-foot section of the four-foot-high wire fence around the former garden patch.

The sheets and blankets had been stripped off the beds and taken by the raiders. But he found more of both among other household items boxed in a storeroom. He also found old and damaged blankets in an outbuilding. With one of these, he made a pad to fasten behind his saddle and carry the roll of wire. He was tempted to take a great many more things. But on this trip he was not prepared to carry or drag them. All around him, in addition to tools, he began to recognize a number of other items that would be useful in building or furnishing the cave.

He looked enviously at a waterwheel-driven electric generator beside the small stream that flowed near the ranch. It had obviously supplied power to the buildings during power outages or other emergencies. There were poles carrying wires to the house and outbuildings that must run out to a power line along a road too far away for him to see from here. The wire would have connected with rural electricity, back when current had been still coming into this area.

Aside from things he need merely pick up, there was a remarkable amount of wood siding on the house that had escaped the flames. Much more than he would need. In addition, there was a store of unused two-by-fours and planks in one of the outbuildings. Even if the nails in the keg turned out to be less than he would need, there was a wealth of them, as he had anticipated, in the still-standing walls of the buildings.

With some kind of hauling sledge, which he could build of materials here, there were larger or heavier things to take apart and transport up into the hills. With both horses pulling the sledge once snow fell, he could move a good load at a time.

He even looked at a bedstead, which could be taken apart for transporting.

Something like that was a ridiculous luxury—at least at this point. He could, however, make use of kitchen chairs and a table. Also, there were cooking utensils, as well as tableware and some dishes, which he would take. Most of what the ranch house had owned of these items had been taken, but much remained, particularly the cooking utensils, large spoons, spatulas, and other things.

On a sudden inspiration, he checked the number of vehicles still standing about the ranch-house area. There were four cars, three of which looked as if they had been in running condition when the supply of gas had dried up. Also, there were one large and one small tractor and a couple of pickup trucks. One of the trucks still had a blade, for snowplowing or some other use, attached to the front of it.

In addition to these, there was a snowmobile vehicle, and tucked inside its basket was a pair of heavy snowmobile boots large enough for him to wear, which would be invaluable when winter set in. There was also a two-wheel fence-sided trailer and a massive, rubber-tired four-wheel flatbed trailer that would need either a tractor or a heavy pickup to pull it, loaded.

There were both skis and snowshoes, as well as a toboggan. But it was none of these that interested him as much as the batteries in the cars and trucks and tractors. They were all dead, of course. There had been no gas available for any motorized vehicles for over a year. But it had occurred to Jeebee that since they were all late-model sealed batteries with their acid locked inside them, he might be able to use the solar-cell blanket to bring them up to charge again. Then he could use the batteries themselves to run the interior, ceiling lights of the cars for ordinary illumination in his cave. He could even use them to run one or two of the headlights from the cars, briefly, if for some reason a very bright source of light was needed. It was the way the wagon had run light bulbs off a generator attached to its turning wheels that had turned his mind in this direction.

All of the batteries that he found seemed in good shape. They were all sealed, which meant that the acid would still be safely inside them. He tried turning on the lights of the various vehicles, to see if there was any life in any of them. But, of course, there was not.

It was tempting to take a single battery and headlamp from one of the tractors, where it was easy to get off, and carry it back up to the campsite with him. Up there he might be able to monkey with it and the solar-cell blanket to see if he could not charge up the battery and get the headlamp to light, even if dimly, for a short while.

But it would be wrong to put that much unnecessary weight on Sally in addition to his own; on this first trip at any rate. The horses were his most valuable possession. He must not risk hurting or overworking either of them.

It would be much better to take a few useful but light things in addition to the wire. He ended by bundling a number of small tools into one of the blankets, including paper and some pencils that had been ignored by the raiders. These, in particular, he grabbed up happily.

From his young days, when he had first tried to make drawings of the inner workings of the clocks and radios he worked with, he had developed a habit of thinking with a pencil in his hands. He was used to thinking on paper—or on a computer screen. Now he could sit down and draw plans, not only of the cave, but of the means of bringing up to it some of the heavier, or more awkward, items.

To these items, wadded in the second blanket, he added only one old, tattered blanket-coat that he had found in an outbuilding. All other clothing had apparently been taken by the raiders, who would probably wear it without taking it off until it fell apart on them, then throw it away in the expectation of replacing it from some other looted place down the line.

This bundle he put inside the roll of wire, to secure it for the ride, tying it tightly into place. Happily, the raiders had evidently had no use for most of the light and heavy rope to be found in the outbuildings.

Once more in the saddle, he took the same route back to camp. When he got there, he enclosed everything, including the blanket he had used as a pad for Sally, in the middle of the roll of wire.

Once more, he pulled his trick of kneeling on Sally's back. It was a great deal more comfortable this time, now that his kneeling was being done on the saddle. He tied the stuffed wire roll up in a different tree from that which held the packload, using some of the extra rope he had brought back from the ranch. He fastened it at a height where he was pretty sure it would be out of reach of Wolf. In any case, there was nothing in the bundle that resembled food, so Wolf's only attraction to it would be curiosity. That might be enough to keep him from trying to climb the tree just to get his teeth into the bundle.

Wolf had not been there when he got back, and still had not returned by the time he had put the bundle up and unsaddled

Sally. In the last few days, Wolf's unusual, frequent visits had lessened in number, until he was coming in only two or three times a day. It occurred to Jeebee that he might have visited the campsite while Jeebee was gone. If so, any feeling his partner might have that Jeebee was no longer able to find his own food would have been eradicated. Now Jeebee thought that most likely Wolf would probably not return again until his usual time of twilight.

Jeebee spent the nearly two hours of workable daylight at a sketch of what he would build on the front of the cave.

There had been a posthole digger in one of the outbuildings. That, quite naturally, had been one of the things for which the raiders had no use. He decided now that one solution to the problem of bringing long lengths of plank from the ranch up to the cave was to bring a larger number of short ones. As a result he had sketched out a series of postholes running along the face of the bluff, in which he could stand upright lengths of doubled two-by-fours nailed together. Then he could nail the short lengths of planks between them to make a solid wall.

There were some twelve-foot lengths of two-by-fours stored in one of the outbuildings. At least enough to build the series of posts Jeebee had in mind.

He would space his posts not more than three feet apart. Twelve of them, therefore, should mark out the front of his cave-home-to-be. That would include those needed for the extra small wall that would tie the far end of the front into the bluff to make the blacksmithing area.

He was still refining his sketch of this, squinting at the much-erased paper of the large pad he had brought back with him, when a furry face pushed itself between the paper and his nose. Wolf was back.

Jeebee welcomed him with unusual exuberance.

After the greeting ceremony was over, Jeebee got the fire going and began to realize that he had not eaten since morning. He had prudently resolved not to try to get at his cooked meat while Wolf was around. Unfortunately, in this case he had waited until too late in the day.

He was tempted to take Sally over to the tree and reach up into the bag of meat enough to get out several handfuls of the cooked chunks. Then he could stay where he was, throw some of the chunks to Wolf, and eat the rest himself, seated on horseback.

The plan was theoretically workable, but it would draw Wolf's attention particularly to the bag of cooked meat. At Jeebee's best estimate, it was out of Wolf's reach and he already knew it was there. But Jeebee had the sneaking feeling that the less attention paid to it, the better. He did not know how Wolf might find a way to reach it, but he had gotten to the point where he believed almost anything was possible to the other.

Besides, it would not be the first meal he had skipped.

He put the thought of eating out of his mind; and after a while of sitting, gazing into the fire and half thinking, half dreaming of the cave home as it eventually could be, he rolled up in his blankets, ready for sleep. It would be two or three days anyway before his left ankle would be strong enough for him to risk trying to ride Brute and handle the more temperamental horse in the matter of carrying or dragging things back from the ranch.

He could use those days by riding Sally down, having her pull back a bundle of the twelve-foot-long two-by-fours, with the front ends elevated and the back ends scraping along the ground, plus a few other things that he could not only keep safe from Wolf, but use right away. It was a temptation to bring the posthole digger up without further delay. But it would be awkward to drag, and it was too long and rigid to be carried conveniently behind the saddle.

He reminded himself sensibly that the only way he could use the tool would be by standing firmly on one foot while driving the spade end of the digger into the ground with the other. The sprained ankle was probably still some days away from being used either way.

The thought of redamaging the ankle by trying to drive the posthole digger into the ground, or of turning it again by trying to stand on that foot alone, was unnerving. The last thing he needed now was to be laid up again for another long period.

He measured and marked the spots to erect the two-by-fours before settling down with the fire and Wolf for the night.

The next three days, he was busy bringing up equipment from the ranch, and he brought the posthole digger after all, as well as a saw and other tools and a collapsible metal ladder he found laid up on the rafters of one of the less completely burned outbuildings. He hid the ladder under the two sleeping blankets he lay upon, and was lying upon them when Wolf showed up, the third evening.

He had not been at all sure that Wolf, scenting or otherwise figuring out that something was there, would not root between the blankets to investigate, but Wolf did not. Three days later, using the hole digger by standing gingerly on his bad ankle, he successfully had four of the posts up at the campsite. Wolf investigated these with great interest when he came back, urinated on them, and gnawed on a few of them, but without doing any great damage.

Jeebee, looking over the tooth-marked pieces of lumber, decided that they were usable as they were, after all. Gradually, the rest of the postholes got dug. Wolf showed up at one time when he was still using the posthole digger, and when Jeebee had laid it down for a moment, tried to carry it off. But it was both heavy and awkward, and when Jeebee pretended to become very interested in something at the other side of the meadow, paying no attention to him at all, Wolf dropped the digger and trotted over to find out what was attractive there.

When Wolf came up, Jeebee engaged him for a little time in play, and then lay down on his blankets. Wolf lay down also. But it was still only late afternoon and whatever impulse had brought him back had now been satisfied or forgotten. He disappeared again.

In spite of the fact that Wolf was gone, however, Jeebee prudently ignored the posthole digger, letting it lie where it was overnight. The following day, after Wolf had disappeared, he tried something new. He got down the roll of fencing and fenced himself in against the face of the bluff with the wire in a semicircle around him, held upright by angle-iron posts from the garden patch, its end stakes driven into the vertical face of the bluff.

Jeebee had no doubt that if Wolf made a serious effort, he could pull the stakes out, one by one, but he hoped that organized an effort would not occur to his partner. Certainly the fence was now fastened firmly enough to stand up against being pushed or pawed by Wolf in any less-than-serious fashion.

He went back to work. Eventually Wolf did come, and prowled along the fence. He pawed at it once or twice and whimpered at Jeebee. Jeebee stopped work and stepped over the fence, to greet him, leaving the posthole digger inside. Jeebee greeted him, and in the process moved away from the fence. For a while he enticed Wolf as well as he could into forgetting the fence. Then, while Wolf was still there, he deliberately went back to it, stepped over it, and returned to work.

Wolf came up to the fence once more, and once more protested at it keeping him out. But when Jeebee continued to work, paying him no attention, he turned suddenly and trotted off with an exaggeratedly indifferent air. He went off to lie down in a little hollow among the roots of a tree at the edge of the meadow near the fire, which he had sometime since picked as his favorite resting place.

CHAPTER 28

So began some of the busiest weeks of Jeebee's life.

Late summer, if not fine early fall weather, clear and warm, still held the land. The days were still long, and it seemed to Jeebee that most of their useful length was in the afternoon hours.

He took the utmost advantage of this, rising before daylight to make his arrival at the ranch as early as possible. Every trip down there, now, he brought back something; even his backpack would be stuffed full of small items such as used nails, screws, or cloth in any size and shape.

Actually, in these early days, his time was spent mainly in working at the ranch itself. In addition to its tractors, cars, pickup trucks, and the one snowmobile, there were the two wagons of different sizes. Both ran on regular car axles and had Y-shaped hitch devices so that they could be pulled by trucks or tractors.

The larger wagon was a flatbed affair, high-sprung to ride over small obstacles, but built to carry heavy and bulky loads. It had a plank bed, ten feet wide by twenty feet in length. Possibly, Jeebee thought, it had been used to bring fodder out where the range cattle could get at it at times of the year when ordinary graze was scarce.

In winter, with snow on the ground, it must have had its wheels changed for the equivalent of skis. He went looking for some such things, and found them, together with skis for the other, much-smaller, two-wheeled wagon, up on rafters in a half-burned outbuilding.

He left them where they were. He had no time to waste even examining them now. In any case, the larger wagon was no use at all to Jeebee. His two horses could certainly pull it across the flatlands, but not with a load of any weight on it.

Even if they had been able to, it would have been impossible to pull it up the open slopes of the foothills, where there were no roads, or even tracks on which to travel. He turned to examining the two-wheel trailer.

It was obviously homemade, mainly of metal. It had the shortened axle from some car, with two ordinary automobile wheels and extra-thick clumps of leaf springs between them and the trailer bed. The bed itself had been made of thick planks, covered with sheet metal to take the wear of use.

It was surrounded by a four-bar railing of welded, one-and-a-half-inch pipe on posts of heavier pipe placed vertically, three feet high. The railing at the back was a gate that hinged at the base and had both planking and sheet metal across it so that it could be let down as a ramp up which the trailer could be loaded. The scraped and worn metal sheeting of the bed was about the dimensions of that in the back of a small pickup truck.

The hitch on its front was obviously designed to be fastened to the back of a tractor or a truck. Probably, thought Jeebee, a tractor. Its heavy construction would make it capable of carrying equipment, and other small but heavy loads, out into open areas where it was needed.

Someone had also welded a skid to the middle of the back bar of the frame that held the trailer bed. Jeebee had no idea why. But the skid was ideal for his needs, pulling the loaded wagon up slopes where its back end might otherwise drag on the ground.

As it was, when the two-wheeled wagon stood unhitched on the level, as now, it was tilted only slightly to the rear, resting on the tip of the skid. Obviously, with a tractor pulling it, it would move forward with its bed level and the end of the skid would ride half a foot above the ground.

This was something that Sally and Brute might be able to pull together, if they were willing to work as a team. Also, something they might be able to bring up the untracked slopes between the ranch and his cave.

Jeebee went searching for some sort of double yoke the two horses could wear to pull in tandem. He found nothing, however, and decided he was just as glad he had not.

On the uneven footing of the slopes, where the two horses might not have their backs level at all times, they were probably better off in separate harnesses. With such harnesses, closely tied together, but not so close that one would pull the other off balance by stepping downhill suddenly, they would be much safer.

Accordingly, he made two harnesses out of rope, wrapping soft cloths around any parts of the rope that might chafe. He also worked out a fairly complicated rope tie that would fasten both harnesses to the Y-point of the hitch.

The tie would undoubtedly wear thin and break from time to time, but the ranch had plenty of rope, and the tie could always be replaced.

The day he finished all this it was barely noon. He had come down alone on Brute, so he spent the rest of the day scouting the area between the ranch and his meadow to find a route that followed the gentlest possible slopes. He did not have a great deal of choice in most places. Still, he ended by finding a route that he estimated would probably take three hours or more for the horses with the trailer loaded. But at least it ought to be possible to them.

He had been riding only Brute lately to give Sally a rest after her recent days of having to carry both him and what he was bringing back from the ranch. But the day after scouting the new route, he brought both horses down early.

At the ranch, Brute objected even to being put into his harness. But then, Brute could be expected to object to about anything. Sally was clearly not too pleased with hers, either, but she made no important protest.

The real test came after they had both been harnessed to the empty trailer wagon and Jeebee tried leading them with the wagon behind them. It was well that he had taken a close grip on their halter ropes, because Brute's first impulse was to bolt. He was clearly under the impression that if he ran quick enough and far enough, he would get rid of the obnoxious device that was trundling behind him.

Jeebee ended by spending most of the afternoon leading the horses around. It was not until late afternoon that he got to the point where he thought he could try standing in the wagon and driving them.

He had rigged long, double reins to each horse. It was not so much that he felt that he needed to hold all four lines in his hands at once as it was the fact that both horses had been trained to neck reining, in which the rein was merely laid against the side of their necks to signal a turn. He had considered that on the slopes with the trailer, a rein could easily fall against the side of a horse's neck accidentally. Jeebee wanted to take as few chances as possible. If he could train them to mouth reining when they were pulling together like this, it would be safer.

The driving was only partly successful. Jeebee at last gave up trying it. He told himself that in any case, he would not be riding in the trailer when they were actually going up the slopes. He would be walking and leading the horses. Not only was that safer, but they would have load enough without adding his weight to it.

It was getting late in the day. He gave up his original hope of bringing the wagon back to the cave this trip, and unhitched both horses. He rode Brute back, with Sally on a lead rope, as usual.

The next morning early he took them down again, harnessed them to the trailer, and was about to take it back empty as a practice run. But the sheer need to make each trip count as much as possible caused him to put a few items in it.

He bundled these in an old blanket and tied it down to the trailer bed, above the axle. Rope anchored the bundle to the metal railing on all four sides.

Feeling reasonably certain that it would not shift, he began driving the horses along the flatlands, northward, for a little distance. His newer, easier route did not begin until they had reached a sort of cut into the foothills, about half a mile from the ranch house.

Moving across the open flatlands, Brute settled down somewhat to pulling with Sally. Jeebee was optimistic that with time the male horse would become completely used to the work.

When they got to the cut, Jeebee got out of the wagon and began leading the animals. Brute was, if anything, relieved to be led. Still, there were problems of turns, and places where their path was along the bottom of one slope with another at an angle to it, so that the trailer traveled tilted up on one side for a little distance. About twenty minutes into the foothills, the rope hitch broke and had to be retied, so that they were a good four hours finally getting to the cave.

The final half hour of daylight barely saw them into the campsite. Jeebee unhitched the relieved horses inside the closed wire fence to protect the trailer and its load from Wolf. Then he put them in the wooden corral he had been building and carried the bundle into the inner room of the cave.

He started a fire and went back outside to the trailer, closing the fence behind him.

The moment he did, Wolf materialized out of the last of the gathering gloom, and Jeebee came back out of the fenced-in area to go through their regular evening set of greetings. Then Wolf, after some hesitation, gave the trailer as thorough an examination through the fence as he could. Jeebee had carefully placed it so the rope of the harnesses and the trailer hitch were beyond his reach.

Satisfied at last, Wolf came to the fire and lay down.

Sitting, watching the other, Jeebee told himself that Wolf must almost certainly have been following him, out of sight, down to the ranch these last few days, or even weeks. In fact, Wolf had probably been making the route down and back to the ranch parallel to him on many of his trips.

He had certainly not appeared where Jeebee could see him. But that was Wolf's nature. He had been equally slow to approach Paul's wagon. He would not want to come into any un-

known place until he was sure it was safe to do so, no matter
how used he was to seeing it from a distance. Undoubtedly,
Jeebee thought as he finally rolled himself in his blankets, Wolf
would end up in the long run coming into the buildings with him.
Which might pose a problem in Jeebee's gathering and collecting
things he wanted to take back to the cave.

He turned out to be right within the next week. Five days
later Wolf appeared just before he got to the ranch and came
with him to the edge of its inhabited areas. In the next couple of
days he came increasingly closer, until he was actually in among
the buildings.

However, after a certain amount of limited exploring, staying as close to Jeebee as he could most of the time, Wolf made
himself scarce once more. In the days that followed, Jeebee found
that the problem he anticipated never really materialized. Wolf
remained shy of entering any enclosed area. Also, many days he
simply was not there.

Jeebee realized after some thought that most of his partner's
days needed necessarily to be given to hunting for needed food.
Wolf might take some time off from this, but he could not take
much. Normally, Jeebee ended up alone with the horses, in his
process of getting what he wanted from the ranch.

He blamed himself for not thinking of making use of the
two-wheeled wagon before. With it, he could have brought up
the two-by-fours and much of the other lumber in just a few
loads, if not in one large load. He had carefully been increasing
the amount carried in the trailer, and watching the horses to be
sure he did not work them too hard. It was as necessary to him,
as to them, that they keep their strength.

Now he got into necessarily heavier loads, and into loads he
had not thought of carrying originally. Ignored by himself as well
as the raiders was an aluminum building set off at some distance
from the rest of the ranch structures. This was something he recognized as a pole barn, a structure made of poles and aluminum
sheets solely for the purpose of housing and protecting baled hay
from the weather so that it could be stored into the winter and its
contents available for use to whatever horses or other such ani-

mals were at the ranch. It had been set apart like that simply
because hay caught fire very easily, and the whole structure could
be destroyed in a twinkling by a carelessly dropped cigarette.

Now, on seeing it, he realized that he would have to lay in a
supply of fodder for the two horses during the winter months up
at the cave. Here was the fodder, ready for him, and the trailer
could transport it. Not only that, but he found his attention attracted by the pole barn itself. Its doors, sides, and roof were
modular, light enough to carry, and of a size that could be carried in the two-wheel trailer.

The side poles were set in the earth. The rafters were attached to horizontal boards nailed between the side and corner
poles of the barn. The wall and ceiling strips of aluminum were
four feet wide to bridge the distance between poles and some ten
feet in height. All together they enclosed a remarkable amount of
baled hay.

He could strip the siding and roof off, take the rafters and
dig up the poles and simply transport the whole thing to the cave.
On second thought, he need not even dig up the poles. He could
cut and set log poles at the cave to attach the aluminum strips to.
All in all, it was well worth the days it would cost him to take
apart and transport the movable part of the pole barn and its
contents.

He did so, accordingly, during part of the following week.
The segments of the pole barn made an awkward, but not over-
heavy load for the trailer. The hay was a slower business, not
only to transport but to load—and it drove him crazy with the
chaff and straws that worked their way into his hair and through
his clothing to itch him to a frenzy.

Nonetheless, finally it was all done, and he had a strange
sense of pride at looking at it, set up, filled with fodder, and
ready to take care of the horses during the winter.

He turned back to moving his other necessities up to the
cave and getting the cave itself finished. He was racing against
the calendar. He wanted all his needed materials up at the
meadow before snow came.

Two of his most difficult trips came when he began to break

loose both the front and back doors of the ranch, complete with their frames. One of these at a time was a full load for the horses to pull to the cave. He was forced to make two trips to get them both up.

It took a good deal of muscle on his part to transfer each one to the trailer, even once he had loosened them from the house. But he must have them. He had decided he would need solid-core, outer doors for his cave because he wanted them to be as resistant to low temperatures, wind, and snow as possible.

The frames were necessary because Jeebee had no faith in his ability to either build a door frame or hang the door within one. He had heard once that it was a tricky thing to do. The door had to be hung just right, both vertically and in the frame. In the end he got both of them up to the cave, where he put the first one into the opening he had left for it in the outer wall.

His weather front for the excavated home was now complete. Only the interior remained undone. But he could take his time about the work inside, he told himself.

He celebrated that day by taking down the wire fence. It was only late afternoon, but Wolf had already returned and watched him remove it.

To his surprise—although afterward, thinking about what he knew of wolf behavior, it should not have been—Wolf did not at once enter into the territory that the fence had guarded.

Instead, he began by taking his time about making a leisurely approach to the now rolled-up fencing, lying in the meadow a little way from where it had been set up. Finally, he got close enough to sniff it over completely, both the fencing and the angle-iron posts that had secured it. But then, little by little he came deeper into the earlier-denied space until he reached the wall itself, which he then examined closely, from one end to the other.

The next morning, after Wolf had left, Jeebee began work inside the wall.

His last work outside had been to put a roof over the end of it that was far enough away from the face of the cliff so that the space needed bridging—that space where he hoped to set up his smithy. He had needed to fit the rest of the roof tightly against the face of the bluff, digging into the actual earth, with wood slanting upward into it so that any rain would run off. Later on he would undoubtedly find chinks and openings in the roof and wall, but he could then patch them with clay. When winter came, snow and ice would help by filling any openings and freezing them shut.

He was so concerned with having the structure tight that when he finally went in at last to start work on the inner cave section, he discovered something he had completely forgotten. With the wall up and the roof in position, it was too dark inside to see what he was doing.

He had already established that the solar blanket would charge the car batteries, even if it took some time to do it. But he found that working in constant gloom, he used up the batteries' charge faster than he could replace it.

He found his solution in connecting the batteries to the ceiling lights of the cars. The idea of using these had occurred to him earlier; but he had forgotten it. Now, it turned out to be ideal. The automobile interior lights gave him more than adequate illumination, and drained a battery only slowly.

But in the end he finally gave up and went back down to take out one of the ranch house's unbroken windows and bring it back to put it in a space he cut in his front wall.

Accordingly, he lost another day and a half of working time before he was able to resume excavation of the cave's interior in earnest.

He had made some preliminary sketches of how he might do the timbering. Now he began work by digging back the earth that faced the front wall from a few feet short of the end opposite to the blacksmithing area and over to the point where the bluff itself curved back to make the smithy space.

He had to pause occasionally to let dust clear the air of the cave and settle. This slowed him down still further, but he developed the habit of stepping out and doing some other little chore for a while. Eventually, however, he had created a space about four feet deep with a level floor. It was as far as he could go, simply digging.

He began the putting up of two-by-fours as studs, and building a second, interior wall, topping it off with an inner roof to hold back the sandy soil of the bluff above him. He would timber a bit, dig a little further, then timber again. Eventually, he planked between the studs of his inner wall as far as the curve of the bluff, leaving a space in it three feet in from the outer wall, and leaving a space in both outer and inner walls that would be filled by the two doors he had brought from the ranch house.

Once he had done this, he was ready to dig and timber the inside room of his cave. But his estimate of materials had been woefully short. He was forced into more trips to the ranch for used lumber and nails.

With these up at the meadow, finally, he began to work through the space of the door opening he had left in the inner wall.

He timbered as he went, and gradually excavated a room about eight feet wide and ten feet deep, with an interior ceiling over his head, both to support the earth above and keep it from trickling down upon him.

He had begun the interior room deliberately at a level a good two and a half feet above the level of the front room he had made with his two walls. Now, he was attempting to put to use something he had read about, which evidently worked in the building of igloos and snow caves. An igloo, he had read years ago, had its entrance, and a small interior area, below the level of a higher shelf on which much of the actual living was done. This arrangement caused a cold air barrier to form in the lower area. The heavier cold air below could not rise; so the warmth above was not lost to the icy outside temperatures.

The theory was undoubtedly excellent, but he found that in practice, even with both doors open to the outside, after he had worked a short while, the air began to grow bad. There was no real circulation into the area where he was digging.

He was forced to stop. Clearly he would have to provide some air circulation to the cave.

Happily, he had already made some plans to solve not only the circulation problem but the problem of heating the cave at the same time.

He went up to the top of the bluff, and by measuring, positioned himself over the space he had already cleared in the original hole, below. He began to dig a slanting hole down from there for about twelve feet. At this point he was sure he was well below the ceiling he would be excavating up to for the inner cave.

He went back to digging within the cave and soon, at what would be the left side of the inner room, as seen from the entrance, broke through to the point where the hole had been opened to the top of the bluff. He had brought up a length of chimney pipe from a dusty, long-unused, potbellied heating stove in one of the outbuildings of the ranch. He poked this up through the hole to just above ground level at the bluff's top and anchored the pipe in place. Then he began building a clay-mortared stone fireplace and chimney up to and around the pipe.

Now that he had ventilation in one wall of the cave, he returned to the digging. Air came in through the open doors and was warmed by his body heat and exited up the pipe. When he experimented with the doors closed, still enough air leaked in to keep it fresh while he worked. Whether it would be safe to build a fire in the fireplace was another question.

He was extremely doubtful that his crude heating plant would work at all, or that if it did, it would not also smoke him out or otherwise asphyxiate him. But he built a fire in it with the doors open and there was a moment of extreme jubilation on his part when he found that it drew quite well. Even with both doors closed, it would draw, and the firelight within it illuminated the cave somewhat.

The illumination was not great, but it was enough to let him do without even the interior car lights if he had to.

It was only a stop-gap form of illumination, but would have to do for the moment. It was time for him to go hunting again. He had been doing a minimum amount of gathering meat, grudging the time that it took away from his work. But he was now scraping bottom from his last slaughtering trip to the flatlands, and the last of the meat had not really kept too well. It had not made him sick. But even though the nights were much cooler, outdoors it was still nowhere near refrigerator, let alone freezer temperatures.

Accordingly, that evening, by an outside fire—for Wolf would still not go into the inner room of the cave—he made plans to go down to the flatlands for at least a couple of days. The first he would spend hunting. The next would be at the ranch, gathering up at least several more of the vehicle batteries.

The air was chill in spite of the fire and he thought he felt a hint of snow in the dark night air around him. He changed his mind. He had originally been thinking of riding Brute down and taking Sally along as a packhorse to carry the meat and the batteries—which together would not make too much of a load for her.

Now he decided to take the trailer. He had put off bringing up the skis for it. He should get those and keep them with the trailer; after first finding out how they went on. He would need to have the necessary nuts, bolts, and wrenches—or whatever—with him to put them on in case he was caught unexpectedly by snow.

The next morning was frosty. He harnessed both horses to the trailer and started down. It was now only mid-September. He had thought about the possibility of freakish early snowstorms, but it had really not come home to him until now what a difference it would make for him if one caught him unprepared, with wind and an abrupt, steep drop in temperature.

Even on the drive down to the ranch, the wind picked up and became colder. He was glad, and he was sure the horses were glad as well, to get to the ranch. He tied them in the shelter of one of the partially burned outbuildings, and went himself to look in the outbuildings where he had seen the skis for the two wagons. He had merely looked at the skis the time before, registering the fact they were there. He had not examined them.

Now that he climbed up to the rafters and looked at them closely, he discovered that the skis for the larger wagon were unusable. One had its tip ruined by fire, the other was half burned away. The skis for the small trailer were untouched, but as he looked at them, common sense suddenly shoved his imagination aside.

He could use them on light snow over level ground. But in

deep or slippery snow and upslopes, the weight of the trailer alone would be too much for the horses to pull.

He took them down anyway. Tied to one of them, in a large and strong cloth sack that had printing—now unreadable—stamped in black upon its once-white surface, he found all the necessary parts to connect them in place of the wheels.

He took them to the trailer, and put them in it. A few solitary but heavy flakes were drifting on the wind now and one lit on the back of his hand to touch him with a sudden sensation of an icy fingertip.

He looked at it in the moment before it melted from the heat of his body and disappeared. After a moment's thought, he took the hitch of the unloaded trailer and pulled it himself into the same outbuilding that was sheltering the horses.

If it turned into a real snowfall, they might all have to hole up here at the ranch for a day or so. He still found it hard to imagine a real blowing blizzard this early in the year. But the sky above him seemed to sag low with the weight of the dark clouds that hung overhead from horizon to horizon, and the snowflakes were coming at him more thickly.

He decided to ignore the storm, for the moment at least. He was dressed warmly, and by turning the collar of his jacket up around his neck and ears, he could ignore the cold wind. He had already started to think of what he could do if the trailer proved unusable. Not only the trailer, he reminded himself, but the horses. Deep snow would make it almost impossible for them to get through. Certainly, it would make it impossible for them to drag any amount of weight.

What he would have to do was build a light sledge that he could pull himself. Then he could go on foot down into the lowlands on snowshoes, which were one of the things he had found in the house here. That was handy, though he had re-searched them before leaving Stoketon. He knew two patterns for building them, including a temporary, emergency kind that could be built by someone who was lost in wilderness in sudden snow.

He didn't have to try to make them now, and in fact had already removed the snowshoes he had found, along with the skis, to the cave—as well as the heavy snowmobile boots.

He went now to look for lumber that he could peel from the outbuildings of the ranch, lumber that would make it possible for him to build the kind of one-man sledge he had in mind.

As he had begun to cannibalize the ranch house to provide materials for his cave, he had discovered that there might be benefits in leaving the undamaged parts of the house and its outbuildings as intact as possible, for purposes of further shelter or use. Accordingly, he examined first the outbuildings that had been most damaged by the fire.

The worst off of these was a building that had originally, evidently, been little more than a roof and a couple of walls. It had been either the blacksmithy for the ranch or the building in which a portable forge had been set up to do blacksmithing. He had already discovered an anvil there, which he meant to bring back to the cave for his own use once he got down the list of other priorities to it. Right now, the need for it was far enough in the future not to concern him.

There was almost nothing left of this building. Certainly there had been nothing about it of the kind of material of which he was most in need.

What he had hoped for was to find a couple of six-to-eight-foot planks, both at least an inch in thickness. If he found them he could saw their ends on the diagonal, or if he could discover a saw around the place that would let him saw in a curve, he could put a continuous upward curve to the bottom edge at the end of each plank. The two planks could then form the runners of his sledge. After that it would merely be a matter of bracing between them with a few two-by-fours and putting light planks across the two top edges to make a bed. The whole thing need only be heavy enough to carry about a hundred pounds of beef, or an equal load.

But there was nothing left in the smithy outbuilding. He went on next to the most ruined shed, which had evidently been a storeplace for odds and ends of small equipment and tools in need of mending, or merely those that were potentially too useful to throw away.

This building had been only about half destroyed by the fire. Jeebee looked it over, but saw nothing of the thickness he wanted. He was just about to leave when he realized that what he was looking for was under his feet.

The floorboards of the shed, in fact the floorboards of all the sheds, were of thicker planks than those used in the sides of the buildings or the ranch house.

He had already taken a number of hand tools up to the cave. But lately he had seen the wisdom of keeping at least one of each of the more common tools down at the ranch, for work there as well. Accordingly, he went to his store of these things and found a claw hammer and a crowbar.

With these he pried up a couple of the floorboards. He found that there was a bonus attached, once he had. For not only were the planks as thick as he wanted, but they had been put down with nails larger than any of those he had so far salvaged from their original places in the house and other buildings.

He went to work with a saw that decidedly was not made to cut curves. Not only was it a straight-cut saw—unthinkingly, earlier, he had taken the best saw with him—but it was rusty and dull. But as it got close to noon, he finally got the sawing done and began to join the two planks with the heavy nails driven through their sides and into the ends of a couple of braces made of two-by-fours.

Planking over the top of the sledge with the lightest boards he could find took less than another hour. He attached a towing rope to the front ends of the runner planks. The end product was good. But he began to be a little worried as he looked at it and realized how much dead weight he would be pulling, even without any load on it. Heading into a blizzard with this dragging behind him, fully loaded, might be more than he could manage. He needed to save weight some way, but certainly he could not save it either on the runners or on the bracing boards.

He went looking for something else to cover the body of the sledge. He found it in a piece of half-inch plywood that had been used in a building that had evidently done double duty as a temporary barn for about three horses or three head of cattle. The plywood had been used to form partitions between the stalls.

Swearing under his breath at his waste of time, he removed the boards and replaced them with the plywood.

When he was done, the sledge was still not what might be called "light." But it was the best he could do. Wrapped up in his work, he had almost forgotten the weather. But now he stepped outside the building in which he had been working and saw that the day had grown very dark. The snow was no longer a scatter of soft flakes, but hard, almost invisible pellets of ice. There would be no trying to get back up to the campsite and the cave today.

When the morning dawned, there were a good four inches of grainy snow on the ground. But the wind had ceased, and although the temperature was low, the absence of movement in the cold air made it bearable. It was even more bearable as the last of the clouds disappeared, and the sun came out.

The snow was not so deep and the temperature was not so low that what had fallen might not quickly turn into slush or ice, which could be slippery underneath the hooves of the horses. Still . . . he made a quick decision to load the sledge on the trailer and head back to the camp.

Once there, he could find shelter for the horses in the corral he had built abutting the small, right-angled wall of his smithy-to-be. The trailer would be safe at the campsite, and he would also have the sledge on hand. So that if the weather continued to be bad and more snow fell, he could head down into the flatlands with it alone.

On foot. As he had early imagined himself doing.

CHAPTER 29

I t was a long, hard struggle back to the cave. In spite of the fact that the air temperature stayed low, the horses found most of the going slippery, and the trailer was evidently a problem to pull, particularly when they ran into smaller drifts.

Jeebee went ahead of them to break trail and to make sure that the horses did not wander into a drift too deep to pull the trailer through. Its only load was the sledge, but under these conditions that was enough.

They reached the meadow in late afternoon. The bright, cloudless sky overhead, and the fact that the surrounding trees blocked out much of what little wind stirred, gave the meadow an appearance of being warmer than it actually was. Jeebee unhitched the trailer without bothering to take the sledge out, unharnessed the horses, and put them in the corral.

He went directly to the shelter of the cave for himself and built a fire in the fireplace. Wolf, who at first had been reluctant to venture inside the newly built wall at all, had some days since worked himself up to coming into the outer part. He had inspected every feature of the space minutely. Much of the wood bore exploratory chew marks, and one of the vertical studs had obvious stains. Wolf had found a corner of the wall where Jeebee had built a rough frame for a cloth weather barrier to stand between the smithy and the rest of the lower front room, and adopted it as a nice place to curl up and sleep.

Jeebee closed the outer door, now, but did not latch it; merely pulling it to, and fastening it with a loop of leather thong after Wolf followed him in as far as the front room. He was confident that Wolf would push on the door if he wanted to get out and would discover the thong. Even if he didn't recognize that it held the door closed, he would almost certainly bite it—and thereafter Wolf would go for the thong whenever he wanted the door open.

Jeebee lit one of his battery-fed interior car lights and kept it lit long enough to get a fire started in the fireplace, using the dead wood and tinder he now kept stored beside it, ready for use.

The fire blazed up. It began to warm the interior room almost immediately. Jeebee turned off the electric light. Looking around in the firelight at the unfinished cave, he thought that it was not much of a place to come home to, offering little more than warmth and shelter. Only its front wall was finished. Its two side walls, including the one with the fireplace, were still in process of building, and the innermost wall was simply a slope of dirt and sand that every so often crumbled loose and slid down to join the dirt underfoot. Jeebee told himself that he must get around eventually to flooring the interior room, once he had finished sealing the walls, ceiling, and all else.

Meanwhile he had his fireplace. He had moved his packload bed inside and put those things like bacon, wrapped, up on the yet-unceilinged rafters, out of reach of anyone but himself.

Feeling secure, therefore, in a sudden burst now of good feeling at being out of the weather and warm again, Jeebee left the interior door open and tried to coax Wolf to come in by the fire. But the most he was able to achieve was a hesitant muzzle thrust partway through the door opening, just above the threshold.

Jeebee gave up on his coaxing. He turned his attention to moving his bed close to the fire for the night. Near it, even with the inner door open, and the outer one barely closed, he was comfortable enough. There was plenty of draft coming in to keep the fire going. The only thing to concern himself about was that he might run short of firewood in the night.

He went forth into the cold once more to gather sufficient heavy pieces of wood to last the night, and went to bed. He knew he would be roused by the increasing chill from time to time to add wood to the fire before it went out.

The last thing he remembered before dropping off was a bit of dirt falling from the unfinished ceiling into his hair. He brushed the sand and dirt away, sleepily, and muzzily reminded himself that he needed to make himself a cap for winter use. Fully dressed and feeling the warmth of the fire on his face, he drifted off, thinking that he would try out the snowshoes tomorrow.

But even during the night, the weather warmed. Jeebee woke up, with the fire out entirely, but was still comfortable underneath the two blankets over him and inside the clothes he was wearing.

He felt his way across the short distance of earth to the inner door and opened it to see the early-morning light. The outer door was standing wide, and the chewed remnant of the thong still hung from the jamb.

Wolf had wanted out, but he had not left the meadow. He was curled up in the sunlight outside. He got to his feet, shook himself, and came over to greet Jeebee as Jeebee stumbled out of the door. They had the brief interchange of greetings that Wolf usually insisted on before leaving mornings. Then he was gone.

Jeebee went through his own private morning process. He had changed his mind about the snowshoes. The day was warming up toward normal autumnal temperatures, and the snow was not so much melting as simply evaporating about him. A soft wind blew.

The most urgent thing, he realized, was what he had set out to do the day before. That was hunt for food. He hated to impose on the horses after their long haul through the snow of yesterday. But if one of them could stand the imposition better, it would be Brute. So it was Brute he saddled, and took Sally on a lead rein, not toward the ranch at all, but directly down and out into the flatlands to look for cattle.

Once down on the flat, however, he changed his mind. He angled southeastward until he hit the line of poles that had once carried electricity to the ranch. They paralleled a road that he had assumed was the ranch's access to some main highway, somewhere to the east. The snow was now only a thin coating of icy crust on the land.

It had occurred to him that with the landscape suddenly all the same color, landmarks he had unconsciously become used to would be either hidden or changed, and it would be wise to have an anchor point. He could use his orienteering skills, but the poles were visible for some distance and could serve as an easy reference line. He could go out along them, and if he felt like looking northward for possible cattle, he could go in that direction with the assurance that if he only turned back southward, he would eventually come upon the line of poles again, which would lead him back to the ranch and familiar territory.

With the mountains behind him there would be no lack of at least two high points that could be seen for miles. If he took bearings on two such points, this would give him a point he could always get back to. It was almost impossible to get lost if you had a compass and a mountainous horizon.

It would not be the most direct route if he had to do that, back to the meadow and his cave, but it was a sure way of getting home again.

He followed the line of poles and rode slowly out along it, slightly south of east as to direction, according to his compass.

He stayed with the poles, but both south and north of them he swept the horizon steadily with his binoculars for any sight of cattle.

About midday he spotted some specks south of him, in the distance. He had counted poles as he went and he was just past the two hundred and sixteenth of these when he spotted whatever it was he was seeing to the south.

Now he wished he had had the forethought to bring along the hatchet he had found at the ranch and carried up to the cave, where it had proved to be very handy indeed. However, he had the next best thing in his smaller, working sheath knife at his belt.

Using this, he hacked a strip from the two hundred and sixteenth pole, exposing the lighter color of new wood by removing gray, weathered surface. The slash was on the south side of the pole, and should be recognizable through his binoculars from some little distance. He put the knife back in its sheath, redid the button closure, and once more located the specks with his binoculars.

They had moved, if at all, not very far from where he had first seen them. He rode toward them.

He was lucky. It was a cow accompanied by her almost full-grown calf. The calf had nowhere near the weight that it would carry once it was full grown, but it stood nearly as tall as its mother, and its frame was nearly as large.

Like the other cattle he had found and shot before, these two let him get quite close before they showed signs of moving off. Nearly all these cattle must have been used to being approached by humans on horseback and in vehicles, up until just a few years before, and there were not that many predators around that came either with horses or with vehicles to threaten them.

Jeebee killed the calf with a single shot, which was not only easier on his ammunition supply, but more merciful to the animal. From this short distance there was no problem in making such a quick kill with a single bullet.

For a few minutes he thought he would have trouble getting the cow to leave the dead calf so that he could safely get down and begin butchering. But when he untied Sally's lead rein and galloped Brute at the cow, whooping and waving his cap over his head, she took fright and lumbered off in a clumsy gallop of her own. He got down and began the messy business of slicing through the skin of the calf and butchering off as much meat as possible, to be carried back in one of the plastic tarps again.

Done at last, he was ready to go. He found, as he had suspected, that in the process of chasing off the cow, getting down, and butchering the calf, he had lost his bearings in the still-white wilderness that surrounded him. On the off chance that he might not be too far away to see it, he unslung the binoculars and looked for the slash that identified the two hundred and sixteenth pole. But he could not even see the poles.

He secured the load of fresh, slippery, warm chunks of beef in its plastic and net on Sally's back, tied her lead rein back to its anchor at the back of Brute's saddle, mounted Brute, and using his compass, headed northward.

Either the cow and her calf had been moving away from him, all the time he was bearing down on them, or else the road had taken a turn to the north on its way to the highway—he had never been out along it this far before—but he rode for some little while before he began to pick up what looked like a row of black dots right on the horizon.

Reasoning that these would be the tops of the electric poles, the greater part of their length cut off from him by some swell in the ground ahead, he put aside the binoculars and simply rode directly toward where he had seen them. In about fifteen minutes they became visible to the naked eye, and then seemed to grow up longer and longer from the ground beneath them as he got close.

He rode right up to them and began to hunt to his left, which was westward and back toward the ranch, for one that bore the slash mark he had made. He did not find it and it occurred to him that he might well have gone toward the cattle on more of a slant back westward toward the foothills than he had thought, so that now he had come back to the line of poles behind the two hundred and sixteenth one.

But in any case, his compass showed him the way westward, and he knew he was heading toward the ranch and the foothills. That was all he really needed to know. He rode past several poles before he noticed something that caused him to rein Brute in sharply.

He was astonished at his lack of observation in not seeing it before. On the other side of the poles, there was a track in the snow. It was a track of boots, going in the same direction he was now going. He lifted the reins and Brute moved forward until he halted him again right over the track. The boots were small and tended to shuffle through the snow. Whoever it was, was walking—which should not be happening in this territory, where even if there were no vehicles that ran anymore, there was an abundance of riding horses. And it was headed toward a ruined ranch, which any neighbor by this time must know had no life left within it.

The track could only be that of a stranger, as he was a stranger, to this area. And any stranger was a possible danger. His first instinct was to turn and run. Then curiosity got the better of him.

He unslung his binoculars and looked ahead. Clear in the binoculars was a figure, heavily muffled in clothes and trudging, as the tracks indicated, toward the ranch—which was still out of sight. There was a pack on its back, but it seemed to be empty, and the figure was not carrying a rifle, or in fact any other visible weapon.

Jeebee reminded himself that the other could well have something like a revolver tucked into his belt in front. A revolver that could be pulled as the figure turned to face him, if he came up to it.

But at the same time, by contrast, he himself was almost a traveling armory of guns and knives.

He decided to catch up with the figure, but as quietly as possible. He took the horses forward warily, still at a walk, but at a fast walk—a walk faster than the pace the person ahead of him was making.

The sound of their hooves on the ground was muffled by the snow above it. Jeebee and the two animals went forward very quietly indeed. Still, he could hardly believe it when he came closer and closer to the walking figure and the other did not stop and turn to see who was following.

Now that he was only twenty or thirty feet behind the intruder, Jeebee began to read the expression of the other's body. Whoever it was, his shoulders slumped, and he was pushing forward as if at the end of whatever strength was in the body above the legs that kept moving.

If the other was really ready to drop from fatigue, as he well might be if he had been going any distance through this snow from the time the sun had risen, then perhaps he was too worn out to hear Jeebee approach behind him, or to look around and take ordinary precautions. Loosening his rifle in its holster,

Jeebee closed the gap between himself and the plodding shape. He moved up right behind it, then level with it, before, at last, the figure stopped, raised its head, and looked at him.

It was Merry. Her eyes were like black holes in a face that was as pale as the face of a person in a coma.

For a long moment she stared at him unbelievingly. Then immediately he was off his horse and had his arms around her. The minute she felt herself held she sagged so suddenly that he found himself holding her whole weight. He realized suddenly that she must be on the ragged edge of exhaustion, only being driven forward by whatever had kept her moving so far.

His arms holding her had pushed her clothing up around her face. He kissed the icy tip of her ear, which was all he could see.

"Merry," he said, with his whole heart and body speaking the word. He felt her arms try to reach about him and drop.

"Are you able to ride?" he asked softly with his lips right next to her ear.

There was a moment, and then she nodded. He lifted her up on Brute, a dead weight at first, and then she tried to help him— but weakly. He got her into the saddle, then put his own left foot into the nearest stirrup and swung himself up behind the saddle, putting his foot into the other stirrup and pushing away her own right foot, which was instinctively feeling for the stirrup.

"Just sit," he said softly into her closest ear. "We'll ride together and I'll take care of everything. Just lean against me. It's going to take an hour or two to get where we're going. So just take it as easy as you can, and remember, I'll hold you. You won't fall."

He held her to him with one arm and handled Brute's reins in the other hand. Brute was not pleased to be carrying double, but Jeebee responded savagely with rein and voice at Brute's first movement to protest.

"Damn you," Jeebee snarled, "walk straight!"

The surprised horse was remarkably obedient from then on through the trip to the cave. Sally followed on her lead rein with her usual good temper.

They rode forward at a walk because for all Jeebee wanted

to get Merry back to the cave as quickly as possible, he felt it would be much easier on her if he did not even put the horses into a trot. In any case, they would have to slow down to a walk to climb the foothills.

After a while, he got his glasses out and looked ahead along the line of poles. Sure enough, his glasses picked out the dark tiny shapes of the ranch buildings up ahead. He turned and angled off in the northerly direction. As he got closer to the foothills, he steered for the cut up which he had begun his route with the trailer to the meadow. The easier slopes would be the easiest on Merry.

The route was still slippery, but the horses were more surefooted without the weight of the trailer pulling them back. They came eventually to the meadow and the cave, and Jeebee got down from Brute to carry Merry inside. He lit the electric lights with a reckless disregard for depleting the batteries and got a fire going in the fireplace. Only then did he think of unloading or unsaddling the two horses. They could wait a little longer. Merry came first.

He shut and latched the inside door, leaving the outside door open. He looked at the fire apprehensively. But apparently with the outer door open there were still enough air leaks, in and around the inner door as well as through the inner wall, that the fire continued to have enough draft to burn cheerfully.

He felt Merry's forehead and it felt hot to him, but then his hands were still cold from being outside.

She grabbed his hand fiercely as he started to move away from her.

"Don't leave me!" she said.

"It's all right," he told her softly. "I'm just going to get a thermometer to take your temperature. We're home now. You're safe. I'll take care of you."

He took the thermometer from his backpack, the same one he had carried in his medical kit from Stoketon, and put it in her mouth. After five minutes by his watch he took it out. She was not running a fever, as his cold hands had led him to believe. Instead her body temperature was a full three degrees below normal.

He piled everything warm he had upon her and built up the fire in the fireplace.

It came back to him then that the first thing to do with a person who has been overchilled is to get hot food into her. He had kept a soup continuously making over the fire when it was lit—a sort of pot-au-feu—using a bent metal rod from the ruined ranch house. He had stuck the rod into the ground beside the fireplace, its upper six inches bent at a right angle out over the flames, with a hook bent into its further end to hold the wire handle of a pot he had also taken from the ranch house. Swiveling the rod now, he put the pot above the flames.

Having done this, he went back and sat holding Merry's hand while the soup heated. She lay with her eyes closed, and he did not try to talk to her. When the soup was heated, he filled a soup bowl and brought it to her.

The packload bed was so low that even kneeling beside it, he was too high. Still kneeling, he sat down on his heels and put the bowl of soup on the ground beside him. With his left arm he lifted her upper body into a half-sitting position and lifted a spoonful of the soup to her lips.

At first she seemed only able to take small sips. Then, she took larger ones. After a bit she was swallowing eagerly. But abruptly she closed her lips and shook her head slightly.

"No more," she said. "Let me down."

He laid her back on the bed. She closed her eyes and went almost immediately to sleep. He continued to sit beside her, feeding the fire and making sure the covers stayed piled on top of her. She had volunteered nothing about Paul, Nick, and the wagon. It was obvious something had happened to them or she would have mentioned them by now.

Plainly, there was a reason for her not speaking of them. Jeebee understood this out of his new knowledge of the world and himself. So he would not ask. When she was ready to tell him, she would. He suddenly remembered the horses.

It was probably better to take a chance and go out now to take care of them.

He did so, first unloading the bundle of meat from Sally. He put it safely within the latch door of the inner room, then took both horses to the corral and removed their saddles and blankets. He left them there and returned to Merry, who seemed not to have stirred. He took the pot of soup off the fire, and kneeling by the fire, filled a larger pot with chunks of the recently butchered calf meat and water.

This time he used another rod, bent roughly into a Y-shape at one end, to help support the increased weight of the bent-over end of the first rod. He hung the pot with the water and raw meat in it above the flames and began the slow process of cooking the meat he had just butchered.

CHAPTER 30

Two hours later, when Jeebee took Merry's temperature again, it was up to normal. He breathed a sigh of relief and went on with his business of cooking the meat. Wolf came and scratched at the door, but Jeebee ignored him, and after a while the scratching ceased.

Merry slept steadily through that night and through most of the following day, waking for only short intervals. With the second evening, however, he took her temperature again on general principles and found it slightly up. It was only a small rise, barely over a single degree when Jeebee checked it shortly after eight o'clock on his watch, but it concerned him. She seemed no more than exhausted to him, but he did not trust his medical knowledge to be sure that the small temperature increase might not have some unrecognized importance. But by dawn she was a half degree below normal, which Jeebee took to be as much a sign of health as any temperature reading could be.

Wolf scratched on the door again and whimpered outside once more.

"Are you up to seeing him?" Jeebee asked Merry, and then realized he had mentioned Wolf in exactly the same way as he might have brought up the topic of a visiting relative, who wanted to visit.

"Yes," said Merry, "for a few minutes, just. But I'd like to see him."

Jeebee went to the door to open it. He did not know whether Merry realized that part of Wolf's importuning to be let in was probably because of his curiosity. He would have become highly interested on scenting and hearing Merry here in the cave, when he had last seen her many days and miles away.

"Tell me when you want me to get him out," he said over his shoulder to Merry, and opened the door.

Recently, Wolf had summoned up courage to venture first into the inner room of the cave, then to investigate all of it, and finally to make himself at home there. Jeebee had had to work out a method of evicting him, when his visits became too extended, or whenever he looked suspiciously like he was about to defecate or urinate. Wolf was inclined to relieve himself wherever he happened to be at the moment, and accounts Jeebee had read by people who had reared wolves in their homes agreed that wolves were extraordinarily resistant to housebreaking.

Jeebee opened the door, and Wolf bounded up inside, boldly enough, but checked after entering. He stood, with his attention riveted on Merry in the bed and his head cocked in an attitude of uncertainty, as though he didn't quite recognize her.

"Hello, old Wolf," Merry crooned softly. "Did you come to see me? Come on, Wolf. I haven't seen you for a long time. . . ."

As soon as she spoke, Wolf pushed past Jeebee and shambled toward the bed. His ears were rolled back deferentially and his tail wagged slightly, but his head was high, signaling neither timidity nor appeasement—just a friendly and comfortable renewal of old acquaintance.

Arrived there, he licked at her face. She tried to dodge the tongue and reached out to scratch in the winter-thick fur under his neck. Wolf slipped quickly into the enthusiasm of his normal greeting, and the more Merry tried to restrain him, the more insistently he pressed his attentions.

"That's enough," Merry said finally.

Jeebee stepped forward and scooped Wolf up, one arm under his belly and the other between his forelegs. Wolf's chest was cradled in the crook of his arm, and his neck was jammed against Jeebee's shoulder, so Wolf could not turn and snap at his face in protest. Carrying the other so, Jeebee pushed his way through first the inner door, then the outer one. Outside, he kicked the outer door closed hard enough so it latched behind them. Then he set Wolf down.

Wolf tried to get back in through the front door, but Jeebee stood where he was.

"It's no use," Jeebee told him. "She's got to rest. Later on you can see as much of her as you want to. How about that?"

As usual, neither the words nor the tone of Jeebee's voice made any visible impression on Wolf, where they might have soothed the ruffled feelings of a dog. But, also as usual, Jeebee felt better voicing his thoughts aloud. After a few seconds, Wolf gave up trying to open the latched door, gave Jeebee a petulant stare, and stalked off. As suddenly as ever, he pulled his vanishing act, and the meadow was empty.

Jeebee waited a moment more to make sure he was gone, then let himself back in through the outside door, latching it behind him again and returning to Merry.

"I guess I'm weaker than I thought," Merry said as he came in.

"You've got plenty of reason to be," Jeebee said. His voice sounded gruff in his own ears. "Sleep, now. Or would you like something more to eat first?"

"No more food," said Merry. "You've filled me up to where I could go five days without eating."

"You'd probably gone five days without when I met you," said Jeebee.

"Not quite," said Merry. But her eyelids fluttered as she said it. A second later she was asleep again.

On the morning of the fourth day, her need for sleep and her general exhaustion seemed mostly to have left her. She woke when Jeebee roused himself. They could not see out the window he had put in the front wall with both doors closed, but Jeebee knew from habit that it was barely dawn. This morning saw Merry bright-eyed and looking almost as he had last remembered her at the wagon.

She insisted on rising, and frying some of the bacon herself, then making what she christened as their "deprived" form of pancakes, with the melted bacon fat, flour, and water.

Jeebee ate, feeling extraordinarily domesticated, and went out to harness the horses to the trailer. It was a bright morning. Cool now, but it would warm with the day. When everything was ready, he left the revolver with her. "I'll hunt in close to the foothills," he said. "I ought to be back by midafternoon."

"I wish I could go with you," she answered.

"In a day or so, when you're stronger," he said.

They clung together tightly for a moment.

It was with an effort on both their parts that they let go of each other. Jeebee picked up the reins of the two animals shortly in front of their mouths, wrapped the excess around his arm, and led them away across the meadow and down toward the flatlands.

When he got back, in midafternoon as he had promised, he found the cave and its contents straightened up and as cleared of loose sand as possible. He delivered his raw meat, which she started cooking, and they went through the ending routine of the day, including Wolf's twilight return and greetings and finishing up the cooking of all the meat he had brought back.

Jeebee had been sleeping rolled up on the earth floor of the cave so as not to disturb her during the first few nights. This night, she made room for him in the bed. For a moment they lay looking into each other's eyes in the firelight, then came together as naturally as shadows from the sun outside a room approach each other and merge at the end of a day.

It took her a full week to recover to anything like normal activity. They had no way of weighing her until she could get down to the ranch, or Jeebee could bring back up the bathroom scales that he knew to be down there, ignored by its attackers when the ranch had been looted. It was obvious that she had lost more than a little weight. Her clothes hung loosely on her, and she looked even more lost in some of Jeebee's clothes she borrowed to wear while she washed her own.

She urged Jeebee to return to his normal routine, whatever that was.

"I'm just fine by myself," she said. "I can make a fire if I want. I can cook anything I want to eat. I'm completely taken care of here. You can keep leaving your revolver with me, if you're worried about my being safe. But the snow will be five feet deep before you turn around. I want to get down to that ranch with you, too, as soon as we can. I'll bet I can find a lot of things you didn't think to bring up here."

"You might," said Jeebee.

He thought he heard a note in her voice that was somehow wrong, and could be connected to whatever had happened to Paul, Nick, and the wagon—and to her as a result. It was as if she was trying hard to act as if there was nothing unsaid between them—a sort of unnatural brittleness. But he said nothing. He took the rifle, the horses and trailer—for the snow was now almost gone and the good weather held—and went back to his hunting. Now that she was here to do the cooking for him, he could simply drop off a load of raw meat at the cave and return to the flatlands without waiting. With the two of them and winter coming on, there was a more urgent need for stockpiling meat than ever.

The days were still sunny, but it was getting colder. It was now frosty in the mornings, and the cooked meat could be hung in places where it was in the shade all day. So it could be kept at close to ordinary refrigerator temperature.

So Jeebee spent the next few days hunting. Up at the cave, Merry gradually recovered her strength, although the strange brittleness of character stayed with her. She was almost overbusy, cleaning and recleaning the inner room, cooking the meat he brought in, and—although he did not know about this until she was halfway into it—she began enlarging the hole in the cold front room, at the opposite end of that long, narrow passageway from the blacksmithy, and had it half-dug before he found out.

Still, she seemed finally to have become fully rested. So that, while Jeebee by himself had been in the habit of going to sleep shortly after sundown and sleeping until just before dawn, he now took to staying up later in the evening with her, talking before the fire. In these talks, finally, little by little, without any coaxing from him but as if the memories were painful, the story of her journey to find him came out.

It came in bits and pieces. Clearly, she found difficulty in winding herself up to the point of telling it, and she was starting with those things that were easier to tell, first.

For Jeebee it was a little like reading a book, or watching a movie, which had been chopped into sections, each section being read forward in the ordinary manner, but with the sections not necessarily in order except that they generally revealed themselves in reverse order.

She had known, she said, in any case roughly, where Jeebee was headed, and thought she knew which way he would go. Although of course she had assumed he would be going directly up into Montana after leaving the wagon. It had not occurred to her that he might backtrack, cross the Powder River Pass, and take a side trip to get the wolf books. As a result, she had gone up the other side of that particular range of mountains and not crossed his trail until she was above Billings.

She had had an advantage over him. She was more confident about asking her way as she went.

When she started, the people she stopped with overnight and questioned as to whether they had seen anyone like Jeebee or signs of his trail, or even heard of such a person, were either people who had at one time been customers of Paul's or who knew of Paul.

When she got beyond the point where Paul was known, she still continued by a chain method, in which she would ask the last family to welcome her whom she might contact farther north. So, equipped with a name and some information that would help introduce her to someone who did not know her, she had moved on, and on; each time, upon leaving she asked for the name of someone yet further up.

None of those she asked or visited had seen Jeebee, or knew of him directly. But she did pick up word, late in the trip, of someone glimpsed moving northward with a couple of horses.

Even this information was told her only from time to time. But since she knew she was headed in the right direction, she continued northward. Her figuring was that since Jeebee would be fighting the clock of the seasons to get to his brother's ranch in time, he would keep moving in the direction she was taking herself. Her only fear was that he would reach the area of his brother's ranch, then start to wander around trying to find it, and she might overshoot him at that point. Her hope was that she still could overtake him before he got too far north.

She was still feeling relatively safe when her chain of references, from household to household, broke.

She had already decided that if the worse came to the worst, and she had not caught up with Jeebee before winter started, she would try to find some family that would take her in until the spring. One which would be willing to trade food and shelter in exchange for the work she could do for them.

She knew that she had a good deal to offer in her knowledge of horses, of herbal and general medicines, and a multitude of other things useful to know around a farm or ranch. She knew she could be an asset to any such place and more than earn her keep. The only danger was finding herself stuck with people who would not give her a chance to prove what she was able to do.

". . . and that's more or less what happened," she told Jeebee, staring into the flames in the fireplace of the cave. "I finally got sent on by one family—their name was Henderson, they were nice people—but they sent me on with only one name, a name for only one person in a family. He was an old man named Gary Brutelle. I was told he didn't have any wife or children, but he was supposed to have a couple of younger men, nephews or cousins or something like that, living with him."

She had always been wary of stopping with any family or group that had no woman among them. But the Hendersons had assured her that old Gary Brutelle was the nicest of men. In addition, he would be definitely in control of anyone else living under his roof.

It was the only lead she had. So she went forward, particularly feeling that she must be very close behind Jeebee, since at the Hendersons' there had been talk of some sign found that somebody with horses had camped in the willow bottoms of a small river nearby. A camp, she was told, of which the sign had been recent.

So if that was Jeebee, he must be fairly close ahead of her.

Jeebee was tempted to tell her about the bear, but he did not want to interrupt her, now that she was talking.

She did not even glance at him, but continued with her eyes on the fire.

"But when I got to this Brutelle place," she said, "the old man had died. There were only the two cousins there. They were men in their forties, and they seemed decent enough. I was going to move on anyway, except they seemed very good, and really insisted on my staying overnight."

She paused.

"I shouldn't have trusted them."

Jeebee tensed. This time she did look at him.

"Oh, they didn't do anything to me personally." She looked back at the fire. "But when I got up in the morning and moved out into the kitchen, I found one of them holding a rifle on me. The other took away my revolver. They told me they'd talked it over last night after I'd gone to bed. I was to stay with them— and work for them. They needed a woman around the house. As long as I didn't give any trouble to them, they wouldn't give any trouble to me. But I was going to stay, and that was that."

She hesitated.

"In some ways," she said, "I don't think they were really so bad. It was just that they really wanted to keep me, and they knew I'd never stay of my own free will. So they took my guns and my horses—everything I owned—and made sure I wasn't carrying anything else, even a knife I might use against them. And kept me locked up nights. Daytimes, there was always one of them with me and he had a gun."

She stopped, and stayed stopped so long that Jeebee finally prompted her.

"What happened then?"

She looked at him.

"Well," she said, "I thought it best to seem to go along with them and maybe they'd relax and I'd have a chance to slip away.

And that's pretty much what happened after several weeks. But I had to run at night, with nothing more than that packsack on my back, with a couple of blankets and a little bit of food that I stole from their kitchen. I headed north blind. I didn't even get to keep my binoculars. With those I could have waited my time to come up and watch a ranch house from a distance until I was sure there was a woman there, or else there was some sign that it'd be safe to go up to them. As it happened, I'd only passed a couple of places—and that at night—before this snow caught me. I sneaked into a barn at one of the ranch houses, but left that morning before anybody was up, so I don't know what they were like. I headed on north, but finally, I knew it was no good. I was out of food and desperate. Even if they made a slave of me, the next place I came to, I had to go in and throw myself on their mercy. If I didn't find a place, I was going into the hills, the way you have, and see if I couldn't set snares for rabbits and small animals and find someplace to hole up."

She looked at him.

"Well, you know the rest," she said. "It was then you found me."

"You were really ready to drop," said Jeebee. "I don't know how you went that long before turning in somewhere."

"I kept hoping to catch up with you," she said, looking at him. "It's funny. I didn't really find you until after I'd finally given up hope I'd find you."

"You were out on your feet," Jeebee said gruffly. "You'd have died that night if I hadn't found you."

"Maybe," she said, looking back at the fire. "Maybe . . . but maybe not. I had a lot of reason to want to live."

She sat without saying anything more for some seconds. Jeebee waited her out, listening to the crackle and snap of the burning wood in the fireplace. Finally she shook her head, as if she was putting the whole memory she had talked about out of her mind. She looked over at him and smiled.

"Have you looked for an outdoor thermometer down at that ranch?" she said. "That's not the sort of thing people raiding a ranch like that would particularly think of taking. They must have had a thermometer to see what the outside temperature was like. Did you see one?"

"No," Jeebee said slowly. The fact of the matter was it had never crossed his mind to look, either. Or if he had seen one, he had paid no attention to it. He was long past the point where he thought of the weather in degrees. It was cold, it was hot, it was bearable, it was unbearable. These were the things he concerned himself with, as exclusively as Wolf might.

"You're probably right," he said. "There's got to be one. I can look for it. But what do we need a thermometer for, particularly?"

"You shouldn't have to ask me that," said Merry. "You know I've been digging that pit in the cold room up front for the meat storage. We're almost to the point where it's going to be cold enough to keep meat frozen down there. But we want to be sure. If you can get a thermometer from the ranch, we can check the temperature at the bottom and know."

Jeebee felt stupid.

"Of course," he said. "I'll swing by there tomorrow, long enough to see if I can find one without a lot of searching. I'd still like to get more in before the weather breaks."

"I'd like to get down there, too," said Merry. "Why don't you let me go down with you, and leave me at the ranch while you go out hunting, then come back and pick me up along with whatever I've found to take back."

Jeebee was tempted to point out that taking her there and then going back to pick her up would limit the amount of ground he could cover out on the open range looking for cattle. While he hesitated, she spoke again.

"As you say, this good weather isn't going to last, perhaps not more than another day or so—if that. In fact, it could snow tonight and we'd be into winter," she said. "I want to get down and comb through that place before everything gets covered."

"All right," said Jeebee.

But, almost miraculously, the weather continued to hold. Not only was it warmer than it had been—and warmer than it should be for this time of year—but the sky remained clear of clouds and they had relatively long hours of daylight in which to get things done.

Jeebee was making progress in using the solar-cell blanket to charge all the batteries. Evidently the converter that was built into the blanket would work for car batteries, although it was, as he had expected, no better than a trickle charger. It was very slow to get a battery up to working level.

Nonetheless, he kept the blanket spread out where the sun could reach it all day long, and continuously connected to a battery, so that one of them was being charged all the daylight hours. Eventually they had four fully charged batteries in reserve, which could be turned on for extra or emergency lighting during the night or early morning, if the fire was out or for other reason they needed extra illumination. Using the cars' interior lights had allowed the batteries to charge faster than Jeebee depleted them by use. Also, the light from the fireplace had helped.

Accordingly, both Merry and Jeebee went with the horses and the trailer down to the ranch the next morning. Merry finally let herself be persuaded to ride in the trailer, though this was anything but a comfortable way to travel.

The springs on the trailer were very stiff, designed for heavy loads, like machinery or equipment that needed to be hauled about the ranch. So they were very little use in cushioning the bumps and jolts along the way. Also the trailer was continually tilted either upslope or downslope or sometimes toward one side or another. The result was that Merry had to ride holding on to the top pipe of the fencing that enclosed the body of the trailer, to keep from being thrown off her feet.

In fact, part of the way down there, she got so thoroughly sick of the jolting that she insisted on stopping, getting out, and walking. However, she recognized shortly that she was still not up to an extended tramp of any kind on foot. They compromised by stopping for short rests and Jeebee promised that he would build a sort of padded chair-harness that could be put in the trailer for anyone who wanted to ride in it. It had not occurred to him before, but either one of them could be hurt away from the cave, and need to be transported back to it in the trailer. He began to think about some way of anchoring down and cushioning a bed that could be fastened to the floor of the trailer as well as the harness.

He dropped Merry off at the ranch. He had taken the place so much for granted, he was a little startled to see Merry reacting to it as if it was some sort of potential Christmas tree full of presents. He left her there, worrying a little that she would be disappointed with what a small amount of things there were to find, and went about his hunting.

It turned out to be one of his unsuccessful days. Most of the time he could find cattle fairly easily. But occasionally, from some instinct of self-preservation, they either all seemed to have gone into hiding, or else he was somehow perversely threading a path through all the places where they weren't.

He had given up and headed back toward the ranch when he found himself startling jackrabbits with the horses and the trailer as he advanced. Apparently, as inexplicably as there were no cattle, there was this area that was suddenly full of the large rodents. The .30/06 was really too heavy a weapon to use on such small animals. A direct hit on the body of one of them simply blew the animal apart. But there were enough of them so that he could try for head shots; and he did end up killing three this way, gutting and cleaning the carcasses and bringing them tied to the railing of the trailer, back to the ranch.

He had hoped that Merry had found a satisfying number of some small things, like the thermometer, so that she would not be disappointed with her visit to the ranch, but he had completely underestimated her.

She apparently caught sight of him while he was still a distance away and came out in the open to wave at him to attract his attention. He waved back and continued on in. She met him happily.

"Bring the trailer around and we'll load up," she said.

Jeebee followed her around to the back of the ranch house and found a pile of filled plastic sacks. The sacks he already knew about. There was a stack of them in one of the outbuildings, and no one among the looters had apparently been interested in them. But she now had six of them stuffed full of various things, the actual identity of which he could not see through the milky semi-transparency of the plastic.

CHAPTER 31

"What's all this?" he said, for there were six of them, the equivalent of large leaf bags, filled full and fastened with wire ties. "I don't have anything in the trailer. We can carry them all right. But where will we put them when we get back up there?"

"You'll see," said Merry. There was very nearly a gleeful look on her face. "Most of it's light, anyway, and some of the other stuff won't have to go into the cave at all."

"What is it?" Jeebee asked.

"Odds and ends—useful things, though," said Merry, "and a lot of root vegetables from the garden. Some we'll eat, but a lot we'll keep as seed to start next spring."

Jeebee opened his mouth to tell her they would be moving on as soon as the weather was good enough to travel in the spring. But he was stilled by the thought that after what she had been through, it would be wrong to rob her of this moment of pleasure. There would be plenty of time for her to find out that wherever they would be, it would not be around here, when any vegetables they had planted in the spring were ready for harvest.

He had been surprised by the amount of things she had gathered. But he was more surprised—and impressed—when they got back to the cave and she showed him exactly what she had found. The variety was large, from the outdoor thermometer she had talked about earlier, to a number of small cans of various spices, including supplies of salt, sugar, baking powder and baking soda, sacks of dried beans, peas, and other dried vegetables that Jeebee had not even thought to look for.

In addition to these were a number of other small but useful items, including hooks that could be screwed into their plank walls so they could hang up things, and old throw rugs full of holes or half worn away, which had been ignored by the looters—but which Merry now pointed out would be useful not to only make the floor of their cave's inner room warmer but possibly the walls as well.

She had also brought back a great deal of yarn of various colors.

"Have you done any knitting?" she asked Jeebee.

Jeebee guiltily remembered her pushing knitting needles and yarn on him when he was ready to leave the wagon and emphasizing that he knit things like gloves and caps for his own use.

"No," he said, "I haven't had time."

"Well, you'll have time this winter," she told him.

Merry was right about what she had said about the things she had gathered not taking up as much room in the inner part of the cave as Jeebee had expected, once they were stored in an orderly fashion. This was mostly around the walls, except for those things that would be of direct use in the cooking, and these she put next to the fireplace, saying that she would build shelves within reach of the fire to put them.

"In fact," she said, "we could use a lot of shelving in here. That's something else I can do while you're busy with other things."

Jeebee had to agree with her. Shelves were an obvious thing. He had even thought of them, but not as anything he would get to in the near future. Other things—even the forge for the smithy he needed to build—ranked before such things. But now, of course, the situation was changed.

Jeebee skinned the rabbits—it was a small pat to his ego that he was more experienced at this than Merry. She freely admitted this, saying that she was quite at home with cleaning and preparing domestic animals for cooking, but had little experience with wild game simply because at the wagon they had not eaten much of it.

They put the rabbits on to boil, and Merry cleaned and cut some of the vegetables into the pot with them. Jeebee had taken some from the garden himself, but only from time to time, figuring that it did not have enough vegetables in it so that he could eat them regularly without exhausting the supply.

The vegetables, with the rabbit, therefore, were a treat. The long-term problem of balancing their diet had also been met by Merry in an unexpected way. It had never occurred to Jeebee to look for vitamin pills down at the ranch.

Merry had gone looking and found nearly a year's supply. She had also come upon a greater find. Jeebee had stared earlier when she pulled a number of bags of dried beans and dried peas from one sack. He had stared harder when, after that, she pulled a good six-inch-wide two-inch-thick wheel of paraffin-covered cheese out of one of the other bags.

"Where did that come from?" Jeebee said. "I could swear I went through that house a dozen times looking for some food that had been missed by the people who robbed it; and they'd taken everything that was ready to eat. I did find some flour, and things like that. But I even looked for a root cellar all around the place and couldn't find one."

"Did you think of looking under the kitchen floor?" said Merry.

"Under the kitchen floor?"

"Of course," Merry said. "Where else would you put foods that you might want to get at in a hurry, but wanted to keep out of the way in the kitchen? Someplace cool but dry, and sure not to freeze?"

"The kitchen . . ." said Jeebee thoughtfully. "I didn't notice anything in the kitchen that looked like it was a trapdoor to a place below it."

"The trap door was in that little pantry area with all the shelves around it," Merry said. "The people that went through it simply grabbed what they wanted off the shelves and never

looked down. You did the same thing, didn't you? You looked
into the pantry, saw practically nothing there but these spice
cans, and gave up. Right?"

Jeebee nodded slowly.

"Yes," he said. "I didn't check the floor there. What made
you do it?"

"I was just pretty sure that there had to be something like
that. I've seen a lot of entries like that in the kitchens of houses
off by themselves. It's a natural thing to have. By the way, there's
a lot more still down there that we'd better pick up and take
away before the really cold weather comes. Things that wouldn't
have frozen, ordinarily, because the house above them would be
heated. But now it's just a ruin, stuff will freeze as hard there as
they will in our meat pit in the cold room, out front. There're
more cheeses for one thing. Oh yes, and more of this."

It was then she had held up a large bottle full of long, dark
tablets.

"Vitamins," she said, "the one-a-day kind. We're both going
to take them from now on, as long as we have to live on so much
meat. And the cheese'll help. Good source of vitamins C and D."

While the food cooked, Jeebee stepped into the outer room
to see how far Merry had gotten with the freeze pit she had been
digging in the floor of the cold room. It had occurred to him that
he might use his time right now to finish it. But he saw that she
had done remarkably well with the time she had. She was either
stronger in some ways than he had thought, already, or else she
had a particular pride in being able to do this bit of excavation.
In either case, perhaps it would be best not to seem to step in and
finish it for her.

Since he was outside and had the time, he went along the
length of the cold room, past the corner where Wolf was now in
the habit of curling up, and stepped into the area that would be
the smithy.

There was nothing here yet but some stones he had already
gathered, and a large pile of clay. He had found a clay deposit
after searching down the bed of the larger stream for some distance and brought what was there back, load by load, in a couple
of the buckets from the ranch.

The two full buckets each time had been a good load to carry that distance, but it was invaluable. The stone, mortared by clay, would make an excellent firepit. But it struck him now that he had better get the clay to the inner room before it froze where it sat. Or else he would never be able to break it into chunks to warm up, soften, and mix with added water for use as mortar.

The two buckets were still here. He got a shovel from the inner cave, where he kept the tools so that Wolf would not chew their handles to bits, and went out to load buckets and start bringing the clay inside.

"What's that?" Merry demanded when he brought in the first two buckets.

He told her briefly.

"And you were worried about me filling up the space in here!" she said.

That was all she said, however. He managed to transfer the clay before the food was ready. He made a rough pyramid of it against their innermost wall of sand, the one wall of the cave that he would be excavating further once he was confined to the cave by weather and could only work inside.

The rabbits were tender and tasty.

"A change for the better, from beef all the time," Merry said as they were eating, "don't you think so?"

"Yes," Jeebee answered.

The truth was, however, the change did not make a great deal of difference to him. Sometime since he had left Stoketon, appetite had become unimportant to him. Hunger was important, and food was good when he ate it. But he did not miss any particular taste, or regret things that he used to be able to eat that were no longer available.

The fact of the matter was that the feeling he looked for was that of a full stomach rather than the satisfaction of a particular taste.

But Merry had gone to some trouble with the rabbits, including using some of the spices she had brought back up. Jeebee did not want to hurt her feelings. But privately, he would have been as happy with anything else that was meat, along with the vegetables.

That evening, as they sat before the fire, she began for the first time to tell him about some parts of the last few days of her search for him.

Most of the people she had stopped with had been very helpful. Some had been indifferent. Some had been hospitable only out of a sense of obligation, or a consideration of the future contact they might want to have with Paul and the wagon.

Nearly all of them had thought Merry was foolish to go looking for someone who had probably vanished. Somebody, who under the new conditions of the present time, was not likely to be found. But until she passed out of the area in which she, Paul, and the wagon were known, the visiting had been pleasant.

What struck Jeebee as she talked was a sense of wonder. Not just a wonder that she should venture on such a search for him, but that she should stick so single-mindedly to the goal of finding him. There was a driving force in her he had never really appreciated.

"You know," she told him as they finally banked the fire and started to bed, "we ought to change places for a few days. Let me take over the hunting. You work up here, or down at the ranch, whichever you want. Which *do* you want, by the way?"

"There's things I ought to get started on here, like building the forge," he said, because that was at the top of his thoughts, "before it gets too cold out there. The clay'll freeze on me, if I wait too long."

"It's strange you didn't find some kind of forge down there in that outbuilding you said must have been a blacksmithing place for the ranch," said Merry. "A forge wouldn't burn."

"They may have used a portable forge, and the looters took it with them," said Jeebee. "Nick told me about the portable forges. Sears, or Montgomery Ward's, used to sell them, once upon a time. Maybe they still do—I mean, did right up until the Collapse. It was a sort of three-legged metal bowl that you could pick up and carry, and build a coal fire in. It wouldn't be hard to carry that off."

"Maybe you're right," said Merry.

The next morning she left with the two horses and the rifle.

She did not take the trailer, planning to use Sally as a packhorse instead. The weather was still good, if crisp, and the sky was clear. Jeebee worried about her, in spite of himself. Still, she had said she would stay close to the foothills.

Left alone at the cave, he began work on the forge. It was a matter of building up a round, well-like affair out of stones he had gathered. They were all about six inches in diameter, and as close to roundness as he could find. He built a small, circular wall with them, packing the spaces between with mortar. The sides went up around a log that he had laid in at an angle when the walls were about six inches off the ground so that its upper end would project into the firepit at the top.

The space left by the log when he took it out would be the channel for the draft of forced air he would provide with the foot bellows he planned to build later.

In the next few days, while Merry gathered meat, he built the wall up until it was about three feet off the ground. Then filled it with the remaining rocks to the level at which the angled log came out and the firepit had its bottom.

He pulled the log out, finally, and coated the firepit and the inside of the air passage with a smooth coat of clay.

By the third day, the forge itself was done and the clay of it drying. Meanwhile he was hard at work building his bellows. These he made simply of two large triangular pieces of plank, joined together along the sides with leather that widened from some three inches at the wooden nozzle that fitted into the air channel, to a good twelve inches around the broad end of the back, where he had attached two solid handles ten inches long, each to one plank side.

Pulled apart by the handles, the bellows sucked air in through the leather valve on the underside of a hole in the top wooden side of the bellows, then forced the air up the channel in the forge when the two sides were pushed together again with the handles.

He had planned to fasten one handle and side by staking it into the earth floor, and pump the bellows by stepping on the top handle to force the two wooden sides together, once the bellows had inflated. For that, however, he needed some mechanism that would pull the upper side away from the lower to inflate it.

He solved that by attaching to its top side a rope that ran up and through a pulley screwed tight to one of the two-by-four rafters of his slim roof. The far end of the cord through the pulley was counterweighted.

Now he could push the top handle down to the floor with his foot, collapsing the bellows, and the counterweight would pull it up again, inflating them, when he took his foot off the handle. He could now pump air into the fire, once he had one going in the forge, while still having both his hands free for work.

All this took a little better than the three days. Every evening, after Merry had gotten home, they ate; and after, as they sat with the fire, Merry spoke a little more freely about her long trip to find him. It was as if she could not leave the trip alone, but at the same time he had the feeling that she was dodging around a part of it, something to do with it that she found hard to tell.

Jeebee began to feel uneasy about what might be bothering her. But he had now grown so unused to asking questions that he could not push her to tell him.

The day after he finished the forge itself, he rigged a hood over it with a length of leftover stovepipe to carry the vapors from the fire out the front wall. He could not remember, and his one course in undergraduate chemistry was not good enough for him to figure out, what kind of dangerous vapors his homemade charcoal might put out.

But with a draft from the bottom and the stovepipe open to the outside above the forge fire, most of its gases ought to be carried out, and the unchinked walls around him should let plenty of air in. At last, he built a small fire with wood in the forge, and when it was going well enough, added the charcoal.

He was both excited and pleased at the way the charcoal caught from the small wood fire. He had brought up the anvil from the ashes of the ranch's smithy some days before. He had kept it ready by the forge; and now simply as an experiment, he tried heating and bending a piece of angle iron, using the six-pound hammer from the ranch once the iron had turned a bright cherry red.

The angle iron bent. Not elegantly but more easily than it ever would have cold, it responded to the hammer blows.

He was full of triumph. Merry was not home yet, or he would have gone to get her immediately to show her that his smithy was now a working device.

He stopped pumping the bellows, and left the charcoal to die down by itself.

Theoretically, it should go out before it had burned itself completely to ash. He must remember to check, later. He had been making charcoal regularly by the old-fashioned method of getting a fire stoked with well-dried wood well started, then covering it with earth so that it burned slowly, away from the oxygen of the open air. The wood should have been from hardwoods like oak. Unfortunately, all he had to work with was pine, but dead wood, if it was firm and dry, seemed to make at least a usable charcoal.

Working this way, he had accumulated a fairly good pile of fuel for the forge. But, going out to look at the pile of it he had built up against the outside of the smithy wall, he realized that he would have to continue making it all winter long if he intended to use the forge at all regularly. With the bellows pumping air into it, the forge ate fuel.

He went back to work in the interior room of the cave. His plan since he had found Merry again, had been to dig back further into the sandy wall so that later on he would be able to build a somewhat larger inside room. Merry had not yet put down the layer of worn-out throw rugs she had planned, simply because he had told her that he intended to do this digging. There was no point in laying rugs and then strewing sand on top of them.

He worked as neatly as he could, but dust quickly accumulated in the air and fogged everything in sight under his dim illumination from the car-interior lights. He was tempted to use the yard floodlight he had found at the ranch. The solar blanket did an excellent job of charging up the rechargeable battery of that device. Some daylight was coming in through the front window of the cold room and the door of the inner room which he had left open, but it was not enough to help much. He needed to see exactly where and what he was digging.

He gave up at last to give the air of the inner room a chance to clear before Merry got home, and went out to his unending job of accumulating and chopping firewood for the fireplace.

They could not have too much of this and he was piling it ready against the outside wall of the cave, where it would act as an extra windbreak, if not extra insulation against the cold, later on. Merry came home eventually, with a good load of meat, as well as some light things from the ranch, to top out a fairly good-sized packload on Sally.

"I was lucky," she told Jeebee as they were unloading and unsaddling the horses together. "I found a calf by itself, almost the minute I hit the flat down there. So I spent the rest of the time at the ranch. How's the forge coming?"

"It's done," said Jeebee. "There's no time tonight to rig lights in there, so if you can wait awhile in the morning before you go out, I'll show you how it works."

That afternoon and evening after she got home Merry did not talk about her journey to find Jeebee. She talked about everything else, about her hunting, about the ranch, about several dozen things. Her tone was excited and cheerful. She bustled about the interior of the cave. Finally, almost regretfully, she agreed that they should probably turn in for the night, since they were always up by dawn.

Jeebee fell asleep almost immediately, as had become a habit with him. He was roused to find Merry holding herself tightly against him and crying into his chest.

"What is it?" he said, putting his arms around her.

"Just hold me," Merry choked.

He tightened his arms around her. She was crying very hard indeed. It was the kind of weeping that tears apart the one who weeps.

Once, Jeebee thought, his mind would have been flooded with a number of questions and guesses as to what was troubling her. But the past months had changed him in this, too. Her explanation would come eventually. There was no need to try to hurry it. She was being attacked by something, something her mind remembered; and all he could do was be a fortress about her and wait. So, he would wait.

He laid his cheek down tenderly upon the top of her soft hair and tried to encompass her as much as he could with his presence. For no reason at all, he thought of how Wolf had come to him in the river bottoms, and also when he had turned his ankle. Often Wolf had come when he was asleep, or when he was so caught between wakefulness and sleep that he was hardly conscious of the other appearing. Invariably, Wolf sniffed him all over and then nose-prodded at his arm or body. "Nose-lift," he told himself, would be a better term, since essentially what Wolf did was slide the top of his nose under an arm or a leg and push upward, to see if Jeebee made any reaction.

The moment Jeebee did come full awake or respond, Wolf either greeted him or—more often—simply seemed to lose all interest, turned about, trotted off, and disappeared.

If it had not been for the wolf books, Jeebee would not have recognized what the other was doing. But with the help of the books, he now understood. Wolf was simply making sure that he was still alive. At first, his sudden switches to total indifference had been shocking to Jeebee. Yet this was the same animal who had brought him food the only way he could—in his own stomach.

Wolves dealt with things as they were, and, Jeebee told himself, he now had come to do pretty much the same thing.

He waited. Merry cried for some time. Eventually the emotion went out of her, her body relaxed, and the tears gave way to dry sobs, the sobs to silence. She lay still for what seemed a long while, simply holding to him. Then, almost abruptly, she took her arms away and sat up, wiping her eyes.

"Let's get up and build up the fire," she said.

She got out of the bed without waiting for his answer, wrapped a blanket around her, and went over to hunch down before the fire and feed its still-glowing coals. Jeebee rose, pulled on his pants and jacket, and went to join her.

The fire blazed up and they sat down together on the two chairs he had brought back from the ranch, just before the fireplace. Merry took the coffeepot off its hook and weighed it in her hand. Evidently satisfied that there was still tea water in it, she put it back on the hook and swung the rod about so that it was over the flames.

She continued to say nothing, so Jeebee did not speak, either. They sat together. After a while, when the water was hot, she filled his cup, then hers, and sat back in her chair, not sipping from the cup, but holding it in both hands as if to warm herself. The fire was now throwing enough heat so that extra warmth should not be necessary, but still she cradled the cup in her grasp.

"I haven't cried," she said to the fire. "I wasn't able to, until now."

"Do you want to tell me?" Jeebee asked.

"Yes," she said, "I wanted to from the first moment I found you. But I couldn't."

She paused.

"You remember the horses?" she asked.

"Yes," said Jeebee, understanding which particular horses to which she referred.

"You know the ones I mean?" she persisted.

"The ones always saddled and ready, tied to the end of the wagon as you went," Jeebee answered.

As he said the words the memory of them came back to him. The three horses—four, after he had joined the wagon's crew—all saddled, the full pack behind the saddle, a loaded rifle scabbarded at each saddle and the ends of their reins tied to holding bars at the back of the wagon. He remembered that whatever horse Merry would be riding also always had a rifle at its saddle. Just as she at all times had a handgun in the holster of the gunbelt around her waist and a filled pack behind her saddle. These packs, he had learned, on his third day with the wagon, carried the essentials for survival, insofar as Paul could supply them. They carried some of Paul's hidden store of antibiotics, ammunition and extra handguns, which were always valuable trade goods, bedrolls, clothing, and other needs. The horses that bore these things were for escape.

Merry had looked at him for a second as she asked the last question, but now her eyes were back on the fire.

"They were waiting for us," she said in a steady voice. "We were on a pretty good highway—not a two-lane freeway, but a good local highway, with the ground clear back fifty to a hundred feet on each side and trees beyond—"

She laughed, unhappily.

"If it hadn't been like that, I wouldn't be here," she said. "They would have got me, too—"

Her voice died. He waited. Finally he spoke.

"The people in the area didn't warn you that there was danger?" he asked.

What she wanted to tell him was not even now coming easily. It was up to him, plainly, to draw her out gently, to make it possible with questions for her to tell him.

"Nobody local had told us anything," Merry answered dully. "I don't think they knew themselves there were raiders around."

"Someone local must have known, if they were waiting and ready for you."

"Yes," she answered, "they were waiting. I don't know how they knew. Maybe they'd been camped nearby, in a patch of woods somewhere, or perhaps in some place that'd already been raided. Just—there was no warning. No warning at all. Just all of a sudden they were there, coming out of the trees on both sides of the road."

"Then it was planned," Jeebee said.

"Yes," Merry said indifferently. Her words were still addressed to the fire. It was as if all that mattered could be seen there, among the alternately fading and bright-glowing embers, where the greatest heat of the fire was, under the flames.

"It was an ambush." She shook her head, very slightly. "There were way too many of them for us, but they wanted it easy."

She went silent, again. Jeebee waited. But this time it was as if she had run out of words to go on with. He prodded her with another question as Wolf had nosed up one of his arms when he was bedridden and unmoving.

"How did they think it'd go?"

"I don't know," Merry said in the same dead voice to the flames. "Easy, I suppose. There had to have been more than a hundred of them. They let the wagon get right into the middle of where they were waiting, before they came out of the trees. It was just luck I was back, further than usual, heading in Missy"— she glanced for only a second at Jeebee—"you don't know her. We traded for her after you left us. She wasn't full-trained to staying with the wagon and so she'd stray—"

Merry paused.

"If I hadn't gone back after her . . . but I did, and when they swarmed the wagon, they were all up ahead of me. I heard the alarm siren when Dad pulled it; and I looked back, to see them riding in on it from both sides. Then the siren quit; and I knew Dad must already be inside with Nick. Almost at the same time, I heard our machine guns, both of them. . . ."

She ran down. Jeebee waited. "You know what he always said," she went on dully. "'*Ride, fast as you can. Don't look back.*'"

She stopped speaking. The firelight glanced off her hair. She was sitting with her elbows on her knees, apparently all her attention concentrated on the fire. The moments stretched out.

"I rode," she said at last, in a monotone. "I think some of them even chased me a little ways—I'm not sure of that. But I rode; and after a while I was too far away to hear the firing. . . ."

She broke off. Again, a silence. Only the fire crackled and snapped.

"They couldn't have known how well Dad and Nick were prepared to fight them off," she went on finally. "They must have been surprised. . . ."

She lifted her head slowly and looked steadily at Jeebee.

"You know what else he said." She waited.

Jeebee nodded and she went on.

"'*Don't try to come back*'—that's what he always told us. '*Never come back.*'"

Her eyes were still on Jeebee. He wanted to reach out and touch her, comfortingly, but he was afraid that even that might be wrong at this moment.

"You went back," Jeebee said.

She dropped her eyes and nodded.

He waited.

"I went deep into some woods and waited there—oh, a couple of hours perhaps," she said to the embers. "Finally, I went back . . . slowly. I had the binoculars. I found a good spot I could see, from maybe a hundred yards or more away. I could have been even closer. They weren't paying attention to anything but the wagon. They'd tried to burn it. The front seat was gone, the wooden facings over the front and back ends were gone, the canvas with our sign on it was burned away and so were the tires. All that was left was the steel underneath. They were up by the steel box of the wagon itself, and they must've realized by that time that it wasn't the ordinary sort of thing they went after. The machine guns would have let them know that. It wasn't going to be that easy for them to get at Dad and Nick."

Her eyes clung to Jeebee's now, as if she was holding on to him with her gaze alone.

"They'd spread out in two fans front and back so that they were out of traverse range of the slots the machine guns could fire through," she said. "And the fire they'd started at first had gone out. But just as I started watching they got a new fire going, between the wheels and under the bed of the wagon. They were going to heat the metal shell of the wagon, until it drove Dad and Nick out, or cooked them alive.

"I could see them there. They were as thick as crowds used to be at circuses when I was a little girl," she said. "They were waiting for the fire under the wagon to do their work for them. There was nothing I could do; and I didn't know what Dad and Nick could do anymore. But he had something to do. He'd just never told me, Dad hadn't."

He waited. She bit her lip.

"You didn't know either what they'd planned, did you?" she said to Jeebee. "They didn't tell you? No. No, of course, if they wouldn't tell me, neither Dad nor Nick would ever tell you that. They didn't tell me because they didn't want me to know, for fear I might not have ridden off then, in the first place."

She took a deep breath.

"All of a sudden," she said, "there was an explosion. It was as if the wagon was one large stick of dynamite. I saw a bright flash for just part of a second, then even from where I was standing, I could feel the air push me, and the sound of it made me deaf for a moment. I was deaf and blind, both, there for a bit—and then I could see that the wagon was gone. All gone. And the raiders who'd been close to it were gone, too. Fifty feet or more away there were things lying that were other, dead raiders. There was no one moving. No one. It was all over. It was done."

She closed her eyes and sat back in her chair as if she were very weary.

Jeebee got out of his own chair, knelt beside hers, and put his arms around her, holding her head to his head, with the palm of one hand.

"They did it to make sure you got away," he said.

Against the side of his head, he felt her head move in a faint nod.

"Yes," she whispered.

They stayed together, not moving for some little time. Then Merry stirred, pulling herself out of his arms, and turned to look into his face. She smiled and took his arm, pushing him upward and back toward his seat.

She smiled at him.

"It's all right now," she said, "it's all right now I've told you. It'll never be that bad for me again, now that you know, too."

Jeebee seated himself, still looking back at her, trying to think of something to say.

There was nothing. After a while she took the coffeepot and filled his cup carefully, then poured a little more into her own and sipped it. They sat there in silence, both of them watching the fire, and from time to time Jeebee bent down to pick up another piece of wood and put it on the fire.

CHAPTER 32

Within the next week, actual winter moved in. It began with a three-day snowstorm that kept them cave-bound. That was followed by a spell of open weather, then by storms at about two-day intervals, on the average, and lasting anywhere from a few hours to a couple of days.

The snow cover on the ground built up rapidly. Jeebee was only able to make two more trips with the trailer. After that, he was reduced to going on snowshoe, without the horses, and pulling the sledge behind him.

In the foothills, particularly among the trees, the depth of the snow cover was exceedingly varied. Some areas were only very lightly covered. Others were ten feet or more deep in drifts. The shale slope was now a single glistening slope of unknown depth, and the less steep slope at the top of the bluff that crowned it was beginning to build up a massive, many-feet-deep cliff of drifted snow, which overhung all the slope below, threateningly.

Jeebee, after checking the area from a respectful distance, ignored it completely. It might be safe to try to cross it with the sledge, but there was no point in taking unnecessary chances. By this time he was familiar with the foothills in the area in any case, and had a variety of routes available to him down to the flatlands.

He settled on one that took him by means of folds of land, either through relatively sheltered, treed areas or down open slopes that were gentle enough so that he would be able to get the sledge back up them.

Several times, he had tried riding the sledge like a child's sleigh down a slope. But it was almost impossible to guide. The fourth time it landed him deep in a drift that it took him some minutes to dig himself out of. He did not try again.

The ranch, when he had time and reason to visit it, was effectively being buried. The part of the ranch house that had been opened to the elements by fire was drifted deep with snow. Most of the outbuildings either had drifts within them or about them. No part of it any longer offered the shelter that it had given from wind and sleet, on the occasion of his overnight visit, a little earlier in the fall.

His life became a simple one of working on the cave and at the forge. He steadily enlarged and boarded in the cave. He also began real work at the forge, as much to learn from experience as to make what they needed—but in want of both.

Most of what he hammered into shape were things for the inner room in the cave. He made a more sturdy and permanent support for the hooked rod that had suspended kettles and pots over the flames of the fireplace. He also made brackets and support for shelving. Little by little, the inner cave was becoming more homelike.

Wolf had furred out magnificently with the cold weather. He still slept in his favorite corner of the cold room up front. It was evidently uncomfortable for him, fur-coated as he was, to stay in the warmth of the inner cave for any length of time at all. Still he insisted on coming in for his morning and evening greetings, particularly if he had been away from the cave.

Most of the storm time, however, he spent in that same corner, sleeping. It amazed Jeebee that he could sleep so much. When there was nothing going on, apparently, Wolf could sleep for sixteen or more hours, though his sleep was periodically interrupted by small wakings and movings around.

It was hard to keep him out of the inner room, particularly

when they were stormbound for more than a day. But he was completely undisciplined as far as his bowel habits were concerned, and Merry now had the throw rugs down on the floor. Jeebee and Merry had gotten into the habit of going into the outer room, dressed for its temperature, to be with him at dawn and twilight, and he would join Jeebee in the smithy, until the heat of the forge drove him back out again.

In fact, the front room was not all that unpleasant. Its walls kept the wind out, and the pale, but sometimes bright, winter light came through its one window and illuminated even its further corners.

The cold-storage pit for the frozen cooked meat was finished and doing its job admirably, protected by the section of fencing Jeebee had brought up from the ranch. It was that same length of fence that had protected him from Wolf's teasing playfulness while he built the front wall of the cave.

The books had been right. The fencing effectively guarded the pit from Wolf. Wolf tried to pull it out of place. But he was frustrated by the way Jeebee had anchored it, with large, metal, forge-made anchors, like spikes with their ends turned up. Plainly he did not like to walk or stand upon it. The books had been right in that. Also, they had been right in that he did not try to dig under the recommended three-foot skirt of it, that Jeebee had pegged down outward over the bare earth floor.

The storms tailed off. They became occasional. Sometimes a week or ten days would go without one. Jeebee had been unsure how successful Wolf's hunting had been under these winter conditions. His conscience prodded him into sharing some of their stored meat with Wolf at intervals.

He had tried to do this always by taking the meat out of the pit when Wolf was away and thawing it in the inside room. Then, after Wolf had returned, Jeebee would carry it outside the front wall for some little distance and simply drop it in the snow. Wolf was never slow in collecting it for himself.

This worked well. But Jeebee could only guess whether he was merely supplementing Wolf's diet or whether he literally needed to feed Wolf to keep him from starving. But in any case,

Jeebee kept on doing it. The one natural and inevitable result was that they went through their stored supply of beef faster than Jeebee had expected. This forced him into taking more days to go on hunting trips.

He made a number of these during clear spots in the weather. Using the sledge to pull back the meat and sometimes the skin from more than one head of beef, however, turned out to be more than he could handle. The loaded sledge was a bastard—that was the only word for it—in the hills. He might have managed it with twice his usual load down on the flat surface of the plain. But going uphill, and over surfaces that frequently tipped sharply and unexpectedly to right or left, the double load was too much.

He had grown accustomed to the feeling that he should be able to make the trip down and back without trouble. Then came a trip on which, the second day out and having found no food animals, he was caught by a storm.

It came too swiftly for him to even think of getting back to the cave.

The first warning he had was a vague difference in the light. He looked up at the sky and saw, he thought, no clouds. But the blue overhead seemed more pale than usual, as if a layer of white gauze had been drawn over it. When he looked at the sun, its outline was unclear, as if a faint haze had developed, high up between him and it.

He took the glasses automatically to skim the horizon and found that the horizon was now indistinct. There was no line where sky and land should meet.

He had been out in the open for more than half a year now. There was nothing specific to fasten on, but an uneasy feeling grew in him as of something titanic and inimical looming over him. If he had been Wolf, Wolf would have been sniffing the still air tensely.

Where he might not have a year before, he now paid attention to that uneasiness. Stopping the sledge, he got out the tent and began setting it up alongside the sledge.

He had barely gotten it up with his blankets inside and one

side staked down, when a thick mist seem to congeal around him all at once. The feeling of uneasiness grew. He drove the stakes on the other side of the tent and hammered its poles even tighter into the packed underlayers of hard snow. Taking the blankets out again, he scooped out snow inside to make up for the space he had taken away from the height of the tent.

He climbed within and fastened the ends of the tent as tightly as he could. He slid into his roll of blankets. The enclosed air space warmed quickly about him. Outside, the air remained still. But the uneasiness he felt was still with him. He kept on all his clothes and boots, and waited.

He did not have long to wait. Within minutes he heard the wind in the distance, like the sound of a hunting animal. Almost as soon as he heard it, it hit the tent, rising from a light push to a heavy fist blow of air that turned the tent's interior icy cold, all at once. With it came the sudden rattling of ice particles against the tent fabric.

He pulled himself up partially out of the blankets so that his arms were free. He dug his mittened hands into the snow on the tent side away from the sledge and took hold of the stakes he had driven in there, putting his weight on them to help hold them down. The walls of the tent sucked inward, then billowed out again suddenly, with a crack. He could feel the pressure of the wind only inches from him, not touching him, but as if a great hand had taken hold of the tent with him inside.

He lay, the tent cracking and vibrating wildly around him, satisfied to just hold on if he could, until the gusts should pass.

But they did not pass. They came at slightly longer intervals for a while and then picked up again more fiercely than before. The foot end of the tent blew out suddenly and flapped wildly in the wind; its inner corners yanked by the force of the wind out from under the heels of his boots, with which he had been pressing them into the snow below.

There was nothing he could do but let it flap. He pushed down with one elbow on the flaps beyond his head, feeling the icy air reaching all around him. The storm was like some enormous living creature, trying to snatch the tent from him and tear it to shreds; to tear him, the sledge and everything else to shreds, leaving only the white sterile world of snow and snow-filled air.

He held on—he held on. But at last the outer side of the tent was snatched from the snow and a moment later the whole tent flew wild, flapping like a mad thing.

He grabbed and caught the inner edge, rolling on it to hold it down, rolling until he wrapped it all around him like an untidy cocoon.

He rolled backward until the low edge of the sledge stopped him.

Squirming around, bound by the rolled tent about him, he got his mittened hands free enough to dig into the snow under the runner.

Like a burrowing mole, he excavated until he could squirm in with the tent wrapped around him. He crawled until he was under the sledge, putting it between himself and the wind, cocked at an angle over his body.

He lay, gasping for breath.

The snow was blowing thickly now. It began to drift around him and around the sledge.

Soon they were completely enclosed; and the fierce tearing of the wind began to be muffled by its thickness. The wind sound grew more and more distant until he could barely hear it. In his heavy clothing, wrapped in the tent and the snow, he was almost warm.

"I mustn't fall asleep," he told himself, "I might suffocate."

He lay there awake, accordingly, staring into an unchanging darkness. It was completely black around him now. It occurred to him that perhaps so much time had gone by that the sun was going down, the daylight leaving as the snow drifted deeper and ever deeper, over him. He could still hear the storm distantly, but now it had softened to a sound almost like a lullaby.

He woke with a start.

He had fallen asleep after all. But he was still breathing. Evidently the drift had not been packed so tightly by the wind that air could not reach him. Perhaps grains of hard snow, like those which had rattled against the tarpaulin tent when he had first been underneath it, would not pack like softer flakes.

He wriggled and pushed his way through the snow surrounding until he suddenly popped out into brilliant sunlight.

The sun was just rising in a bright blue sky. The air was so cold that his first breath of it seemed to shock his lungs. But—it was morning. Habit had woken him close to his usual time of rousing.

Nothing had ever looked so good to him as that sun, and the brilliant blue sky overhead. There were no clouds anywhere in the great blue bowl above the white land. About him, except for the drift that had enclosed and protected both himself and the sledge, the vast snow plain looked unchanged. Only a few small, dark nubs, the tops of frozen vegetation, still protruded through it at large distances from each other.

After a long moment, creakily, he turned to the business of excavating the sledge. He was grateful for the fact that he had not had time to acquire a load, so that he had been able to lift it enough to crawl under it.

He suddenly realized he was ravenous.

His pack was the only thing that had been on the sledge. He looked, and it was still there, securely tied down. He untied it and got out the food he had brought along for the trip. It was frozen as hard as a rock.

Sensibly, Merry had packaged it in small chunks. It was a mixture of dried beef and cooked vegetables with a good deal of beef fat included. Each chunk was about the size of a golf ball. He put half a dozen of these inside the top layers of his clothing so that his body's heat would thaw them. Stiffly, he got to his feet, took up the reins of the now-freed sledge, and started heading back toward the cave.

The weather, though frigid, had turned good again. Theoretically he could now continue hunting. But he felt in no shape to hunt at the moment. The time he had spent under the snowdrift, and fighting the storm before that, had taken something out of him. He wanted only to get back to the cave, warm up, and rest up. He turned toward the foothills, pulling the heavy, unhandy weight of the sledge along with him only because he could not afford to leave it behind.

It seemed he pulled for some time before he reached the first

slopes of the foothills. He had felt barely up to the work of getting here when he had started. But the labor had warmed him.
He felt better, instead of worse, for the struggle. At the bottom of
the first slope, he stopped and checked the frozen food inside his
clothing.

It was thawed enough to eat.

Sitting down heavily on the sledge, he chewed and swallowed. The food seemed to bring him the rest of the way back to
life. Particularly, the fat Merry had mixed into it tasted sweeter
to him than any sugar, and he could almost feel it refueling his
weary body.

When he had finished eating, he felt almost strong enough to
go back to his hunting, after all. But caution laid a hand on him.
He had barely survived one storm, as much by luck as anything
else. He was in no shape to risk another. Before he went down on
these winter plains again he must work out, not only a plan, but
all the things he would need to carry with him to dig in properly
and survive future storms.

For one thing, in the future he should take along more food,
extra clothing, and anything else that such an emergency might
call for. Thinking of this, he made the long, panting climb back
to the cave. It was only a little past noon when he got there, but
he felt as if he had barely had the strength to make it home.

He mumbled an explanation to Merry as she helped him off
with his outer clothing. He was too worn out to eat even the
food she offered. All he wanted was to crawl into their bed under
a mountain of blankets; and when at last he did, he dropped
immediately into deep slumber.

But this time, as dreamless sleep enclosed him, he was conscious of being finally, undeniably, completely warm.

When he woke, it was in a slow float back into awareness
and the realization, from Merry's activity around the cave, that
he had slept only about three or four hours. Wolf had apparently
not come home yet, to rouse him for the regular twilight greeting
ceremony. Still, Merry had food starting to cook for what must
be their evening meal.

"Feel better?" she asked now as he got up and began rub-
bing the last of the sleep from his eyes.

He sat on the edge of the bed.

"A lot better," he said. Indeed, he was surprised just how much better he felt. It was as if his sleep during the storm and under the snowdrift afterward had been no real sleep at all. But the few hours he had just passed felt as if they had been some of the most restful unconsciousness he could remember in years. He told himself that the feeling was probably just the fact that he was safely back inside the cave, with her.

"Nothing like home," he told her.

Merry smiled. The smile was her usual bright smile. But, in addition, there was some sort of glow about her that was brighter than usual. As if someone had just given her a much-wanted present.

He found the lighter pair of pants he normally wore in the warmth of the cave, taking them down from their hook where Merry had hung them, and pulled them on, tucking his shirt in. He had slept in his shirt over her objections, not wanting to give up anything that might help bring warmth back to his body. Dressed, he went over and kissed Merry gratefully, and she kissed him back with particular enthusiasm.

"Have we time?" he asked. Her glow had invaded him.

"Yes—no," said Merry. She pushed him toward his chair at the table. "Sit down. Dinner's going to be ready in a minute."

He sat.

"Wolf hasn't been around?"

"He got back about half an hour ago," she answered. "I went outside to be with him for a bit and let you sleep. He was walking sore-footed—you know the way he does when he's covered a lot of distance. He curled up in his corner. I think he's still there."

Jeebee stretched without getting up from his chair, pushing his hands high above his head, which was something he could not do standing upright. The ceiling was still too low. Someday, he told himself, he would fix that.

Sitting there while she got the meal on, he told her more about the storm than he had done in his brief mumble on getting home. She was sympathetic, but he noticed that the glow about her did not diminish. It puzzled and intrigued him. Aside from the fact that he could feel that it would not be right to ask the reason for it, his own nature was not one that asked personal questions easily. So, as he had waited for her to tell him about what had happened to her father and Nick, he waited now for the explanation of why she glowed.

She sat down with him at the table. As they ate, the talk switched to things needing to be done in the cave. Their meat supply called for at most only a couple more successful hunting trips, one being to replace the one he had just aborted because of the storm. He began to tell her what he had in mind to add to his supplies for any such trip, from now on. One would be a sort of homemade sleeping bag, rather than the blankets he usually rolled himself in. Two, he should put a series of blocks or handles on the side of the sledge that would allow him to lift it, even if loaded, while he was lying flat on the snow surface beside it.

Also, he wanted an extra-light emergency pack, in addition to the one he wore always on his back. Another one that would carry only some food and perhaps a few other necessary things. Just such a sudden storm as he had experienced could last up to two days, under the sledge and the snow. He ought to be prepared with adequate means to keep him warm and fed that long.

His curiosity over this glow of hers went unsatisfied all through dinner and until Merry had cleared the table, scraping what little was left to scrape off their dishes into the coals of the fire and putting the dishes themselves to soak in a warm pot of water.

Having done this last, she wiped her hands on one of the cloths from the ranch she had chosen and laundered to act as dish towels and turned from the fire to confront him, still in his chair.

"I've got something to tell you," she said.

Jeebee's heart skipped a beat. In spite of himself a feeling of alarm kindled inside him. What might be good news from Merry's viewpoint might well contain the seeds of something that would mean trouble for them both, seeds she might not suspect were there. But he smiled up at her.

"What is it?" he asked.

"I'm pregnant," Merry almost sang.

"My God!"

Jeebee erupted from the chair. The glow had suddenly gone out of Merry. She stared at him grimly.

"What do you mean, '*My God*'?" she said. "Here I tell you I'm carrying our child, and you say, 'My God!' What's that supposed to mean?"

"There's no hospital! No doctors!" Jeebee said almost wildly. "We probably couldn't even lay our hands on a nurse if we searched for miles around! All you'll have is me, and I'm not worth a damn when it comes to something like having a baby!"

The breath went out of Merry in a long relieved sigh.

"So that's it," she said, in a calmer voice. She pushed him backward. "Sit down."

Numbly, almost tripped up by the edge of his chair seat behind his knees, and under the impulse of Merry's not inconsiderable strength, Jeebee sat down abruptly.

"Now," said Merry, sitting down in his lap and speaking directly into his face from only about six inches away, "let me tell you a few things. First, I helped at a birthing the first year Dad had the wagon going on its route, five years ago. I was fourteen. Since then I've been at dozens. In fact, I deliberately asked about possible births at every place we stopped, asked if I couldn't be useful so I could learn as much about what had to be done as possible. Lots of times there was at least a neighbor who was due to give birth, and Dad would hold the wagon there until I had a chance to be part of it. What do you think was one of the things on my list of recommendations to people I might have asked to hire me this winter, if I hadn't found you? I'm the closest thing to a trained midwife that they'd be likely to find. Now, what do you think about that?"

"But I—" Jeebee began.

"But you, nothing!" said Merry. "Let me tell you as well that Dad not only waited for me when it was necessary so that I could be at a birthing and help and learn, he also got me three books as soon as he could find them, after that first birth I was at when I was fourteen. He came to me and shoved them into my hands. *'Learn these,'* he said. *'I mean, memorize them. You're going to be in situations where maybe there'll be no one around to help you. I want you to know what's in them by heart.'* And I did. I memorized every word in those three books. What's more, I'm going to teach them to you, starting now. By the time I'm through with you, you're going to have them memorized, too. Now, what do you think of all that?"

"Fine," said Jeebee, "and believe me I'm going to learn every word you know. But it's still not going to make me into the equivalent of a real doctor, or even a real nurse. What if something goes wrong?"

"Sweetheart," said Merry, "nothing is going to go wrong. I'm young, I'm strong, my hips are wide. What with the cheese, the beans, and the rest of the food we've been able to put together, and the vitamin tablets, I'm going to have proper nutrition during the months I'm carrying the baby. Nothing is going to go wrong. Just remember that women were having babies, sometimes all by themselves out in the middle of nowhere or in some cave, thousands of years before there were doctors or nurses or midwives. Besides, it's not something you can change your mind about now. The baby's on the way and I'm going to have it. Also, it's going to be the best, prettiest, strongest baby that ever was. So you might as well just get used to the fact."

"I will," Jeebee said somewhat feebly, "just give me a little time, will you? I hadn't thought about anything like this at all."

Merry kissed him and got up off his lap.

"No, I don't suppose you have," she said. "Well, you can sleep on it tonight. But I'm going to start teaching you the first few paragraphs of the first book tomorrow."

"That's fine," said Jeebee. But his voice still sounded a little weak in his own ears.

She grinned at him, her fists on her hips.

"You're scared," she said.

"Damn right," Jeebee answered.

CHAPTER 33

He remained scared.

Meanwhile, the winter wore on, the temperature lowered, and the snow grew deeper, until at last the curve of icy temperatures turned upward, the snow cover gradually began to decrease again, and they moved at last into spring. Throughout all this time, there were no lack of problems and emergencies that for the moment had been able to shove Merry's condition out of the immediate center of his mind.

But the moment any of these were past, it returned to center stage in his thoughts, as the Powder River Pass had both filled him with foreboding but drawn him toward it.

As soon as he was free to think of something other than immediate necessities, the fact of the approaching birth would come back to him, inescapable, ominous, beckoning.

Face it any way he might, it remained a certainty that he alone was the only person Merry would have to turn to for help when the hour came. He was far from confident about how much help he would be then, in that time in which the life of not only the child growing within her, but her own, would be at balance.

It was something he had never imagined having to face. He, Jeebee, with a critical responsibility for the safe birth of a child and its mother. Nor did it help that the child would be his own, and the mother of that child the one person he loved most on earth.

There was no way he could alter or control what would happen. He knew that; but knowing this did not change his feelings. He took his fears out in a savage attack on what would be needed when the time came. Even the temporary relief this work gave him had to come in the intervals between his normal duties of keeping them fed, housed, and protected.

Survival required that he keep up his hunts down on the flatlands. Half a dozen more times before spring came, he was caught by storms while he was down there. On five of these occasions he managed without trouble. He waited them out, warm enough—if not exactly comfortable—in his homemade sleeping bag, under the shelter of the sledge and the snow that quickly drifted over him.

But the sixth time, the storm lasted sixteen hours, and after the first ten switched direction a quarter of the way around the compass. So that from this new angle the wind blew clear the drift that had accumulated over him and the sledge.

He had to wrestle the sledge into a new position, with the numbingly cold wind and snow pushing against him as if the sledge were a wooden sail, fighting him every inch of the way.

He had been exhausted when he finally established his new position and the snow began to build about them again. He did not think he could have worked another fifteen minutes before reaching the limits of his strength. But as it was, he saved not only himself, but the load of frozen meat he already had on the sledge. A load, unfortunately, which had made the sledge that much more difficult to shift.

On one other trip he had missed his shot at a range bull, which had been the only animal he could find. He had wounded it, but not enough to even slow it down. It had charged him. Only the fact that he had dodged behind the sledge and the bull had tripped over a snow-covered corner of it, trying to get to him, had given him time to pump another shot in just behind its shoulder and bring it down. At that, it was still not dead. He had to fire another shot into it before it finally lay still.

In the same icy months of January through early March, up at the cave, Merry had experienced her own near escape. Investigating a slight noise in the outer room one afternoon, she had all but stepped out on top of a cougar, who had come in through the swinging wolf door that Jeebee had built for Wolf, into one wall of the smithy.

The cougar had been attracted by the smell of the stored meat. Frustrated, like Wolf, by the wire netting over the storage pit, it was hooking its claws into the mesh and trying to pull it up, and this had made the sound Merry had heard.

Merry reacted without thinking. She had been drying the last of the morning dishes when the noise caught her attention, and still held the dish towel. She ran at the bewildered cat, flailing at it with the towel and waving her arms wildly.

"Get away from our food!" she screamed.

The mountain lion bounded back past her, back along the cold room and through the wolf door into the smithy, and vanished from there into the brush. It left behind a few hairs on the wooden framing.

The look on its white-haired face had been one of sheer terror, in the face of the flapping dishcloth, and Merry found herself leaning against the frame of the inner door, laughing hysterically at the poor creature's obvious stark fear and comical retreat.

The image of the predator fleeing from a furious, dish-towel-waving woman sent her into another bout of nearly uncontrollable laughter when she later told Jeebee the story.

Jeebee was not amused. Any wild animal, particularly one hungry enough to enter a place that must smell so thoroughly of humans and Wolf, was unpredictable. Any wild animal was dangerous if cornered, and Merry had very nearly cornered the cougar in the end of the cold room. Moreover, if it was as panic-stricken as Merry had said, it could have injured her just in its efforts to escape. The next day he tripled the two-by-fours reinforcing the vertical sides of the doorframe. Then anchored deeply in them two U-shaped iron hooks, which would hold a bar of axle iron to lock the door.

From then on, Merry kept the door barred, opening it only to Jeebee's voice, or the whining and scratching of Wolf. Even then, before unbarring the door, she belted the revolver around her waist.

But in spite of the episode of the cougar, the glow that Jeebee had noticed in her on the evening he had learned he was to be a father, remained and deepened. Jeebee found it hard to describe, to himself or her.

"It's a sort of happiness-of-satisfaction look," he told Merry once.

"No," she had answered, patting the beginning bulge of her belly complacently, "it's just the mother-feeling.

"Isn't that right, baby?" she said to the child inside her.

But then she looked up into Jeebee's face.

"You know," she said, "you look different, too."

"I do?" Jeebee asked, astonished.

One of the things Merry had brought up from the ranch was the only mirror that had escaped being smashed by the raiders, the cover of the medicine chest in the ranch-house bathroom. Later on, when he was able to do so without Merry catching him at it, Jeebee looked at his bearded features in the glass. He tried very hard to see the difference Merry had mentioned. But as far as he could tell, it was the same old face.

Merry happened to come back to the inside room just as he turned from the mirror.

"Finally decided to shave it off?" she asked.

Merry had never liked Jeebee's beard, but they had come to a compromise. He could wear it through the cold winter months. He had found it an actual asset in warmth for his face, particularly down in the open winds of the flatlands. But with the melting of the winter's snow, his beard would also disappear.

"In the spring, as I promised you," he said now.

He went out to check on his current charcoal-making fire. During his time back up at the cave, his days were filled with things like making more charcoal for his forge. This, and an ever-increasing list of other matters, always needed to be attended to. The consumption of charcoal had gone up because of the many things needing to be made of metal, particularly with the improvements they were both now adding to the interior room.

By the end of March, he had finished excavating back another five feet and walling in the final side of the room. Another week and the ceiling was completed. He and Merry had discussed a number of ways of sealing the walls, floor, and ceiling so that they would be able to keep the area clean. Jeebee had laid down a plank floor. Now even this should be sealed in some fashion that would keep the dirt from working up through the cracks between the planks.

Merry's original use of old blankets and the like for throw rugs, while successful in creating warmth underfoot, particularly when feet were without boots or socks, was not a practical way to ensure cleanliness. This was because, in their limited space, it was impossible to do the constant, large amounts of washing and rewashing needed to keep the floor coverings fresh and safe.

It was finally decided they would put down a second floor on top of what was already there, with a sheet of plastic as a sealing layer between it and the underfloor. To do this they would have to wait until spring had advanced far enough to make the outbuildings at the ranch clear of drifted snow.

The sealing layer, Jeebee thought, could be made by joining the large plastic bags, each bag measuring three feet five inches by two feet ten inches, of which there was a tall stack, laid flat, in one of the outbuildings. He had come up with the idea of melting the edges of some of these bags together into one large sheet, using an iron rod, heated at the forge. The tricky part would be to get the rod at the right temperature and hold it there.

A sandwich of layers like that might keep dirt from working up into their rooms from underneath; both at the time of the birth and after the baby had come.

Finally, they were at the end of April, and the snow was rapidly disappearing. It seemed to evaporate almost as much as it seemed to melt. In fact, thought Jeebee, considering their altitude, a good deal of straight evaporation might indeed be removing it. Regretfully, he shaved his beard, and decided it was time to have a look at the ranch.

He chose to ride Sally, as the steadier of the two horses— particularly after a winter in which they had had no work at all, being neither ridden nor fitted with a packload—down to see how the buildings had weathered the winter.

It was necessary for him to pick his way with Sally. There were still spots where he had to get off and lead her, through drifts that still lay fairly deep in places where two slopes came together, but they made it down successfully. Out of curiosity he passed the shale slope and saw, surprisingly, that it was entirely clear of snow in certain places. The hole to the den, or whatever it might be high up on it, was now completely exposed.

That should have prepared him for what he would find at the ranch. But in spite of his realization of the dryness of the air, compared to what he had been used to in Michigan, and the effect of the recently sunny and warm days, he was surprised when he got there.

The ranch was already mostly clear of snow. It lingered only in shady places or where drifts had piled high. He was able to get into the outbuilding with the plastic bags and check the stack of them. Laid empty, and then piled, one on top of the other, he estimated the stack must contain at least a couple of hundred bags. He thought fleetingly that if the sealing of the floor worked, he might also eventually seal the ceiling, then after that, possibly the inside walls.

After a cursory look around the other buildings and what was left of the ranch house, he headed back to the cave, returning with as many bags as Sally could conveniently carry behind the saddle. He had more than enough to let him experiment at finding the right temperature to seal them.

It was something that would have to be discovered by trial and error. He remembered, almost wistfully, electric devices for sealing food-storage bags for the deep freezer. Once they had been for sale everywhere. If the ranch had owned something like that, perhaps with the solar-cell blanket he could have used it to seal the bag edges together.

In the next few weeks he experimented with his heated rod. The work was frustrating. It seemed the iron was always either too hot or too cool. If he got it to just the right temperature for a few moments, it had cooled again before he had completed what he had set out to do with it. But, eventually, he found the right temperature and built a rack over the forge. Then, by resting the rod in hooks on the rack at just the right height, for a specific time, he was able to get it warmed, or rewarmed just enough, but not too much, to work.

In the end he became expert at this, too.

He sealed enough bags together to make a plastic sheet a little larger in area than the floor of the inner room.

Together, he and Merry laid it down, sealing it with strips of narrow boards nailed on top of it at the bases of the vertical walls. After that, it was merely a matter of bringing up and nailing down the planks of the upper floor. They used the trailer to carry the planks. For by this time they were well into April and the ground was dry enough to hitch both horses to that vehicle for trips to the ranch.

Merry went with him on these trips. While there, she carefully planted sections of the potatoes she had saved in a cool corner of the inner room through the winter, for seed in the garden. She had some other seeds, which she planted as well, but Jeebee was too involved in his own concerns to pay much attention to what they were.

"Why do you want to do anything like this?" he asked her. "We'll be gone by the time fall comes around."

"You don't dig and eat new potatoes in the fall," Merry said.

She was right, of course.

He made no more objections to anything she decided to do, after that. In any case, there were other matters to occupy him.

With the total vanishing of the snow, Jeebee's inner unease shifted unexpectedly into high gear. With the earth bare and new green stuff sprouting, it was now undeniable that time was on the march.

Until then he had been able to look out on the snow and say to himself, "It's winter still. There's a while yet. I've still got time to get ready."

But the sight of the naked, burgeoning earth was like the

ticking of a clock. They were little more than two months from the expected birth date.

He had memorized the books that Merry had taught him, line by line, like someone from a time before the written word had been invented. She would give him a sentence, have him repeat it back to her, then repeat it to himself again and again, until it came automatically to him. He found the repetition of the words comforting, even after he already knew the books backward and forward. Their words were something of authority, something to cling to.

At the same time, it did not tell him what he really wanted to hear—the fact that he would be able to handle his share of things when the time came. He searched between the words for that kind of reassurance, but could not find it. Then his mind went off in a dozen different directions to worry about a dozen other, different things.

He worried about Wolf. A pet dog could be jealous when a new baby came. That was common knowledge. Wolf, of course, was no pet. On the other hand, while a pet dog might be jealous, he was not likely to look on the baby as possibly something to eat.

"It's good you're going to have the baby in June," Jeebee said to Merry. "It's a stroke of luck."

"Stroke of luck, nothing!" Merry answered cheerfully. "It's a matter simply of counting the days forward. It takes nine months to produce a baby. That's all you need to know."

"Yes, yes," said Jeebee, "I know that. That isn't what I'm talking about. June's the time when the testosterone in wolves is at its lowest. They're at their least aggressive then."

Merry, who had been cutting cloth for clothes for the baby, stopped abruptly in what she was doing.

"Aggressive? What do you mean—aggressive?"

"Oh, just what I say," said Jeebee. He was suddenly upset at having mentioned the matter at all to Merry. "The high testosterone season is during the early winter months. January, February—like that. That's when the wolves in a pack compete for position and breeding rights. Just the opposite in May and June.

June more than May is the time when they're least competitive, and it's at that time that the pups are born. Then all the wolves in a pack are concerned with all the pups. I've told you about this. They all help to feed the new ones, and baby-sit them if the mother has to go off for a while. What I was saying, was that we'll be having our baby at just the time when Wolf is at his most friendly and helpful."

"You mean he's the least likely to be aggressive toward the baby?" Merry looked at him with narrowed eyes.

"Well, yes," said Jeebee, "but aggressive isn't the word. Just the opposite. It will be a time when Wolf will be most likely to be protective and helpful."

"I see," said Merry, and the frown that had drawn a line between her two eyes smoothed somewhat.

Jeebee still felt uneasy at having perhaps planted a worry in her mind. He made a mental note not to bring the subject up again. Merry was perfectly capable of making sure, permanently, that Wolf was not a potential danger to her baby. He did not want any reaction as drastic as that.

On the other hand he, too, was determined that Wolf must be agreeable to adding this newcomer to their pack. It would have to be a matter of being completely on guard against him when the time came. Jeebee primed himself for that moment, among his other preparations.

Meanwhile, there was an endless list of things to make. He built a framework around the bed, and an extra area of floor next to it that would be the actual birthing area. He set up sheets of plastic made from the bags that could be used to enclose it completely, like a tent within the room, if necessary to protect against dirt or sand.

He had already put a plastic layer tight against the ceiling and the top of the walls of the room. It was impossible to double-plank from underneath, but the ceiling was already as well sealed as was possible. Now, in addition, this tentlike affair would be ready. Merry would probably not want it with its sides down most of the time, simply because it would become intolerably hot inside and possibly shut out a sufficient air supply.

At any rate, there it was, ready to go. It was not difficult to build or to make, after his experience in plastic-coating the floor.

Merry had also wanted an enema syringe for herself, when the pains would first begin. First births, according to the books and her experience, were usually more prolonged than the births of children born later to the same mother. They found such a syringe with a plastic nozzle and a rubber bulb down in the ruins of the ranch house, but the rubber was so old that it had cracked and no longer worked. They kept the nozzle and instead attached a bag Jeebee made up from plastic sealed into the shape of a long, rectangular bag, fastened to the nozzle with tight thongs of rawhide that had been allowed to shrink around the inner end of the nozzle to the point where it was watertight.

Filling the bag was a laborious process of immersing it in a container of warm soapy water and simply holding it under the surface until the air escaped upward and water took its place in the bag. Once the bag was full, it could be emptied simply by rolling up the bag.

Merry had also asked him to build what was in effect a type of birthing stool that had been used for centuries under primitive conditions, with a solid vertical rod before it, with a solid crossbar she could cling to, to help in the muscular effort of the delivery.

Jeebee eventually came up with a tripod with the requisite bars. She drew him a sketch of the birthing stool she wanted him to build for her. This was simply a three-legged stool with a seat. However, the seat was to be cut out in half-moon shape to give the baby room to emerge and to give Jeebee room to reach in and help when the time came.

He had been lucky enough to find a keyhole saw down at the ranch, and with this, since it was small and rather a flimsy saw, but would cut in a curve, he carved out three identical seat shapes from light plywood and glued them together, reinforcing the glue by nailing them together and countersinking the nails. He finished by padding the seat with cloth covered by leather they had tanned themselves from cattle hide.

The tripod, the bars, the stool with its special seat ended up as sturdy pieces of equipment, and Merry was pleased.

His final and most important concern, as they moved on into May and then through May toward the early June date of the birth, was for the lighting in the cave.

He had kept as many as possible of the batteries on standby at full charge ready for use.

He estimated that he had battery enough for light, even using the headlamps, for at least thirty hours.

Still, the illumination he got this way, while good, was not what he might need at the actual moment of birth. For that time he was relying on the solar-powered yard floodlight that had apparently been overlooked by the raiders.

Why this was, Jeebee did not really know. It was true the floodlight had been tucked up under the eaves at the back of the house. But unless the defense of the ranch house, together with the fire, had kept the raiders from looting until daylight when the floodlight would have automatically shut itself off, Jeebee had no idea how they could have missed it.

However, the fact was they had. When he first found it, and tried it, it was dead. He had been about to give up on it when he noticed that its receptor surface had been completely coated with a sort of tarry black substance, which seemed to be ashes mixed with a resin that had possibly bubbled out under the heat of the fire from the roofing material of the ranch.

Carefully, he cleaned this off and exposed it to sunlight, and was impressed at the bright light he got from it, after a full day of exposure to the sunlight.

Its battery was only good for about ten hours; but it would not be required, he thought, until the moment of actual delivery itself, so all its power could be kept in reserve.

Merry was equally delighted with it. Like the bike Jeebee had ridden out of Michigan, it was powered by the most advanced type of solar cell, and it could be switched to various intensities. At high intensity it would be a good equivalent for what would effectively be an operating-room light. He rigged this to its own bar on the tripod, near the top, with a clamp so that it could be rotated into any position necessary. Meanwhile, Merry had finished making baby clothes and blankets, and had insisted on building, by herself, a small, high-sided crib to keep near the fire so the baby would always be warm. It was late spring now, and to Jeebee the nights were only pleasantly cool. But he could understand how a baby might have different needs as far as warmth was concerned.

Unexpectedly, Jeebee found himself with nothing more to do but wait. He puttered around with the bed, the stool, the tripod, and the lamps, essentially making work for himself, until Merry literally drove him out of the inner room.

"Go find something to do someplace else!" she said finally. She was not angry but she was definite.

"What, for instance?" said Jeebee. The expected date of birth was only a week away.

"Find something!" said Merry. "Build something in that forge of yours!"

Jeebee went to the forge and found himself with no ideas whatsoever. Running through his mind were only the words of the various books that Merry had made him memorize. For want of anything else to do he built a fire in the forge. Some weeks since, he had removed that part of the roof that was closest to the bluff, preferring to be soaked by an occasional sprinkle of rain to being roasted alive by the heat of the forge in the enclosed space.

With the fire going, he examined the pieces of metal he had brought up. There was some angle iron, some steel rods, some lengths of steel water pipe, and a couple of pieces of axle stock from one of the older cars.

He examined the shorter piece of axle stock, which was about a foot and a half long and about an inch and a half in diameter. It suggested nothing useful to be made from it, and he looked at it morosely. It was too bad, he thought, he did not have some means of drilling it out and then tightly wrapping it with wire. He could make at least, then, some sort of single-shot equivalent of a rifle, which Merry could have with her after the baby came, when he was gone and had left her only with the revolver.

The episode with the cougar had made a large impression on both of them. The big cat might run away from a full-grown adult—or might not, next time—but if cougars were like wolves, a child would be in worse danger.

Jeebee still felt guilty for being absent at the time. His conscience had been troubling him ever since. He had considered—and discarded—a number of possible ways to leave Merry adequately armed while he hunted down on the flats. He had even considered leaving the rifle and trying to get cattle with the revolver alone.

Now, as he looked at the piece of axle stock, a wild idea came to him. Merry had told him to find something to do. He might as well do this. He had envisioned something like a long spear before this. Something with which Merry could at least hold off an animal like the cougar.

As the image took a firmer shape in his mind, he began to envision the axle hammered out, drawn and flattened to perhaps half again or more its length, and then perhaps cut in half and formed with a spearhead. Spearhead, and part shaft, of metal, that could form the front half of such a spear. The back half could perhaps be made from one of the pieces of water pipe, cut to length and one end fitted around the butt end of the front piece and then forge-welded to it.

He started heating the axle stock in the fire and hammering. As it began to flatten under the hammer blows he had a further inspiration. The spear should have a crossbar. In fact it should be something like the boar spear of the Middle Ages, in which a crossbar kept the boar from charging up the shaft of a spear embedded in the animal, in its frenzy to get to the man holding it and use its tusks on him.

The piece of axle stock was approximately one and a half feet long and one and a half inches in diameter and round. He hammered it out until it lengthened and flattened into what looked like a two-and-a-half-foot metal paddle with a one-inch-square handle some six inches long. The paddle end was three inches wide and three-eights of an inch thick.

He made two lengthwise cuts in the paddle end, using the hardy, that same small chisellike device that Nick had given him back at the wagon to start him in backwoods blacksmithing. The hardy had a square handle about an inch in diameter, which fitted through a hole in one end of his anvil with its triangular head pointed upward, its chisel edge providing a blade against which he cut the forge-heated metal. The paddle had now become a handle that had three pieces running forward from it.

Two of the pieces he spread out at ninety-degree angles, then cut them off at lengths of three inches. What he had left looked something like a rough metal blank for a sword, or cross, the handle being the top leg of the cross, the three-inch extensions on either side forming what would be its crossbar and the center section of the original paddle being either the long leg of the cross or the rough for the blade.

In this case, it was neither. The long leg would form the spear shaft and head.

He used the hammer to make this shaft definite, and hammered the far end of it into a wickedly barbed spearhead with backward-pointing tines a good four inches in length.

From one of his lengths of one-and-a-quarter-inch water pipe he cut off a two-inch length and fitted it over the short handle end of the front spear piece. Heating pipe and end together in the forge, he set them together on the anvil and hammer-welded them until they were one piece.

Finally he had a finished spearhead, ready to be mounted on a shaft, which preferably should be hardwood.

The woods all around the cave were pines. But he had brought up from the ranch last fall a number of the tools, including a rusty hoe, with a metal blade that was half broken off. He had had thoughts then of mending it in his forge; half as an experiment, half as an attempt to produce something useful for gardening.

Now he decided to sacrifice it as a hoe and simply cut off four feet of its wooden handle. Trimmed down somewhat, this slid into the end of the hollow pipe section he had just welded to his spear. After that it was merely a matter of using a punch to make a couple of holes opposed to each other on either side of the water pipe and then hammering a nail through the holes and wood. When it protruded through the further hole, he cut off the nail and flattened both ends so that it became a rivet, fastening the wood shaft into the metal spear end securely.

By the time he had reached this point it was just about noon, four days later, and he had become completely engrossed in making the spear. He was just flattening the ends of the nail he had cut off to use for a rivet when he heard Merry calling.

He threw the spear aside and ran back to the inner room. Wolf had already greeted them and left some three hours earlier, for which Jeebee now was grateful, because there was a note in Merry's voice that had suddenly driven thought of everything but her from him.

He burst into the inner room, distractedly shoving the door to behind him, to find Merry sitting on the bed, smiling happily at him. The smile lasted for just a second before it disappeared in a moment's stare of great intensity.

"It's time, Jeebee," she said in a remarkably calm voice. "The pains have been coming for some time, but I wasn't sure. Now, I think the baby's really ready to come!"

Jeebee stared at her. Abruptly, his mind was a complete blank. He could not remember the words of the books he had memorized, he could not remember what he was supposed to do.

"But it's supposed to be three days yet—" he said stupidly.

"Well, it isn't," said Merry. "It's now. Come, help me up on my feet. I've got to walk as much as possible."

CHAPTER 34

In the inner room, only two of the car interior lights were lit. The other two, headlamps and floodlight on the tripod over the birthing stool, were still dark. There was no fire in the fireplace, and to Jeebee the air seemed cool after being in the smithy. But by the light of the lamps Merry's face and arms gleamed with a sheen of perspiration.

"I've had the enema," she said, "about half an hour ago. I'm all cleaned out and ready. I've been resting a bit, but help me up now. As I say, I've got to walk."

He moved to her automatically, but his mind was still adjusting to the fact that the baby had decided to put in an appearance three days ahead of schedule. He was grateful to Merry for being able to think for both of them in this first moment—for him of disbelief that the moment had actually arrived.

He took her hands and assisted her up off the bed. She could, he knew, have made it to her feet herself, but from here on she should save her strength as much as possible. The walking was good and necessary for her. Standing up from the bed was an unnecessary waste of strength.

She began to walk. "I've been having contractions for a while now," she said. "They were about eight minutes apart to start. Lasting about a minute."

Jeebee turned to a pad and pencil he had laid ready on a

wall shelf, the pencil from his backpack, the pad made of paper scavenged from the ranch. He made a note of the time.

"How fast are they now?" he said with the pencil still in his hand. He looked at the faithful old watch with its hundred-year battery, still on his now sun-browned right wrist.

"Time them," she answered, "Now. And . . . now!"

"Six minutes, fourteen seconds," said Jeebee, looking up from the watch. "How long did you wait before calling me?"

"Not long. Calm down," said Merry.

Jeebee made himself take a deep breath, "I'm calm—calmer," he said, "I think."

"Good," said Merry. The ending of the word was a little tight between her teeth as a contraction hit her.

"Is there anything at all I can do?"

"You can walk along with me," said Merry. "I'm a little clumsy."

Jeebee walked with her.

For the next six hours Merry walked, and intermittently rested, sitting on the side of the bed. Jeebee checked for probably the twentieth time that he had triple sheets below her. Triple sheets with a plastic tarp between each. And he checked both bed and birthing area for cleanliness again. Everything seemed to be the way it should be. Above the birthing stool was the tripod with the crossbar that Merry would be able to hold to during the actual birth.

Her contractions gradually increased, and although she continued to walk, with only short rests, Jeebee himself became worried that she was spending too much of her strength this way. After six hours she gave in to his suggestions and agreed to sit on the edge of the bed for a good fifteen minutes.

The contractions had speeded up now. They were coming more often and lasting longer. They had both thoroughly absorbed the idea that a first birth would be slow, but secretly Jeebee had expected things to happen faster than this. He made an effort of will to put a damper on his imagination, which was threatening to envision all sorts of complications. He reminded himself that now was far too early to start imagining that sort of trouble.

"Sit down, yourself," said Merry from the bed. "You've been on your feet as much as I have."

"I don't have a baby inside me fighting to get out," Jeebee grumbled, still standing in front of her. "Besides we've got to keep that bed and stool area sterile."

But he sat down on the floor at her feet, anyway, crossing his legs and telling himself that she had enough to deal with herself, she did not need to put up with his nervousness.

After a while she got up and walked again, for a little while, and then sat down once more. The contractions were now down to four or five minutes apart and stronger. Jeebee made a note of it while she was resting and before he sat down again himself.

The truth of the matter was he did not really feel like sitting down. The walking was nothing. He was used to walking all day on snowshoes or in his boots if necessary. But with the tension added on, he found a moment of sitting down was welcome, even for him, and certainly it masked his concern for her. He strove to exhibit the same matter-of-fact way in which she seemed to be taking matters.

It's being helpless, not being able to do anything, he told himself. Men aren't built to be helpless. Of course, women aren't either. No creature is.

His concentration on her was so exclusive that he was not aware of the rest of the room. He was standing over her about 5:00 P.M., as she was sitting on the edge of the bed again, and without warning a wedge-shaped, furry head suddenly pushed past his left leg, plunging its nose toward the very center of everybody's attention.

Wolf had appeared, and evidently Jeebee had failed to latch the inner door. In any case, Wolf had now slipped in without either Jeebee or Merry noticing it. Once inside it was inevitable that, with the active curiosity he had always shown, and that the books had told Jeebee was a prime characteristic of wolf behavior, he had tried to get in on the act.

"Wolf—" Jeebee shouted—and at that moment Merry's water broke.

The short single shiftlike garment she had made to wear during the birth process was up above her knees. Her amniotic fluid stained the sheet and some even splashed onto Wolf's intruding face. He disappeared like a flash of lightning, jerking backward out of Jeebee's sight.

"Are you all right—" Jeebee began to Merry.

"Yes, I'm all right!" said Merry. "You might get me something to clean up a little with—and get Wolf out!"

Jeebee reached to the foot of the bed where he had piled a number of freshly laundered and boiled small pieces of cloth somewhere in size between a washcloth and a towel. He handed one to Merry and, now having a second to spare, glanced over his shoulder. Wolf was clear across the cave, as far as the small dimensions of the cave would let him be, down on the floor licking at his paws and using the dampened paws to scrub at his face, washing it like a cat.

"Get out of here!" said Jeebee. He remembered that a better way of talking to Wolf was, in effect, in Wolf's own language, essentially. He snarled at the other. And the snarl was possibly one of his best efforts.

Wolf stopped washing his face and looked up. Merry snarled, too, and there was no doubt about the meaning behind Merry's snarl.

Wolf got to his feet. After they had first met, it had taken Jeebee a few weeks to appreciate how expressive a wolf's face and body could be. Now, Jeebee read absolute outrage in them. Wolf got to his feet and literally stamped toward the door, looking back over his shoulder with a snort and a facial expression that clearly said, *"I don't have to stand here and take this kind of treatment!"*

He made a stiff-legged exit through the partially opened door into the lower room beyond. Jeebee turned back to Merry.

"Are you really all right?" Jeebee asked. "I could shut the door, but it'll get awfully stuffy in here."

"No," said Merry, handing him back the cloth with which she had been cleaning herself. Jeebee threw it out past the tripod on to the open floor by the fireplace. There would be time to pick it up later. "He won't bother me again."

"No. He won't!" Jeebee said, with feelings that had not reached that particular depth of sincerity since he had climbed up out of the root cellar where he had found canned food, and seen Wolf waiting, possibly with the intention of trying to take the food from him. He had been ready to kill Wolf then if he had to, and he found he was feeling almost as strongly about the other now. Undoubtedly, the moment and feeling would pass, but right now Jeebee was pure animal himself.

Jeebee told himself to forget Wolf. He was gone now. Being the practical sort of individual any wolf was, he had probably just curled up in the front room in his normal sleeping spot. Jeebee could forget about him and concentrate on important things. He turned back to the bed to strip the stained sheet and the first plastic underlayer from beneath it.

Merry got up and continued to walk. Jeebee walked with her for three or four minutes. Then a strong contraction stopped her. She sat down on the edge of the bed once more.

At twelve minutes after 7:00 P.M. she had two even stronger contractions, one and a half minutes apart, and then went almost immediately into contractions one minute apart and lasting a full minute.

From that moment on, time went by in a blur for Jeebee, and he was sure the same thing was happening to Merry. She sat on the edge of the bed and the contractions speeded up. He checked occasionally, as the words of the books he had memorized had taught him, using two fingers to see if the cervix, a little less than four inches inside the vagina, had opened to its full aperture. So far, it had not; nor had its ring of muscle thinned in stretching, to the point where the passageway was completely open and free for the baby to emerge.

By some time after 10:45 P.M. (Jeebee's note on it was scribbled so badly that later he was unable to read what he had written), Merry's contractions became very strong indeed, lasting a minute and a half.

She sat continuously on the edge of the bed now, and was having a strong urge to push at the end of the contractions. It was strange, thought Jeebee, because Merry knew what he was telling her better than he knew it himself, but the urge to push down in her was so close to being on automatic and out of her conscious control that it helped her to have him keep cautioning her against it.

"No, don't push. Not yet," he said, again and again.

At first, when he said this, she had nodded, but after a bit she stopped doing even that. She was panting like a puppy now, to keep from pushing, because she knew, as Jeebee also had learned, that if she pushed at this time, she might tear membranes, which would mean bleeding and possible infection.

Sometime—Jeebee later estimated it as being almost midnight—the contractions had become very strong indeed; and reaching in to check the cervix, he could no longer feel it as a ring of muscle. It had thinned to the point where it would allow the downward passage of the baby. The road from the uterus was finally completely open, and the tips of his fingers at last felt something that could only be the crown of the baby's head. Thank God, it was head-down!

It was time for Merry to move to the birthing stool. Jeebee carried her to it; for she was now exhausted from the labor. Her mouth was dry from the panting and he held a cup to her lips so she could take another of the small sips of water he had been giving her. She was very exhausted now, and she was just passing into the stage the childbirth books had warned about, called transition. That point at which the body shifts gears, giving up the labor of the cervix, which is now completely dilated. Merry looked at the end of her tether, worn-out, depressed, and desperate. She was past the point of being reasonable, and she glared at Jeebee.

"I've got to give up. This is all your fault. I'm never going to do it again."

"It won't be long now," said Jeebee, "it won't be long. Just hang in there a little while yet. You don't want to stop now . . ."

At this point she was shivering, and when Jeebee touched her, her skin was icy cold. He wrapped layers of blankets around her. Time moved on. Gradually, warmth began to return to her, and the period of depression passed.

Suddenly she had one great contraction that made her gasp. She had pushed involuntarily, and now Jeebee no longer encouraged her not to. From now on pushing was appropriate. Now, it only hurt her when she was building up pressure to push. This was as the childbirth books they had memorized had told them. When she actually pushed, the pain would go. Jeebee was to ask her about this afterward, and she would tell him, then, that she didn't know if it had. She just hadn't remembered.

She had a death grip on the crossbar, now almost hanging with all her weight from the tripod.

The baby descended still further. Now it was crowning, beginning to show its forehead at the enlarged entrance of the vagina. Jeebee was busy gently helping the opening, pulling back Merry's body from around the emerging head.

Before his eyes, he saw the first of the miracles happen. The birthing books had warned that he might have to help position the baby, but this time at least, it was not necessary. Before his eyes the physical part of the head and the body behind it rotated by itself, so that the shoulders were now up and down vertically.

The head began to emerge, and Jeebee cupped it softly with his hand, supporting it and holding it back a little so that it would not come too fast and tear membranes in Merry's body. With his other hand, the right hand, he continued to help pull back the body around the opening, and Merry pushed with all her strength, pushed and pushed. . . .

It was at this moment, in just the flash of a second, that Jeebee saw Wolf once more back in the room. Wolf was just putting his shoulder down to shoulder-shove-and-roll on the stained blanket Jeebee had ripped off the bed earlier after Merry's water bag burst. But Jeebee had no time to waste on Wolf now. All of his attention had to stay on Merry.

When he was once more free to flash a look in Wolf's direction for another split second, he saw Wolf lying in watching position, paws crossed in front of him and his eyes taking in the whole process.

The head was all the way out now and Jeebee was still supporting it, kneeling and sitting on his heels so as to keep himself and the baby below Merry and the stool top. Suddenly, the lower shoulder emerged at last, and with that, everything suddenly began to move quickly.

Jeebee tried to keep the baby from coming too fast, but it came swiftly, nonetheless, now that the difficult parts of it were past the narrowest part of the opening passage.

Almost immediately it seemed he held the baby in both hands. He continued to sit on his heels, making sure he held the baby below Merry's body and watching the umbilical cord to see if it was still pulsing.

It was. But as he watched, the pulsing gradually slowed and ceased.

Cradling the tiny naked figure in his left arm with his hand still half enclosing and supporting the head, he reached blindly back behind him to the foot of the bed and got one of the sterilized, boiled, still-damp cloths off the pile he had left there. With it, he gently cleaned the baby's nose and mouth of mucus.

This was the point at which the books had called for suction to completely clear the nose and mouth of the newborn. But they had nothing of rubber or other elastic to make one. Jeebee put his mouth over the tiny nose and mouth and sucked gently. He felt only a touch on his tongue to tell him anything had come out. He spat sideways onto the plastic sheet.

As soon as the baby was able to breathe he took in a deep breath and uttered a tiny, immediate wail of a cry. Softly, with the cloth, Jeebee continued cleaning the rest of the little face. As soon as the baby's eyes were uncovered they flashed about, incredibly blue.

With the flash of the eyes, something expanded powerfully in Jeebee, a silent explosion of emotion that he would have not believed possible, a connection of himself with this child of his he was holding.

He had identified his earlier feeling of protection with the moment he had been ready to kill Wolf to protect the food he had found. He changed his mind now. What he felt at this moment in protectiveness toward the infant in his hands was much greater. It faced outward, like an armed wall against the world and anything that might threaten his child.

He continued, wiping clean the little body.

It had been, on emergence from Merry, a plainly blue color, beneath a thin white covering that looked like nothing so much as cream cheese. It was a boy, Jeebee noticed for the first time. Now, unexpectedly, rapidly, it began—and this was the second miracle—to turn pink. Jeebee, cautiously supporting the baby with both hands now again, lifted him and laid him on Merry's chest. Her arms came up wearily but immediately to enfold it, and to direct its head toward her left breast, which was closest. Immediately, instinctively, the baby found her nipple with his mouth and began to nurse.

For his first moment of relaxation from tension, as he watched the two of them, Jeebee began to realize that he was reeling from fatigue and emotional backwash from his emotional experience just now, which he suddenly realized had been foretold in the childbirth books. It had been his moment of instinctive bonding with his son. Now it would never leave him.

Jeebee stayed, kneeling where he was by the birthing stool, caught for a moment in a half daze, mesmerized by the timeless picture of Merry feeding her child. Then his sense of urgency jerked him out of the daze suddenly. There was still work for him to do. He looked at the bed now and located the scissors he had boiled, before he had laid them there on one of the boiled cloths; and next to them an adjoining cloth supporting two clean strips of rawhide cord, almost small enough to be fish line.

With one of these he tied off the cord about an inch from Merry's skin, and then tied the other cord about an inch and a half beyond that. Then using the scissors from a sewing box they had found at the ranch house, he cut between the two ties and the baby was free.

He rose unsteadily, suddenly aware that he could hardly stand on his cramped leg muscles after having sat in a kneeling position so long. Blood flowed back into his legs.

Gently, he picked up Merry with the baby from the birthing stool and laid them both, just as they were, on the clean sheet he had exposed in that moment in which he had stripped the stained top one and the plastic sheet after Merry's water had burst.

Merry accepted the move without seeming to notice it. She was half sitting up now, with double pillows between her and the head of the bed to support her back. She was still having mild contractions, and every so often, a small flow of red-stained fluid that Jeebee remembered was called *lochia* drained onto the sheet beneath her.

It had been in preparation for this that Jeebee had sandwiched several layers of plastic between alternate layer of sheets so that when the sheet became too dampened, he could clear it away down to another, dry one.

A moment later, as he watched, the afterbirth, slippery with blood, emerged. He wrapped it in plastic and put it aside on a high, overhead shelf, to be taken out later.

The baby stopped nursing and closed his eyes. Merry, who had been watching him, let her head loll back against the pillows with a sigh of happiness. Her baby was alternately feeding and staring about, his blue eyes flickering here and there, then closing as he seemed to doze for a short while, then waking to search for the nipple again and feed some more.

With one of the boiled cloths dampened in warm water, he cleaned the rest of the baby and wrapped him in the warmest and softest cloth he could find. Then he wrapped both the baby and Merry in their softest blanket.

He turned away to start to clean up. Little whimpering noises of the kind Wolf would make in certain social situations made him spin back. He had forgotten all about Wolf being there.

To his surprise, Wolf was slowly approaching Merry and the baby in the bed, in his most submissive and ingratiating of postures. His head was held low, his ears were back, his tail wagging, wolf-style, and he was making the little whimpering sounds of reassurance and promise of the best of all possible intentions.

Merry, totally exhausted but fully alert, snarled at him with surprising strength and intensity. The snarl was so reflexive and real that it startled Jeebee. He did not have to be a wolf himself to read it very clearly. Merry was a mother and Wolf was not going to get any closer to her baby.

Wolf stopped immediately and Jeebee, suddenly coming to his senses, woke up and moved toward him to throw him out, bodily, if necessary.

But Wolf was gone through the door before he had fully taken the first step toward him. This time, however, he did not leave with any show of temper, but rather with a quick self-effacement that was almost magical in its speed.

"Take him," Merry said, lifting the baby from her body. "Would you bring me that chamber pot? My teeth are floating."

Jeebee moved to take the baby from her.

"Carefully!" Merry's voice was almost as sharp as when she had snarled at Wolf. Jeebee felt a momentary flicker of indignation, which was gone as quickly as it came, as he moved over to accept the baby into his arms. He had handled the baby carefully enough before Merry ever held him, he thought. But the thought remained unuttered.

"Oh," said Merry, getting out of bed slowly and painfully. "And will you get me some food, now? I'm starving! And I want a large cup of water—and maybe five more after that."

The chamber pot was handy, the cup and the water were available. Merry got back under the covers and took the baby back again. He had woken when he was passed to Jeebee, and when he came back to his mother he searched once more for her breast. Then she sighed happily, again. A very, very deep sigh.

Jeebee was busy bringing her sandwiches made by putting a slice of cold cooked beef between two slices of cheese. They had been hoarding some of the cheese against this moment. Merry bit into it voraciously.

"Do you know, when he suckles there's no pain at all?" She spoke with her mouth full; but that was all right. It was all right, Jeebee thought, with the world.

CHAPTER 35

Jeebee was exhausted, ready to take a couple of blankets, roll up on the floor, and try to catch at least some sleep.

Merry, however, was still hungry. He built a small fire in the fireplace to heat a good-sized cooking pot of the thick soup he had prepared. It was made mainly of root vegetables, because the garden down at the ranch had not yet begun to produce much in the way of this summer's eatables. But they still had some carrots, beets, and rutabagas, plus dried peas from the ranch's fruit cellar, saved for important occasions.

The root vegetables, dug the fall before from the garden there, had been kept with their tops chopped off, and buried in a box of sandy soil. They were a little dried and tough, but in soup form they became tender, and something to balance the animal protein of the cheese and meat.

Eventually, Merry's hunger was satisfied. A little more than three hours after the birth she dozed off, then dropped into what seemed to Jeebee like a normal-to-heavy sleep, with the baby beside her in the bed.

Jeebee had worried before the birth about the business of her sleeping with the newborn child in the bed with her.

"You'll be pretty worn-out," he had said, only a couple of days before, "and you'll probably sleep pretty heavily. If you roll over in your sleep, you might—"

"I'm not going to roll on my precious baby!" said Merry. "How can you even think something like that!"

"You might not know—"

"I'll know!" Merry had said. "No one is going to have that baby with them but me, until I say so!"

Jeebee had necessarily left it at that. Later on, he had remembered something in one of the wolf books and looked it up. Sure enough, there was a statement there about surrogates, people who volunteered to take care of and raise very young animals from zoos and similar places that could not keep them safely with the adults of their own species, or where the animal mother was dead or incapable.

These humans often needed to sleep nights with the very young animals, and it was noted that they could do so safely. It had been established that as long as the human being was neither sedated nor affected by any drug or medicine, there was absolutely no danger of one of them rolling over in their sleep on the young creatures.

Now, looking at Merry sleeping with one arm still holding the sleeping baby close to her breast, he felt reassured and happy.

He finished cleaning up and went outside, stepping for a moment into the summer morning.

Wolf was gone from the front room and was nowhere to be seen around the cave. Nor was he visible in the meadow outside. About Jeebee, the early day was warming as the sun rose, and he found himself thinking that he had never felt quite so happy as he did at this moment.

In a sense, his world was complete. He felt enclosed in happiness under the straight-back pines, with the sound of a small breeze going through their branches and the two streams slipping by with other light sounds between their banks. Above him white clouds sailed demurely across the blue June sky. He felt fulfilled. In this moment, life seemed finally, utterly purposeful, and overwhelmingly satisfactory.

He was, for the first time since Merry had called him in, conscious of his own tiredness. Merry had evidently been wired up during those hours following the birth when she had been so hungry, and apparently he had picked up some of the wiredness from her. Now he himself wanted only to sleep.

He went back inside, leaving the outer door open but closing the inner one and making up his own bed on the floor with his body against it, the door itself open just a tiny crack for air. To get in, Wolf or anything else would have to push him aside. And that would wake him. Merry and the baby were protected.

He was woken for short periods at indefinite times after that by Merry wanting something more to eat or drink. Each time, he felt his way to the nearest electric light and switched it on. The second time, Merry suggested a light be put down where she could reach it herself. All the headlamps were on long cords and easy to move. He shifted the one closest to the bed; and, momentarily while awake, as long as he was up, he stepped outside again and found that Wolf had come back. He was curled up in his usual corner of the lower room. Beyond the open outer door, the day showed itself at mid-to-late afternoon.

He went all the way outdoors, to feel again the summertime and reach for a trace of the remarkable feeling of completeness he had felt earlier. Turning back in, his eye caught something by the side of the door and he remembered that sometime after the baby was born, he had wrapped the afterbirth in plastic and put it out here, to dispose of later. It was still there. But the plastic had been neatly ripped away from it. It was completely exposed, but untouched.

The ripping away of the plastic was clearly Wolf's work. But he—who would eat anything that was eatable—had not touched the afterbirth. Jeebee's heart gave a curious lurch in his chest. What could have made Wolf respect that, where normally anything eatable would have been snatched up and carried off by him?

Jeebee tried to remember something in the books about wolves that he had read which could explain this. But there was nothing. Slowly the thought formed in him that he was doubtful of accepting, because it simply might be a matter of sheer wish-fulfillment. It had occurred to him that perhaps Wolf might have respected the afterbirth because he had made an association of it with as much of the birth scene as he had witnessed, and with Merry and the baby itself.

If so, then it could have been the beginning of a recognition that the baby was part of their family, part of the pack, as Wolf would have thought of them. It was a long jump into sheer supposition. Jeebee was only too aware of how little he knew about wolves. But he wondered if perhaps Wolf's experience with the amniotic fluid in his face, and his later shoulder-rolling in the sheet that had been stained when Merry's water bag burst, as well as his watching of the birth—plus Merry's warning him off—if all these things had not acted as a form of something like imprinting.

It was pure guesswork, but maybe it was a possibility. When he went back in, he located the chain he had found at the ranch and that he had equipped earlier with a snap on one end so that it could act as a leash, as the storekeeper woman had walked with Wolf on a leash in the town where Jeebee had lost his motorized bike. He had never gotten around to trying whether Wolf would remember and accept the leash with him. Now Jeebee hung it from a nail in the frame of the inner door, where it would be close at hand. Later on, he would try out the leash.

It seemed he had hardly closed his eyes before he was wakened by scratching at the door and Wolf whining and snuffling through the crack, it seemed right into his ear. He sat up as Merry turned the light on, having herself been woken by Wolf's demands to enter.

"Do you want me to let him in?" said Jeebee, putting his hand up to the chain. "I've got the leash here now. I can keep him on that. I really think we want to start getting him used to the baby right from the start."

He thought fleetingly again of the afterbirth outside with the plastic carefully peeled away from it.

"Shall I leash him and then let him in, just close enough to see you and the baby again?" Jeebee repeated when she did not answer.

"Yes," said Merry, "but don't let him get any closer than the edge of the bed."

Jeebee got up, holding the door shut by leaning against it with all his body weight. He unhooked the chain, and then, still holding the door shut, moved around and opened it only enough to push himself through the opening and push Wolf back. Jeebee looped the ready-held chain loosely around Wolf's neck as he imprisoned him with his arms and snapped the snap into one of the links. It was attached to Wolf now, but it hung loosely around his neck and the snap would keep that looseness so the chain would not choke him. Wolf did not seem to object. Beyond the wide-open outer door, twilight held the sky. It was the regular time for Wolf's evening visit.

Still holding tight to the chain and keeping Wolf from pulling away from him, but allowing him into the room, Jeebee stepped backward one pace. Wolf strained against the chain, not fighting it, but trying to get to the inner room. Jeebee let Wolf pull him into the inner room, and only stopped him with the chain some three feet from the near edge of the bed. Merry was sitting up, eyeing Wolf narrowly, with the baby on the far side of her, lying out of sight beyond her body.

Jeebee allowed Wolf to go a step forward; he was still about a foot and a half from the bed, whimpering now, wagging his tail and looking both agreeably and appealingly at Merry.

Without warning, the baby cried, a thin wail, and tossed its arms in the air so that they appeared on the other side of Merry's body. Merry turned and took the tiny figure up into her arms, laying the little head against her breast.

Long before she had lifted the baby fully into sight, Wolf had jumped backward, and hidden behind Jeebee.

"Will you look at that!" said Jeebee. "He's afraid of the baby!"

"He's hungry," Merry said softly, to the baby rather than to Jeebee or Wolf. "Is he hungry?"

She had lifted the baby to her breast and it found the nipple and nursed—but just for a few moments. It was evidently not as hungry as it thought it had been. It let the nipple out of its mouth and turned its head away toward Jeebee, small blue eyes flashing about.

A long gray muzzle sneaked around the side of Jeebee's leg. Wolf was peering at the baby.

The baby jerked up an arm in a sudden motion like a reflexive wave, and Wolf's muzzle was gone behind Jeebee's leg once more, almost before the arm had started to lift.

The baby looked around for a moment more before deciding to find the nipple again, and went back to nursing. The gray muzzle crept out again.

Silently, almost imperceptibly, Wolf emerged from behind Jeebee, his neck outstretched, his nose flared toward the bed, and his eyes on Merry and the baby. Merry herself was looking down, watching the baby, absorbed in the process of nursing.

Wolf floated gradually forward until most of his body was past Jeebee. The chain, which Jeebee had kept slack, drew tight and stopped him a foot from the near bedside.

Jeebee moved forward a little, himself, slackening his chain; Wolf started to take up the slack and suddenly froze. Jeebee looked at Merry. Merry's eyes and attention were all on Wolf. Her face was fixed in an expression and her lips had drawn back from her teeth. It was not a welcoming face. The glitter of her teeth in the fluorescent light was like the glitter of the teeth of any carnivore mother. Wolf's ears had flattened to his head, his head itself had lowered, and his tail had begun to wag as he moved forward. Now he stood still in his same position and began to make little appeasing whines.

"Let him come as far as the edge of the bed?" Jeebee said.

"As far as the edge"—Merry's face had not changed—"but no farther!"

Jeebee stood where he was, with a slack chain. Gradually Wolf inched forward until his nose was barely inches from the bedside.

"That's enough!" Merry said suddenly.

Jeebee checked Wolf. He only twitched the chain taut for a second, but Wolf had stopped even before the words were out of Merry's mouth. Now, Wolf backed a step and then turned to leave, out of the inner room, through the outer door and into the open air.

Outside, Jeebee took the leash off.

With the leash off, Wolf appeared to lose all interest in the cave's interior. He greeted Jeebee in the usual fashion and tried to get Jeebee to play with him and chase him. Jeebee, however, was too wise in Wolf's ways by this time to be drawn from his post in the doorway. Wolf had left the inner room on his own decision. But it was one of his oldest tricks to see if he could not get Jeebee's attention away from something that Wolf himself wanted, and then beat Jeebee back to whatever it was. Wolf might actually have been wanting to romp and roughhouse in the usual fashion; but he could equally well have been trying merely to draw Jeebee out of position so he could slip past him and in through the door again. Perhaps he thought that Merry might let him come closer to the new pup if Jeebee was not there.

In any case, Jeebee stood his ground, and after a while Wolf, panting agreeably, suddenly turned and pulled his usual vanishing act through the trees. Jeebee turned, himself, closing both the front and inner doors behind him as he went back inside.

He doubted that Wolf would still try to come back for a while, or that his disappearing just now meant that he had given up trying to get in. But just to be on the safe side, Jeebee made sure the inner door was firmly latched.

Back inside, the light was still on and Merry still sat up in bed, holding her child.

"I hope it didn't worry you to have him that close," said Jeebee.

"Worry me? No," Merry answered.

Her right hand came up from the hidden side of her where the baby had been lying. It was holding Jeebee's revolver. "I'll be carrying this from now on."

Jeebee gazed at the gun and at her and let out a deep breath. He remembered the moment coming up out of the root cellar with the cans, months before.

"Yes," he said. "Well, I don't really think he'll be a danger to the baby."

"No," said Merry.

She put the revolver away, laying it back down where it had

been, and her mood changed as abruptly as Wolf's had seemed to, outside.

"Isn't he beautiful?" she said fondly, looking down at the baby.

"Yes," said Jeebee, wondering a little to find that he really did think the baby was beautiful. He was not used to thinking in those terms about men, boys, or even male children. But Merry was right. Their baby was beautiful.

"We've got to name him," Merry said decisively.

There was a little lift to her voice at the end of the sentence. Not enough to make it a question, but enough to invite comment from Jeebee. Or, if not, some kind of response.

"What do you want to name him?" Jeebee said diplomatically.

"Paul," she answered immediately. Her gaze clouded a little. "He'll never know his granddaddy, but he can carry his name."

She looked up at Jeebee.

"You don't like Paul for him?" Merry asked.

"I hadn't even thought," said Jeebee. "No, of course I like Paul."

His answer was completely truthful. He simply hadn't thought that far ahead; and in any case, he had no objection to the baby being named after Merry's father. The thought came to him, too late, that he might have put forward the name of his own father. But Merry had never known his father. In fact Jeebee had all but forgotten him in the years since his father's death and his own maturing.

Paul, he thought now; Paul was a name he probably would have picked himself, given time to think about it.

"Turn out the light," Merry said sleepily, settling down with the baby in her arms and closing her eyes. "Leave the doors open a little, though."

Jeebee did as she had said and went outside again. If Merry was not concerned about Wolf returning, then it was foolish for him to worry about it.

The evening was warm. He looked around at a meadow in the full stride of a northern summer. The pines stood up, straight and dark-needled around a green meadow in which the two streams ran down the natural slope from their point of divergence. The waters were deep blue under a sky that was darkening steadily, enormously high, with a few large clouds at a distance from each other, high to still be bathed in the light of the sun, and moving steadily together like a fleet of treasury galleons sailing eagerly before a westering wind to the lands of gold and promise.

All about him he could feel the world turning forward through time, out of the darkness that had brought him here toward a brighter future.

The warmth, the soft air, the scent of the summer day now ending, filled him, enlarging him as if he was a balloon. He drew it deep into his lungs, feeling as if he grew with the inhalation. He must tell Merry about this moment, later on when she was rested and there was time. In fact, there would be a great deal for them to tell each other about this tremendous achievement at the height and best of the year. He drew the air deep into his lungs for another enormous breath. He was ready to build the cave behind him into a palace. He was ready to rebuild the world. He felt like a giant.

He let the air out, checking on a sudden thought. One other thing he had not talked about with Merry was his original plan of going on after the baby was born to finish finding his brother's ranch. That whole part of their future had been pushed into the back of his mind as the birth of the baby came close, and he had almost forgotten it himself.

The truth was, he had never really faced the problems of traveling with the new baby. Now that the child was actually born, he could fully realize what would be involved in that. He, Merry, and infant Paul would necessarily be wandering about the higher plains, possibly to be shot at on sight by local ranchers, and living as people on the move had to do. It was suddenly clear how foolish the idea had been.

There could be no moving from here until next summer, at least, when Paul would be a good deal stronger and bigger, even if still young for travel, even carried in a basket of sorts, hung on back or chest, as the Indians had carried their youngest children. Merry must have simply taken it for granted he would eventually realize this. It must have been so obvious to her that he would eventually see this for himself that she had not bothered to point out the impossibility of it. She was very like her father in that.

Consciously, he had not confronted these facts. Unconsciously, he realized now, with all his plans of building the forge and adding on to the cave, he had come to terms with it long since. Jeebee looked around him again. The evening was glorious. He still felt like a giant. It was ridiculous for him to feel so, he thought suddenly. It had all been Merry's accomplishment, not his. But that was the way he felt, nonetheless. Also, he abruptly recognized, he was hungry.

He went back in, turned on one of the interior lights that was farthest from the bed, and cut some meat and cheese for himself. He made his bed again on the floor against the door and turned the light out. In no time whatsoever, he, with the other two, was sleeping the sleep of the successful and the just.

CHAPTER 36

With the baby's birth Jeebee went into a blur of activity. They had been concentrating so hard on the birth that they had almost forgotten the inexorable march of the seasons. Now it was as if young Paul was a calendar clock, who by his growth measured off the days for them and emphasized how much was to be done before the snow flew again.

Jeebee found himself coming to begrudge the necessary day a week he spent down on the flat, hunting meat. He could still generally locate at least one cow or calf within the sweep of a day's ride under good conditions, but the supply would not last forever, although now there were young calves, which would be growing up and providing a future supply.

Still, though these promised well for the future, there was also the possibility that at any time a neighboring rancher might move in to take over this territory. In which case, without warning, he might someday discover armed men on the flatlands directly below him; and hunting would no longer be the safe thing that he had begun to take for granted it would be.

He started giving at least another half a day now and then to checking the foothill and mountain territory within several hours' ride of the cave, looking for sign of deer travel or presence. He not only found what seemed to be deer trails, but sighted a number of deer.

Aiding him in this, of course, was the fact that fawns had been born with the spring. While these had already grown considerably, still to a certain extent they restricted the travel of their mothers and of such barren female deer who had stayed pretty much together during the winter past.

He decided that there was a fair amount of meat supply in wild game, which could be harvested if he needed it. He could even start harvesting them now; but there was an excellent reason for his not doing so.

The fact was, he had underestimated the amount of work he had planned to get done after the baby's birth and before cold weather set in.

If he was going to stay here another year, there were needs he had to start facing now. One of these was ammunition for his guns, particularly if he was not going to reach any place where he could get more powder and possibly more shells.

He knew how to load his own cartridges, simply because Paul had carried the materials in his wagon, and Nick had shown him the technique. Paul had sold the cartridge makings cheaper than the finished cartridges themselves, partly because the materials were easier to transport in bulk.

He had become used to saving most of his brass for reuse, but neither primers nor modern smokeless powder would be easy to find, and they were impossible for him to duplicate.

Possibly he could make black powder, if he had to. But to the best of his present knowledge, he would have to be willing to make a long and probably perilous trip through strange territory, south, to get sulfur. The silver nitrate for the primers was there to be extracted from bird droppings. But gathering the droppings would require more time than he had to spare.

A much better alternative would be to have something else to kill cattle and large game with—something for which he could make the missiles himself. Something that would have the additional value of being silent so that he would not attract attention by the carrying sound of firing a firearm if someone was down, out of sight on the flatlands but still within hearing.

The ideal answer to all this would be, he thought, a

crossbow. He had once handled and even shot a handmade crossbow, its bow part made of a steel leaf from an automobile spring. Its short, heavy bolt—or arrow—with its metal broadhead arrow point, had gone completely through a target of three-eighths-inch plywood. With the forge now operating, he could build himself such a weapon and missiles. By using the crossbow for hunting whenever possible, he could considerably stretch his remaining ammunition supplies.

In addition to this, he had planned, ever since it was clear they must stay, to make an addition above their present cave. He planned to use window frames and glass scavenged from the ranch, which like most isolated dwelling places, had its own supply of extra glazing materials.

So he could even put glass in one or several of those window frames that had had their glass knocked out by the raiders or destroyed by the fire. It would only require that the frame itself be solid. What he intended was to build a sort of skylight window in an upward-extended section of the wall of the cold room, which would let outside sunlight over a floor, sealing it off from the cold room, below, directly into the inner room.

The window he had in mind would actually be three of the ranch's windows fastened, one on top of the other, so that essentially he would have triple glazing to keep the cold out and still let the daylight come through.

But both the crossbow and the skylight would be time-consuming jobs, and with the hunting and other necessary duties, it was hard to believe he would get them done as fast as he would have liked. The sooner he got the crossbow working, the sooner he could start saving on his firearm ammunition. On the other hand, the window would have to be finished before winter.

The work did not seem like much compared to what the two of them had accomplished the past months, Jeebee thought, but now Merry would have her hands full most of the time taking care of Paul.

It was only gradually, in the weeks and months that followed, that he learned differently.

Out of his almost nonexistent knowledge of women who

had just had children, Jeebee had rather fuzzily assumed that Merry would be, except for feeding young Paul, something of a near invalid for a month or more after the birth. Able perhaps to get around in the cave and just outside it and do minor things there. But not up to any kind of ordinary work that might require heavy exertion from her.

To his surprise, by a week and a half after the birth, she had not only rigged a carrying chest pack for Paul, but was doing a number of light jobs. They had reached the point where some of the seeds that she had saved from the ranch's garden and re-planted in its rich topsoil (possibly trucked in for the purpose) had begun producing food ready for harvesting.

As a result, even now, in midsummer, they had a quantity of homegrown foodstuffs to bring back to the cave from below, and to cook and store. Apparently the people of the ranch house had regularly put up much of their garden produce in glass sealer jars, in the fall. Merry also knew how to do this. While Jeebee hunted and did other necessary things, she was busy cooking and sealing a great deal of what could be preserved this way.

Where there was more of certain vegetables than they had jars for, and some that could not be stored well in sealer jars, these Merry cooked. Some of these were cooked into forms more fit for such storage. From ripe tomatoes she made tomato sauce, and even a variation of catsup. Carrots, rutabagas and such other root vegetables would keep well with their stems cut off and bur-ied in open boxes of dry sand.

These boxes, like the sealer jars, they stored in a cool area. Jeebee had opened up the inner room's back wall and dug the equivalent of the ranch house's fruit cellar in the soil behind it, to house them.

Meanwhile Jeebee was busily at work at the crossbow. Hap-pily, on the occasion in which he had seen the crossbow demon-strated and had a chance to shoot it himself, he had also been shown the plans from which the crossbow had been made, and his memory was good in that respect. He redrew them on some of the paper he had gotten from the ranch, just to make it all clear in his own mind before he began work.

The wooden stock required something stronger than pine, in his estimation, and the ordinary two-by-four would not be wide enough at the butt end for him. Happily, over the fireplace that had been at the ranch was a mantelpiece of varnished wood, which Jeebee identified as oak. It was a foot wide and some eight feet long and about two inches thick.

With a little labor he removed it from its position and brought it back up to the cave. There he sweated to saw off a length of thirty inches, which he then roughed out into the wooden part of the crossbow with an ax.

When he was finished, he had a wooden stock about six inches wide at the butt and curving up underneath to its narrowest point. The material for the bowstring he had already obtained, the brake cable from one of the cars, the loop of it at each end of the bow—a leaf from one of the automobile springs—held by the small set screws that already existed with the brake cable to hold it taut and in place in its original duty on the car.

Next he drilled upward through the stock at its narrowest point, making a place to set the trigger. That trigger would release a nut—he would have to make it—which would hold the bowstring in place when cocked. From the notch that held the nut, forward to the front end of the stock, he cut a groove in which the bolt would lie when the crossbow was strung and ready to fire.

This groove notch and the passage for the trigger needed only another slot across the stock near the front of it into which he could mount the lower edge of the steel leaf spring, once it was ready to act as a bow; plus a couple of slots lower on the stock near its front, to which he would be fixing a forged steel stirrup.

This would be needed so that he could put his toe in it to hold the weapon down while he pulled its string back into cocked position on the nut. There would be two more holes needed through which leather thongs could go, to lash the bow stave firmly in place once it was in its slot. On second thought, he decided to use animal sinew, put on wet and allowed to dry-shrink to the point where it was as tight as necessary.

The rest of the work was all at the forge. He had to do some forge work on the steel spring to put it into a slightly recurved bow shape. He also had to make the steel stirrup and the rivet that would hold it. Then, there was the trigger, which was a length of metal bent twice, once semiparallel below the stock to be pushed up against the stock to trigger the nut above in the opposite direction, pivoting over a pin halfway up the slot and pressed against a notch in the bottom of the nut, where it was held in place against the tension of the bowstring, once it was strung. To fire the bolt, he could then just pull up on the trigger, depressing the sear at the trigger's far end and releasing the nut, which would then rotate and let the bowstring fly forward.

The last part of the mechanism he worked on at the forge was the nut itself. This was essentially a thick circle of metal, as wide as the stock, and with a pie-shaped cut taken out of it where the bowstring would loop over it, and a slot through it so that the bow could notch to the string, ready for firing.

He also added the useful, though not completely necessary item of another spring-steel finger bolt, secured on the bottom of the stock, to provide cocking tension to the exposed part of the trigger to fire the bow.

There was only a little extra forge work required once the bow itself had been made and assembled. This consisted of forging broadhead points for the hardwood shafts—made from left-over parts of the mantel—together with a forge-rolled section behind it that could be glued to the front of the shaft. The shaft also had fins, where a plain bolt would have had feathers, and these he made of wood and also glued on. The glue was something that Merry knew how to make out of cattle hooves.

The glue gave off an almost unbearable smell in the making—which fascinated Wolf—but when done worked very well for Jeebee's purposes, not only in making the crossbow but in other instances where glue was useful.

All in all, the making of the crossbow was a fairly straightforward procedure. But it ended up taking Jeebee a number of weeks, counting the time involved in obtaining the necessary parts from the car and the ranch house and doing the work of assembly. One of his last jobs was stringing the bow before it was attached to the stock.

Since the bow had, he estimated, between eighty and a hundred and ten pounds of pull, he would barely be able to cock it with his foot in the stirrup and lifting up on it. Stringing the bow in the first place was therefore a problem. It was solved by putting the forged bow stave across a couple of logs and placing on top of it a long lever of a narrow log, with a rock holding down the short end of the lever that was heavier than the bow pole's weight.

With this done, Jeebee was able to push down on the long end of the lever and weight it with another rock. This bent the steel bow stave to the point where he could loop the ready-made brake-cable bowstring over its tip, onto the leather cushioning that he had wrapped around the bow ends where the loops of the string would rest.

Finally assembled, and with about a half-dozen bolts made, with the broadhead points, the wooden vanes glued in, and butt caps made of cartridge casing, he tried it out.

He had brought a piece of three-eighths-inch plywood up from the ranch that compared, according to his memory, with the one that had been used as a target when he had first seen and fired a crossbow. He cut it in half, putting one piece loosely behind the other, since he did not want to lose the bolt if it indeed went all the way through, as he had lost the first bolt of the crossbow he had been allowed to fire several years back. Now, he cocked the device, put the bolt in the slot, and aimed at the plywood from an easy fifteen yards of distance.

The crossbow exceeded expectations. It went clear through the outer piece of plywood and its point penetrated at least a third and possibly half of the way through the second piece, so that he had to cut the wood around it before he could wriggle it out.

In the immediate days following, he practiced with his crossbow whenever he had spare time; and at last became reasonably accurate with it.

He was very pleased with this addition to their armory. He

had wished for another rifle that Merry could keep with her while he was gone. While making the crossbow, he had thought that perhaps he could leave the crossbow or the rifle with her. Accordingly he let her try her marksmanship with the crossbow. But it soon became obvious that if he left either weapon with her, it would have to be the rifle.

It was strange. Merry, who was literally a superb shot with both rifle and pistol, was much more erratic and inaccurate with a crossbow than Jeebee himself. Jeebee puzzled over this. But the only answer he could come up with was that, since he had envisioned the crossbow and wanted one since he was a child, he might have approached the use of the weapon with more enthusiasm than she did. Either that, or else she was trying to use it the way she used a firearm, which fitted the shoulder differently, as well as having a definite kick and a different flight pattern to its missile.

In the end he was glad she was better off with the rifle. The bolt of the crossbow was a penetrating missile, rather than a smashing missile. For that very reason, it was slower to kill. It achieved its end by internal bleeding of its target, unless whoever fired it was lucky enough to hit dead on a vulnerable spot like the heart or an eye socket. That meant it produced a wounded animal, which could be more of a threat before it finally died.

Jeebee was in the smithy, engrossed in making some more bolts, in preparation for his first attempt with the crossbow on a hunting trip to the flatlands, when he heard a curious thumping sound from overhead. He listened tensely for a second. It was not coming from directly above him but was being transmitted to him through the earth and the wooden walls he had put around the forge. He dropped his work and ran to and out of the outer door, snatching up the rifle from just inside the door of the inner room.

Outside, the rifle held ready for use, he swung about to look at the bluff above the cave.

There, just above the cave, Merry was digging into the cliff and into the bluff face.

His hands sagged with the rifle as the tension abruptly went out of him.

She was beginning, he saw, the last of his projects for him, the putting in of the skylight to the inner room. The first step in adding the skylight was, of course, to dig an opening into the bluff above the ceiling of the inner room. An opening in which the window of the skylight could be put.

She had put the metal ladder from the ranch up against the front wall of the cave; and climbed up it until she could step out onto the sloping face of the bluff above. There, she was busily at work with a shovel. Jeebee stepped hastily back to avoid being hit by a shovelful of earth and took a calmer look at what he was seeing.

Next to where she was digging on the steep face of the earthen bluff was something that Jeebee squinted at, not understanding what he saw at first glance.

Then he recognized that it was a platform of stakes driven at a slight angle deep into the bluff face. Supported by those stakes and firmly tied to them was the chest pack in which Merry normally carried Paul, outside the cave. It was just possible to catch sight of Paul's face above his wrappings, and then his arms waved suddenly.

He was dressed inches thick in warm clothing, and seemed to be enjoying the open air, the sunlight, and the vigorous activity of his mother, next to him.

"Merry!" Jeebee shouted to her. "What are you doing that for? That's my job!"

"When you're ready to get to work on it, fine," Merry said a little breathlessly, without stopping her digging. "Meanwhile, I'm making a start. Don't worry, I won't dig down into the top of our room."

"Well, I'll take over now!" Jeebee shouted.

"When you're done," Merry called back. "Until then I'll keep on working."

"I'm done now," Jeebee said, guiltily conscious that he had been lingering over last-minute touches on the crossbow bolts.

Jeebee went up the ladder after her. She continued to work until he was right beside her, but then stopped and passed the shovel over without protest. It was not one of the tools he had gotten around to making at the forge yet. This was a rather rusty one they had been fortunate enough to find in the ruins of the ranch. They also, of course, had the small collapsible entrenching shovel that Jeebee had carried down with him on the horse or sledge when he went hunting over the snow on the flats in wintertime. But this old, full-sized shovel was a great deal more effective up here, moving several times the load of earth that the entrenching tool was capable of lifting.

Jeebee took over and was soon hard at work digging back into the bluff over the ceiling of the inner room. The supports he had put up earlier to hold back the earth above them were probably sufficient so that he would be able to stand and work on the two-by-fours that made the rafters of the ceiling, but just to be on the safe side he added a few extra supports and planks between them.

The result was that the outer room's ceiling became a solid floor as he gradually cleared dirt out to a height of about five feet at the front of the opening in the bluff, shallowing down until it met the wall in the back of the ceiling.

In this new space he set up new shoring timbers and support for the earth that would be above it.

He was still hard at work, but ready to quit, when Wolf returned with the evening. Seeing him up there inside the hole he had made, Wolf was instantly interested and started to climb the ladder toward him, then changed his mind before his hind legs were off the ground. His partner, Jeebee had found out sometime back, could climb ladders with no trouble or worry at all, but he was not at all happy about climbing down them.

Jeebee shouted the news of Wolf's arrival to Merry inside, went down the ladder, and after preliminary greetings, the two moved inside the room where Merry and Paul were.

Merry had gradually relaxed her concern over allowing Wolf close to Paul. Far from being a threat to the child, Wolf was very gentle and solicitous toward Paul. He would, in fact, endure more from Paul than he would from Jeebee or Merry. He insisted on sniffing the youngster over thoroughly each time he came in for greetings; and if one of Paul's waving arms happened to stick a finger into his eye while he was doing this, he merely squeezed the eye half shut and went on about his examination.

Wolf's fascination with Paul did not seem to fade with familiarity. He was clearly ready to continue being full of wonder about him. From the wolf books, Jeebee had learned that this was typical of wolves, that they were all very interested in the young of their own species and would be both caring toward them and willing to play with them for hours at a time. From Wolf's point of view, Paul was plainly one more member of the community.

This attitude had been very clear in all of Wolf's behavior toward Jeebee and Merry, but it evidently had some stretch in it as regards Paul. Not that Wolf was ever close to the baby without Merry and usually Jeebee hovering over the two of them. Wolf's instinct, for instance, had been to try to pick up Paul in his jaws. But Merry put a stop to that.

Wolf was apparently ready, at least within limits, to adapt to Paul, who was still lying there in his crib, not yet up to crawling, when young wolf pups would already have been tumbling around outside the den in which they were born.

According to wolf rules and patterns they had become a pack. Wolf and Jeebee by themselves had simply been a traveling pair. Fixed in position, territorially, but with the addition of Merry and now Paul, the social climate had changed. Wolf clearly looked on Jeebee as the alpha male, Merry as the alpha female, and himself as the beta male of the pack. Paul, he probably considered a somewhat strange wolf pup—that was, if he had ever had any acquaintance at all with wolf pups himself from the time he had been very young.

If he had been raised almost completely by humans, thought Jeebee, he might even not recognize a real wolf puppy for what it was, at first seeing. Though, once he had gotten over his initial caution toward it as toward all strange things, he would be sure to investigate it and come to accept it quickly enough.

CHAPTER 37

The end of summer, fall, and winter abruptly accelerated, the one into the next just after it. Suddenly there simply was not enough time for everything.

The business of building the partial room above the old ceiling of the inner room and putting a triple window in a new wall across the front of the bluff higher up turned out to be more complicated than Jeebee had thought. One of the problems he ran into was shoring to hold up the ceiling of the skylight room, the floor of which was itself firmly supported by the shoring and the walls of the inner room below. Also, with the best of his intentions, his work caused sand to filter down into the inner room below while he was busy, and Merry had to carry Paul in his chest pack or in his crib, either outside entirely or into the forge area, to get him away from it.

Meanwhile, there was still the hunting to be done. The crossbow turned out to work very well as a cattle killer, but as he had expected, its bolt killed by internal hemorrhage, without the shocking power of the much-faster bullet from a gun. The result was that on several expeditions, Jeebee needed to be thankful for being on horseback and therefore more able to dodge the charge of a wounded cow or steer.

However, Jeebee was learning how to use the weapon accurately from a greater range. As a result, with luck, if he shot the animal from far enough off, it did not connect the arrow hitting it with the distant sight of him. It also put more space between him and the wounded animal, if it decided to charge. This difference would become critical once he was back to pulling the sledge down over the snow to the flatlands for his hunting, and facing his prey on foot.

In the meantime, back up at the cave, he had to take time out to thoroughly clean the chimney he had built and erect a small but strong-roofed enclosure over the point where it emerged from the ground so there was no danger of it getting blocked by snow or windblown debris. He and Merry were one thing. But he did not want young Paul exposed to a sudden stoppage of the chimney and smoke billowing out into the inner room.

With all this handled, one way or another, Jeebee had still not finished the skylight when the first flakes of snow began to fall. Luckily it was just a snow shower, which lasted for perhaps twenty minutes and then stopped, but it told him his time was limited. He burned his electric lighting recklessly in the upper room and worked into the night. He had chosen his three windows and set them in place. Now he began the finish work around them, and the last sealing of the wall outside, working by artificial light.

He managed to get it done by morning, but he had exhausted all but one of his batteries, and he himself was ready to drop. He slept for about four hours, then went to the final job of mortaring it weather-tight. This meant taking clay, which now could not be left outside for any length of time without freezing, mixing it with water, and carrying it outside a load at a time to seal the edges around the window and the new section of upper wall.

Merry would have helped him, but there was not enough room for both of them to work up there. By late afternoon, snow had started again. He got the work finished, just in time, and nearly fell off the ladder, trying to get down it.

He came back inside and started blindly to go to work at

finally opening up the ceiling above their heads. Merry stopped him.

"Have you no sense left at all?" Merry said. "You're so close to being unconscious, you don't know whether you're standing on your head or your feet."

He turned around to argue with her, and found that the movement made him dizzy. Subsiding, he let her pilot him back to the bed, and lay down on it.

"Just give me an hour," he said, "then I can finish it."

"Hour, nothing!" Merry retorted. "You've got us sealed in up there now. You've got all winter to take down the ceiling of this room. You sleep and just let yourself sleep as much as you can."

He still felt that he should be arguing with her, but somehow the strength was not in him. He did not remember any more until he woke, finally, to find sunlight in his face.

He came to, startled, opening his eyes and sitting up on the edge of the bed at the same time. Above him the ceiling had been half torn down toward the front of the inner room, and daylight was streaming through and down upon them. There was a fire in the fireplace, Paul was silent in his crib, and Merry was busy sewing something at the table.

"You opened up the ceiling—" Jeebee said stupidly.

Merry bit off a thread.

"And I can do the rest of it without your help," she said without looking at him. But her tone was soft. "Go back to sleep."

He tried to stand up, found he was still dizzy, and lay back down on the bed. Sleep came again, at once. However, this time it was not a deep unconsciousness, in which he would even lose track of time. This time he dreamed; and it was the old nightmare that he had carried with him out of Michigan into northern Indiana and westward.

He dreamed again that he was working in the study group, and that the screen in front of him was full of the symbols of his equations. Suddenly a darkness, just a pinpoint of darkness at first, appeared near the middle of the screen to obliterate some of them. But it grew, spreading and wiping out all his work.

It was, as he had long since figured out, his consciousness of the Collapse, in retrospect coming to interrupt and destroy all that he had tried to do—he and the others. Again he dreamed of the black shape that pursued him, cornered him, over and over, looming closer and closer, to blot out everything as it came close to blot him out also.

He woke, sweating.

Merry was seated on the bed beside him, her hands on his shoulders. She had been the one who had seized him, not the darkness.

"You had a nightmare," she said, relaxing her grip and letting him sag back against the pillow. "You were shouting—something about iron."

"The iron years," he said dully.

"The iron years?" She looked at him narrowly.

"It was just my name for this time we're in, that's followed the Collapse," Jeebee said. "That's all. I thought—I told myself we'd gone back to the time of iron. You understand?"

Merry nodded her head.

"I think so," she said. "You mean we've moved into a time when things are hard, when everything is hard, like iron?"

"That's it," Jeebee said, remembering even as he spoke to her. "Maybe a little more than that. I meant—you know, there was a time once when iron ruled the world. Men with iron weapons, in iron armor, ruled everything. And in some ways we've gone back to it now, and it will last at least for decades, maybe for a couple of hundred years—"

He broke off, looking up at her concerned face.

"Oh, we'll go back to civilization, back to technology," he said. "It's inevitable. It won't be exactly the same, but the knowledge'll all be built up again. It's always been that way."

"Always?" said Merry. "This never happened before—the Collapse with everything falling apart, the whole world going bankrupt, transportation and communication and everything failing, all at once."

"No," Jeebee answered, "but that's just the shape it's taken in our time. Before that there was pestilence, or barbarians who took everything, including life, from all but a few lucky ones, and each time the race built back to get pretty much on the track it'd been on from the start. We'll do it again. But it's going to be a hard time, in between. That's what I was thinking of when I started calling them 'iron years.'"

She took a corner of the top sheet and wiped his damp face, gently.

"It's my fault," she said.

"Your fault?" Jeebee stared at her.

"Oh, I don't mean the iron years. I mean, you overworked. You drove yourself to the dropping point. And that was my fault because I started you out by shoving you in that direction. I was so full of thinking what we needed for Paul through this winter. I should have known you don't need prodding, that you'd go to your absolute limits anyway, without anyone shoving you from behind."

"Well, then." Jeebee reached up and pulled her down to him so that he could kiss her. "I would have done the same thing anyway then, wouldn't I?"

"Maybe," Merry said, laying her cheek alongside his, "but if you do, from now on, you'll only have yourself to blame."

Jeebee looked around him. There was a strange quality to the light coming down on them from the skylight. It could not be just that they were later in the afternoon; the angle of the light had not changed that much. He could have only been asleep another hour or so at the most.

"I've got to get up," he said.

Merry's hands pressed his shoulders softly back toward the bed.

"It's snowing. Snowing heavily," she said. "We're locked in for a while. Besides, it's time for you to do nothing for a few days and mend. Give yourself time."

"Still, I—"

"No still," Merry interrupted. "It'll be hard to stop the wheels spinning at first, but you'll just have to wait until they do. Now lie back, take it easy, do nothing; at least till the storm stops and probably for the next few days. We're in no hurry, now. We're sealed in, nice and tight and warm, the three of us.

We've got plenty of meat and vegetables stored. There's all the time in the world for us, now."

She was right, of course. It took Jeebee a little time to admit it to himself, but the way he had collapsed physically before his first long sleep was something with which he could not argue.

He worked at resting. For the first two days, it was indeed work. He had to fight to keep from getting up and doing things; and in the end, about the third or fourth day, he did let himself finish opening up the whole ceiling of the inner room to the skylight. He also let himself do small things like bringing in wood to keep the fireplace fire going, and making sure the solar blanket was not covered by snow, but hung up against the front wall of the cave, where it could get the full benefit of the sun to recharge the batteries he had depleted during his last orgy of work.

Little by little, he relaxed. It did not come easily, but gradually the urge crying out inside of him to be busy, always busy, muted and fell silent. He reread his wolf books, he watched Merry, he thought, and above all he studied young Paul, sitting in a chair by the cradle and watching the baby, both asleep and awake, for long periods.

There was a healing element in this period. He could feel it, but the machinery of it did not come out into the open of his conscious mind until he felt Merry's arm around his shoulder one day as he was sitting watching Paul and saw her gazing down at him.

He looked up at her.

"You know," he said, "I told you about that moment I had with him during the birth, when his eyes opened? That moment of bonding?"

Merry nodded.

"He gives me something every time I look at him," Jeebee said slowly. He looked back down at Paul now. "It's strange . . . I'm just trying to put things together, trying to figure out how something as large as this could happen to me—you, and then him."

He looked back up to Merry.

"I'm just trying to make sense of it," he said.

Merry leaned down and kissed his cheek.

"That's one of the things that's so lovely about you," she said. "You're always trying to understand."

She ruffled the hair on the back of his head with her hand softly, and left him for some knitting she had been working at over a period of time. It was to be a warm, balaclava-type helmet, leaving only his eyes, nose, and mouth uncovered, to wear while hunting. It was being made of dark blue yarn. Not, he thought, as bright as those flashing eyes he'd uncovered just after Paul was born. Not as blue, because nothing could be quite like that in his experience again.

The snow had stopped after several days and it was followed by unusually intense cold. He stayed in the cabin, intending to wait this out, but when it did warm, it warmed in the night along toward morning, and with daybreak, snow was beginning to fall again.

It was not a heavy snowfall, but it lasted. It was the second day after that before he finally went outside to see how things were. The weather was cold, but normal for this time of year, climbing a few degrees above freezing in the daytime and dropping to ten to fifteen degrees below zero, Fahrenheit, at night. However, the snow was not so deep that he would not be able to ride one of the horses through it.

As Merry had mentioned, they were already well stocked with meat, and the freeze hole held the nighttime ground-level temperatures all day long at the bottom of the pit, so that the meat stayed frozen hard.

They did not need a hunting trip, therefore, but there were some small things he thought he might want to bring up from the ranch, and he wanted to have a look at how thickly the snow lay in various parts of the foothills and down on the flat itself, since this would give him an idea of how it would build up and drift down there in future hunting trips.

He saddled Sally accordingly and set out. He intended to take only the revolver and the crossbow, but Merry insisted on his leaving the pistol and crossbow with her and taking the rifle instead. It was possibly more sensible, but he had an uncomfortable feeling at leaving the two of them alone there, with less defensive firepower than he was taking along himself, particularly since he did not intend to hunt.

The sky was almost clear of clouds. It had that high blue look that sky gets in winter, where it seems to go on and on forever upward. In many places the snow was only about four to six inches deep. Only under the cliffs and in blocked corners had drifts piled up. He had to descend from Sally's saddle and lead her by the bridle in only a few spots.

One of these was the shale slope. Ordinarily he went around this. But it remained the most direct route to the ranch. Now, as usual, it was a slanted white sheet from far below up to the bluff where already a drift had piled high. The mouth of the hole that he had guessed had once been a den was still visible as a blackness about halfway across it, but to his surprise, and with a certain amount of shock, he saw animal footprints leading to it—leading to it only.

He examined the prints. He was even now not an expert in reading prints to know what animal had made them. But these, he could be fairly certain, were bear-paw prints, and they were prints made by the feet of a bear much larger than the one who had attacked him down in the willow bottoms. It could even be that they were the prints of a grizzly.

He shied away from the thought. Blowing and drifting altered prints in snow, but these were fairly fresh and he was almost certain they were bear tracks.

No tracks led out at all. If it was a bear, it had already begun to hibernate. In any case, the damage done by leaving his own and Sally's trail was already done.

But he had stopped to examine the prints at a point a good twenty feet from the entrance to the cave. He now turned about and led Sally softly back the way they had come, while making a mental note not to venture near this area again until there had been at least one other snowstorm to cover his tracks. There should be no trail then, for whatever was in the hole to follow back to the cave.

By the time he left the shale close to where he had originally stepped onto it, his first fears had subsided to a great extent. If the bear had not come out—he might just as well assume flatly from the start that it was a bear of some sort, grizzly or black, though it was hard to believe a black had left tracks that size—it had to have already started its hibernation. And it was not likely to break that hibernation until spring. Unless something disturbed it, they could forget about it until then.

His first impulse had been to return himself and the rifle directly to the cave so that Merry and Paul would not be at the mercy of the bear, with nothing but the revolver and the crossbow to hold him off—and little good a .38 handgun would do against something like a grizzly. In fact, Jeebee doubted that any weapon they had could do him any real damage, unless a bolt from the crossbow, planted into its lower body area, would eventually bleed it to death. But by that time he could have destroyed not only the cave but both Merry and Paul.

But it was ridiculous to return, he thought, now. He could not stay forted up with them all winter. He would have to leave on hunting trips and various other things. It was not even sensible to go back and sit tight until it snowed again. They might, at this time of year, go as much as a couple of weeks without even a light snowfall.

Accordingly, he continued on his swing down to the ranch, which had been lightly touched by the snow, except for those corners where it had drifted into the exposed parts of the house or outbuildings. He got the small things he had intended to pick up—they consisted of some shingles he had rescued from the ash pile on the floor of the ranch's former smithy and a bathroom scale that he and Merry had talked about bringing up to the cave several times but somehow had never gotten around to taking.

With the relatively light weight of these, he made a swing out into the open range and found as he had expected that except where the land dipped enough to accumulate drifted snow, the going was not bad at all. With little deep snow, and without a strong wind to herd them in a particular direction, his experience now told him, the wild cattle would be following their normal pattern of roaming freely. He swung back into the foothills at last and returned to the ranch by a route that avoided the shale slope entirely.

CHAPTER 38

Back at the cave all was well. Jeebee congratulated himself silently on having the common
sense to continue his sweep instead of simply heading back here.
He unsaddled Sally, put her in the corral, and returned with the
saddle and the things he had gathered from the ranch to the inner
room.

"We've got a hibernating bear for a neighbor," he told
Merry, once everything was put away.

"Bear?" Merry said, frowning. "Where?"

"More than half a mile from here," Jeebee answered,
"maybe a kilometer, or even a bit more than a kilometer. You
know, the hole in the shale slope?"

"That?" said Merry.

"That," Jeebee answered. "You remember I thought it
might've been used as a den, before. I saw the tracks going in,
just today. There weren't any coming out. It must be a pretty big
bear. It might be a grizzly."

"Grizzly!" Merry stopped what she was doing. "I don't like
that. A grizzly, this close!"

"You know, the year round," Jeebee said, "they could come
within fifty yards of the cave here and we'd never know it. There
can't be too many grizzlies, and bears move around a lot anyway.
They have to find food. Besides, remember I told you that the

tracks led into the hole but not out? Whatever it is, if it's a bear, it's started hibernating and won't come out until spring. We'll just keep it in mind, and I think I'm going to insist on going hunting with just the pistol and the crossbow. You keep the rifle here from now on."

"There ought to be some way of killing it while it's still asleep in there," said Merry, "if it's a grizzly. I don't want a grizzly anywhere near Paul."

"I can't think of any way," Jeebee answered, "but if it is a grizzly, the .30/06 is rather light to kill it with a single shot unless you reach a vital area. And I don't like the idea of trying to hit a vital area in a pitch-dark hole, particularly if it's curled up, the way I imagine it would be if it was hibernating."

"We could take the floodlight with the battery," Merry said. "I could hold the light on it, while you shot it—as many times as it took."

"And what if it came out after us in spite of the fact it had been shot several times? I'd have a rifle that was already proving it was too light, and you'd just have a revolver."

"I could take that crazy spear of yours," said Merry.

Jeebee snorted.

"If it came to that," he said, "I'd take the spear and the light. You'd do the shooting. You're the better shot."

He took a deep breath.

"In any case," he said, "the very idea of trying to shoot it now is ridiculous. We'd just be borrowing trouble. We'd be giving it a chance to kill us both—and then what would happen to Paul? On the other hand, if we just leave it alone, it'll sleep till spring. Then when it comes out, it's likely to go in any direction but here. It wouldn't have denned up here unless it belongs in this territory. If it does, then it knows that there's cattle down below, and its first instinct on waking is going to be to head down onto the flat. It'll know that after a winter there'll be a number of dead cattle that're still eatable because they were frozen and covered with snow until spring. A hungry grizzly that's been hibernating is going to think of that dead meat first, and go for it. There's every reason he should go straight down there, and no particular reason to come our way."

Merry plainly was not convinced, but neither did she continue to argue. Jeebee had a sneaking feeling that it was his question about what would happen to Paul if they were both killed that had really changed her mind about going after the bear now.

He felt a little guilty, as if he had unfairly bludgeoned his way to winning the argument. But he consoled himself with the fact that after all, what he said was no more than the truth. A bear that size had to be more than a year old. If it was in this district, it knew about the cattle and had seen more than one spring, with its frozen carcasses gradually being uncovered as the snow melted. It would certainly head for the flatlands when it woke.

So they left the matter there. Jeebee sat back and waited for the next snow. Once his tracks were covered, he could relax. But instead of producing more snow, the weather perversely decided to get warmer.

Not only that, but the warming weather continued into the next day, the next, and the next. This unusual spell was then interrupted by a sudden cold snap lasting overnight, followed the next morning by a heavy, but short-term snow shower, the results of which lay on the ground for perhaps half an hour in the already bare spots exposed to the sun, and then vanished. The days went back to being warm again.

The renewal of the warm spell was an unexpected gift from the weather that gave them time to do the last-minute things that Jeebee's collapse and the first snowstorm seemed to have lost to them.

In one of the outbuildings of the ranch, there had been the dusty, obviously long-unused potbellied stove from which Jeebee had gotten the flue for his forge. For the sake of young Paul, Merry had wanted to bring this up and vent it out their chimney as a replacement for the fireplace. As she pointed out to Jeebee, it would be much better for cooking, and much more efficient at providing heat to the inside of the cave.

During the warm days of fall, Jeebee had put off bringing it up from day to day, until suddenly he had found himself racing the onset of winter to get the skylight finished in time. By the time he did, it had been no longer possible for the two horses to take the trailer down.

The trailer had been absolutely necessary. The stove was too great a weight for either horse to carry alone. The feet would come off it, and a few other extraneous parts, but the main weight of the cast-iron body was more than even Brute could bring up the slopes. With the trailer, on the other hand, the two horses could transport it handily, provided snow had not made the slopes impassable.

Now, thanks to this freak warm spell, there was enough bare ground all the way down to the ranch so that Jeebee could try to take the trailer for it. So he did. Meanwhile, up at the cave, Merry was busy taking down some shelves and putting up new ones, to fit the cooking process more conveniently around a stove rather than a fireplace.

There were a few slippery spots and patches of ground that had been iced by the freeze, then lightly covered with the new snow, that Jeebee had to get the horses and trailer over on the way down to the ranch. Otherwise he had no trouble and found nothing that would keep them from pulling the stove back up.

On the way down, at a point at which he could do so, Jeebee used his binoculars to check on the shale slope from a distance. To his relief, there were large bare patches on it, too, and with the powerful binoculars he was able to focus in closely on the mouth of the hole. All sign of his being near it had already gone.

He noticed for the first time that on top of the bluff that crowned the slope, there was still the unusual, tremendous accumulation of snow. More than he would have thought would have come from the snowfall alone. Perhaps there had been a snow-slide from the slopes higher up, which were more steep, and it had found a natural barrier to pile up against in the upturned lip of the bluff.

He continued to the ranch. It was even more clear of snow than he had expected. He loaded the stove with its flue, and everything else that belonged to it, on the trailer, and lashed the pieces tightly into place. Luckily, all its necessary parts were there, including lids for the two cooking surfaces in the top of the stove, through which fuel could be added, as well as through the door in front.

The horses made relatively easy work of getting back up to the cave. Jeebee, with Merry's help, spent the rest of that day and the next two, setting the stove up and getting it working.

Jeebee found he regretted losing the open fire of the fireplace. On the other hand, there was no doubt that the stove was more efficient, more practical, and a great deal safer to use. He was pleased that he did not have to rob his smithy of flue sections to get enough to vent the stove up the chimney, and more than pleased to be able to get rid of the smoke up the flue of the fireplace rather than up the nakedly clay-mortared stone walls of his homemade chimney.

He set up the flue within the chimney, pushing it up until it poked into the little weather top he had built aboveground on the top of the bluff for it. The flue would be easier to take apart, section by section, when spring came. It would need to be cleaned then of tars and possible flammable soots. Just as the interior of the chimney had been, though he had done his best to scrub the latter as clean as possible.

The batteries were mostly back on full charge. As a result, he and Merry could work into the evening if they wanted to. After they got the stove set up and cooked their first meal on it, they did just that. There were a number of odds and ends to finish with Merry's new shelves, and a rearrangement of furniture to be made and distributed around the stove rather than the fireplace. Jeebee promised himself to dig the room bigger during their stormbound days in the winter.

Wolf had had more than a few opportunities to investigate the stove while it was being moved in and set up. He had been wary of it at first, as he was with anything strange. However, by the time Merry and Paul had eaten their first meal to be cooked on it, he had become more or less reconciled to it. Although Jeebee secretly felt that Wolf, like himself, missed the open flames of the fireplace—to lie before and gaze into.

One of the reasons it had taken them so long to put up the stove was the fact that the flue of the original chimney started relatively low down, and the flue, the round flexible piping from the stove, had been designed to go out through a wall at about head height.

Jeebee had needed to remove a section of the wall and dig into a point at which he could make a new entrance into the chimney for the piping of the flue. It had also been necessary for him to go on top of the bluff and partially dismantle his weather cover in order to fasten the flue at its top. Moreover, the round metal piping had to be secured to the chimney wall, below, where it entered it.

For this, Jeebee had already forged thin metal strapping, lengths of flat metal that could be bent around the pipe and anchored by spikes driven into the clay between the rocks, and then mortared tightly with fresh clay. Luckily, the metal-clad asbestos collar that had been designed by the stove factory to protect the wood of any wall it went through—as it did in the inner room before reaching and entering the chimney further up—had been among the rest of the dusty parts available. Jeebee could have forged a metal collar, but no insulating material like asbestos was to be found anywhere around the ranch.

As a result, that last night, they ended up working almost until midnight.

Luckily, Paul had finally taken to sleeping straight through the night, now. They both tumbled gratefully into bed and Jeebee fell soundly asleep.

He was wakened, unexpectedly, and sat up in the darkness to switch on one of the headlamps that was within arm's reach of the bed, its light directed away from their eyes. Merry was also awake and starting to sit up beside him.

"What was that?" Jeebee said to her.

"I don't know," Merry answered. They looked at each other. It had been an extended roar, far off, like the sound of a freight train, amplified and compressed. Now everything was utterly silent once more.

"Whatever it was," said Jeebee, "it was some ways away from here."

"Yes," said Merry.

Slowly, they lay back down on the bed again, side by side.

"I'll take a look around in the morning," said Jeebee.

"That's a good idea," Merry said. "Whatever made that noise, I want to know what it was."

Jeebee lay for a little while before he could drop off again. Long before he managed it, he could hear Merry, breathing slowly and steadily in her own sleep beside him. He had switched off the headlamp, and they were in utter darkness. Finally, slumber claimed him also.

He woke again—suddenly.

There was early dawn light coming through the skylight above him, and Merry was not beside him. For a second he lay, wondering what had woken him. Then he heard it again, and recognized it as he had, even in the depths of his slumber. It was a frantic almost-scream of horses, neighing in terror from the corral. In the same moment he heard Merry's voice from beyond the wall that separated him from the front room.

"Jeebee!"

The word was no scream. It was a shout. But it carried the same note of alarm that had sounded in the voices of the horses. At the same time, he heard the bark of the .30/06 from beyond the wall at the head of their bed.

His reaction was instinctive and immediate. He grabbed the revolver from the two pegs on the wall behind the bed, as two other pegs above these had held the rifle, now gone.

Holding the handgun, he flung himself out of bed and through the door to the outer room. Merry was firing the rifle through one of the loopholes he had built into the front wall for that purpose. The outer door of the cold room was slightly ajar, showing a slice of gray, beginning daylight through it. He made two racing steps through it, out into the open, and saw, less than fifty meters off, the massive shape of a grizzly, coming toward them fast on all four legs.

"My God!" he said out loud, without thinking. "It's the horses! It's come for the horses!"

"Get back in here, Jeebee!" Merry's voice cried behind him. But the bear had already seen him, and was now aiming, not in the general direction of the cave and the corral, but directly at him. Jeebee ducked back into the outer room, swinging the outside door half closed, but leaving himself room to fire through it with the revolver. He and Merry fired almost together.

"You were right, Jeebee!" Merry's voice was tight. "It's like throwing rocks at him, using this rifle!"

It was true, Jeebee saw through the crack in the door, even as he was aiming with the pistol and firing again. The grizzly was paying no attention to the bullets that must be hitting him. Even if he was missing, Merry would not be. Not at this short range and with a rifle.

"Try to get him in the eye or mouth!" said Jeebee. Where was Wolf? It was dawn, his time to come in. If nothing else, he could harass and distract the grizzly, as he had the black bear down by the willows.

The pistol clicked empty in his hand. He threw it away, snatched up the crossbow, then threw it down again. The single bolt he would have time for might damage the bear enough to kill it, eventually, but it would not slow it down now. A wildness exploded in Jeebee. He snatched up the boar spear from where it leaned against the front wall beside the crossbow and burst out again through the door out into the open.

"Jeebee, come back here!" he heard Merry shouting. But in this moment he knew enough not to listen.

Just then, as if out of the dawn light itself, Wolf did appear. He burst onto the scene from between the trees behind the bear and to Jeebee's right. It was his usual time, and he came.

The dawn wind was from the cave to the bear. Wolf could well have scented the other creature from several hundred yards behind on his way home—scented it attacking his pack territory—and come instinctively to its defense.

Now he was coming at the bear from behind, not as he had come at the one down in the willow bottoms, but as he had attacked the part-collie at the station, in his fantastic ground-eating leaps of approach.

The grizzly heard him and whirled, standing up on his hind legs, but not before Wolf reached it and made a dart at its hindquarters.

The bear struck at him. Not so much batting, as reaching suddenly with both great paws, as if to catch Wolf between them. But Wolf was already back out of reach, changing his angle of attack, and as Jeebee shouted and the bear looked for a moment at him, darting in on the larger animal once again.

Once more the grizzly grabbed at him, and missed. Still at full extension, it threw one paw outward, catching Wolf with the back of it, high on one shoulder—just barely touched him, it seemed, but Wolf went tumbling down the slope of the meadow toward the nearby stream.

The grizzly, still on its hind legs, turned again toward Jeebee. Merry's rifle continued to sound, and the bear continued to ignore the bullets that must be striking it. It came toward Jeebee on its hind legs.

Jeebee saw it coming, appearing to grow enormously as it got closer. Head and shoulders towering over him, it seemed to swell to mountainous proportions, blotting out the earth and sky, black and invulnerable.

Its blackness was the blackness of his dreams, but now, here in daylight and reality. As a formless void in his dreams, that blackness had destroyed all his work. It had ridden his sleeping hours and pursued him out of Michigan and westward across the devastated land. It had never left him permanently, and now it had taken living shape. Merry and Paul were behind him, and he was the only thing that stood between them and it. A wildness inside him picked him up and drove him. He lifted the boar spear and ran toward the grizzly.

In that second there was no fear or fury in him, nothing but purpose. What was, was before him; and their coming together was inevitable. He ran full at the bear with his spear in one hand.

In the moment before they reached each other he jerked the spear up into both hands, hurled himself forward—"Aim for the balls," Nick had said. He remembered the black bear in the willows. As they came together at their combined speeds, he shoved down the butt of the spear to brace it against ground.

It was like hurling his body against a wall of rock; and then the spear, its point now buried deep in the soft lower body of the grizzly, kicked in his grasp so strongly that it threw him away, tumbling as Wolf had tumbled.

He scrambled back to his feet and saw the grizzly, all its attention now removed from any human target and focused only on the visible shaft of the spear that stuck out from its body. Wolf was dodging in, out, closing his jaws on the thick legs from behind; but the bear ignored him, also.

All its attention was on the visible part of the spear. The shaggy black head and open jaws were lowered to bite at it, but the jaws could barely reach down that far, and its teeth scraped ineffectively upon iron. The bear battered and pulled at the shaft with his paws, roaring each time he struck it, and the point tore and cut inside him. The wooden part of the shaft snapped and splintered, but the backward-pointing tines of the spearhead kept it from being pulled free.

It fought the embedded spear like an enemy, the only enemy there was. Wolf continued harrying from behind, and from the loophole Merry was still pumping rifle shots into the great body. Jeebee stood, empty-handed, less than four paces off, staring, hypnotized by the massive, wounded creature.

The bear began to stagger, still struggling to rid itself of the spear with teeth and claws. It stumbled drunkenly for several steps as if fighting to keep its balance. Then it lifted its head, opened its mouth, and gave utterance to a strangely humanlike, moaning roar of agony and frustration.

One of its legs buckled. It fell to the ground on its side, with one spasmodic jerk moving its hind legs up toward its belly like a man with a cramp. It lay still.

Merry's rifle stopped firing. Wolf darted in, snapped at the throat of the fallen animal and leaped away before it was possible to know if his jaws had actually touched it. He made another snarling, half dart forward, then checked, still some feet away, tensely staring, bright-eyed, at the still beast.

For a long moment he stood there, jaws open and panting, gazing at the bear with a sort of alert disappointment. As if he waited for the dead animal to get up and threaten them again.

The grizzly did not move. Wolf stepped closer and sniffed at it, waited, sniffed again. Suddenly he darted his nose under one heavy forelimb, lifted it slightly and dodged back—all in one quick movement. He waited. The foreleg lay where it had dropped.

His tail and ears rose. His head lifted. The tension began to leak from him.

But Jeebee was already heading away, back into the cold room. He was just in time to catch Merry as she turned toward him. She dropped the rifle and her knees sagged. He caught her and held her tight against him. Her arms wrapped around him and clutched him, with the grip of someone finding refuge, at last.

CHAPTER 39

As he turned toward the door to the inner room of the cave, however, she stiffened suddenly.

"You don't have to carry me!" she said. "I can walk!"

Jeebee grunted a negative, pushed through the door with his shoulder, and laid her down on the bed. At his refusal to let go of her, she had relaxed against him again, with a little sigh; but the minute she touched the bed she bounced up off of it onto her feet as if it had been a bed of live coals.

"Paul!" she said.

She darted past Jeebee across the room, switching on the small lamp over Paul's cradle. But it was not really necessary. Jeebee blessed the skylight. The daylight coming through it now was bright enough to see the interior of the room clearly.

In that second, Merry reached the crib where Paul lay, checked herself with her hands on the side of it, and gave a long, slow sigh of relief.

"He's still sleeping," she said fondly. "He slept through it all."

Jeebee sat down on the edge of the bed. A weakness had suddenly taken him. He was lost in the moment in which he and the grizzly had come together, and he stayed lost in it. He was only dimly aware that Merry had come back and climbed past him onto the inner side of the bed again.

"Well?" she said warmly, after a long moment. "Are you just going to sit there?"

The imprisoning shell that was his memory of the moment that held him, broke. He felt a sudden deep hunger for her flooding all through him. At the same time the weakness he felt was still there. Numbly he became aware that the stockings in which he slept for warmth were soaked through from the snow. He was still in the underwear he had been sleeping in and in which he had fought the grizzly. His feet felt cold—they had not felt cold until now. It was almost like being two people at once. Numbly he bent to strip them off and lay back on the bed, rolling over on his right side to face Merry. He put his arms around her, abruptly with the same kind of urgency and need with which she had held him, when he caught her turning from the loophole. She put her arms around him now again, and the palm of one hand up against his face.

"You're like ice," she said.

It was true. He felt chilled all the way through now, but he had not noticed it until she had mentioned it just now. He held her warmer, living body close to him.

"It must be the reaction," he said dully. Something wet, rough, and almost hot stropped the back of his neck and he almost leaped from the bed at its touch, spinning around to receive Wolf's tongue, this time right across his face.

Jeebee spluttered and sat up, holding him off even while falling into the familiar pattern of stroking and scratching his back and behind his ears that was part of the regular dawn and twilight greeting ceremonies between themselves and this four-legged partner.

"Can't you put him out?" Merry said, behind Jeebee, and Wolf switched his attention to her, attempting to climb over Jeebee and upon the bed to get to her.

"Not now," said Jeebee, holding him off. "Not after what he's been through right along with the rest of us. He'd never forgive us."

He was himself again. The weakness was gone. Merry lifted herself up and moved around to sit beside him on the bed, and Wolf crowded against her, making greeting noises and licking at her hands and face. She, too, responded as Jeebee had, and the normal routine of the greeting ceremony—that was now also a general congratulation ceremony—continued, with Wolf ending by rolling over on his back and exposing his belly to be scratched.

"The bear caught him on his left shoulder," Jeebee said. "Feel it down there. It's a considerable bruise. At that, he was lucky he got hit with the back of the paw instead of the front, otherwise those claws would have ripped him up."

Merry scratched along Wolf's side and, under the guise of grooming motions, explored the stricken area.

"You're right," she said. "It's a bigger swelling than I can cover with my hand. And he isn't even limping!"

"He's probably just ignoring it, the way he's feeling right now," said Jeebee. "He'd react fast enough if we made a fuss over it."

"You're right," Merry said, taking her hand away from the injured area. She glanced at her fingers. "And no blood. That's just fine."

Jeebee nodded. He knew what she was referring to. He had not only found it in the wolf books he had rescued, but he had had some experience with it in the case of some minor cuts and illness in Wolf's case. The only way to get a pill into Wolf was to hide it in a piece of meat that he would swallow whole. Also, even if he would have stood still to have a wound cleansed and bandaged, the bandage would come off more quickly than it went on, the minute he was able to get his teeth on it. Happily, there was no worry about that just now, as Merry had said.

At their feet, now, Wolf decided he had had his fill of belly scratching, scrambled to his feet, gave Merry's closest hand a perfunctory farewell lick, and trotted, grinning, over to the crib to thoroughly sniff over the sleeping Paul.

Merry, long satisfied now that Wolf had accepted Paul as one of the family, made no move to stop him. A few weeks earlier she would have worried about Wolf licking the baby's face and waking him. But Paul had recently graduated to the clutching stage, and he found Wolf's muzzle irresistible. His small fist had learned to fasten on the hair there with surprising strength, and consequently, Wolf now only made a few small sounds to encourage the pup from a safe distance, then headed for the door.

"Will you look," Merry murmured, "at who killed the bear all by himself."

And, indeed, Wolf was visibly strutting as he left.

Jeebee got to his feet, and hastily, by the gentle illumination of the morning light, stripped off his clothes. As he turned back to the bed, he saw Merry had already gotten rid of hers. She lay under the bottom blanket of the number they used to cover themselves at night in colder weather, the edge pulled up to her chin and her eyes bright in her face above that edge.

Jeebee slipped in under the blanket himself and reached for her, feeling her turn toward him as he did so. There was a deeper longing in him now than he had ever felt before, and a pleasure greater than any he had ever experienced as his upper arm closed about her body and back. In fact everything was the same, but at the same time everything was different.

There was a preciousness to her, now that they were both alive and the bear which might have destroyed them both was dead. They were alive because of each other, and it was as if they had gained each other fresh for the first time, with the gaining bringing them both something of far greater value.

He had known that he had loved her since long before, back during the days at the wagon, but never had he loved her as much as in this moment, just after a time in which he might have lost her forever. Her skin was like silk under his hand and her breasts fitted the curve of his fingers, their nipples waking desire even, it seemed, in his fingers. When, after they had held each other, and touched each other for some time, he entered her, there came for him a new sense of blending together—a climax, a unification between them that seemed to make them for the first time actually one living being bound and made into a single person.

Their time together was timeless. But when they released each other at last, and lay, side by side, still holding each other, weary and happy, that singleness still held them in one indivisible unit. And together, like one person, they slid imperceptibly into sleep.

When Jeebee woke again, the day was far advanced, but still the whole room was illuminated. For the cave faced westward, and now the light of late afternoon was striking at a long angle through the skylight he had built above them.

Merry was up and dressed, stirring something in a pot on the stove, her hand moving almost automatically while she crooned softly and tunefully to Paul hidden within the high sides of the crib beside her. A Paul who was evidently awake, for he giggled and made small noises back from time to time—obviously wanting to sing, himself, as his mother was doing.

Jeebee lay there, still feeling the wonder that had been the feeling of oneness, which still enclosed him and Merry—and also Paul, now that he was awake and contributing to it. It was, Jeebee realized suddenly, the beginning of a new appreciation of being alive. They all became closer now, and would continue to be so from now on, than they had ever been before; because they had defended all that was valuable to them, and won in that defense.

Just about then Jeebee may have made some small noise himself in his throat, because Merry looked over toward the bed and saw him lying there with his eyes open.

"No hurry about getting up," Merry said softly. "We'll have something to eat in a little while, but not just yet."

Her face held the same softness that had been in the note of her crooning to Paul, and in the gentleness of her touch—the sometimes fierce gentleness of her touch—when they had been in the bed. Jeebee, who had, indeed, been planning automatically on getting up and dressing, suddenly realized that there was indeed no hurry. She was right. From the angle and color of the light, it was still some little time until twilight. Wolf would not be back for a while, scratching and whining at the door for his regular day-end greetings, if indeed he came at all. It was true there was work to be done. There was always work to be done. But there was nothing immediate calling him right now, and even the bear carcass could wait to be taken care of.

All the pressure he had felt the last few long months of breakneck struggle to get the cave ready for winter was gone from him.

He luxuriated in this sudden rare and wonderful idleness, lying in the bed, feeling his wife and child close to him, enjoying the light and the moment. And there grew within him a kernel of discovery that expanded abruptly all through him, to burst out and encompass the cave, his life, and all their lives, together.

He had faced, through the summer now gone, the fact that it was impossible to continue the search for his brother's place with Paul so young. But he had taken it for granted, as if it was still a fixed and unchangeable element of their plans, that they would all three take up that search next summer when Paul would be older and stronger.

Now it burst on him as an entirely new thought—an understanding like that of someone who becomes suddenly aware that the world is round when he had always believed that it was flat—that they need not go next summer, either.

They need not go on at all.

Why leave here? They would be giving up all that they had made together, all that was familiar and useful, and which had now proved its ability to survive in the face of an attack by a creature that could have destroyed both them and it.

Small as it was, it was a fortress. Armed, only as they were, he and Merry could defend it. Here, Paul could grow older in safety, instead of running the risks of traveling through unknown territory, where people might shoot all of them first, and come to find out who they were later. It was even not beyond the bounds of possibility that they might actually win to the very borders of his brother's ranch and be shot down there by men who worked for his brother, but did not give Jeebee time to explain who he was.

Why leave all they had made here, to go hunting an uncertain future? Why take on a journey in which the three of them, and particularly Paul in the helplessness of babyhood, would be at the mercy of strangers whose attitudes and reflexes they had no way of knowing in advance?

Even if they were safely welcomed at his brother's, once

there, they would be bound to whatever the ranch itself was committed to. If Martin was at war with another rancher for some reason, Jeebee and his family could end up trapped in that war whether they liked it or not. Here, Jeebee was his own master, and Merry her own mistress.

Also, here they were safely hidden. No one knew they existed. No one was likely to come searching for them or expecting to find anyone here. If anyone did stumble across them, it was not likely to be more than a single person—and any single person they need not be afraid of, with the two of them together.

Moreover, here he had his forge, and much to learn and do with it and the cave. There were problems to be solved, of course, but none he now felt he could not handle.

He must carefully get to know his nearest neighbors below and find ways to trade forge work for things he might need from them. He must learn to make black gunpowder and firearms that could use it.

There would be much to do, beginning right away.

Then, in the long run, there were many more things to be done or to make in order that this home of theirs would be more livable. He could put to use a great deal more from the ranch, like its backup, water-driven electric generator, which he had originally believed was too heavy to carry up here.

He could bring the generator up piece by piece and dam the stream to make an artificial waterfall. Here, anything was possible. Away from here, everything would be limited.

Here they were free and life was good.

Jeebee smiled, abrim with gladness, gazing up into the sunshine from the windows.

"What are you so happy about all of a sudden?" he heard Merry's voice asking.